Faoii Betrayer

Tahani Nelson

For Mike Cole

The ranger who believed in me when I didn't believe in myself.

1

Today was the day that Calari would become Faoii.

Ali tried not to feel jealous as she waited impatiently for her friend to come through the little gate at the edge of their farm. She knew it would be the last time she got to see Calari for a long time, and she wanted to be happy for her. But that didn't keep her stomach from twisting with envy. Ali wouldn't get to be Faoii for six more years. She'd be so *old* by then.

It wasn't fair. She wanted to be Faoii *now*.

Ali paced back and forth on her hay bale, clutching her Faoii doll in one hand. She wondered if Calari would already be wearing her breastplate and ivy helm. Or would she get that at the Monastery? Maybe they magically appeared in your room the morning you become Faoii. Or maybe you got your sword first. That would make more sense. A Faoii is nothing without her fantoii.

Ali paced faster, full of questions and excitement. But still Calari didn't come. She checked the horizon. The sun was almost up. Calari should be here by now. Ali wrinkled her nose and paced faster. She was about to walk to the edge of the fence to wait for Calari near the road when the older girl finally appeared around the bend, silhouetted just as the sun crested the horizon.

Ali tried to shield her eyes as she jumped excitedly on her hay bale, hoping to catch a glint of Calari's new breastplate and sword. But as the older girl came into view Ali realized with dismay that she was only carrying a worn sack and wearing sturdy travel breaches. No sword. No breastplate. She didn't look like a Faoii. She just looked like the same old Calari.

Ali tried not to show her disappointment as she sat back down on the haybale to straighten her doll's hair that had come undone while she was jumping. She finished the last plait just as Calari reached her.

"Whatcha got there, Ali?" Calari asked as she set down her sack and sat next to Ali. Disappointment already forgotten, Ali smiled and held up the little Faoii doll for her to see.

"Papa helped me make a sword and shield for her" she said proudly, displaying the little wooden trinkets she'd carefully tied onto the doll's arms. Calari looked it over approvingly.

"Very nice. And your mother did a fine job on the hair, too. She must have worked really hard to make such nice thread."

Ali nodded, her smile widening as she showed off her treasure. "It was my birthday present!"

Calari smiled again at the little doll. "Was it? How lovely! Are you the one that braided her hair, too? Or did your mother help you?"

"I did it all by myself!" Ali beamed, glad that her hard work from a few minutes before had already paid off. "I even put the iron rings in it, too!"

"Really? All by yourself?" Calari frowned thoughtfully and put a finger to her chin. "That gives me an idea, Ali. Do you know what today is?"

"Of course! I've waited for you all morning! Today is the day you go to the Monastery of the Horned Helm! You're going to be a Faoii!"

Calari nodded. "That's right. But I think I need a little more help looking like a Faoii, don't you? Now how do you think people will know who I am if I don't look the part? They won't even let me in the gate if they think I'm just a beggar, now will they? What do you think I should do?"

Ali frowned and looked her friend over for a long moment. She wanted to point out that Calari still didn't have her breastplate or fantoii, but she didn't know where to get those things if it wasn't by magic. Her face lit up when she realized what was missing.

"You need to braid your hair!"

"What? I do?" Calari feigned surprise and pulled the long, black strands over one shoulder, peering at them carefully. "Eternal Blade! I think you're right, Ali. Do you want to help me before I go?"

Ali nodded fervently before climbing up to the haybale behind Calari's head. Carefully, methodically, she plaited her friend's thick locks. It was harder than it was on her doll, and it took her three whole tries to get it right, but when she was satisfied, she patted Calari's head twice and smiled—just like her mother did when she was finished with Ali's hair before trips into town.

Calari pulled the finished braid over her shoulder and felt the plaits at the back of her head. "This is lovely, Ali. Thank you."

Ali climbed back down and picked up her Faoii doll again. "Are you going to miss me when you're in the Monastery, Calari?"

Calari laughed and put one arm around Ali's shoulders. "Not for long, Ali. You'll be there with me soon enough, right?" Ali beamed and bobbed her head up and down. When Calari said it, six years didn't seem so long.

"Yes! You'll see me there very soon! I promise!" Calari smiled and ruffled Ali's hair.

"Then I'll make sure to save all my hugs for when I see you again. But one more before I go, okay?" Ali giggled as she was enfolded in Calari's tight embrace. When she finally let go, Ali wasn't sure if she was more excited or sad.

After she had run into the house and brought out the biscuits her mother had made for Calari's journey, Ali sat on the haybale and watched the hopeful young Faoii walk down the road until she was nearly out of sight. Calari turned back to wave one more time before cresting the horizon and disappearing toward an adventure that Ali could only dream of.

"Someday…" Ali whispered to herself as she shook her own blonde braid back and forth, pretending that it sported iron rings that bounced against a bronze breastplate. "Someday I'll be Faoii, too."

2

Ilahna Harkins always associated Faoii with fire.

The Proclamatic Order of Truth had a long list of characteristics that told them if a person was Faoii—weird symbols, breastplates, swords, braids, spells, lies... but not every Faoii had these things, and some had different incriminating items or behaviors altogether. Over the years Ilahna had learned that no single thing could tell you someone was a witch—except that they all ended up engulfed in flames.

That's how it had always been. That's how it was even now, as Ilahna watched one of the cloaked Proclaimers set his torch to the base of the pyre in the temple square. The two witches lashed to its towering stakes, a man and a woman, cried out at the sudden crackling tinder at their toes, and Ilahna focused on their faces for a moment. They were middle-aged and seemed normal enough from the outside. No armor. No shields. The woman didn't even have her hair in a braid. But the Proclaimers had found them guilty of some sort of crime against Clearwall (Ilahna didn't think that the exact accusations mattered anymore), and now the citizens of Clearwall had gathered to watch the cleansing purge of yet another threat. Ilahna crouched on the roof, watching the flames engulf the witches' feet. Around her, other children dotted the roofs that surrounded the temple courtyard, their small, round faces bright in the light of the pyre.

One of the urchins nudged her, pointing into the crowd. Ilahna followed his finger and locked on two children standing not far from the pyre. Madame Elise, the First Proclaimer, watched the two youth, as well, searching their faces for a reaction from her raised dais. Behind her, the witches screamed louder as they burned.

The two children stood motionless, hands clasped. There were no tears or sniffles. No pleas for mercy or screams for their parents. In fact, the darlings didn't show any emotion at all, their stoic faces reflecting the light of the fire. Ilahna shuddered despite herself. It was the unofficial trial of Clearwall. Someone that showed remorse or anger at a Faoii pyre was automatically declared guilty for crimes against the Kingdom of Imeriel and Her capitol city. These were not the first children who had turned inside of themselves while they were forced to watch their parents burn.

Ilahna nodded to Kilah next to her. "Go get them. They're one of us now." The urchin nodded and bounded into the crowd. It wasn't much, but all of the mazers in Clearwall knew what it was like to be abandoned. They could at least make sure that no one was alone during those first terrible nights when everything changed. And being part of their little group of petty thieves or moss gatherers was safer than being sucked into one of the more violent aspects of Clearwall.

Ilahna didn't know anything about the witches on the pyre. She didn't care. But she wanted to make those children feel a little less destroyed when morning came.

Kilah was already talking to the siblings in the crowd, but his whispers were lost amongst the triumphant screams of the surrounding mob as the flames caught the witches' clothing. They weren't moving anymore, and Ilahna turned away.

Kilah and the other mazers would take care of these newest urchins. Ilahna wasn't even sure why they looked for her approval each time rumors spread of children being left to the Maze in the wake of a pyre. But so many of the younger mazers took comfort in her presence, and she had taught most of them how to survive in a world that didn't care whether they lived another night. She would help to teach these two, as well, now that Kilah had pointed them out to her. But not tonight. She'd already left Jacir alone for too long.

Trying to brush the smoke out of her eyes and the smell of burnt flesh out of her hair, Ilahna turned and leapt across the rooftops, leaving the temple and the triumphant screams of its people behind her.

3

Nearly a month had passed and Ilahna figured that Corey and Belinda, the newest urchins of Clearwall, were going to be okay.

Or as okay as any of them were, anyway.

She whistled three sharp notes as she tore across the marketplace. The newly-minted mazers whistled back as they disappeared into the crowd, their stolen loot in tow. They were not very fast or sure on their feet, but Ilahna had high hopes that they would learn, with time. Mostly, she was just glad that they seemed to eat when she or one of the other urchins offered them food, and she'd seen them playing with other children in the evenings. These were good signs. They had not lost themselves into the darkness that every person in Clearwall had discovered somewhere inside of them after the light of the pyres faded. And that was the most any of them could really ask for.

Jacir appeared next to her, pumping his frail legs as they flew across the worn, cracked cobblestones of Clearwall. His pale, too-thin cheeks were pink with exertion and exhilaration as he clutched a loaf of bread to his chest and pushed himself harder. Ilahna flashed her younger brother a smile of encouragement before glancing behind them at the merchant still in pursuit.

The man was old and frail, but he still clung to what he had with everything that was left within him, and he forced his weary legs after the urchins as they wove through the market square. For a moment, Ilahna was almost afraid he'd catch up to Jacir, and some part of her wondered if the merchant had been a mazer in his youth. It was rare for anyone to keep pace with them for any length of time.

Ilahna whistled at Jacir, signaling him to split up. He whistled back his acknowledgment and pressed forward, disappearing into one of the alleys behind the market as Ilahna feigned a stumble, somersaulting over one of the market stall's jutting supports. Behind her, the merchant released a relieved cry and pressed forward, screaming for someone to grab her. A man nearby heard the command and yelled for a guard as he grasped at Ilahna's tunic. Ilahna nearly laughed as she twisted away from him and contorted around his bulky frame with one fluid motion. He stuttered out a shocked protest as she took off towards the edge of the market square again, flashing a smile at both merchants as they stood, mouths gaping, in her wake.

Ilahna searched for her little brother's shock of red hair as she darted for one of their regular escape routes towards the Maze. At the far end of the square, she caught sight of him well out of reach of the merchants, scrambling over a fence and through the dilapidated remains of what had once been a sewer grate when Clearwall's sanitation system had still been functional. Ilahna had just enough time to hope that he'd shove that loaf down his shirt to keep it out of the mold and grime before she vaulted off one of the street carts and onto the smithy's roof. Eitan, the blacksmith, yelled something at her, but she only had time to smile back at him before pushing ahead.

It's not like Eitan actually cares, she tried to assure herself. He was just giving her a hard time in case the guards or Proclaimers were watching. But they both knew there would be no actual damage and that it was better that she used his smithy as a springboard than some poor housewife's. As one of the few buildings in town to boast shingles rather than thatching, Eitan's home had often supported her nimble feet.

But he was still yelling at her. Ilahna shrugged internally and pressed on. *I'll make it up to you tomorrow, Eitan. I swear.*

Springing off his overhanging eaves, Ilahna's worn boots hit the cobblestones again and she sprinted for the safety of the Maze.

Clearwall was a nightmare. Its twisted, broken streets and half-finished alleys wove around each other in indiscernible patterns. Ilahna knew every warped pathway and strange side passage that made up the indecipherable labyrinth of Imeriel's capitol city. She had memorized every turn and low-hanging eave.

People said that it had been built that way to fend off invading armies, but Ilahna had only ever seen it used as a shelter and escape route for beggars and thieves. Most of Clearwall's citizens had grown up in or near the Maze, but no one knew it like the urchins. And Ilahna was one of the best. Jacir was getting there, but her little brother hadn't grown into his legs yet, and his gawkiness made him look more like a newborn colt than a true mazer.

As though on cue, Jacir appeared from the grate at Ilahna's feet, and she knelt over to pull him out by his sinewy arms.

"You'd better not have ruined that loaf down there," she said as she playfully cuffed him on one too-large ear. "We have a deal with Trisha."

Jacir frowned as he pulled the crumbling bread from under his shirt, doing his best to hold it together as he presented it for her approval. Ilahna feigned disgust for a moment before finally clucking her tongue at her brother with a proud smile.

"Looks good to me. Good job." Jacir grinned up at her as they turned towards the center of the Maze, but Ilahna caught the scent of something unexpected. She twirled back to her brother. "Holy god spit! Is that pumpkin bread?" Jacir nodded excitedly.

"I couldn't believe it when I saw it, either. Aren't you glad you let me pick the mark this time?"

"Glad? I'm ecstatic!"

"We should get something for Corey and Belinda, too. They helped a lot by distracting that guard. And I think they only got a few lengths of rope."

"We will! With a prize like this it'll be easy to pay them for their help." Ilahna stared at the loaf again, unable to conceal her amazement. "Can you imagine what we can trade for even half of this? And we'd still have some left over!"

"Funny, girl. We were just thinking the same thing." The voice that rolled towards them from the shadows of the alleyway was deep and gravely, and Ilahna spun on her heel at the sound, pushing Jacir behind her on instinct. Three tall, gangly young men stepped from the shadows and glowered down at her. Their faces were ridged with deep lines that could only come from years of hardship, and their eyes were dark and cold, though Ilahna doubted they could be much older than her. However, like everyone who had lived their entire lives in the Maze, the strangers had the look of people that were past the point of regret when it came to survival.

"We'll take that loaf, girlie. You and your brother can run off with no harm done. Just hand it over." A flash of a knife in the darkness accompanied the words this time, and Ilahna knew it was a generous offer in the Maze. People had been left to die in the street for less than this.

The man gave Ilahna what once might have been a kind smile, but its effect was somewhat eroded by the mouth filled with broken and missing teeth. Ilahna could smell the rot of decay and malnourishment from where she stood, and she bit back bile. She shook her head and pushed Jacir back another step. Generous offer or not, she was not one to make deals with thugs.

"Not a chance. This is ours."

"Come now, girl. Be reasonable. You won't like your other choice." The leader of the little gang took another step towards her, and Ilahna instinctively reached for the dagger attached to her trinket belt. All three men chuckled, and the sound caressed something in the back of Ilahna's memories. She looked the band over carefully but couldn't tell if she had ever known any of them. You don't really memorize faces in the Maze.

The two men closest to Ilahna took another step forward, but the one in the back of the group, apparently the youngest of the three, was staring intently past her, towards where Jacir still cowered.

"Hey, Jerrik. I recognize that kid. He's that freak. The one who whispers. Think the Proclaimers—?"

That was enough for Ilahna. Now these three were more dangerous than they'd been a moment before, and she would not wait to see how bad things could get from here. She spun and shoved Jacir forward. "Go!" she hissed.

Jacir took off, scrambling down the alleyway and flinging himself over a low wall. The men sprinted after him like hounds on a scent, and Ilahna only had enough time to stick out a foot and trip one of them before springing forward as well. The men were taller than her and had longer legs. On normal ground they'd outpace her easily.

But this wasn't normal ground. This was the Maze. And no one could traverse it the way Ilahna could.

The tallest of the three was already over the wall, but his companion needed three extra steps with one of the encroaching buildings as a springboard to cover the same amount of ground. Even as his foot barely lifted off the cobblestones at the beginning of his leap, Ilahna knew his path and knew with certainty that she could overtake him. A quick, strong-legged hurdle brought her to a higher roof that shadowed his trajectory. Four running steps and

Ilahna tumbled off the gable, one leg outstretched with an aim based primarily on instinct.

The stranger was midleap when the heel of Ilahna's boot struck the top of his head, driving him downward and into the cracked cobblestones beneath the wall. Teeth scattered across the alleyway, but Ilahna didn't even notice them as she continued forward without losing stride. Ahead of her, the leader of the little band was right on Jacir's heels. Her brother was fast for his age and knew the Maze almost as well as Ilahna did, but his movements were still gawky and coltish. He'd be caught in a moment if Ilahna didn't act quickly.

Without giving the idea enough time to fully form, Ilahna let out a desperate, reckless, high-pitched whistle. It was unlike any of the birdcalls that she and Jacir usually used to communicate during a run, and it was one that she seldom had need of. Jacir responded immediately, trusting his sister completely, and dropped to the ground.

At Jacir's heels, the stranger clumsily tried to jump or sidestep the bony lump of boy that was suddenly on the ground in front of him. The movement was awkward, and it took the thug nearly four full steps to catch himself.

It was enough. Ilahna was already leaping over her ungainly little brother, her dagger flashing in the sunlight as she brought it down. It sank deep into the lithe man's shoulder, and he screamed in surprise and pain. Ilahna pressed her feet against his back, grabbing his ring belt with her left hand and pulling at the dagger with her right. Then, using the strength of her calves, she backflipped off his shoulder blades, leaving the sound of his moans and curses behind her as she and Jacir escaped deeper into the Maze.

A few minutes later, the siblings crouched behind one of the double-spouted chimneys of an ancient, groaning building, panting hard. "You okay, Jacir? Did he hurt you?" Ilahna gasped out, brushing down her brother and checking for injuries.

"I'm okay. He only tripped over me. I'm okay." Ilahna smiled in relief, leaning against the chimney with a heavy sigh. She held up the ring belt and its few paltry trinkets.

"Today wasn't a complete loss, at least," she said, looking over the meager prize she'd ripped from their adversary. It was standard fare: a tin canteen, a ball of twine, flint and tinder, and a few scraps of dried meat were fastened to the strip of worn leather.

"I don't think it was a loss at all." Jacir grinned as he pulled the mostly intact loaf of pumpkin bread from his own belt pouch. Ilahna let out a little whoop of glee at the delicacy and ruffled his hair.

"You amaze me sometimes, little brother. Come on. We promised Trisha a trade." Jacir's smile stretched his already-thin face even tighter, and his eyes lit up as he followed Ilahna towards the center of the Maze.

4

It was nearly sunset as Ilahna and Jacir made their way through the twisting streets of Clearwall's Maze and past the throngs of bent, dreary people making their way back to their shabby homes. Most of those scurrying through the streets wore small disks with a picture of a fish around their necks, though Ilahna had never believed that the little tokens were necessary. You could tell a dockworker by the smell alone—the stench of fish and silk strand moss wafting from their thin tunics was nearly suffocating. But it was the most common job in Clearwall and was sometimes even profitable—a few of the dockworkers had a meager portion of the day's catch with them, the dark, oily fish pulled from the Starlit River gleaming in the last feeble rays of sunlight.

These lucky handful of fishermen that had been able to pull in enough fish to reach the Proclaimers' high quota and still procure something extra for their family carried their prize with quickening footsteps and attentive glances. Ilahna knew she was not the only one who eyed the rare delicacies meticulously fastened to their triumphant owners' belts but dared not try for the tempting bounty. She and Jacir had already had enough encounters for one day.

Ilahna slowed as she and Jacir reached their destination: a tall, quickly deteriorating building that towered near the southern wall of the Maze. The old guard tower had probably been a grand structure when it was built, but it had fallen into disuse in her grandfather's time as fewer and fewer people cared what happened to those who lived beneath its shadow. Now it was nothing more than a crumbling monument to eyes that no longer cast their gaze on the decrepit rats of Clearwall.

Ilahna slunk around one side of the crumbling tower, peeping up into one of windows on the ground floor. "Damn," she whispered angrily. "The Sarrin family is already home." Jacir stretched on his toes next to her in order to peer over the frame.

"That's okay, Ilahna. The Sarrins like Trisha. They won't tell on you if you use the stairs. Lots of urchins do it."

"Yeah. But they all pay for that silence." She cuffed Jacir fondly on the ear. "Why pay twice for one trade?" Jacir looked at his feet and fidgeted for a moment.

"But... But I can't make it up the side like you can." The disappointment on his face was nearly palpable and she sighed deeply, casting a longing glance towards the crumbling façade of the old watchtower. So many of the chipped bricks made perfect handholds, and she itched to scramble up the wall and drop through the trapdoor at its top, where Trisha lived in a little alcove that even the deftest mazers hesitated to risk.

Ilahna glanced at her brother again, unable to ignore his pleading look. She groaned.

"Oh, fine. Come on." Jacir smiled broadly and led the way to the lopsided door at the front of the guard tower.

The Sarrin family answered Ilahna's knocks promptly, peeking out from behind the ill-fitting door. No doubt, the original iron-wrought one had been stripped for metal by desperate hands. "Yes?" Mira Sarrin asked in a quacking voice. "Can I help you?"

Ilahna rolled her eyes. "Come on, Mira, you know why we're here. We want to talk to Trisha and we'll pay you for your silence." Mira pretended to think for a moment, ignoring Ilahna's impatiently tapping foot. Finally, she moved away from the door and allowed the urchins inside, moving with an aging gait that Ilahna doubted was sincere.

The inside of the old guard tower was shabbily furnished, but the Sarrin family had tried to make it brighter with colorful blankets they'd woven in better times. Mira looked over the knickknacks on Ilahna's trinket belt carefully.

"Ilahna," the aging woman finally asked softly. "Do you have any thread?" Ilahna pursed her lips and drew her last spool from one of the pouches. If she gave this up, she'd would have to nick some more off the wealthy tailors in the temple district—a much more difficult feat than stealing bread from an aging merchant in the market square. But she sighed as Mira's dark eyes lit up at the sight of the tiny spool of thread. She didn't like the Sarrins very much, but outrunning the Proclaimers really wasn't a high price to pay if it made the Maze a little less terrible for someone, even for a minute.

"Yeah. Sure, Mira. Here. Can we go up now?" Ilahna sighed, tossing the spool towards the quiet woman. Mira nodded, secreting the thread away into a hidden pocket beneath her apron.

"The landing at the top is getting worse. Be careful."

Ilahna and Jacir climbed the creaky wooden stairs of the old guard tower with soft steps. As they rose higher, sunlight seeped through bits of brick and mortar that had chipped away over time, and the steps began to bow beneath their feet. They trod carefully, finally stopping at the groaning landing about three quarters from the tower's top. Above them, uneven beams and odd supports jutted from the stonework of the tower, all that was left of the original stairs.

Ilahna let out a soft bird call, and Trisha's round face popped out from the landing far above. "Ilahna! Jacir! You remembered!" she smiled broadly as she waved. "You coming up or do you want me to come down?" Ilahna looked to Jacir, who eyed the beams carefully.

"I want to try."

"Are you sure? Some of the jumps are pretty far."

"Trisha can do it, and she's smaller than me."

"Yeah, but Trisha is more cat than girl." Jacir laughed and shook his head.

"I can do it, Lana. I promise."

Ilahna thought about it for a long moment before finally nodding. She thought he could do it, too, and it was time he started pressing his skills a little further. Clearwall was getting more desperate, and the Proclaimers were catching more mazers each year. She didn't know what happened to those who were caught, and she didn't want to find out. Especially not with her little brother. "Go on, then," she finally relented. I'm right behind you."

Jacir did not make his way up the protruding beams as quickly as Ilahna had at his age, but Ilahna had always been more reckless than he was. Jacir focused primarily on wall runs and vaulting with outstretched arms to catch the edges of beams with his fingers before scrabbling up and moving towards the next. It was a slower ascent than was strictly necessary, but it was safe. Ilahna followed her brother deftly, leaping from plank to plank with a graceful ease.

Jacir almost made it to Trisha without incident, but his final jump was too quick. Too unsteady. He leapt into the nothingness, arms outstretched, and Ilahna could tell halfway through that he had misjudged. In a moment filled with terror and the desperate sound of her own heartbeat, Ilahna watched as Jacir barely managed to reach the final landing with one uncertain, groping hand, the other swinging wildly behind him. Ilahna bit her lip hard enough to draw blood as she clambered frantically upwards through the cloud of drifting dust her brother had dislodged, her mind screaming. *Get to him. Save him.*

She'd already reached the warped beam Jacir was clinging to before Trisha even had time to yelp, but to Ilahna it felt like hours had passed. But Jacir still clung, and Ilahna wrapped her fingers around his wrist until her nails bit into his pasty skin. The pain seemed enough to center him because he opened his eyes.

"I've got you. Stop flinging your arm and focus. Come on!" The terror in Jacir's eyes didn't fade and he still swung his arm behind him, desperate for balance. "Come on!" Ilahna repeated, her voice harsher this time. Jacir's entire body jerked at her tone, and he stopped struggling. With a concentrated effort, he got his other hand onto the beam and pulled himself up to the landing. Finally, Ilahna let her heart climb back out of her throat and released his wrist.

"Wow." Trisha laughed nervously behind them. "That was the closest I've had in a while. Maybe I should have come down." There was a tiny edge of squeaky terror in her voice, and her legs shook a little bit as she approached. "You okay, Jacir?"

Jacir nodded, still on hands and knees. "I'm fine," he finally replied, though his voice pitched and shook. "I should have made that."

"We're going to wait a few years before you try that again. That was too close," Ilahna growled.

"No! I can do it! I know I can. I just…miscalculated."

"Miscalculations are what kills an urchin," Ilahna said pointedly, but at the pleading look in Jacir's eye, she softened a bit. "But… that was pretty good, Jacir. You did really well up until the end." She sighed and let the tension ease from her shoulders. "Did you drop Trisha's gift?"

Jacir pulled out the loaf of bread from his belt pouch, looking sheepish. Despite everything, however, it was still mostly whole, and Ilahna felt a surge of pride. As clumsy as he seemed, Jacir knew exactly where his body was in relation to everything around him, and could bring a clutch of eggs across all of Clearwall without breaking a single one.

At the thought of eggs, Ilahna turned to Trisha, seeing if she would approve.

"Pumpkin bread!" the tiny, cat-like girl squealed with joy. "I haven't had pumpkin bread in so long!" Her moonlike face lit up excitedly, and Ilahna was suddenly reminded that Trisha was just a girl, still. Barely a year older than Jacir. But she was quick and lithe and could climb any building in Clearwall with her eyes closed while carrying a basket.

More than that, though—Trisha was a happy, bright child who had hope for something other than what she'd been born into, and you could see it on her face whenever she grinned. It was... refreshing. A shining beacon in the darkness of the Maze.

Ilahna supposed that little ray of hope was why Trisha had never joined the roaming gangs of the other parentless urchins in Clearwall; grungy packs of starving, fearless scavengers that dug through trash heaps and stole into poorly-locked houses when they weren't cornering people for coin or to sell their own meager possessions back to them. Instead, Trisha seemed content here in the old guard tower with her pigeons and her broken stairway, trading eggs for bread and trinkets. Watching the sunsets from atop her tower.

Ilahna pulled out her cleanest dagger and used it to cut the loaf in half. "What can we get for this, Trisha?" she asked, holding out one portion.

"For a half loaf of pumpkin bread? I'll give you both of the hawk eggs I got from the southern portcullis! And a pigeon egg, too!"

Ilahna was so shocked she nearly dropped her dagger. "What? The portcullis?" Her eyes lit up with newfound respect. "You actually climbed the wall?"

Trisha shook her head. "Not all the way. I'm not crazy like *some* people around here." Ilahna rolled her eyes and Trisha laughed. "I was up around dawn yesterday. I scaled it on a lark while Zaho was on watch, since he's always asleep when the sun comes up. Grabbed the eggs and ran." She smiled broadly. "Pretty good, huh? Maybe someday everyone will know *me* as the best mazer in Clearwall!"

"Only if you actually make it to the top and see the trees. Until then, that title's mine." Ilahna winked at Trisha, who laughed again as she climbed up to the woven baskets where she stored her precious treasures.

Ilahna was about to bargain for an extra pigeon egg when a sudden whisper slit through the room like an icy tendril. She froze. *No. Not now. Not now.*

"Someday…Someday we'll all see trees. Green and gold and orange." Ilahna's hair stood on end at the sound of Jacir's ghostly whisper, her heart hammering in her chest. She sidestepped behind Jacir quickly, trying to inconspicuously smother his mouth with her hand as Trisha crept back down the wall with a basket.

"The pigeon egg's a couple days old, but it's still good," she said, smiling.

"That's fine, Trish." Ilahna responded quickly, still trying to drown out Jacir's whispers. "Mind if we use one of your ropes to go down? We promised Jorthee we'd be back before now." Trisha didn't respond and stood watching Jacir with a curious look, the pumpkin bread and eggs forgotten. Ilahna sheepishly pushed Jacir behind her as he continued to mumble under his breath, forcing her way into Trisha's attention. "Trisha? The eggs?"

Behind her, Jacir stopped whispering, and Trisha took a step back uncertainly. "Uh… yeah. Eggs. Here you go." She carefully handed Ilahna a woven basket. "There are a few for the kids that collect the silk strand. Would you drop them off for me?"

"Of course. Can we use the rope? Don't want to break them." Trisha nodded, but her eyes were still trained on Jacir.

"What was he talking about?" she finally asked, her voice filled with a child's curiosity. "What's green and gold and orange?" Ilahna's heart thudded in her breast again. She liked Trisha, but anyone who asked questions about Jacir was a danger. People like Jacir—people that whispered of strange things into darkness—did not last long in Clearwall.

Ilahna tried to hide her nervousness with a chuckle. "Just an old rhyme we heard the gang kids singing," she covered, pushing Jacir towards the landing as she reached for one of Trisha's riggings. "If I learn all of it, I'll teach it to you. I promise." Ilahna gave her most disarming smile as she took the rope in her hand. "Ready, Jacir?"

Without waiting for a response, Ilahna thrust the rope into her brother's hands and nudged him towards the landing. Luckily, his eyes had cleared, and he nodded before stepping into the empty space at the center of the tower. The weight that Trisha had attached to the other side of the pulley lifted lazily under his light frame, and a few moments later, Jacir was deposited safely at the bottom of the warped steps. Ilahna didn't wait for it to return, still nervous about the little egg hunter's curiosity. Instead she smiled, gave Trisha a little wave, and swung off the ledge. With more surety than she felt, she slid to the bottom and ushered Jacir out the door.

They were several blocks away before Ilahna felt like she could breathe again. Jacir seemed lucid now, and he very carefully pulled out one of the eggs set aside for the silk strand gatherers. He held it up to the light, peering through the holes that had been drilled into the ends. A small piece of sail cloth was rolled up inside. Ilahna didn't know what the message was or who it came from, and Trisha would never tell on someone she traded with, but these little secrets in eggshells were not an uncommon way to pass correspondence in Clearwall.

Ilahna carefully placed the hollowed-out shells in the empty nest carefully hidden beneath the eves of a warehouse in the docks district before turning and smiling at Jacir, grateful he'd come out of his episode without further incident.

"Come on," she said. "Let's go home." Jacir smiled at the idea and trotted off towards the Maze. Ilahna trailed behind, her thoughts dark.

Twice in one day someone had mentioned Jacir's strangeness. Ilahna felt sure that a third would be their undoing.

5

"Home" for the urchins was really the blocky remains of a long-abandoned tannery. Some of the supporting walls still stood, and a modest amount of roof offered sufficient protection from the elements, but the earthen floor had long since been stained with the noxious scent of its previous occupation, and few traveled near it. Ilahna knew they'd probably be more comfortable in one of the larger buildings that the gangs of mazers had taken over as their own, but it wasn't worth the risks. Besides, Ilahna and Jacir had grown used to the acrid stench of ancient alkaline lime, and neither doubted the safety of seclusion that the little shack offered. They would not be safe in a building filled with others. Ilahna was barely sure that they were safe now.

Old Jorthee offered a warm smile at their approach, and Ilahna tried to return it. Their uncle was the only other person in Clearwall who knew about Jacir's whisperings and often watched over the young boy when Ilahna couldn't. Ilahna and Jacir clasped their hands together and bowed their heads in greeting before offering him his share of their prize. "We brought dinner, Uncle."

"Eggs? Pumpkin bread? Where did you get all of this from, children?" Jorthee asked in surprise, holding Ilahna's eyes with a piercing gaze. Ilahna met his stare evenly.

"One of the traveling merchants gave it to us after we brushed down his horse." The words came out more easily than she'd expected, and Ilahna broke eye contact in order to settle a dented tin pan over their little fire. Jorthee's gaze narrowed.

"Your eyes still darken a shade when you lie, Little Bird. You are getting better at deceiving the Sight, but you cannot fool me." Ilahna felt her cheeks burn, and Jorthee laughed. "And if I wasn't sure before, I definitely am now. You must keep practicing."

Ilahna bristled in shame, knowing that her freckled cheeks were still turning a deeper red with each passing second. She tried to hide her own body's treachery by pulling her fiery curls forward to hang at either side of her face as she poked at the fire. It didn't seem to work very well, but Jacir saved her from further embarrassment.

"Where did you learn how to use the Sight, Jorthee?" he asked from around a mouthful of pumpkin bread. The old man turned one steel-grey eye towards the gawky urchin.

"I've told you this before, my boy. Your great-grandfather taught me."

"Yes, but where did he learn it?" Jacir's eyes were wide with innocence and curiosity. In contrast, Jorthee's face was an unreadable mask in the semidarkness.

"From a young woman that he cared about very dearly," he finally responded quietly.

Jacir smiled and nodded, evidently content with this answer, but Ilahna wanted more. It wasn't often that Jorthee talked about how things used to be. Old Gods only knew when she'd get another chance to hear his stories.

"Your grandfather was a soldier, right?" Ilahna tried to ask neutrally as she scooped one of the hawk eggs onto Jorthee's worn plate. She gave half of what was left to Jacir before taking the remainder and sitting on the floor near Jorthee's worn chair. "Did he fight in any wars?"

"Only the one," Jorthee responded in weighted tones. The words hung heavily in the air and Ilahna pressed her lips together, not needing to ask what he was referring to. The citizens of Clearwall knew very little about Imeriel's history, being unable to read the ancient texts locked within the temple, but the Proclaimers made sure everyone knew about the Godfell War—the great conflict 200 years before in which the Faoii had killed the Gods and cursed Clearwall to centuries of suffering.

The silence stretched on for a long time before Jorthee took a bite of his egg and smiled. "Your great-grandfather was a master bowman," he said, almost to himself. "One of the bravest men in Clearwall."

A surge of pride welled in Ilahna's chest at Jorthee's words. Their ancestor had been there for the greatest war in history. He had tried to protect Clearwall from the Faoii witches. Had tried to save Clearwall from magic. Facing dark powers and evil spells with only a bow and a sense of duty. In the end, he had failed, and the Faoii had killed the Old Gods, but Ilahna still felt a thrill of amazement at the idea that their family had tried to hold the witches back. That once they were something more than… this.

"What was it like?" Ilahna asked, unable to suppress her curiosity. She knew that the Godfell War was a taboo subject in Clearwall—too close to trying to learn more about the Faoii witches of old—but she yearned to hear about worlds beyond this one and a time when their family was comprised of heroes rather than thieves.

Jorthee must have recognized her thoughts (he always did), because he simply shook his head in response. "Not now, Little Bird. Maybe some other time." With that, he leaned back in his rickety chair, rested his head against the old tannery wall, and seemed to fall asleep. Ilahna frowned in disappointment but said nothing as she ran a bit of crust through the runny yolk on her plate. Above them, the faintest hints of far-off stars twinkled down through the holey roof.

Ilahna waited for a long time in case Jorthee changed his mind, but eventually gave up when their uncle did not stir. She nudged her brother with one shoulder. "They're constructing another pyre tomorrow. I know you don't like the burnings very much, but maybe we should go. Maybe get some extra wood. Or grab some things off the people in the crowd. I think you're good enough now to do a run right under the Proclaimers' noses." Ilahna assumed that Jacir would be excited about this newest rank she was offering, but instead her brother wrinkled his nose in disgust.

"Who are they burning?" he asked.

Ilahna shrugged. "I don't know. Some Faoii. Crazy witch drew symbols all over her walls. But that's not what I'm talking about. Jacir, I think you're finally good enough to work one of the pyre crowds. You did really well today. I'm proud of you." Jacir frowned, still not showing the excitement Ilahna had expected.

"What did they look like?"

"What?" Ilahna replied, exasperated. "Why does it matter? I don't know. Old, I guess? Not the oldest witch we've seen, but not young anymore. Greying hair. Probably dumb enough to put it in a braid." Jacir shook his head.

"No. Not the witch. The symbols. What did they look like?" Ilahna threw her hands in the air.

"How the Old Gods should I know?" Ilahna's voice was more exasperated than she'd intended. She immediately felt bad about her outburst, but Jacir didn't even seem to notice. Instead, he just kept watching her with intent curiosity.

"If we don't know what they looked like, then how do we know they're Faoii?"

Ilahna's heart thumped in her chest. She'd heard Jacir start this line of questions before. It never steered them to safe conversation topics. And even though Jorthee had seemed sure that the Proclaimers were not listening during the few moments he had discussed their ancestor and the Godfell War, Ilahna knew there were always ears in Clearwall. She tried again to steer the conversation in a safer direction.

"Come on, Jacir. You've heard the Proclaimers. All symbols are Faoii symbols, right?" Ilahna cast a sidelong glance at her brother, trying to force a laugh. "It's a good thing the Proclaimers found her before she could do anything terrible, right? They're protecting us." She said the last part loudly, just in case there actually was someone within earshot, but she dropped her voice again as she put an arm around Jacir's shoulders. "Say it," she whispered. "In case they're listening." Jacir didn't reply, staring forward with eyes that didn't seem to focus on anything at all.

"No," he finally whispered, his voice as distant as his eyes. Ilahna's heart sank in dismay as she lost her brother to a place she couldn't reach. "No. They're not protecting anyone. Those symbols weren't just for Faoii. They weren't even bad. Everyone knew them, knew how to tell what they said. They communicated that way—Faoii and commoner alike. But the Proclaimers took that away."

On reflex, Ilahna whipped her head up to look towards the open street outside. There was no movement in either direction, and her heart slowed a little bit. But her brother's words still frightened her. People had been lashed to the pyre for less than this. Witches did not get trials.

Stop. Please stop.

Ilahna gently rubbed her brother's back, willing the blank look in his eyes to fade. From across the room, Jorthee had opened his eyes again and was casting wary glances towards the door. "Can you wake him, Little Bird?"

Ilahna tried to shake her brother from his trance, but he was still whispering about impossible things that he claimed the Proclaimers had stolen over time. She put her hands on both of his cheeks in desperation. "Shh. Shhh. Don't say those kinds of things, Jacir. The Proclaimers say that the weird drawings are Faoii symbols, and we have to agree with them, okay? That witch drew them all over her house and now she's being burned for it. And that's the right thing. Say it. Say it out loud. Look at me." She pulled Jacir towards her and forced his unfocused eyes onto her face. "The Proclaimers are always right. Say it."

It took her little brother too long to refocus his eyes, but when they finally did, he shivered. Ilahna let out a breath she hadn't been aware she was holding and wrapped her arms around him, relieved. Jacir's frail frame shook beneath her arms. "Say it," she whispered in his ear again. "In case they're listening."

"The Proclaimers are always right," Jacir finally said, loudly enough to drift out the glassless windows. Ilahna relaxed a little, still hugging him to her as she rubbed his back. Outside there were no sounds except for the whistle of wind through the Maze.

"You okay?" she finally asked. He nodded into her shoulder. Behind her, Jorthee released a quiet sigh of relief.

"Yeah. I…" The child took a deep, shuddering breath. "Lana, I don't know why I do that. I don't know where it comes from. I want it to stop. I want it to go away!" He buried his head in her shoulder, his entire body racked by sudden, rushing sobs.

Ilahna rubbed his back in slow, comforting circles. "I know, Jacir. I know. We'll figure it out. We just have to be careful. The Proclaimers won't understand if they hear you talk like that. They'll think you're a Faoii, too. So, we just have to figure out how to keep quiet when it happens, okay? We can do that."

Jacir shook his head, trying to keep his voice low around his sobs. "I don't want it to be quiet, Lana! I just want it to not happen anymore! I know how dangerous it is. I know that it's bad. And I know how scared it makes you. I don't want you to be afraid of me. I don't want to be scary. I don't want to be a Faoii." Ilahna hugged him closer, mumbling into his hair.

"Oh, Jacir. I could never be afraid of you. Ever. And you are not a Faoii." She repeated these things over and over until her brother finally calmed slightly with a hiccup, but he did not try to raise his head. Ilahna sat with him, rubbing his back and whispering comforting nothings into his ear until his shivering changed from that of a sobbing child to that of a cold one, and Ilahna reached behind her and pulled their thin blanket off their pallet, wrapping it around his little frame.

"Let's go to sleep, okay? It will be better in the morning." She tried to sound confident, but the words were bitter on her tongue. *It'll be better in the morning.* She said it every night, even though they both knew it never was. But it was a pretty lie that every urchin in Clearwall desperately wanted to believe.

Shivering under their blanket from either cold or fear, the two siblings drifted into a night comprised of uncertainty and nightmares while their uncle stared on, watching for the dangers that lurked in Clearwall's shadows.

On the other side of Clearwall, *the last creaking cart of the evening rumbled to the city gates. The cloaked traveler inside pulled her hood forward, hiding the contours of her face in the shadows of its oilskin fabric. Next to her, a farmwife cooed at the wiggling mass in her arms, her heavily-tanned skin made darker next to the pink fists that pumped the air. It was one of the things that had made the cart nearly ideal for this unwanted passage. The hooded traveler's own dark skin did not seem so out of place next to those who worked in the fields all day. It was not perfect, of course. But in the dusk, it would suffice.*

The farmer at the front of the cart pulled his horses to a stop and turned in his seat to talk to the Proclaimers at the gate. The traveler ignored their conversation and risked a glance at the high portcullis. It was different than the last time she had been here. Clearwall had obviously expanded in her absence. She resisted the urge to spit over the side of the cart at the thought.

"Your disks only account for three," the Proclaimer growled from beneath his shining helm, holding up the farmer's necklace and its three passport disks accusingly. The farmer cleared his throat.

"Ah. Yes. But, as you see, we did not have our son during our last visit."

The traveler smiled from beneath her hood. Lies came easily to the poor when they were profitable. Of course the farmer had arranged for his offspring well in advance. But she was paying well for this slight inconvenience. More than enough to cover whatever fee this small exchange would require.

The traveler watched the proceedings with lazy disinterest. She had seen it many times before. A slight disagreement for show, an exchange of bribe money, a promise to purchase the proper disk at the temple, and a long, careful tally of the root vegetables in the cart. Only once did the Proclaimer at the gate try to meet her gaze, and her hand snaked toward the hilt of her blade on instinct. But a sudden wail from the baby next to her broke the tension and the guard turned away without incident, finally relenting to wave the cart through.

The traveler watched the gate as they passed under it. There were other ways into Clearwall, of course. Many would call them easier. But this route demanded the lowest cost. Gold was not such a heavy price to pay.

Finally clear of the Proclaimers' watchful eyes the little band found themselves inside the towering walls of Imeriel's capitol city. The traveler could not refrain from spitting over the edge of the cart this time. It didn't make any difference. All of the refuse in the world would hardly be noticeable next to the grime and sludge that was the city of Clearwall.

6

Ilahna's dreams that night were not the abstract fantasies of brightly colored imaginings that she longed for every time she crawled onto their worn pallet at the end of the day. Instead, moments after she closed her eyes, she knew that she was once again reliving a memory that had replayed over and over a hundred times before. There was never a way to change it, though Old Gods knew she'd tried. Dejectedly, she watched the familiar scene unfold before her.

She and Jacir had been playing in the Maze—racing across rooftops, chasing birds. His childish squeals of delight were the brightest sound she'd ever heard in Clearwall, and she couldn't help but whoop in solidarity. This was life. This was everything she could ever want. Clearwall did not offer much hope for its citizens. But moments like this made you forget that for a while.

Smiles plastered across windswept faces, the siblings tore across the city side by side. Young, free, and—above all—together, the sludgy puddles of piss and dreck on the cobblestones below seemed to Ilahna like quaint ponds reflecting rays of golden light. Their laughter warmed the chill in the air and echoed through alleyways. In that brief span of time, Clearwall was a paradise. Ilahna remembered hoping that they could live like this forever.

But then, just as the thought occurred to her, the town grew quiet, and Ilahna could no longer hear her brother's laughter by her side. She skidded to a stop and spun to ask him what was wrong, but the rooftops were empty. Heart racing, Ilahna searched for her wayward sibling, but her familiar taunts and birdcalls went unanswered as she tried in vain to get Jacir to respond. A million terrifying possibilities paralyzed her. Had he fallen? Had the Proclaimers caught him? Had one of the merchants recognized his red hair and decided to act on an old grudge? Ilahna retraced her steps at breakneck speed, her heart hammering in her chest. She called for her brother, using all the languages they'd made up over the years, all the whistles and secret codes. But all his usual routes were empty. No one answered her cries.

The silence was broken suddenly when the hollow clanging of the temple bells sounded over Clearwall with an ominous toll. The birds that she and Jacir had not already startled from their roosts filled the air with a fluttering of wings in the aftermath of the bells' mournful peal. *The bells. Maybe he'll follow the bells.* Sliding across roofs and flinging herself off of gables in desperation, Ilahna chased the echoing chimes until she found herself in the marketplace at the opening of the temple district.

Consciously, Ilahna knew that the market leading to the temple's courtyard was always filled with chatter and merchants shouting their wares. There had never been a time when Clearwall was truly silent. But as she dodged through the ghostly people of the marketplace, tripping over baskets of fruit that were both there and ethereal in this foggy dreamscape, everything was muffled. She could only hear her own frightened, desperate calls and the impossibly persistent echo of the great iron bells that still reverberated in the gloom. Ilahna ran recklessly between the stalls, still screaming Jacir's name. The people of Clearwall, their bodies wisplike and cold, passed her without noticing before dissolving into the mist that had spread from nowhere.

Finally, Ilahna passed through the market and came to the temple courtyard, settled now without even the echoes of the bells to fill the silence. The world that had been so bright only a short time before now seemed faded, worn.

In the open area at the bottom of the temple steps, a solitary figure stood, staring upward at the grand building that dominated Clearwall. From far away Ilahna consciously tried to stop her feet, tried to keep her ghostly self from reopening that terrifying box that still, after all this time, haunted her memories and dreams. But she was compelled. She approached her brother with a shaking hand.

"Jacir? What's wrong?" The words slipped from her lips just like they had that first time and a hundred times since. She tried to pretend she hadn't said them. Tried to change the insistent nightmare that had gripped her innumerable times before. But there was no escaping it, and for the first and hundredth time she saw her brother's unfocused eyes as he stared vacantly at the temple and its alabaster columns looming against the slate-grey sky. Ilahna had always been fascinated by the temple's façade. It seemed beautifully easy to climb. A tempting test of her skills. But she knew that Jacir wasn't seeing a mazer's dream. He was just... staring.

The temple's beautiful, disfigured statues and carved, irregularly jagged front stared impassively back, and in that moment Ilahna somehow knew with a dreaded certainty that Jacir saw it without the chips and chiseled scars. He saw something that he shouldn't. Something that was both old and unforgivable.

Desperately, Ilahna tried once again to pull him away from this place of power and secrets, afraid to see his eyes, afraid to hear the words she knew were coming. But he was like a pillar in himself, and a sudden wind howled around them, tousling his hair as she touched his shoulder.

And in that moment of contact, she *saw* what he saw: a temple unbroken. Its face adorned with deep rigid symbols she could not comprehend and its disfigured statues whole with braids and breastplates carved from gleaming stone. Even in her dream, Ilahna repressed a scream, slamming doors shut inside her mind with all the willpower she could muster. It worked, and she forcefully shoved the ghostly image back out of existence, leaving only the stark, unaltered image of the defaced temple. But Jacir still stood, staring at the fuzzy, dreamlike differences that she could no longer see.

Ilahna wished that Jacir would try to shut the doors that let him see such things. She wished that he understood how much danger there was in knowing. Once again Ilahna tried to spin Jacir towards her. To tell him not to look at the things hidden by that great stone door behind his eyes. *Shut the doors. Close your eyes. Please, Jacir. Please don't see.* But Jacir's unfocused pupils roamed tirelessly over the defaced surface of the temple. They were so intent, so piercing, that she knew he was looking at something specific, tracing it with his eyes as he sought to understand what only he could see.

Ilahna hated this memory. Hated this dream. She didn't even think it had happened in the real world at all, that she had somehow slipped across the veil with her brother in the night and now was haunted by ghosts that fled with daylight. She hated all of it. Hated whatever magic drew them both here when her guards were down.

She knew what was coming, and Ilahna wanted to run, screaming, before the next event could unfold. But she was powerless as Jacir's mouth opened. Ilahna tried to cover her ears, but the first true crack in the dam slipped between his lips in a whisper.

"Li…Library." A pause. A scrunched-up face. "Ilahna. What's a library?"

Ilahna's guts filled with cold water. It was the first witchy word Jacir had ever said, but she knew in that moment that things would never be the same. She'd never be able to slam the doors shut for Jacir now that he had entered them willingly and pulled something back through the other side. She would never be able to protect him from the ghostlike world he'd brought them both to unintentionally. She'd cut herself off from that shifting, superimposed realm out of fear and willpower in the first instant she saw it—but Jacir had seen the cracked door and chosen to open it further.

It might be a dream. It was always a dream. But from the temple, Ilahna could feel the First Proclaimer's eyes on both of them.

Ilahna woke in a cold sweat, shivering under their blanket. Next to her, Jacir exhaled silently through parted lips, and she slowly relaxed as she watched his frail chest rise and fall. After she was confident that he was resting peacefully, Ilahna sat up and wrapped her arms around her knees.

Every night she relived that first moment of failure: When she had been unable to shut the door for Jacir during that frightful experience in the dream temple courtyard. She had wanted to protect him from those visions that were both real and imagined. But she had failed, and now the door would not shut at all. Jacir walked back and forth through its gaping, terrifying maw without awareness, and with ever-increasing frequency. Half-heartedly, Ilahna prayed to whatever Old Gods were left that she could protect him from it, but she doubted anyone still heard.

Just in case, however, she prayed a little harder. Then she waited, trying not to let her heart thrum too hopefully in her chest.

There was no response except for a flutter of ashes in an icy wind as she stared upward into a godless sky.

7

Ilahna must have drifted back to sleep eventually, because she woke when Jacir stirred. She tried to smile for him as she stretched, and they spent the early morning huddled on their pallet, exchanging stories and playing games. It was not as fun as their races across the rooftops would be in a few hours, but it was too cold before the sun rose, and staying huddled together beneath the thin blanket made it impossible for them to accidentally break their necks in the dark.

Ilahna had just exchanged one of her twigs for Jacir's third-largest rock and was waiting for him to take his turn. She knew she had him, but they always played the game to its conclusion, and there was still a chance she would change her mind about her victory and let him win, just to see his bright smile. But as the minutes passed and still Jacir did not make his choice, Ilahna looked up from their assortment to ask him what he was planning.

She froze at the vacant stare in his eyes. *No. Not again. Not so soon.* The episodes were happening more frequently, and it twisted her heart. She cast a frightened glance towards Jorthee across the room. He met her eyes sadly but did not rise from his worn chair.

"Jacir? What is it?" Ilahna whispered, gently putting one hand on his arm. He turned his unfocused eyes in her direction.

"It's cold now. We missed the trees changing colors." Ilahna let out a bitter laugh and tried to smile for him.

"Trees? Betrayer's blade, Jacir. You've never seen a tree in your life." In all truth, Ilahna had never seen one up close either, but she had spied a faint line of green on the horizon once when she'd climbed the fort's western wall on a dare. Clearwall's guards and even a Proclaimer had lobbed sling bullets at her and chased her all across the city for her trouble, but for those few moments she had seen the world outside of Clearwall. She was about to remind Jacir of this tale, since it always seemed to delight him, but his eyes remained unfocused. She bit her lip nervously and was about to say something else to change the subject, but Jacir's unfocused eyes stilled her. *I could never be afraid of you.* She released a deep sigh.

"Okay, fine. It's just us, right? Jorthee, will you… will you keep watch?" Her uncle nodded and rose to stare out the window. He appeared to idly smoke his pipe, but Ilahna saw the concerned look in his eyes as he scanned the darkness. Feeling stronger, Ilahna took Jacir's hand. "Okay, Jace. Tell me about the trees."

From far away, Jacir smiled. "There used to be trees. Or… there will be. Or both…?" His sky-grey eyes twinkled for a moment as Jacir looked somewhere that Ilahna couldn't see. "They're beautiful! And they really do change colors. Orange and red and gold!"

For a long time, Ilahna listened to her brother talk about things he shouldn't know about, listening to his voice fill with a happiness that wasn't known in Clearwall. She smiled for him and pet his hair as he whispered nonsense into the darkness, telling her about a beauty that could not possibly be real. She hoped that he could let this run itself out and then they could go for days or even weeks without the fear that came with his ghostly visions. And, as much as she hated to admit it… it was a pleasant picture he painted in the dark. Ilahna wondered if there was anyone in Clearwall who still believed in the changing of the trees. That seemed like Faoii magic.

Had she looked up, she might have seen the tears at the edge of Jorthee's eyes as he listened to Jacir's stories of forgotten times and far-off forests.

The weather was unseasonably cold when the sun at last rose to light up Ilahna and Jacir's third game of Kings and Witches. Jacir had finally come out of the trance on his own, and Ilahna was hopeful that the curse would not manifest again for a while. Now, as the sun crested the eastern walls, they were free to begin their daily run.

"Be safe, children," Jorthee said as he returned to his chair. "The roofs may be slick."

"Do you want us to bring anything, Uncle?" Ilahna asked from the doorway. Jorthee shook his head.

"No, Little Bird. I will procure our dinner for today. Stay away from the market, lest you be recognized." Ilahna nodded and, with Jacir beside her, took off over Clearwall's Maze.

The urchins spent the day fighting off the chill by pushing their bodies to run faster and climb higher than they normally did. They were almost reckless in their takes that day, filling their pockets and trinket belts with an exciting array of baubles and dried goods, though they did as instructed and stayed out of the market proper. It was exhilarating, and Jacir's cheeks were still pink with exertion when they finally returned to the small tannery that evening, the day's acquisitions in tow. Jorthee was already cooking some sort of small fowl over the fire, and Ilahna eyed the dwindling supply of wood they had pillaged from one of the pyres two weeks before. There wasn't enough to make another week. She'd have to go to the pyre tonight whether Jacir decided to join her or not.

Now they sat, shivering on the side of the tannery that had the most cover, savoring the freshly cooked meat that Jorthee refused to answer any questions about. There was no snow this evening, but the air was frigid and biting, somehow so much worse without the buffering flurries and layer of insulation that a snowy day would have provided. Ilahna felt the ice in her bones, and Jacir's teeth chattered violently as he chewed. Ilahna had managed to get them a second itchy horse blanket when the stable boy was distracted by one of the street whores, but the paltry rag was not as thick as she had hoped. The winter air still poked its bony fingers through their skin as the sun sank below Clearwall's western walls.

Jorthee stirred the fire in their makeshift hearth, and its weak glow strengthened a little. Ilahna clenched her teeth. "Jorthee," she ventured. "How do the Proclaimers always have so much wood when everyone else has to depend on dung or silk strand?" Many of the urchins in Clearwall pulled silk strand moss from the bank of the Starlit River, which, once dried, burned hot and fast and was nearly impossible to put out as its tendrils unraveled and spread out in every direction. It was dangerous, but it was warm.

"I do not know, Little Bird. It is not for us to decided what the resources of Imeriel are used for. The Proclaimers have decided that the wood must go to the pyres, and we must obey."

"I know, Uncle. I just…" She lowered her voice, glancing to the glassless windows. "I just think that the people of Clearwall deserve leaders that focus more on life than death."

Jorthee didn't respond and Ilahna clenched her teeth at the memories of the dozens of witches Clearwall had burned in her lifetime. It was the smell, mostly, that got to her, but even that was less potent after years of living in the disused tannery that sat open to the ash-filled sky. She wasn't sure what about the burnings made her so uncomfortable, while the rest of Clearwall saw them as a form of harmless entertainment. Better than harmless, even, as every discovered witch supposedly made Clearwall a safer place. But the practice still unsettled her. It felt like something far more important than wood was wasted needlessly on the pyres. And it was far too easy to picture Jacir lashed to the stake each time.

Ilahna shook her head violently, purging the dark thoughts. She might not like the pyres, but as she sat with her shuddering brother even before the sun had completely set, she didn't think they had a choice. They needed wood. And Jacir did need to learn how to work the pyre crowds. She straightened her shoulders and licked her lips.

"Jorthee? I think I'm going to take Jacir with me to the witch burning tonight. Sometimes there are unused logs at the end, or at least spare kindling. I could grab some." Ilahna didn't mention that it would also be nice to stand next to the blaze for a while and let it thaw the aches in her fingers and ribcage. She rubbed at Jacir's shoulders as he quaked violently.

Jorthee's eyes were sad as he nodded. "It makes the most sense, children. Be safe and watch each other. Try…" He paused, and for a moment Jorthee looked even older than before. "Try not to listen to her screams."

8

Ilahna and Jacir tied their thin blankets around their necks like capes as they leapt from roof to roof on their way to the temple courtyard, only slowing as they approached the long edge of houses bordering the open square. Other urchins were already gathered on the worn roofs, unwilling to move closer despite the cold.

"Didn't expect to see you tonight, Ilahna," Kilah said as they crouched on the last house in the row. "There won't be any new urchins in this group. What's up?"

"We need wood. And I'm going to teach Jacir how to work a pyre crowd. Want to join? Get what you can for trinkets?" Kilah shook his head.

"Not tonight. It's too busy for me. I don't think I'd be able to get back to the Maze if I get caught. Happy hunting, though." He turned away from her to refocus on the crowd below, his face reflecting the light of the torches.

Ilahna and Jacir climbed down carefully and joined the throng of people that were arriving. The brightly lit temple towered over the crowd that had already gathered, its alabaster columns reflecting moon and torchlight alike. Ilahna tried not to shudder at the lofty monolith with its impassive statues that stared back at her, daring her to recall the fleeting images that had once superimposed themselves on its broken features. Instead, she distracted herself by tracing paths she would use to climb its scarred surface in an existence where that would not immediately get her killed. Her little fantasy carried her far away from the gathering crowd, and she smiled as her imaginary self was proclaimed the greatest mazer in Clearwall.

A man next to Ilahna spoke suddenly, intruding on her thoughts. "It's beautiful, isn't it? The temple is almost as impressive as the palace itself. The Proclaimers have done so much for us!" Ilahna nodded mutely and cast a glance to the north. Clearwall Keep stared down from its raised dais far above the walled-off city. Moonlight reflected off its colorful, stained-glass windows.

Ilahna rolled her eyes and looked back to the achievable dream of the temple's rooftop. The palace was so unreachable it might as well be that line of trees outside the city walls.

In comparison to the Keep, the temple was staggering in its proximity, terrifying with its chiseled, maimed surface that she knew in her gut had not always been maimed. Its armless, broken maiden statues stared impassively down from underneath jagged, disfigured foreheads, and Ilahna tried not to let herself wonder yet again why someone would carve off a statue's hair? Or arms? It seemed so senseless.

But deep down, Ilahna knew she could answer these questions and more if she just pried at the slab behind her eyes.... Just a little peek through the keyhole...

She dismissed the ghostly echoes with a violent shake of her head and cast a sideways glance at Jacir. He held her hand and stared up at the temple, shifting uneasily from foot to foot as the crowd closed in around them. Ilahna frowned. He seemed normal enough right now, but she also knew she'd only seen a glimpse of what Jacir had experienced before she'd slammed shut the great stone door that protected her from whatever curse plagued her little brother. Now she worried that it had been a mistake to bring him here, where the Proclaimers' ears were closest. But a pyre promised warmth and wood. And her fear for her brother's health was stronger than her fear of being caught.

Maybe we won't even steal anything tonight. Maybe warming ourselves by a fire will be enough.

A tall Proclaimer appeared in front of Ilahna, cutting off her view of the temple and breaking her from her reverie. She met his eyes and glanced down at his gauntleted hands, which held an array of small effigies for the burning celebration. Ilahna quickly plucked a cloth doll depicting a woman with long, braided hair from the pile, then selected a demon-faced warrior for Jacir. Normally they wouldn't get close enough to the flames to use the dolls, but being in the thick of the crowd meant they had to play the part. Not offering an effigy to the flames was almost as bad as crying at the death of a witch. The Proclaimer moved on, his spotless white cloak rustling in the breeze.

Ilahna looked down at the crude doll. Its faceless little head was misshapen, its body a lumpy rectangle with two lopsided arms. But the Faoii symbols—the sword, the shield, the braid—those were well-crafted. The most classic symbols of the Faoii. Even though she didn't trust everything the Proclaimers said, the little symbols woke something in her. They were beautiful in their simplicity and loathsome in their representation. The Proclaimers knew how to burn righteous hatred into their followers, and Ilahna felt it flare up inside her as she stared at the little Faoii doll.

From far away, whispers escaped from a crack in the door. *Why would they work so hard to make you hate a symbol? How could a braid be evil? Or a shield? What are they afraid of?*

But the teachings of the Proclamatic Order of Truth were stronger and louder than the treasonous whispers that drifted to her from across space and time, and a deep, burning rage filled Ilahna as she stared at the little Faoii. It filled the space between her ears and behind her eyes and blasted away the quiet whispers with a rushing roar of heat and fury.

In that moment, as she stared down at the little shield and the single-edged sword, Ilahna wanted them to join with the symbol she associated with the Faoii most of all: the flames. She wanted them to burn.

A sudden commotion from the temple caught Ilahna's attention and she tore her eyes away from the Faoii doll to gaze upon the dais. The raucous crowd, fueled by the excitement and anticipation of what was to come, stilled for a moment as bedraggled woman was dragged out of its front doors and down the steps to the pyre. There was no reverence or sorrow in the crowd's eyes as they watched her walk the worn path between the stairs and the stake on which she would meet her end.

The silence swelled as the witch completed that terrible tread, and as she was at last lashed to the stake, a sudden roar of triumph erupted from the citizens, nearly drowning out her plaintive cries as the Proclaimers undid the gag that had muffled her pleas.

"I swear! I didn't know that symbol was beneath the paint! It's an old house! I didn't know!" Her desperate screams were drowned out by the boos of the people that surrounded her, and the witch let out a frightened cry at their lit torches. Madame Elise, First Proclaimer of the Gods, cried louder than anyone.

"Citizens of Clearwall!" The First Proclaimer's voice cut across the din with a frightening efficiency. Madame Elise placed one gauntleted hand on her sword hilt, and the hairs on Ilahna's arms stood on end as the temple courtyard grew deathly quiet save for the witch's sobs. Madame Elise's teeth gleamed in the firelight. "We had hoped that all witches and Faoii sympathizers had been cast out from our city! We had hoped that all who were guilty had come forward to receive their forgiveness and rightful end! But some have held out! We must offer this heretic and all others like her as sacrifices to the Betrayed Ones! We must remind the Old Gods that we do not condone the actions of the Betrayer so long ago and wish only that They would return to us! That They would guide us once again!

"We all know how the Betrayer cast our world into darkness more than a century past! We know that the world was better before! That people were happier, violence was scarcer, and that peace reigned across the nations! But she—that horrible Faoii, that infamous Betrayer—killed the benevolent Gods and cast our world into disrepair. Now we scrounge for food! For work! For love! But before... before the Betrayer, all people had these things! If we return to the Old Gods' arms, we can have them again!" She turned towards the pyre and its sobbing crone. "By the Proclamatic Order and the hand of King Lucius VII, I condemn this traitor to death! May this remind the Gods that we have cast out those that hurt Them! Let Them know that we stand ready to follow once more! Death to the heretics! Death to the Faoii and the Betrayer's followers! All hail the Old Gods!"

Madame Elise released her sword hilt as she took one of the torches and touched it to the dried kindling that reached the edge of her raised dais. The pyre lit with a crackling pop, and the woman's cries were drowned out by the mob's triumphant howls as they shoved their own torches towards its base. Normally, Ilahna was far enough removed from the crowd not to feel drawn into the fever that consumed them in front of the pyres, but in that moment, she found herself joining in the chorus, her eyes dark with hatred. Her heart clenched in fury as she thought of her great grandfather and of the curse that still plagued her brother. She shrieked with rage as she thrust her little effigy into the flames.

Fueled by bloodlust, it took Ilahna too long to realize that Jacir had not joined the dark chorus of Clearwall. Instead, from several lengths away, he spoke in disjointed, halting whispers. They cut through Ilahna's screams and slivered an icy chill into her intestines.

"There's dark magic in the dolls. They fuel the hatred. They fuel the madness." Ilahna gasped as his chilled words cut through the radiating heat that had soaked into her heart, and she dropped her effigy. The little braid curled upward before catching at the base of the pyre. Feeling hollow and far away, Ilahna tottered a step back towards Jacir, barely aware that he was still whispering things he shouldn't say.

"And she's wrong. The Proclaimer. People weren't happier. The ground here is soaked with blood. And blame. And guilt." Ilahna took another wobbly step away from the pyre, jostled by those clamoring to move past her towards the flames, their own effigies outstretched. The fire tried to call her back, but as she took one more determined step towards her brother a sudden, frosted breeze against her skin woke her fully.

In a rush Ilahna remembered where she was and what was happening. The people around her seemed to be moving faster as they pushed their way to the fire and its screaming victim. The sound rushed all around her, but it wasn't enough to completely drown out Jacir's whispered words. Finally reaching him, she clamped a hand over her brother's mouth.

But she was too late. Somehow, Madame Elise heard, and she turned her steely eyes on the two children. The iron in that gaze pierced Ilahna to the core and suddenly she couldn't remember how to make her legs move as her teeth chattered and her knees shook. The hand she still had clasped over Jacir's mouth trembled and dropped to her side.

From her dais, Madame Elise placed her hand on the hilt of her sword again, and Ilahna's stomach turned to ice water as the crowd around her fell silent, turning towards the children with slow, uncertain movements and glazed eyes.

"How dare you speak against the Betrayed Gods of Old! How dare you question Their benevolence!" Madame Elise pointed a finger in Jacir's direction, her eyes piercing the darkness. Ilahna wilted beneath the gaze, but her young brother spoke on, oblivious to the danger.

"They weren't perfect, though. They were manipulative and power hungry. The Faoii killed Them… to free us." Jacir's words faded away, and he stood silently, staring without seeing into the growing flames. Around them, everything was silent except for the crackling of the fire and the dying woman's screams.

Ilahna tried to breathe around the hammering in her chest, her eyes darting in every direction as she desperately sought an escape route. But her nose was clogged with the scent of burning flesh and her eyes were streaming with smoke. The screams of rage and hatred that had consumed her when she held the doll still haunted her, breaking her concentration. She needed to get them out of there. She needed to move. But Elise was already speaking, her voice quiet and filled with something…different. Certainty? Excitement? Ilahna couldn't tell.

"Who told you this, child? Your sister?" Jacir shook his head, slowly coming out of whatever reverie had enshrouded him. He quaked when he recognized Madame Elise, backing into Ilahna with an unsteady step. Ilahna gripped his shoulders tightly, trying her best not to scream at the Proclaimer's burning stare and too-wide smile.

"We…we need to go, Madame Elise," she managed to quake out. "Thank you for ridding the city of this newest heretic. May the Betrayed Gods' return be swift." Ilahna tried to turn Jacir towards a hole in the crowd, but it was like swimming through deep water. *What's wrong with you? Move! MOVE!* But she couldn't, and the escape route closed quickly as more people shifted to get a better view of the young lunatics that would dare incur the Proclaimers' wrath. Elise descended the temple steps and forcefully turned the siblings back towards her with her bony, talon-like hands.

"Let the boy speak," she snapped at Ilahna. The Proclaimer laid her hand on her sword's hilt again, and an icy cold filled Ilahna more solidly than before. She froze, unable to respond or protest. Madame Elise nodded, content, and turned back to Jacir. Her voice was soft when she spoke again: "Who told you of the dark times a century past, young man? Your sister? One of the other boys that play on the streets of Clearwall? A trusted adult, perhaps?"

"No!" Jacir gulped and tried once again to back into Ilahna's embrace, but Elise held his shoulders and stared at him with eyes that knew too much. "No. None of them. The woman with the hood told me. I see her sometimes. Listen to her. She used to help me, but now…She's so angry. She always shoves me away. But sometimes I can still watch her and… she explains all the things I don't understand." A cold, heavy stone formed in Ilahna's gut. Elise had killed more important people than them for less than this.

Shut up shut up shut up.

Move, Ilahna! MOVE!

"A woman in a hood?" Elise smiled sweetly. Too sweetly. The air suddenly smelled of rusted copper—sickly sweet. Metallic. It turned Ilahna's stomach, and bile rose in the back of her throat. The next words seeped from Elise's mouth like dark tendrils. Or like the smoke from the pyre that still cast long, dark shadows across the First Proclaimer's face.

"It sounds to me, child, that she is misguiding you. Can you describe her for me? Do this, and I will forgive you of your part in this treachery."

Jacir stammered. "I... I..." Elise squeezed his shoulders, her nails biting through his thin shirt until he cried out. "White hair! In a braid! Black skin and grey eyes! That's all I know!" A sudden, familiar bird call from the roofs at the edge of the square snapped Ilahna free from the icy tendrils that held her, and she responded to it on instinct, reaching for Jacir again before she even realized that the call had been the sound for *retreat*—a signal she'd taught all the mazers years before.

"Jacir, go!" Ilahna yanked her brother free of Madame Elise's grasp and shoved him towards the crowd. A man was jostled out of the way, and Jacir scrambled through the open gap, disappearing into the overflowing square. Elise's eyes were first surprised, then livid as they bore down at Ilahna, but the urchin was already bounding away, leaping over strangers and pushing off of broad shoulders as she dodged grasping arms and torches.

When she finally made it to the safety of the rooftops, the other mazers were gone, but she hardly noticed. Legs rubbery, Ilahna escaped into the sanctuary of the Maze, her tears only partially due to the smoke from the burning woman who had finally stopped screaming behind her.

That night, the siblings waited in terror. They knew the Maze better than anyone, and both had taken indirect and twisted routes to get back to their acrid-smelling tannery and its worn pallet, but no one was ever certain of the Proclaimers' reach. The city guards, appointed by the king, had their patrol and their assigned areas. They were fallible and human, prone to bribery or kindness. They never ventured past the tannery or into the Maze's decrepit crevices. But the Proclaimers were different. The Proclaimers appeared everywhere, could be anywhere, and always seemed to materialize at the worst possible moments. The ever-watchful Children of Truth had an otherworldly quality that demanded both terror and obedience. And their conviction was unshakable. There was no bargaining with a Proclaimer.

Ilahna shuddered in the dark. What if they found them? What would Madame Elise do? The pyre and its dreaded stake towered in Ilahna's vision, and she wrapped Jacir in her arms, rocking him gently. Her eyes never left the door.

"Little Bird, what happened?" Jorthee's soothing voice cut through the darkness of their little sanctuary, and Ilahna gulped down her unease before telling him of the night's events. Jorthee listened in silence, not speaking until she'd finished.

"So the First Proclaimer thinks that someone is spreading lies to deface the Gods? That is not so bad, Little Bird. Jacir is young enough that he may be absolved of any wrongdoing." Ilahna looked up, afraid to hope.

"Do you think so?" Jorthee smiled at her as he walked creakily to their pallet and placed one hand on her shoulder.

"Of course. Madame Elise has no desire to harm a child. That would turn the people against her. Instead, it is more likely that she will find someone matching the description Jacir gave and make an example of protecting the city. Guilty or not, there will be another pyre before this week is out." Had Ilahna been listening closely, she would have heard the sorrow in Jorthee's voice. As it was, however, she could only stare down at Jacir's trembling form. He appeared to be asleep, and she released a sigh of relief as she pet his hair.

"What if Elise can't find anyone like that? What then?"

"You worry too much, Little Bird. Clearwall is a large place. And there is always someone guilty of something." Jorthee looked like he was about to say something else, but thought better of it and returned to his usual seat beside the dying fire. "Who does Jacir think he saw?"

"I don't know. He says he saw a woman with dark skin and light eyes. Her hair was in a braid." Jorthee's eyes widened, and Ilahna's blood ran cold. In all the years they'd lived with their uncle, she had never seen him look so surprised before.

"Do you know her, Uncle?" Jorthee shook his head, but the response seemed almost too quick to Ilahna. Too certain.

"No. And the First Proclaimer won't either. She is only searching for shadows that are not there. Chasing ancient myths and long-forgotten ghosts." Jorthee sounded sure when he spoke, but Ilahna saw him glance uneasily at the door before settling his features back into their normal, undisturbed mask. He gave Ilahna a comforting smile. "Do not worry, Little Bird. If the First Proclaimer were going to come, she would be here already. Try to rest."

Ilahna opened her mouth to protest, but Jorthee seemed so calm, so certain, that she could only nod. Slowly, carefully, Ilahna pulled Jacir closer to her and slipped into a fitful sleep.

The woman crouched *on a roof that overlooked an old and putrid tannery. She watched her targets fall into an uneasy sleep on a worn, warped pallet. She thought the old man would follow them into slumber, but instead he rose and padded over to the far side of the little shack, stopping in front of a solitary, rotting cupboard that stood against one wall. The woman narrowed her eyes as the old man reached behind it and, after a moment, drew a battered sword from its hiding place. Its sheath was dented and unpolished, but the woman recognized its hilt instantly, and a sudden jolt of anger and disgust pierced her. The old man carried the relic with him back to his place near the fire and wrapped it beneath his fading robe.*

The woman snarled and stood with a single, fluid motion. Then, the rooftop was barren, graced by only a whistling wind and long-forgotten ghosts fading in the darkness past her disappearing footprints.

9

When the children woke, Jorthee was in his usual spot, resting his head against the back of the worn chair next to the small hearth. Ilahna looked for any sign of unease in his expression, but he remained as unreadable as ever. Slowly, he opened one eye and caught her gaze.

"All is well, Little Bird. Do not fret." Ilahna nodded and looked to Jacir, who groggily sat up on the edge of the pallet.

"How are you feeling, Jacir?" she asked. He looked back at her, bleary-eyed.

"I'm okay." He paused and looked down at his feet. "I'm sorry for yesterday. I'm sorry for all of it."

"Shhh. That was yesterday. Today is today. It'll be better, you'll see." Jacir didn't look convinced.

"What do you think we should do, Uncle?" he asked, instead. "What *can* we do?" Jorthee thought about it for a moment.

"If I were you, children, I would act as though it was just another day. A change in routine is as much a sign of guilt in Clearwall as anything else," Jorthee finally replied in a thoughtful tone. "Most of Clearwall has grown used to seeing two redheads dashing across the roofs in the direction of the smithy at least once a week. You don't want to break that pattern now." Ilahna's heart sped up a little bit at the reminder that they were going to meet with Eitan today. Jorthee smiled softly. "Be safe, children. But... maybe err on the side of legal today, yes?"

Ilahna smiled, already pulling on her boots. "Come on, Jace. Eitan said he'd pay us to move ore today. He might even share his breakfast with you if we get there early enough." Jacir's eyes widened with delight at the mention of breakfast, and he scampered towards the door. Ilahna was about to follow him, but a thought struck her.

"Go on ahead of me. I'll be there soon," she told her brother. "And don't eat too much. I'm going to need your help." Jacir nodded eagerly and sprinted out, clambering over the worn wall of a building that no longer stood and onto what was left of its support beams. Ilahna watched him race across the rooftops until he was out of sight.

"There's something on your mind." Jorthee spoke matter-of-factly, puffing on his long pipe as he watched Ilahna move away from the door to pace in front of him. "You don't normally keep your blacksmith friend waiting." He let his eyes color with curiosity and amusement, and Ilahna knew he was letting her practice the Sight. But she barely glanced in his direction.

"Uncle." Ilahna broached the subject carefully, worried that the thoughts she couldn't shake might displease the elderly man. "You've always tried to take care of us, right? Since we were little?"

"I have tried, Little Bird. Jacir was still in swaddling clothes when that task was left to me. I do little these days, however. You've become an astonishingly adept mazer. I do not doubt that you can take care of yourself, now."

"But what if we get into a situation that we can't escape? What if something like last night happens again?" Jorthee gave her a disapproving frown.

"You must continue to work on your false-facing, Little Bird. And when you have mastered it, you must teach it to your brother so that such incidents are readily avoidable." His eyes colored again, this time with pride. Ilahna shook her head. It wasn't enough anymore.

"No, Uncle. I know you grew up when citizens were still allowed to have weapons. And I know you trained to be a guard when you were younger, back when just anyone could apply for guard postings. So, I know you can do this." She forced as much steel and surety in her eyes as she could muster. "Uncle, I want you to teach us to defend ourselves." Jorthee's eyebrows rose in surprise but settled again quickly.

"No."

Ilahna was taken aback. Jorthee had rarely denied her anything before, and never without reason. This stark and definitive answer left her speechless for a moment, but once she recovered, she pressed on. "Please, Uncle! Proclaimers have swords! If they ever decide to hurt Jacir, I wouldn't be able to stop them! You have to help me!" Jorthee puffed on his pipe again, shaking his head miserably.

"When peasants raise blades against soldiers, people die. Not just one or two, but thousands. It sweeps across the land like a plague, destroying all who could be even a potential threat. I will not let you be the one to light that pyre, Little Bird."

Fuming, Ilahna at last studied Jorthee's face. What she saw there was offensive and surprising.

"You think I'll start a war. Like the Faoii did. Like the Betrayer." She bristled. "God spit, Jorthee! How could you even think that? I'm not a blighted witch! It's not like I'm going to attack the entire Proclamatic Order!" Her uncle looked shocked by that, then hurt. Ilahna lowered her tone, ashamed. "I just want to help Jacir," she whispered. "I can't let them take him. Never."

After a moment, Jorthee's eyes softened. "I know, Little Bird. But there must be another way. Raising a sword against the Proclaimers will only lead to pain and death. Not just for Jacir, or for you. But for everyone in Clearwall. Perhaps everyone in Imeriel."

Ilahna released some of the tension in her back and arms and, at last, nodded. Tears stung at her eyes, but she kept her head down to hide them. She'd tried.

Jorthee puffed on his pipe a few more times before setting it aside. He did not tap out the old leaves in the bowl, as they could not afford new ones to replace them with. Ilahna often wondered how his pipe did not taste like ancient ash by now.

"You know, Little Bird," Jorthee finally said. "Even the Betrayer was only trying to help her loved ones, too. No one starts a war without reason. And everyone thinks their reasoning is sound."

Ilahna stiffened at the words and glanced towards the open windows. "Uncle?"

"I know. It is the exact opposite of what Madame Elise says from her pulpit. It is treasonous and an act of deliberate defiance to even say it out loud. Which is why you must never repeat any of it. But you need to know." He leaned forward and, while he spoke in low tones, his words were so laced with truth that it almost felt like he was yelling. "The Betrayer was just a woman, Ilahna. Just like you or the bird girl in the watchtower or even Madame Elise. Be careful which rocks you choose to overturn, because you don't know who might be in the path of the avalanche it causes."

Ilahna started to argue, but paused, reconsidering. "You think learning how to protect Jacir will cause an avalanche?" she finally asked.

"If you learn to do it with violence, it might. I simply want you *both* to be safe, Little Bird. Whatever it takes."

They stayed in silence for a few minutes, and finally Ilahna turned towards the door. "I'm sorry for asking, Uncle. Thank you for your wisdom and council."

"Wait." Jorthee's voice was old. Tired. "I need something of you. Take whatever job you need to, but find a way to purchase a sturdy wooden chair and enough leather to upholster it."

Ilahna glanced around at the single wooden pallet and weathered cupboard. A leather chair would look ridiculous in their meager home. And, as sure as she was that Jorthee would enjoy the comfort of a new chair, she knew he would never have her work to purchase something only he would use.

"Why?" she finally asked. Jorthee sighed, the deep ridges in his weary face apparent.

"For once, do not question. Just do as I ask."

Ilahna didn't press him. "Very well, Uncle. When do you need them by?"

"As long as it takes." Ilahna nodded and turned again to leave, but the sound of Jorthee's creaking bones behind her made her stop. She turned towards him again, and Jorthee approached her on shriveled legs, his bright blue eyes intense. He gripped her by her shoulders firmly and forced her to meet his gaze. "And, Ilahna, this is very important: Get them by legal means." The urchin started to protest her innocence on reflex, but he clicked his tongue. "Do not lie to me, Little Bird. I know what we've all had to do just to get by in the past. I do not fault you for it, but this is important. Do not steal *anything.* Do not draw attention to yourself." He pondered for a moment. "Buy the chair first. Make a show of measuring it and haggling for the necessary leather. But do *not* let someone else upholster it for you. People must see you enough to believe your story, but not so much that you are remembered. Can you do it?" Ilahna grinned.

"You know I can."

"Good. Go."

Ilahna nodded and dashed towards the Maze. Jacir would already be at Eitan's smithy, and they had a hard day of moving ore ahead of them. But the coin would get them one step closer to whatever it was that Jorthee needed. She stopped to glance back at the old tannery for a moment and saw the old man moving very slowly away from their home in the opposite direction. Ilahna frowned in confusion before dropping off the roof and scurrying into the twisted corridors of Clearwall's Maze.

10

Ali plaited her long blonde hair with swift, practiced movements, her lips pressed into a determined frown. Tomorrow was her eleventh birthday. The last day that a child could be accepted into the Faoii Order. She'd lost count of how many times she'd made the journey to the Monastery of the Horned Helm in order to petition. Each time she had been denied. She had no magic, and the Faoii repeatedly explained that she could not be accepted without a gift that made her worthy.

Rather than being disappointed, Ali had only become more determined. When she couldn't find her own magic, she sought training in other skills, pushing herself to perfect the Faoii arts. Fletching, calligraphy, armor smithing, sword fighting—she'd learned it all, determined to prove that she was more than worthy of the ivy helm and breastplate, with or without magic. And yet, each time she'd approached the gates to the Monastery of the Horned Helm, she'd been denied. Today was her last chance.

Ali internally catalogued everything she'd been taught. As grating as Calari's well-meaning advice and kind platitudes had become as time went on, the unascended Faoii's guidance still gave Ali the best odds at finally stepping into that secretive society she had dreamt of her entire life. Her old friend still came to the little farm several times a year to offer encouragement. At the Faoii's suggestion, Ali had been practicing with a weighted wooden sword for years now, and she sparred with Calari during her visits. Even with all of Calari's Faoii training, it had been several years since she'd been able to best Ali in their duels.

But even that experience had not proven enough, and Ali had finally persuaded her father to allow her to train with a retired soldier in Weeping Glade a few days' ride to the south whenever she was not needed at home. Now her wooden buckler felt as natural as her tunic sleeve, and the practice sword was like an extension of her arm. She was not permitted to own a metal sword or shield, but she had pushed her training further by sneaking as close as she could to the Monastery of the Horned Helm and camping for weeks at a time to watch the Faoii and Croeli practice their stances in the courtyard. She knew the steps. She knew how to hold her body and how to use every piece of it as a weapon when her sword would not suffice. She knew the entirety of the Faoii Oath.

Surely the Faoii would accept her this time. They had to see by now how dedicated she was. And surely that strength of discipline was worth as much as whatever magic was still locked away inside her blood. So much magic was useless, anyway. Her mother could weave little glimmers of light into thread. Her father had a knack for knowing which crops would fare best in the soil. How could such petty tricks be worth more than everything she had learned? Everything she could offer the Order?

Ali straightened her back resolutely and hugged her parents goodbye as she set out purposefully for the Monastery of the Horned Helm. No sneaking to peer over the wall this time. No camping on its borders. She would walk right up to that gate and the Faoii would finally see that she was worthy. This time they would accept her into their ranks.

They had to.

11

Ilahna clucked her tongue as she circled the sturdy wooden chair. Then she circled back the other way. The carpenter crossed his arms over his chest and tapped his foot. "Are you planning on purchasing it or not, little girl?"

Ilahna clasped her hands behind her back and circled once more. "It's a very nice chair, isn't it? But is it really *perfect*?"

She stepped towards the carver and he took a reflective step backwards, eyeing her shabby clothing and tangled red curls with disgust. Ilahna wondered if he saw fleas. She'd just taken a bath, too.

"Explain to me how you plan to pay for this, urchin?" the carver growled. Ilahna faked indignation and stopped her circling.

"How *dare* you? If the Proclaimers' silver isn't good enough for you then I'll gladly take it elsewhere!" She hefted the bag of coins she'd been collecting for weeks through as many jobs she and Jacir were able to take on. Her hands were calloused and bruised from mucking stables, weeding gardens, and building walls, but she finally thought she had enough to do as Jorthee had asked. The merchant's eyes focused on the bag in her hand with a look of panic before easing into a smile.

"My apologies, madam. Of course, I am happy to serve."

"Well, it might not be exactly what the Proclaimers asked for, but we can always upholster it. Let's discuss payment."

They haggled for a while, though on Ilahna's part it was mostly for show. If she went too low, then the merchant would surely remember her as the servant stealing from its master. Too high and it would seem she wasn't trained enough to be a wares servant. It was a tricky line to balance on, but she'd been watching merchants in Clearwall her entire life. She knew all the steps. It was almost comical how easy it all was.

I'm going to make you proud, Jorthee. I'm going to prove I'm capable. I'm going to keep Jacir safe.

The haggling didn't take very long at all, and a quarter of a bell later, Jacir looked even smaller and clumsier than normal as he helped Ilahna move the heavy chair to Eitan's smithy. It was an awkward and grueling walk through the twisted streets of Clearwall, but as they passed yet another Proclaimer in the craftsman quarter near the market, Ilahna began to understand. The leather and metal craftsmen in town were watched closer than any of the other artisans. Their crafts were monitored carefully, each hammer fall noted in books that no one other than the Proclaimers knew how to read. Even horseshoes were tallied carefully, and more than one farrier had been lashed to a stake after having produced too many to account for those the government commissioned for their war and plow horses each year.

Part of Ilahna wanted to question what could be so important that a merchant would dare risk the wrath of the Proclaimers. They had to have made the extra horseshoes for *something*, right? Something worth risking their lives for. What could mean that much to someone?

But as she carefully carried a chair she never planned to upholster to a smith who'd make her a hundred horseshoes if she asked, Ilahna thought she knew. She'd risk anything to keep her loved ones safe. To give them at least a chance at happiness. She didn't know how someone might have tried to do that with horseshoes, but she was once again reminded that there was very little separating her and Jacir from the traitors that had been burned in the temple square. And that the Proclaimers wouldn't see that thin line at all.

And thus they were forced into this ruse. Making sure that the Proclaimers wouldn't accidentally see a crime that wasn't there. Pretending to leather a chair so that it wasn't suspicious that they need leather. Trying to hide her brother's magics in the night.

Ilahna was broken free of the troubling thoughts when a sudden, beautiful song broke over the marketplace, ringing through the streets. Ilahna smiled, thoughts of pyres and treason fading as the cumbersome chair felt lighter in her grip.

Eitan.

While there was no official doctrine that forbade singing in Clearwall, many people had been arrested or burned for singing Faoii songs or rebellious ballads, and over time Ilahna had learned to hate the sound of music. But there was something different about how Eitan sang as he struck his hammer against the anvil. The words were what everyone expected—there would be no reason for the Proclaimers to question him—but something about the tone in his voice, the current that flowed under the notes, made Eitan's songs vibrant and calming at the same time. The hunched bodies of Clearwall straightened a bit when they walked down his street. There was the faintest hint of a smile on people's lips when Eitan's songs drifted through the marketplace. And Ilahna, in particular, loved the way the music seemed to tousle Eitan's chestnut hair.

Eitan looked up from the pounding of his anvil and wiped his brow before setting the rod he was working with into the water. A cloud of steam obscured him for a minute before he emerged from the mist, chest glistening with sweat as he pulled on a worn, sleeveless tunic. He eyed Ilahna with barely concealed humor.

"Whatcha got there, Ilahna?" Ilahna repositioned the chair's weight on her shoulders. Behind her, she could hear Jacir's quiet pants.

"Did you go blind overnight, Eitan? It's a chair. A *heavy* chair." She said the last bit pointedly and rolled her shoulders. "Come on. Help me." Eitan laughed as he moved to take Jacir's side.

"I know it's a chair. I mean, why do *you* have it?" he asked as he steered Ilahna inside. They placed the bulky piece of furniture towards the back of his workshop and Ilahna stretched her arms above her head, feeling her shoulders pop and tingle.

"I need to upholster it for the Proclaimers. I thought you might have the leather for it?" she asked as she rubbed feeling back into her forearms.

Eitan held Ilahna's gaze. "Really, Ilahna? Are you so pressed for money that you'll even do work for the Proclaimers?" He frowned at her, his eyes worried. "You know I would have let you carry ore for twice as much as I gave you last time. I didn't know you needed it that badly."

"It's not that, Eitan. It's…" For a moment Ilahna faltered under the concerned gaze of her best friend's soft brown eyes. She stammered for a moment and felt the blood rush to her cheeks. On instinct she bent her face downward so her hair would cover the increasingly red tint to her features. It didn't seem to work. "It's a long story. You got the leather or not?" she covered, trying to sound impatient.

Eitan chuckled as he brushed the hair back behind her ears. He held her gaze for a long moment before turning towards the back of the shop with a crooked smile.

"You've got it, Ilahna. You know what? I might even have some of the good stuff back here from before Da passed. It's not like I'm getting a lot of customers asking for leatherwork anymore." Ilahna relaxed at his light tone and followed him, the blush finally easing from her features.

"It's a shame you never learned when he tried to teach you, Eitan. You could have twice the business now. He'd spit on you if he still had spit."

Jacir had once said that people before the Godfell War would have been offended by Ilahna's careless treatment of the dead, but Eitan only laughed as he began moving dusty crates out from under the loft. "You should use reverence for those that are gone," Jacir had whispered at the time. Obviously, Ilahna had hushed her brother for using words like "reverence." Every person in

Clearwall had lost someone by now. If you walked softly around every name that could have been carved on a tombstone (if there was enough ground for a cemetery anymore) then there would be no time to do anything other than grieve. Death was just a thing that happened. You either watched someone die—or they disappeared—and you moved on from it. She had done it with their parents when Jacir was still an infant. Eitan did it with his Da. It was something that tied all of Clearwall together, somehow, and Ilahna found that almost comforting.

Almost. Because something in the back of her mind whispered that there was a reason the Proclaimers wanted you to forget the dead.

"Found it!" Eitan called victoriously. One of the worn crates had secreted several sides of cured leather, which Eitan held up for Ilahna's approval. Jacir approached and ran a finger across the leather, his eyes wide. Ilahna couldn't blame him. It was probably the nicest thing he'd ever been close enough to touch.

"Want me to upholster it for you, too?" Eitan asked. "If you mess up the Proclaimers might give me your hide to sell instead. Don't know how it would boil, though. It's not like you have much there." Ilahna rolled her eyes as he moved his eyes down her petite frame with his lopsided grin.

"Don't stare, jerk." She hissed at him, and Eitan averted his gaze sheepishly. "And I can do it just fine by myself, *Eitan*." She stepped up to him with narrowed eyes. "*And* you're going to give me a discount for being an ass."

Ilahna rammed her finger into Eitan's chest with a little bit more force than necessary, and he took a hasty step backwards, making some quip about her being feisty. But he'd apparently forgotten about the lid to the crate directly behind his feet, and he tripped gracelessly backwards, striking the wall with his back and raising a cloud of dust. Ilahna laughed heartily as she pulled him back to his feet and brushed him off.

"You're a clutz, Eitan. It's a good thing you weren't born to the Maze. You would have broken your neck ages ago. How you get away with swinging a hammer all day—" Ilahna cut off suddenly as her eyes focused on the wall behind him. She took an involuntary step away, her face paling.

"Ilahna? What is it?" Eitan was in front of her, his brown eyes concerned again. "What's wrong?"

"Wh-What is that?" She pointed a shaking finger towards the wall, where several unfamiliar drawings composed of straight lines and a few loops peeked out from beneath the smithy's ancient cobwebs. She tore her eyes away from the symbols just in time to recognize the terror in Eitan's gaze as he traced the symbols with his eyes. "Eitan!" she hissed, her heart thumping louder. "What is it? What do we do?"

Eitan blinked hard and shook his head. "I… I don't know. I've never seen them before. The Proclaimers. We have to tell—" He looked around wildly for a moment and Ilahna pounced on him, shoving her hand over his mouth.

"The Proclaimers don't have to know anything, Eitan! They find those drawings and you'll get burned in the square. Just… let's pretend we never saw them, okay? We'll bury them again and paint over them after the rains, okay? Just…" She scooped up a handful of sawdust and threw it at the wall. It rained uselessly down on the floor, failing to stick. She cursed under her breath and rammed her shoulder against the heavy crate. It barely moved. She tried again, straining with everything she had. "Come on! Help me!"

After a painfully long second Eitan pressed his own shoulder against the crate and shoved it forward. Together, they positioned it against the far wall, covering the markings and whatever secrets they hid. But Ilahna could still feel them there.

"You there! What's going on here?" Ilahna's heart jumped in her throat as she spun to face the Proclaimer that sauntered into the small shop, one gauntlet resting on the hilt of her sword. It did not have the same effect as when Madame Elise did it, but on reflex Ilahna took several quick steps backward in order to shove Jacir behind her.

Eitan reacted a tad more gracefully, giving a hasty bow. "Nothing, ma'am. Just saw a rat. The girl here freaked out a bit." He jerked a thumb towards Ilahna who refrained from glaring. Instead, she nodded.

"Yes, ma'am. It was… scary." Her ears burned a little bit as she spoke.

The Proclaimer waited a long moment before nodding. "Try to keep it down. Clearwall is not a place for havoc." She turned away and Ilahna waited a few long moments before releasing a shaky sigh of relief.

"That was too close. I… I think we need to get going before anything else happens." Eitan didn't argue and turned to start binding the leather in straps to make it easier to carry. "Jacir? You ready to go?" Ilahna turned to smile at her brother, but he was staring at the wall, his eyes unfocused. Ilahna's stomach dropped. "Jacir?"

"Ilahna," Jacir whispered, his voice far away. "What does 'Illindria' mean?"

12

Jorthee had told the urchins that they could not bring the chair back to the disused tannery, and Ilahna accepted this without argument. It would have been suspicious for two mazers to carry a nice chair and leather into the slums where even the roofs weren't patched. Instead, Ilahna watched over her shoulder the entire time they walked to a seldom-used warehouse near the docks. Jacir struggled behind her, nearly buckling under the weight of leather slung across his shoulders. Ilahna repositioned the chair on her back and kept going, watching again for any sign of a Proclaimer in pursuit. There weren't any, but she couldn't escape the feeling of eyes all around. She shivered, but not from cold.

Jorthee sat on the floor on the side of the warehouse that was packed with dusty crates and moldy sacks, smoking his dried pipe weed. He smiled brightly at Ilahna's approach. "You've done it, Little Bird. I am so proud of you. No one is suspicious? You didn't draw attention to yourselves?" Ilahna carefully lowered the chair to the ground, her muscles aching. She didn't quite look at Jorthee as she tried to massage feeling back into her arms. Jorthee rose carefully and approached her. "What's happened, Little Bird?"

"We… we saw something in Eitan's shop. A Proclaimer came to investigate. He left again, and I think we covered our tracks, but Jacir…" She lowered her voice. "He's acting… like he does. He keeps saying a weird word." She glanced over to Jacir who had already put his load down next to the chair and wandered to the other side of the building. Now he sat against the far wall with his head on his knees, mouthing silently. "I think it's a witch word, Uncle."

Jorthee puffed his pipe thoughtfully. "What word?"

"Ill—Illindria?"

Jorthee froze, his entire body stiffening. For a man who had taught Ilahna everything he knew about false-facing, she had no trouble seeing the shock in his eyes. He did not even try to hide it. And that terrified her.

"That is… a very old word, Little Bird," he said, recovering. "Of a goddess that even the Proclaimers do not name." Ilahna opened her mouth to reply, but he held a hand out for silence as he puffed a few more times, thinking. Finally, he exhaled a long plume of dry smoke as he sighed. "It is possible, Little Bird, that Jacir is in more danger than I feared. You did not get these things for me too soon. Let us get to work."

Ilahna found her gaze roaming to the warehouse's shut doors more and more over the next several nights as she watched Jorthee boil water and shape each individual piece of leather with his careful, gnarled hands. A dozen times she was sure she heard the Proclaimers rattle the door, but they never came. And still Jorthee continued on, slowly, methodically, and without any obvious signs of fear. He even hummed now and again—old songs that Ilahna thought she remembered from her childhood. Songs that were not allowed in Clearwall.

As Ilahna looked between Jorthee and the doors for the hundredth time since the she had last added kindling to the fire, her eyes happened to fall on Jacir. The scrawny urchin sat with his chin on his knees and his back against the far wall, as always, and Ilahna had assumed he was staring at nothing and listening to things no one else could hear. But as she watched her little brother, she saw the focus in his eyes. The intensity they held as he watched each of Jorthee's careful movements. As he studied and memorized every step.

Ilahna shuddered. Just another piece of knowledge that would eventually get him killed.

No, it won't. Not if I can help it.

Determinedly, she turned back to watch Jorthee work. If this forbidden art would help Jacir, then she would learn it too. Again, Jorthee's careful hands went into the water. Again, he molded a piece of leather with great attention. Ilahna approached him quietly.

"Uncle. Let me help."

Jacir finally stopped mumbling under his breath two days before they had finished their work, and Ilahna was relieved by his silence as she helped enclose him in the leather she and Jorthee had been working on. He looked less coltish as the simple leather breastplate under his tunic forced him to stand straighter and bulked out his frame a little bit. He smiled broadly and turned to look at his reflection in the bucket of water Jorthee had used to shape the pieces.

"Now, children. This is not a perfect fix. These things will not protect you from the full force of a Proclaimer's blade. And certainly not from Madame Elise's mighty sword. But a glancing blow? Perhaps. Mostly, it should give you enough time to run should something happen. And that will always be where your strength lies, my little mazers. With the roofs under your feet and the danger behind you. There is always safety in the Maze."

He helped Ilahna to adjust her own harness. "This is not a replacement for caution, Little Bird. You must still be vigilant. If we are lucky, neither of you will ever have to find out if the armor is effective or not."

Ilahna rolled her shoulders. Jorthee had elected to make her a harness instead of a full breastplate. It would not take long before they had to fashion a new piece as her body developed. The harness already pressed uncomfortably on her tender breasts, and she tried to adjust it to a more comfortable position. She failed, but her discomfort would be worth it if it might keep her family safe someday.

"Uncle, they're so heavy. How are we supposed to run the Maze like this?" she asked, twisting her torso from side to side.

"How did you learn to traverse the Maze to begin with?"

"We practiced," Jacir piped up. "A lot. And sometimes we fell. And then we did it again."

Jorthee laughed. "Exactly." He motioned to the door. "What are you waiting for? Go. Run."

Something about the way he said it filled both children with joy—a longing for the freedom that the roofs offered. Jacir let out an excited whoop and darted for the door. Ilahna followed at his heels, but stopped just before leaving the warehouse, turning back to her uncle. She bowed her head and brought her hands up in gratitude.

"Uncle. Thank you for this."

Jorthee smiled from above his pipe. "It's not worth anything if you don't master it. Run, Little Bird. I will see you at home." His eyes twinkled, and Ilahna grinned as she charged after her little brother.

"Ilahna! Let's look for bird eggs!" Jacir called from a roof across the street. Ilahna laughed and bounded up towards him.

"You know that Trisha has probably already gotten all of them, right?" Ilahna shook her head as Jacir looked at her pleadingly. "Okay, fine," she conceded. "But we're staying near the river district and the docks. The ground is softer if you fall." Jacir whooped again and started running. Ilahna could not repress her own cry of excitement at his joy and followed him, the sun warm and bright on her face.

The exhilaration of the day wore off more quickly than she'd hoped. The Maze seemed so much more difficult than it had their entire lives. Ilahna had always been the best of the urchins—no path was too much for her. But today she stumbled on occasion. She had to take an additional step to get up a wall. She had to use her arms to catch herself on that ledge or to balance on a beam that had been as sure as cobblestones the last time she'd crossed it. And by the end of her run she was exhausted. Straining. Sore. *What are we doing? This is terrible.*

Jacir was even worse. His legs wobbled as he followed her home at the end of the day, his arms hanging limply at his sides. When they finally arrived back at the too-small tannery and its too-small bed, Jacir simply curled on his side and went to sleep. Ilahna muttered to herself and removed his tunic and simple breastplate while he snored.

"Tired, Little Bird?" Jorthee asked, a trace of amusement in his voice. Ilahna shook her head vehemently as he helped her to remove her own harness.

"Who? Me? Never, Uncle."

Jorthee laughed a little at that. "Your false-facing is better. But be honest, Little Bird. Are you alright?"

"I'm tired, Uncle. And sore. But we'll get used to it. We have to get used to it." Ilahna rubbed at the places the harness had dug into. "But I didn't expect it to be this hard. It didn't seem that heavy when we put it on." Jorthee nodded and returned to his chair.

"Sit down, Little Bird. There are many things I want to talk to you about. You might not like all of them. But I think it is time you hear." Ilahna sat on the floor at Jorthee's feet, still rotating one of her shoulders. He looked over the harness she had been wearing and handed it back to her. "You must understand, Little Bird: nothing ever seems like it's going to be hard when you start. Even when you know it will be, there's a part of your mind that says it's going to be possible. If we were crippled by fear from the beginning, we wouldn't ever do anything at all, now would we?"

Ilahna thought for a second, the pain in her arms dissolving into an uncomfortable tingle. "Is it worth it, though? This tiny bit of extra material, even if it is leather… Can it make any bit of difference?"

"You would be amazed at how much of a difference even the smallest things can make." There was a twinkle in Jorthee's eye as he spoke, and Ilahna tried to decipher what that meant, but could not do so. Finally, she looked down, turning the harness over in her hands.

"I don't know, Uncle. Maybe I was wrong. Maybe learning about the things the Proclaimers have banned was a mistake. Especially since the leather makes us slower. Wouldn't it be better to be able to outrun them than to need armor?"

"If you don't give up, you can do both. You can learn to be fast and protected at the same time." He pointed at her with his pipe. "Anyone that tells you that less clothing is necessary for dexterity gave up too easily."

Ilahna could tell that Jorthee was trying to make things seem lighter in preparation for the darkness she could still read behind his eyes. A more somber conversation was coming. But she was not ready for it yet and made a face. "Literally no one has ever said that to me or anyone else, Jorthee."

Jorthee hooted in a puff of dry smoke, and Ilahna waved it away from her eyes. "I am sorry, Little Bird. It is a joke from long before your time." Jorthee was still smiling, but there was a seriousness in his eyes as he leaned forward. "Tell me, Little Bird. What do you think the Faoii looked like?" Instinctually, Ilahna's eyes darted to the window, but there was no one on the street in either direction. She took a deep breath before answering.

"They were witches with braids," she answered after a moment, cocking her head at Jorthee. "Everyone knows that."

"Yes, yes. They had braids. But what did they wear?"

Ilahna thought about it. Creating pictures of the Faoii and their acts was punishable by death, of course. She had never seen one.

Not on this side of the door, anyway.

She shook her head violently, banishing the thought. She had *never* seen a picture of a Faoii, but there were always stories.

"They were nude, weren't they? Or they wore furs and leathers?" The stories always said the Faoii witches were savages. Barbarians. Clothed in darkness and spells and little else.

Jorthee released a deep sigh. "Destroy the schools and dam the flow of information, and you can erase one of the world's proudest people in a generation." He put aside his pipe and leaned forward, all hint of joking gone from his face. "No, Little Bird. The Faoii were never the sex-crazed witches the Proclaimers have painted them as. They wore bronze breastplates and focused on their swordplay more than their magic. They were warriors first and foremost. But they were also women. And if they could change entire worlds while wearing bronze breastplates and heavy sabatons, you can learn to run with a leather harness."

Ilahna's skin crawled. Why was Jorthee talking about the witches and betrayers? Why was he comparing this simple leather harness to something that could get her killed?

And why can you only think of the women carved onto the temple's face?

Ilahna realized that Jorthee was still looking at her with his intense blue eyes. She did not want to offend him, especially after everything he had done for her, but she did not like how treasonous this conversation had gotten. Jorthee knew that people were always watching. He knew there were ears and eyes everywhere. She glanced towards the window again but was greeted by only darkness and a cold wind.

"We shouldn't talk about the Faoii, Uncle," she finally whispered.

"No, Little Bird. You need to hear this. You need to start thinking about these things, even if you make the decision not to act on them. But I want you to make that decision yourself, not because you were never given the choice." He reached over and cupped her chin in his hand. "There are many things we're told not to talk about, Little Bird. Why do you think that is?"

Ilahna thought about it, but she couldn't move past the fear of someone hearing them somehow. Goosebumps rose on her arms and the back of her neck. "I do not know, Uncle."

Jorthee did not release her gaze. "The Proclaimers always say that your tongue is the first step towards the flames. And that's true. But I want you to be aware that the fires lit by words are stronger and brighter than anything the Proclaimers have ever built. Don't let them extinguish those flames before they've even been lit." Ilahna listened to his words and she *knew* the truth in them. It was so bright it seemed to burn into her skull and she jerked her head away, falling backwards and scurrying a few hand widths towards the back wall.

No. I don't want to know these things. I just want to protect Jacir. Isn't that enough?

"Uncle, I don't understand. What do you want from me?" she nearly cried.

Jorthee sat back in his chair, his face sad. "I did not mean to frighten you, Little Bird. I only want for you to listen to yourself first and everyone else second. Not long ago you asked to light the fires of defiance with a sword, and I refused you. But that is only because I want for you to understand that there's a stronger weapon than steel."

"But, Uncle. I don't want to defy anyone! I just want to keep Jacir safe!" Ilahna knew that she broke petty laws almost every day, but the idea of doing something large enough to draw the Proclaimers' eye made her stomach turn to ice water.

"But, don't you see, Little Bird? Keeping Jacir safe is defiance."

Ilahna's heart caught in her throat as she realized the truth in his words, and tears filled her eyes as she slowly returned to her place at Jorthee's feet.

"It shouldn't be wrong to just… live," she finally whispered. "Jacir didn't ask for this. He can't control it."

"Oh, Little Bird. How many of the others that we've seen in the square truly asked to be lashed to the pyre? Even the few that truly had the power that the Proclaimers fear so instinctually were probably no more in control of their fates than Jacir has been. But we all lit the kindling, anyway. It is easy to ignore the fear in someone's eyes when you think they are capable of evil."

Ilahna thought back at the sea of pyres she had watched burn in her lifetime. A flood of screams and pleas accosted her ears, hundreds of witches, housewives, and farmers tearfully proclaiming their innocence with their last breaths. The laughter and triumphant cries of peasants and merchants thrusting their torches and effigies towards the flames.

A dark hatred filled Ilahna as hundreds of screaming, dying *people* passed through her memories, and she rammed her fist into the floor with a sudden, terrible rage. All the emotions and thoughts she'd had for years but pushed down or barricaded behind doors she hadn't wanted to acknowledge came spilling out of her. "It's not *right,* Jorthee! There has to be something we can do!" She didn't hear herself nearly yell the words, so deafened by the cries of burning witches and her heart's own, pained roars. She thought she would drown beneath all the cries and sounds, and a deep, howling wind picked up around them as she sobbed. Somewhere, from across the gale was a single, repeated scream:

You know. You know. *You are the Keeper of Truth.*

Ilahna grabbed her head, trying to drown out the sounds that pressed in all around her. She thought she would drown. That her brain would snap beneath them all. It wasn't right. None of it was right.

A gentle, quiet whisper cut through the terrible wails, and Ilahna focused on the song that Jorthee sang to her in the darkness. Slowly, the din faded, and she opened her eyes to find Jorthee kneeling in front of her, his spindly arms wrapped around her shaking frame. "I know, Little Bird. I know. You aren't the first to feel this way. To feel this rage against what the Proclaimers have done. It always seems like it's the young people who fight the hardest for change when they don't even know what they've lost. They feel a hunger for things that no one else thinks they deserve, and then they're always forced to prove that they're so much stronger than anyone gave them credit for. Too often it ends in tragedy, but if you and the others like you could harness that power and craving for change, put it all in the same direction, you could move mountains."

Ilahna shook in his arms for a moment, letting the tears fall. After a few minutes, she released a shaky laugh. "I don't think you're right, Jorthee. I don't think anyone thinks like me. The Proclaimers would lash me to the pyre if they knew. The other urchins would run from the sight of me if I even whispered it. There is so much more fear than rage. I try to hide the thoughts when they bubble up. I bury them with the thoughts I know I'm supposed to think. And sometimes I can convince myself. But they're always there."

"You don't think anyone else is doing the same thing, Little Bird? Just because they're afraid to say any of it out loud doesn't mean they don't think as you do. They just need to be taught that there is more to gain by winning than to be lost by fighting. And digging out that fear is a very difficult thing. Sometimes, a very dangerous thing. I thought, once, that we had reached the turning point that would send my generation to the war my old bones still hope is coming. But I don't know, Little Bird. I don't know."

Ilahna pulled away from Jorthee and wiped her eyes, the storm inside her calming. "What happened?" she finally whispered, desperate to hear a voice that wasn't screaming from behind a door she refused to open.

Jorthee creakily returned to his chair. He sat there for several minutes, staring off into the distance. Ilahna was almost sure he wasn't going to tell her, but finally he spoke.

"There was a school. Not the morning chapels that the temple district has now, that only preach of the Old Gods and the histories that the Proclaimers tell, but one of the last true schools of Clearwall. Even by then, the emphasis on education was fading. Very few people attended anymore. The Proclaimers had already done a fine job of convincing the public that education was a waste of time and that it was an indoctrination that displeased the Gods. But a few of us still went. Still studied the books and learned the words and tried to become something more than what we were.

"It was difficult, of course. Proclaimers, by then, had started entering the school in droves, chanting and lecturing and doing their best to keep those within from actually learning anything. It was efficient, though, because I had already left the tome I'd been trying to decipher behind and was heading for the door. A particularly large crowd of Proclaimers had entered that day. They filled the school, drowned out the teachers. I don't think I'd ever seen so many armed Proclaimers in one place before, and the constant sound of their spewing platitudes and psalms turned my stomach.

"I regret it now, but something about them made me think I was going to be ill, and I left quickly, so I missed seeing a large group of my young and foolhardy classmates come in after I had gone." A tear leaked from the corner of Jorthee's eye, and he dabbed at it with his sleeve.

"It was a sad day in Clearwall when a group of revolutionists, barely old enough to read the slogans on their crudely-painted signs, crashed into the school with torches and rudimentary weapons. Many people said that they heard chants of 'knowledge above obedience' ringing from the youths that stormed those halls. And while I understood the sentiment at the time, I could not understand why the fighters were so angry. We were allowed knowledge, and all the Proclaimers asked in return was for obedience. To me, it seemed an easy trade.

"But evidently my schoolmates did not feel the same way, for they fell upon the Proclaimers screaming that knowledge was a human right. That they would never blindly accept what was forced upon them instead of learning for themselves.

"The school ran red with children's blood. They were all so young. Barely old enough to marry. A few barely old enough to swear themselves to the Old Gods. Just… younglings. Fighting for something I didn't even realize at the time was worth, or necessary, to fight for.

"The Proclaimers left a dozen or so alive. Those children that, sobbing and terrified, threw down their weapons and begged forgiveness as they knelt in the blood of their schoolmates. The Proclaimers put aside their swords just long enough to build their lonely pyre. And the school closed forever that day.

"It was many years before I realized that the Proclaimers had been planning to outlaw reading and writing one way or another, and that the tiny revolt had only given them a convenient excuse. I still remember the First Proclaimer's speech. Word for word. I don't think I will ever forget it."

"What did she say?" Ilahna whispered. Jorthee released a deep sigh.

"'The words of witches and ancient lies only sow deceit and uncertainty amongst the young and easily-influenced. They divide our strong and proud nation even before the hope of our future can grow old enough to understand what is best for Clearwall as a whole. We do not allow children to play with fire, and yet we let them play with the words that burned away the Gods and brought our great city almost to extinction? No. This death today is caused solely by the misuse of knowledge these poor young souls were not developmentally ready to grasp. And now they shall never have a chance to see the error of their ways. For the safety of our children, and the future of Clearwall, we hereby proclaim these Faoii indoctrination facilities outlawed.'"

Another tear leaked from Jorthee's eye, and Ilahna placed her hand on his. He tried to offer her a smile, but could barely twitch his lips. "Many people cheered. A few mumbled. But none stepped forward as they tore down the school and lit the pyre under those children's bruised and bloodied faces. I don't know what I expected to come from a brainwashed and terrified city, but I knew, even then, that if Clearwall was going to change, there had to be a turning point. And if that catalyst wasn't the pale faces of our own dead children, I don't know what else it could possibly be."

The hut was quiet for a while as Ilahna tried to think of what to say. But how could someone respond to all of that?

Suddenly there was a mumbling from Jacir's still form. Both Jorthee and Ilahna turned to him as he spoke.

"I am the harbinger of justice and truth."

An unexplainable dread that had been driven into her over a lifetime filled Ilahna and she immediately flung herself on the bed, cradling Jacir to her, trying to stifle his sounds. Jorthee's stories were forgotten. Her inner screams of justice and defiance lost to the wind. In that moment, she only cared about keeping Jacir safe. Other people could fight a war. Other people could look at what the Proclaimers said and decide what was true and what wasn't. She only wanted to protect her brother.

Oblivious to her presence, Jacir continued his mumblings. Ilahna did not recognize the phrases that poured from his lips, but she knew she feared them. She feared what the Proclaimers would do if they heard.

Jorthee approached the bed slowly, listening to the mumbled words. Finally he whispered, "maybe you do need to learn how to use steel, too, Ilahna."

Ilahna frowned at the use of her given name. "I don't understand, Uncle. Last month you told me that peasants can't rise against nobles. That I can't be the one to light the pyre. But now you're telling me… all of this."

"Last month the winds were different." Jorthee whispered quietly as he stared out the glassless window and at the wisps of snow that fell there.

The woman watched *the children's escapades. Watched them gather the necessary supplies and be fitted with leather that would protect their bodies. But even if they worked their way out of their coltish, clumsy gaits she knew it wouldn't be enough. Try as they might, it would never be enough.*

She did not forget her reason for being here, the sounds of children screaming and the smell of burning flesh still clear in her memories. Death was coming.

But not yet.

13

Jorthee had always put Ilahna and Jacir's safety above all else, and Ilahna only had kind memories of him in their youth. He had always been slow to answer and slower to anger, always putting deliberate thought into all of his actions and words. Yet now he worked with an unexpected urgency. It was like he could feel something on the breeze. Taste it in the air. And whatever was coming frightened him.

Jorthee pushed Ilahna and Jacir every day, and slowly—oh, so slowly—they got stronger. They moved through the Maze with more agility and in better time. Even Jacir's legs began to look less like sticks and more like actual legs.

But even as their strength grew, so did Ilahna's fear. At night, Jacir continued to mumble things he shouldn't have known, repeating the same group of phrases over and over. The chant became incessant, and Ilahna no longer held out hope for ever having a silent night of true rest. The poem was long, and continuous, each phrase stronger and more forceful than the last. Ilahna prayed to every God she knew of that it would stop, but still he whispered it in the darkness, making the candles flicker and the fire rise just a little higher than it should.

Worst of all, it always began and ended with three dreaded words: "I am Faoii."

Jorthee noticed it, too, and as the nights drew on without Jacir quieting, they eventually moved to the warehouse and its dusty crates. The Proclaimers patrolled here more frequently, and the light was more noticeable in the dark, but at least there were solid walls to muffle Jacir's whispers.

"Come here, Little Bird." Ilahna had been sitting on the cot they'd moved into the warehouse, humming to Jacir more out of routine than actual hope, when Jorthee called to her as he entered the warehouse, closing the door firmly behind him. She rose and crossed the room quietly, leaving Jacir to mumble in the darkness alone.

"What is it, Uncle?"

Jorthee did not answer immediately and instead pulled two wrapped bundles from beneath his faded robe. Ilahna frowned. "What are they?"

"Open them."

Something about the way he said it made Ilahna's heart drop like a heavy stone into her stomach. With trembling fingers she undid the lacing that bound the cloth.

Hidden beneath the oilskin fabric were two sturdy pieces of carved wood, shaped and weighted almost like the Proclaimers' swords, though with a few slight differences. The blades were longer and thinner, and boasted only one "sharp" edge. Ilahna gasped and nearly dropped the practice blades, but Jorthee caught them with surprising agility and gently pushed them back into her hands.

"You wanted to learn, Little Bird. You were right in that I could teach you. And I fear that you will need to know sooner rather than later. Pick your sword. It is time."

Speechless, Ilahna lifted one of the long practice swords by the hilt. It was heavier than she had expected. More solid than she would have believed. Jorthee took the other with a practiced grip and Ilahna watched him carefully. She tried to adjust her fingers to look more like his, but it felt clumsy, despite the obvious quality of the craftsmanship.

"Where did you get these, Uncle? Did Eitan make them?" But even as she spoke, she knew that even Eitan did not have access to such strong wood as this, and even if he did, he would never have been able to secret it away when he was only allotted such a small amount for his forge.

"No, Little Bird. I have always had them. Many times I questioned myself for keeping them. But I did." Ilahna ran her fingers across the carved blade in awe. How many freezing nights could they have endured with the warmth of a fire built with this single secret? She marveled at Jorthee's resolve. She was not sure she would hold on to such relics in a time when their destruction could stave off death in more ways than one.

"Are you sure about this, Uncle?" she asked, raising the wooden sword to chest level experimentally. But Jorthee was already moving, swinging his blade at her wrist. Ilahna moved on reflex and avoided the strike, but only just. She looked up at Jorthee with a shocked expression, but he was nodding, pleased.

"That is good, Little Bird. But you will have to depend on more than swiftness. Watch my stance. Mirror what you see."

The nights grew longer and darker, and Ilahna learned the ancient art of sword fighting by the light of the moon through the window high above the warehouse's loft. At first, she was certain that her lithe body would outpace Jorthee in a short time, but her uncle continually surprised her. After an untold number of decades, her uncle's ancient feet still knew the steps; his arms still moved with surprising speed and strength. As Jorthee's ancient, frail body fell into familiar battle routines with an ease that could only come through muscle memory, Ilahna wondered why she had only ever thought of him as a scholar.

You are from a family of warriors. Not just soldiers. Not just fighters. But those who go to battle with purpose and honor. Those who want to make a difference.

The sudden thought startled Ilahna, and she stumbled as she tried to shake the unwelcome voice that whispered to her from behind the barricaded door behind her eyes. Jorthee's practice sword rapped hard against her shoulder, and Ilahna cried out.

Jorthee paused, giving her a moment to recover. "Can you move your arm, Little Bird?" he asked after a few heartbeats. Ilahna nodded, rubbing the bruise she could already feel forming. "Good. Let's do it again."

They'd been in the warehouse for more than a month. While the days still went on much as they always had, with she and Jacir running across Clearwall with the grace and stealth of starving tomcats between the Maze and Eitan's smithy, things changed once the sun sank behind the western wall. The nights were frigid, and an icy wind blew in from the Starlit River, always accompanied by Jacir's whispered spell.

The sword practice warmed Ilahna's aching bones. Her body was bruised and worn, but still she refused to give up, picking up her practice sword each night with grim determination. Often her arms shook as she raised her carved blade, but she forced it higher—partially to ward off Jorthee's oncoming strikes, and partially to try and focus on anything besides the sounds of Jacir's constant whispers behind her.

Tonight was particularly dark, and only a small fire lit their practice circle. An unexpectedly savage swing knocked the blade from Ilahna's hand, but she was able to jump away before Jorthee could strike her legs or ribs. At his nod, she bent to retrieve it, then returned to her place. She took her stance and motioned him forward. She saw the pride in Jorthee's eyes as he moved his own frail legs back into formation. Ilahna no longer doubted their agility.

The irony was nearly palatable. Not long ago she had begged Jorthee to teach her to fight, and he had refused. She had been hurt at the time, but now that it was actually happening, she did not know how to feel. She wanted this—had always wanted this, deep down—but she still feared what would happen if she or Jacir were ever caught. Would it be enough? Could anything really be enough? She knew Jorthee wondered the same thing; she could see the fear and pain in his eyes each time he taught her a new step. But there was something else there, too. A hope that maybe she could be more than what he had been.

Ilahna hoped so. She wanted their future to be brighter than their past.

And still Jacir's whispers filled the darkness.

Months passed and somehow, blessedly, the Proclaimers never descended upon the warehouse in the night. They had survived the brutality of winter by guile and luck—stealing from the pyres and merchants, huddling in darkness, trying to hide their presence despite Jacir's witchy poem each night. Now Ilahna's harness felt almost like a second skin, and her arms and legs had toned themselves to ivory carvings. Jacir was still small and coltish, but he held his own in their run every day, and he seemed to be made of slightly more than just bones and skin, for once.

Ilahna and Jorthee had been very careful to never let Jacir see the wooden swords with which they practiced. They could not risk him watching with such care as he had when they'd crafted their armor the previous autumn. Ilahna had insisted.

"Jorthee. You know he'll watch us with those eyes. He'll learn everything there is to know about what you're teaching. And it will get him killed one day. Sometimes we can hide what he says, but if he ever starts to move like a fighter when he's not in control of his actions, the Proclaimers will see it. I cannot shield him from both their ears *and* their eyes."

Jorthee chewed that over for a long time. Finally, he simply asked: "Is that your real reason, Little Bird?"

Ilahna almost said yes, but as she looked at Jacir's sleeping, whispering form, she knew it would be a lie. She lowered her head. Did not even try to false-face. "No, Uncle," she finally admitted.

"What is wrong then, child?"

Ilahna looked at the ground. "It's just… I don't want him to know how to fight. I want him to be a kid for a little bit longer. I feel like if Jacir picks up a sword, he'll never be innocent again. And I don't want to lose that. I don't want him to lose that."

Jorthee nodded. "The world is dark enough without losing the ray of sunshine that is our little Jacir. Very well. We will protect him from this darkness for a while longer, if we can. But that means, Ilahna, that it is up to you to protect him." Ilahna nodded vehemently.

"I swear, Jorthee. I'll protect Jacir with everything I am. Forever if that's what it takes."

She had hoped that 'forever' would take a little longer to arrive.

14

Ilahna had just fallen asleep, her arms exhausted and the wooden swords tucked safely into the rafters of the warehouse loft, when Jacir suddenly let out a muffled cry beside her. She turned to him quickly, ready to try and shake him awake, but his eyes were already open in a terrified stare towards the warehouse door.

"Jacir? What is it?"

It was not Jacir that answered her. "There's no time, Little Bird!" Jorthee's urgent whisper from across the warehouse was frantic. "Get dressed! Quickly!"

Ilahna's practiced fingers took no time in getting Jacir into his breastplate. She'd even learned to fasten her own harness without help. But their tunics were barely over the leather when Jorthee was shoving a long bundle into her arms and ushering them both to the back door.

"There's a Proclaimer in the front street. Two more at the end of the block. I don't know where the others are or what they're waiting for. But you must go. Now. Keep each other safe. Remember everything I taught you. You're not ready to light those fires yet, Little Bird, but someday, if you choose to, remember not to be afraid."

"Jorthee, what's happening? What about you?"

Jorthee didn't seem to hear her. "Take the roofs and the back alleyways. You know the Maze like no one else alive. Use that. And never let them catch you. I did everything I could for you. But there's so much more to learn."

"Jorthee! Please!" Ilahna dug in her heels as he pushed her towards the door.

"Go, Little Bird. Go!"

Suddenly there was a forceful pounding on the front door, and Ilahna could tell just from the sound that a gauntleted fist was waiting on the other side. Then the back door was open, and the children were shoved into the cold night air. Ilahna immediately turned back to pry the door open again, but an unfamiliar voice stopped her.

"You there! Stop!"

Ilahna spun, stiffening as a Proclaimer approached them with measured steps, one gauntleted hand already drawing her sword. Ilahna's knees shook as she tried to take a step backwards, clutching the long bundle Jorthee had given her against her chest. Even through the oiled cloth, she could feel the weight of it. Knew where the hilt would be, the pommel, the guard. Her heart leapt into her throat. She didn't know of a worse crime than having a sword in Clearwall.

You are the strength of the weak and the voice of the silent.

The unbidden whisper from across time shattered the ice encasing Ilahna's legs. She gripped the wrapped blade more tightly to her chest with one arm and used the other to spin Jacir away from the oncoming Proclaimer. "Go, Jacir! Go!"

"No! Uncle!" Jacir tried to turn back, but she pushed him forward.

"Go!"

They ran, leaving the shouting Proclaimer behind. They ran in the darkness of night and fear and pain. They took to the roofs and leapt across eaves, their legs pumping incessantly, barely clearing chimneys and uneven tiles as they pushed themselves harder. Faster. Crisscrossing the same paths over and over. Trying to throw any followers off their trail. The bells would start sounding soon. The entire city would start looking for them.

Ilahna's eyes burned painfully, and she was certain that the Proclaimers had already lit their pyre in the square. But eventually she realized that, rather than smoke, it was tears in her eyes that blurred her vision.

The sun was just beginning to light the eastern sky when Jacir stumbled to a halt. "Ilahna. Please," he gasped out between his sobs. "I need to stop."

Ilahna spun, watching the street in all directions. It was quiet. No alarms. No screams. No sabatons on cobblestones. Only the sound of early-morning doves cooing to each other as the first rays of sunlight streaked across the sky.

Ilahna didn't know where to go. Didn't know who to ask for help. They were alone. Jorthee was dead or worse. She had a sword in her hands and a brother that knew more than he should.

A brother she had to protect.

That would be enough. It had to be enough. Above all, at least she still had Jacir.

Ilahna led her frightened, sobbing brother through the Maze with an uncertain step. They crept in shadows and jumped at every little noise even as Jacir repeated Jorthee's name over and over between his stifled sobs. But eventually they found their way to a place they had been a thousand times. A place that had always felt safe.

Ilahna knocked uncertainly, filled with dread. What if he wouldn't help? Who would dare to help two people running from the Proclaimers?

Finally, the door opened.

"Ilahna? What are you doing here?"

"Eitan. We need help."

After Jacir had finally succumbed to an exhaustion that even his tears could not penetrate, Ilahna tucked him into Eitan's only bed. For once, he was blissfully silent and Ilahna hoped her little brother would be able to finally rest.

She turned to Eitan, trying not to crumble as he wrapped his arms around her.

"Ilahna. What happened?" For a long time, Ilahna couldn't respond, and she only sobbed into Eitan's chest as he held her. "Shhh. It'll be okay," he whispered against the top of her head.

Ilahna wasn't sure how long they'd been standing there, his arms wrapped around her tightly as she cried, but suddenly the story rushed out of her, punctuated by deep, racking sobs. Eitan didn't respond or interrupt, only held Ilahna and listened until she had no more words or tears.

When at last she stopped crying and could only stand, hollow and shaking, in his embrace, Eitan gently guided Ilahna to a chair at his kitchen table. The curtains were drawn on the windows, and a feeble ray of morning sunlight struggled to alight the square line of his jaw as he sat across from her. Ilahna stared at the slit of warm sunlight on his skin, feeling the silence between them, as dark and deep as the Starlit River. She thought she would drown in it as she waited for him to say something. Anything.

Finally, Eitan stood. "Let me see the sword."

Ilahna drew back for a moment, clutching the parcel to her. Eitan only stared back, his eyes unwavering. "Ilahna. Let me see it."

Obediently, Ilahna set the bundle on the table and unwrapped it with unsteady fingers. But when the twine finally fell away, Ilahna couldn't help but stare as she saw the scabbard for the first time. She knew it would not be a sword like what the Proclaimers carried, but it was nothing like what she'd imagined.

She knew immediately it was a Faoii blade, and she had expected it to be covered with strange symbols and frightening in appearance. But the scabbard was plain and utilitarian. The blade, after being unsheathed, was long and thin with an unadorned hilt. The entire thing was very practical, and, while she supposed it was probably beautiful in its own right, it still seemed strange to her. She had always been told that the Faoii had wicked blades. Instruments of torture and pride. This was simply a tool.

Eitan glanced to the window before he picked up the sword carefully. He looked it over with a knowledgeable eye.

"This sword is old. But it is well-made. It's better than what the Proclaimers have me make for new recruits."

He turned it over again and his eyes narrowed. He lifted the weapon closer to his face, staring intently. Ilahna watched his face closely, and for a moment there was recognition. Then fear. Then nothing.

"What is it?" She asked, leaning forward. Eitan shrugged and put the blade back down.

"Nothing. I was looking for a maker's mark. There's something there, but it's written in the old Faoii symbols." He looked at her with caring, concerned eyes. "This is a very dangerous thing to have, Ilahna."

"I know. I know we should get rid of it. But… I can't." She felt tears begin to prick at her eyes again and tried to blink them away. "Eitan, I don't know what to do. I don't know why I have it or how to get rid of it. I don't know if Jacir is safer if I keep it or if I throw it away." Eitan took a seat beside her, wrapping one arm around her shoulders. Ilahna clutched his hand in hers. "I don't know what to do. It's not fair. It's not right."

Eitan squeezed her a little tighter. "Hey. It'll be okay. We'll hide the sword. Hide you and Jacir until everything dies down. It'll be okay."

"Not for Jorthee." Ilahna sniffled.

Eitan stiffened a little before softly kissing the top of her head. "No. Not for Jorthee" he agreed sadly.

Then there was only the sound of Ilahna's quiet sniffles as they once again worked to move past the unburied dead.

15

Ali's surety and pride had only grown by the time she finally arrived at the Monastery of the Horned Helm. She harbored no doubts that this time she would finally be accepted, even without magic, and she firmly pounded on the broad iron door with its grand bronze knockers. The ringing echoed in the silence as she waited for a response.

After what seemed like ages, the door finally opened, and two proud figures stood in its gaping maw—a woman and a man, clad in bronze breastplates. Ali held her breath and bowed her head, fisting her hands in front of her like she'd seen the warriors do while she'd spied on them from outside their great stone walls.

"Faoii, Croeli. I come to train in the Order."

The warriors looked her over dispassionately for a long moment, and it was the woman that spoke first.

"I remember you, child. Ali, was it? You have grown since we saw you last."

Ali nodded fervently, encouraged. "I have, Faoii! And I have mastered the art of swordplay." She went to draw her practice sword, but the Croeli raised his hand.

"It is not for you to decide whether or not you are the master of anything, child. We will have to retrain you. Purge you of all the mistakes your inferior teacher undoubtedly instilled in you. But, if she was not completely inept, it is possible that you will have internalized at least the basics."

The Faoii nodded as Ali dejectedly returned her sword to its place at her hip. "It is of no consequence. Of all that is learned within these walls, swordsmanship is the most mundane. That was never our concern with you." The Faoii straightened, her eyes kind from beneath her ivy helm. "Tell us, young one: Have you finally learned of your magic? The powers gifted to you at the fall of Illindria?"

Ali's face fell. She thought her hard work would be enough. She thought they would be able to see. She bowed her head again, her long braid falling over her shoulder.

"No, Faoii. I have not. But—" The Croeli pressed his lips together in a thin line, waving a hand in front of him. The power that rolled from the movement shocked Ali into silence. She risked a glance upward and met the Faoii's softened eyes.

"Are you sure, child? The magic can be subtle, at times, but it spread across all the world. Surely there is something within you, however small?"

Ali looked to the ground and shook her head, trying not to let them see her tears. "No. There is nothing. I have no magic."

The Faoii shook her head sadly. "That is truly unfortunate, child. Go now. Return to us when you know of your innate abilities. Surely they exist and you have just not found them yet."

"But tomorrow is my eleventh birthday!" Ali protested.

The Faoii frowned. "Then I am sorry. But you know our ruling. The ascended will only accept the strongest candidates for training. The ones most capable of defending and helping those under our protection. Go forth, my child, and do good in the world. But you are no Faoii."

The doors closed behind them with a resounding and definitive clang, and Ali, numb, slowly turned back in the way of home.

Ali's parents recognized the look on her face when she arrived and her mother rushed to comfort her, but Ali only shook her head and continued walking. She stopped at the mantlepiece where her little Faoii doll had received a place of honor once she'd outgrown it. With a sudden surge of anger and hatred, Ali plucked it from its spot and threw it violently into the flames.

"I am no Faoii," she hissed as the fire curled around the doll's braid and tiny sword. "I'll never be Faoii."

16

Ilahna and Jacir had lived in small spaces before, but now they found themselves sharing a cramped half-story alcove above Eitan's smithy that secreted an even more cramped crawlspace in the furthest corner behind a false wall. It was bitterly cold at night and unbearably hot during the day, and while Eitan sneaked them food and water once a day under the guise of retrieving the day's supplies from a crate near their hiding place, the weeks of hiding were long and grueling. But, as they had in so many situations before, the urchins did what was necessary to survive.

Ilahna lost track of how many times she heard a gauntleted fist knock on Eitan's door. How many different booming voices demanded to know where the mazers were. Eitan always stated calmly that he had not seen them.

"You can check my home if it helps to ensure the safety of Clearwall. All hail the Proclaimers and the Old Gods."

Ilahna's heart swelled with pride and respect when she heard Eitan address the Proclamatic Order. He always said the right things. Never offended the Proclaimers. Was never dragged into the streets to disappear like so many others before him.

The Proclaimers always came during the day, and Ilahna never had to worry about Jacir's cursed whispers drawing their attention. But sometimes she worried they would hear the quickly-muffled cries she and Jacir could not always stifle as they mourned for Jorthee in the dark.

Eitan never fought or complained about the intrusions, but the Proclaimers were merciless with their searches. They threw metal and boxes aside with reckless abandon. They broke Eitan's dishes as they searched through cupboards that even Jacir could never have fit into. Twice they moved the boxes that had once hidden the Faoii symbols, and Ilahna thanked whatever Old Gods still listened that she and Eitan had found the symbols early and that Eitan had had time to paint over them.

Once, Ilahna heard two of the Proclaimers talking out of Eitan's earshot as they searched the shop. She held her breath and hugged Jacir close to her as she prayed to whoever would listen that the searchers would move on quickly.

"Did you hear about Avirli? The old man managed to get his sword away from him. Spilled his intestines all over that warehouse floor." The other Proclaimer toppled one of Eitan's boxes with an unnecessary force.

"Wounded two more, too, before we were able to take him down. Madame Elise is calling for the heads of his followers before news spreads and people start thinking they can fight back. All of Clearwall is in danger if we don't find those kids. Here, help me move this."

There were more crashing sounds as the Proclaimers searched through Eitan's shop yet again, but Ilahna could not suppress a smile with a surge of pride that Jorthee had made the Proclamatic Order tremble.

Eventually the Proclaimers stopped coming, and for the briefest time Ilahna thought she and Jacir had succeeded and were safe. Until she heard a Proclaimer shouting a new message through the streets one evening.

"A witch and his two brainwashed disciples have been discovered in Clearwall. Come help our beloved city make amends to the Betrayed Old Gods with their execution! And be cautious, people of Clearwall! The words of ancient evil are spreading! The poison seeps so easily from mouth to ear, tasting sweet with honeyed words. But the tongue is the first step to the flames! See those that spread the destruction of Clearwall! Watch them burn! And remember that evil does not have a distinctive face. It is in your neighbors and your friends. Only the Proclaimers can protect you from their lies! So says Madame Elise, First Proclaimer of Clearwall!"

Eitan tried to convince Ilahna and Jacir not to go to the burning. But Ilahna had to know. Who else could they be talking about but Jorthee?

"We'll never be able to rest again if we don't go see. If we don't at least try to say goodbye," she whispered. Eitan had no answer to that. No one ever really got the chance to say 'goodbye' in Clearwall, and those few who did had the rare honor of celebrating an entire life rather than just facing a disappearance or abrupt end. He finally conceded and helped them out of the crawlspace, then hugged her tightly.

"It might be a trap, Ilahna," he whispered without letting her go. "Please be careful. Especially with Jacir… He gets worse at night."

Ilahna nodded. She knew the risks, but she could not deny Jacir this last chance to say goodbye, either. They would not stay long, and she would hide him away again before he could fall through the door that pulled at him in darkness. Just a few moments. A chance to know for sure. A chance to know the truth. To follow something wonderful to its end.

"We'll be careful. I promise. We'll be back before the next bell."

She tucked her sword beneath her cloak and led Jacir across the roofs heading towards the temple district.

The mob that had already gathered in front of the temple was large and violent, and each person jostled the others for space as they thrust torches and effigies into the air with cries of fury and bloodlust. Ilahna and Jacir crouched with the other mazers on a roof at the edge of the square, cloaked in shadow and apprehension. The white alabaster temple looked ghostly in the torchlight. The deep, hollow sound of the temple's bell rattled Ilahna's bones as the Proclaimers and their captives appeared at the top of the steps. The prisoners' hoods cast deep shadows on faces that Ilahna wasn't sure she wanted to see.

The trio marched to the pyre solemnly, barely flinching at the mob's angry cries. They climbed the pyre and stood next to their appointed stakes without raising their heads. The Proclaimers lashed their hands behind their backs to the tune of a thousand angry curses. Then, finally, the three hoods were torn away from the prisoners' heads.

"Look once more upon the faces of those that you have wronged!" Madame Elise yelled from her dais as the hoods fell away. "These are the neighbors and friends that trusted and fed you. You have betrayed all that we are with your poisonous lies. By order of King Lucius VII, for your crimes against Clearwall and the Old Gods, we sentence you to death."

Ilahna's heart sank and she grew suddenly dizzy as she tried not to focus on two blue eyes that stared out across the crowd from the pyre.

No. No no no. Ilahna wanted to pretend this wasn't happening. She'd thought she wanted to know the truth. To know for sure. But it was too much. As her heart shattered in the darkness, she prayed to every God in existence that it wasn't their uncle standing in the center of the pyre.

But Jorthee's eyes roved over the roofs, and even in the darkness he saw the silhouettes of the children he'd raised, hiding in the shadows of the roofs, far from the pyre and the blazing torches.

Ilahna didn't know how, but she knew Jorthee saw them there, and once their gazes met across the plaza square, she could not look away. For a heartbreaking moment she thought she saw disappointment in his eyes. The draining of hope that they'd stayed away. Next to her, Jacir wound his fingers into hers.

"Look what they did to him" he whispered, his voice shaking. "Look what they did!"

Ilahna didn't answer. Her uncle was bleeding from a deep wound in his stomach and shoulder, both of which looked infected and had probably been left untended since the fight in the tannery when she'd run away with his only weapon. Ilahna squeezed Jacir's hand, hating herself more with every second. Jorthee had done so much for them with nothing, and she had never done anything in return. But as she looked into Jorthee's eyes, there was no fear or shame there. Only pride.

Jacir pulled on her hand again. "He wants to tell you something, Lana. I don't…I'm not sure… should I?"

Ilahna didn't even pause. Didn't stop to think.

"Tell me."

The change was instant, and Jacir went stiff beside her. His voice sounded soft. Distant. Ilahna didn't even feel her tears fall as she listened to Jorthee's final message, still holding his gaze across the square.

"Don't worry, Little Bird. There are brighter fires in the world. And the Proclaimers fear them. But the brightest fire of all is the one that starts with that rock you feel in your chest. The one that starts with truth."

Ilahna held Jorthee's gaze as the Proclaimers lit the fire at his feet. The flames reflected in the blood and tears that streaked his face. It licked at his boots and his bound hands. Jorthee gave Ilahna an almost imperceptible nod. The faintest smile.

Ilahna wished he didn't believe in her so much. And she wished she could be as strong as him, whatever end eventually came.

You are the strength of the weak and the voice of the silent.

Ilahna shook the intrusive, ghostly thought away and slammed the door behind her eyes shut, watching the fire twist and change, rising higher until Jorthee could no longer maintain his calm façade. First, he broke from her gaze, turning his face away as he squeezed his eyelids together. When the screaming began, Ilahna could not recognize it for what it was. She stood, paralyzed, staring at the way the flames licked and curled his clothes, his skin. Jacir sobbed in her arms.

Jacir sobbed in her arms.

The unspoken trial of Clearwall.

"Madame Elise! There! On the roof!" The sudden cry of a Proclaimer was jarring, and Ilahna realized a crowd of white cloaks had congregated below them in the square, swords drawn. The other mazers had already dispersed, disappearing into the nights like rats.

"The children are conspirators! Seize them!" Madame Elise's yell cut across the rabble and slammed into Ilahna, and she realized what she'd done. Her heart thundered in her ears as she clutched Jacir closer to her. Eitan was right. The Proclaimers had hoped to draw them out. To trap them. And it had worked.

Heartbeat racing, Ilahna spun and dragged Jacir towards the Maze. The Maze was for urchins. The Maze was safe.

But the Proclaimers had come prepared. Dozens of ladders were set against the walls surrounding the temple square, and people swarmed onto the roofs, blocking their escape. They filled the passageways with furious, pulsing bodies and groping, outstretched hands.

Ilahna searched for refuge, spinning again and again as she looked for a different roof they could jump to, some wall they could climb. But there was nothing. She tried to position herself between the mob and Jacir, but the zealots were everywhere. There was no escape. She would join Jorthee on the pyre. Jacir would be beside her. Desperately, Ilahna fumbled for her sword.

She had nearly gotten her fingers under the folds of fabric when a shape blurred in front of them. A shadow detached itself from a nearby eave and dropped onto an adjacent building, streaking towards the urchins and the mob. A swathe of people fell in its wake, slumping in bloody piles.

"Come with me! Quickly!" Then the shadow was darting toward the Maze again, barely visible in the smoky starlight. A path cleared behind it.

Ilahna did not consider any other options, only obeyed. With Jacir at her heels, they dashed into the safety of Clearwall's twisting Maze.

Jorthee's screams faded behind her.

17

Ilahna thought she knew how to traverse the Maze. She thought she knew how to keep to shadows and use the environment to her advantage. But the person (a woman, she realized at one point when their rescuer's cape had billowed open and revealed a lithe, leather-clad frame) that led them through the twisted streets of Clearwall put even her best attempts to shame. The stranger was like a swallow, swift and graceful, each movement airy and flawless. And the way her feet barely alighted upon the beams or didn't quite touch the walls… it was eerie in its unearthliness. But there was also a determination and strength in the woman's movements that made Ilahna want to be better just for seeing them. The urchin pressed herself harder.

The cries and clamors behind them were persistent, the crowd spreading out into the streets at the Proclaimers' behest, searching for the fleeing mazers and their otherworldly guide. Ilahna's heart thundered in her chest. Adrenaline spurred her forward with each new victorious cry that rose when a searching citizen spotted them, but Ilahna knew she could not keep this pace. And she could already hear Jacir's wretched wheezes behind her.

She was about to cry out to the stranger that they had to stop, but between the need to formulate words and the unfamiliar bulk of the blade in her hands, Ilahna hit a board wrong and stumbled on the thin ledge of the roof beneath her feet. She was able to grab the edge as she passed it, albeit barely, and Jacir was already there to try and help her back up, a mirthlessly ironic reflection of their time in Trisha's tower—but the sword Jorthee had gifted her tumbled to the street below, its scabbard clattering on the cobblestones and the blade coming partially free.

"The sword! We have to get it!" Ilahna cried, trying to pry away Jacir's fingers so she could drop down after it. The hooded figure stopped just long enough to cast an annoyed glance over her shoulder.

"There is no time. There are other—" Ilahna barely caught a spark of green beneath the hood as the woman's gaze focused on the exposed bit of blade in the alleyway below. A throng of Clearwall's citizens was pouring into the opening at the far end, releasing shouts of triumph at the sight of the three fugitives.

The stranger let out a sort of feral hiss before leaping back to where Ilahna flailed. She lifted Ilahna by the collar with one hand and almost threw the urchin back onto the roof and safer footing. "Keep going, girl. Both of you. Get to the docks." The woman pulled her hood back enough to focus a steely grey stare into Jacir's eyes. After a moment he nodded, and she pulled her hood back into place. Then the stranger leapt to the shadowy cobblestones below. The din from the citizens grew louder.

Ilahna scrambled back to her feet and rushed to the ledge to aid their benefactor but was stopped by Jacir's pleas as he pulled at her arm. "We have to do what she says, Ilahna. She knows so much more than we do. And we don't want to make her angrier than she is. Please."

It was the 'please' that brought Ilahna to an uncertain halt, and she glanced nervously between Jacir and the sound of fighting below them. Then, she finally nodded and grabbed Jacir by the hand as they ran in the opposite direction.

Behind them, the sound of screaming and metal against stone rang across the rooftops. And somewhere, deep in the back of her head, Ilahna heard the chant she didn't want to know.

I am Faoii. I am the harbinger of justice and truth.

Ilahna's heart felt like it would burst from her chest when she finally backtracked for the last time, circling once more towards the docks that smelt of dead fish and the putrid silk strand moss that urchins pulled from the river. She guided Jacir carefully, staying pressed against the high wall that kept citizens away from the trade goods and freedom that the Starlit River offered potential stowaways. Far in the distance, people continued to yell to each other across the city.

"How are we supposed to get through the gate?" Ilahna whispered angrily, her forehead sleek with sweat. "Even with most of the Proclaimers searching for us, at least one of them must be guarding the dock gate. The mob will be on us again in minutes."

"I don't think we're supposed to go to the gate." Jacir responded slowly. "I… remember this place."

"You've never even been here," Ilahna whispered back without conviction. Exhaustion borne of something more than physical exertion filled her limbs with lead. There was too much going on, her mind too muddied to talk Jacir out of false memories and witchy words. Her heart was simply too heavy to try. *Jorthee would know what to say.*

But Jacir was already pointing at a deteriorating sewer tunnel in the side of the wall, its stone supports crumbling and its arch uneven. A sluggish stream of brown sludge trickled out of its mouth. Ilahna didn't even try to argue. Didn't ask if he was sure. With leaden steps and drooping shoulders the siblings squeezed between the shoddily-constructed bars that served as the tunnel's only barrier.

They were only able to go a short distance before it was too dark to see, but both urchins were too tired to go much further, regardless. Ilahna found a dry space on the ground and pulled her brother down beside her. They huddled in silence for a few minutes, listening for the voices of the angry mob somewhere above them.

"Jacir…" Ilahna finally ventured. "Who is she?" She didn't bother explaining who she meant.

Jacir clutched Ilahna's hand in the darkness. "I don't know. But she's the one whose story I watch at night. Sometimes I'm able talk to a younger version of her. When she had less scars and anger. The one who wasn't hurt as much. She tells me not to give up. Not to give in. She believes in me. Or… she used to believe in me. I think she's forgotten that part of herself. Because the woman out there now is filled with bitter rage and hatred. And she shoves me away when I get too close. Tries to break my mind from the inside." He shuddered and pulled his legs up to his chest.

"I followed her thread across a huge unending Tapestry. All those nights where I never slept. I was watching her story. And there were so many things to see and learn! It was beautiful. But sometimes I get lost. Sometimes I get wrapped up in the strands. I thought she could help me. She can run across the Tapestry like we run across roofs, Lana. I begged her to teach me, in the darkness. I called out to her more times than I can count." His voice quavered. "But she never came." A flare of anger shot through Ilahna as she imagined someone ignoring her brother's frightened cries, but she stamped it back down, trying to keep her voice even.

"So, what is she doing here now?"

"What, indeed?" A dark, humorless voice echoed into the chamber. Ilahna and Jacir whipped their heads towards the entranceway. A solitary figure, tall and proud, stood silhouetted in the crumbling arch. Her voice was like the velvet a rich man might put in a trapped box—barely covering a hidden blade.

"I remember you, Weaver. I remember you whispering in my head when I was young and foolish. I remember trying to help you, filled with optimism and pride. Know this: I regret that now."

The woman's silky voice hardened. "You just couldn't leave it alone, could you? I sealed it so carefully. I screamed at you not to tread this path. I shoved you away with everything I was. Why couldn't you just leave it alone?" There was a sudden spark, and a torch in the woman's hand blazed to life.

For the first time, Ilahna looked at the newcomer. She could see a dark chin and strong jawline under lips that were pressed into a thin line. There was the faintest glimpse of pale grey eyes that glinted like steel in the sudden firelight. A long, white braid hung limply over one shoulder, its iron rings reflecting the torchlight in muted colors.

With how quickly the stranger had traversed the rooftops, Ilahna had expected someone young. But deep lines creased the dark face, and Ilahna realized that the stranger was older than even Jorthee. She pushed the thought back down before it could form as more than a thick lump in her throat.

With deliberate steps, the woman strode forward, her booted feet striking the water as she walked. In her right hand hung the sword that Jorthee had thrust into Ilahna's hands only a few weeks earlier.

"Why couldn't you leave it alone?" she repeated, nearly screaming. The walls around them shook with the power in her voice, and chunks of rock and moss rained downward.

Jacir pressed himself against the wall, small and frightened. Anger blazed through Ilahna and she rose swiftly, squaring her shoulders as she stepped between her brother and the witch, fists clenched.

"Leave him alone."

The stranger let out another biting, mirthless laugh and looked Ilahna up and down. "Look at this, now. So, the stalwart protector *is* capable of holding her title. Had you shown this strength earlier, then maybe I would not have been drawn here. You had all the necessary tools, but not the willpower. And now I am forced to do what you could not." She threw the blade at Ilahna's feet. "That is a good blade. One of the last ones left. Even I tried to destroy most of those that remained. How did someone like *you* get ahold of it?"

Ilahna's shoulders drooped a little. "Our uncle gave it to me. The man that was… burning. In the square." Despite her rage, Ilahna fought back tears.

The woman did not reply, and for a long moment there was only the sound of falling pebbles and scrabbling rats. The shaking around them eased slowly, and the fury that had rolled off the stranger in waves finally dissipated. Ilahna wiped at her eyes furiously, but she could not stem her tears.

After what seemed like ages the woman turned and began moving deeper into the sewers, rats scuttling away beneath her feet. "Wipe your eyes and pick up your blade, girl. There is much to do, and your kinsfolk will not stop hunting you so quickly."

Ilahna wanted to argue. To leave the blade on the ground out of defiance. "What do you care?" she finally hissed under her breath.

"I don't. But I was compelled to come to your aid. It is my goal to make sure I never have to again. Let's get this over with so I may leave in peace." The woman walked deeper into the darkness, taking the torchlight with her. "You too, young Weaver. It was you that forced me here, and you *will* release me."

Ilahna looked down at her little brother as the torchlight began to fade into the distance. "Jacir, what is she talking about?"

"I don't know. I don't..." Jacir fought back tears, his voice trembling. "I know I screamed to her when they turned on us, but she... she was so fast. She must have already been here." He shook his head, putting his head in his hands. "I don't know, Lana. But... we need her. We'll never survive in Clearwall on our own. Not now."

Ilahna wanted to argue. They'd always made it on their own. But that wasn't quite true, either. Jorthee had always been there for them. Eitan was always around with a song, smile, or comforting hug. But now...

With an angry snarl to hide the sobs that threatened to escape, Ilahna scooped up the sword and pulled Jacir with her as they followed the reflection of the torchlight that still bounced off the tunnel the stranger had disappeared into.

"Wait!" Ilahna finally called into the darkness. The torchlight stopped and they dashed after it. "What should we call you?" she asked as they finally reentered the circle of light. The woman didn't even look back at them.

"Nothing. I will not be staying long."

"We have to call you *something*."

Ilahna felt something akin to an icy breeze before the woman spoke again. The words rolled off her tongue like fob. "If you are so intent on titles and names...then you may call me Faoii."

Goosebumps prickled Ilahna's arms, and she narrowed her eyes. "If you're trying to joke, it's not funny," she said. "A Faoii wouldn't have come to Clearwall."

"Normally you would be correct, but I'm still curious as to what in your great trove of experiences would make you say such a thing with so much surety." The woman glanced over her shoulder. Ilahna met her gaze.

"The Proclaimers of Clearwall drove out the Faoii. Lashed them all to the pyre. If there were any left, they'd be long gone and nothing could have drawn them back. You're no witch. You're just a thief or a con artist. And I know you want something."

The woman's cloak ruffled just barely as she shrugged. "Then stop following me. The world is open to you, girl. I am only here at your brother's behest. You mean nothing to me."

Ilahna clenched her fists. But there was nothing she could do. She didn't know how to protect Jacir anymore. Not now.

So, with more questions than answers, Ilahna and Jacir followed the old woman who called herself Faoii deeper into the sewers beneath Clearwall.

18

Ilahna did not know how deep the sewers went, and as they went further into the darkness, a part of her worried about being buried under rubble, their corpses left to the rats.

This was new territory. The last unexplored crevice of Clearwall. She'd never heard of a mazer who had investigated more than a tiny portion of the abandoned sewer system, though they'd found crumbled openings and treacherous sinkholes during their explorations of the Maze. She'd heard that the more affluent districts near the temple still had water from the Starlit River directed to channels beneath the streets, but no mazer had ever found them, and most of the sewer grates in the Maze had long-since crumbled away or become clogged with sludge and dreck. The few openings that were traversable led to a labyrinth that rivaled even the Maze in its complexity, and even the bravest urchins only went below ground for a block or two at most. It was too easy to become lost or buried in the twisting underground caverns, and there were no roofs to climb if you needed to get your bearings. Usually, the sewers were suicide.

But the woman that called herself Faoii seemed to know the place well, and she took confident strides through its pungent passages, leading the urchins through a twisted path that jumbled even Ilahna's keen sense of direction. The urchins followed, soon so lost that they could not have found the entrance again if they tried. Ilahna tried not to think of it as imprisonment.

At last they came to a dry patch of raised stonework with several branching corridors set into the grimy walls. A sturdy table covered in dust and cobwebs was pushed to one side, and wooden frames supporting the long-rotted remains of moldy mattresses could be seen down one of the adjacent corridors. The woman looked around thoughtfully for a moment before seeming satisfied.

"You are safe here. Tomorrow, we will see if you're worthy of the help you've demanded of me. And of the blade you yet refuse to wield."

Jacir stayed behind Ilahna, his eyes streaming again as he cried softly into the sleeve of his tunic. The Faoii barely looked at him before offhandedly motioning to one of the dry side passages. "Mourne if you must, but get some sleep, young Weaver. If I am to teach you, you will need to be rested. This is far from over." Jacir looked at Ilahna who nodded without taking her eyes off the stranger.

"Go on, Jacir. I'll be right there." Still sniffling, the child crept towards the ancient barracks.

Ilahna didn't move. She was more exhausted than she had ever been, but she could not convince her feet to follow her little brother. She looked at the sword in her suddenly trembling hand, smelled the smoke on her clothes. She could still hear Jorthee screaming in the distance, even though she logically knew that his breath had left him long before. But her mind wouldn't let it go. She clenched the hilt of her sword more tightly.

The 'Faoii' watched dispassionately as Ilahna took three angry steps towards her, raising the blade an inch or so from the ground. Before she reached the witch, however, Ilahna stopped, spun, and stormed her way back in the direction she assumed was the entrance. A few more steps, however, and she stopped again. Again she turned to the cloaked stranger, meeting the grey eyes. Her entire body trembled in rage.

"Are we playing this game again?" The woman sighed. "Whatever you're planning to do, child, get it over with. The world will not wait for you to make up your mind."

"Is he right? Are you the one that's been talking to him? Teaching him… all of this? Did you do this to him?"

"Do what? Allowed him to see beyond what the Proclaimers have taught him? No. He did not need any help for that, though Goddess knows my younger self was overabundant in her advice, useless as it was. But it matters little. He does not listen to reason. For decades I warned him not to pry at the door once I truly understood what resided behind it. Yet he persisted. And now look where you've ended up." The Faoii crossed her arms and leaned against the far wall.

"Don't you blame him! Jacir's only a child. He was normal up until three years ago! You couldn't have talked to him before then!"

The woman spread her hands. "Look at you, knowing so much when you haven't even *tried* to see what your brother sees. You have no idea what he is capable of, girl. But I assure you, it was never my plan to answer his calls. I tried to stifle them for *years*. Tried to escape his inquiries about things too dangerous to know. But your brother's mind is larger than mine. Possibly larger than all of ours put together. His questions are deep and his unconscious need for knowledge and understanding strummed across the Weave, pulling for the answers to questions he didn't even know how to ask. And as the last person tied to it, my life and experiences were pulled forward so that he could examine and learn.

"I did not ask for this. And I do not deny that I would have ignored his pleas had I been able to." Her fist clenched and unclenched, but there was none of the trembling rage Ilahna had seen before. "But he is a strong force. It has taken many years and I have only just begun to build barriers against his will. I doubt there are any who live that could resist the young Weaver's call."

"Don't call him that!" Ilahna nearly screamed. "Jacir isn't a witch!" The Faoii opened her mouth to respond, but Ilahna cut her off. "This isn't Jacir's fault. He didn't ask for any of this! But he's got tangled into all of it. Now he's wrapped up in something he never should have had to worry about and there's no way to untangle all the threads. He's just a kid. This is too big for him. It's not fair!"

"Fair? Child, look at the world around you and tell me what part of it you thought is fair? Tell me which of us asked for any of what we've gotten? That's an immature stance, even for you."

"Don't call me child! I'm old enough to take care of myself! And Jacir, too! I've been doing it for as long as either of us can remember."

"Have you? Were that true, then I would not have to be here now, would I? But no. You couldn't even keep a child safe. So now I'm here to clean up your mess." The Faoii stomped a few steps away and removed her cloak. Ilahna could just make out her leather armor in the darkness.

"I didn't ask for you to help clean it up. I would have rather died on the pyre than take help from someone who doesn't care about him."

The Faoii's shoulders tensed, but she did not turn back around. "Then go meet that fate. There is a ladder at the end of this corridor that exits near the southern gate."

"And leave you alone with Jacir? So you can fill his head with more chants and lies? Never."

The woman released a deep sigh, finally turning back towards the firelight. "Listen, girl. I have no desire to fill that one's head with anything. The world is better without Faoii in it. I would be more than happy to help him close that door. Lead a normal life as an orphaned whelp with a stubborn sister. But that much power cannot be stemmed without the wielder's desire to block it. And the young Weaver craves to know what lies beneath the Tapestry's many strands. Still, though, if both of us try to convince him, we might have some success to stop this flood before it gets any bigger." Ilahna dropped her sword an inch, feeling a tiny thread of hope.

"Say that again. Look at me and say it." The woman's eyes sparked with steel and fire as she took another step forward. The gaze was frightening in its intensity.

"You mean you want to try your Sight on me." Ilahna suddenly shuddered. She felt that this exact conversation had taken place long ago, its echo reaching towards her from across a vast emptiness.

"Yes."

The woman shook her head and flicked her cloak to lay open on the ground before sitting down on it. "I will not play this game with you. Trust me or do not, it does not matter. But do not condemn the Faoii with your mouth and use your eyes to cast their magics. Your hypocrisy is suffocating, even from here."

Ilahna didn't know what to say to that. She had suspected, of course, but she'd let herself believe that Jorthee's teachings were something other than Faoii-based. Just bits of a forgotten past. But the sudden truth hit her with painful intensity and filled her with rage. Rage at him for teaching her. For letting Jacir say the things he said. For getting himself burnt at the stake.

For abandoning them.

Ilahna felt more than heard the sword strike the ground as it tumbled from her grip. She felt her knees hitting the ground next, and then the tears on her cheeks. It seemed like a long time before she heard her own sobs and screeched curses. She cursed Jorthee and the Faoii and the Proclaimers. She cursed the Old Gods and the Betrayer and the strange witch that had pulled them away from the Maze she understood and into this world that seemed too big and dark to handle.

After a few minutes, the woman's booted feet came into view. Ilahna stifled her sobs and forced her eyes upwards. Past the boots and cracked leather armor. Past the stern mouth and flat nose. She hugged herself tightly and forced herself to meet the grey eyes.

"Are you quite finished blaming everyone in the world besides yourself? You've as much to do with this as anyone. The Tapestry holds nearly infinite outcomes for your brother, and an astonishing number of them probably end in death or pain because of the foolishness of his sister. It's quite possible he'd be better off without you. Especially if this is what he can expect when things get difficult." Fury blazed within Ilahna, burning away her tears.

"No! He needs me! I'll protect him with everything I am!"

The Faoii leaned forward and cupped Ilahna's chin. She lifted it until Ilahna was finally forced to stand.

"Good. That's all I want from you. Learn that and I will be free." She pushed Ilahna roughly in the direction of the barracks. "Go get some sleep. Very soon you will have to prove your resolve."

19

Some part of Ilahna had assumed that the stranger would lead them out of Clearwall. That she would save them from the entire town and not just its mob. She did not trust the woman that called herself "Faoii," but she recognized that the tall, stern silhouette that stalked through the caverns had done more for Jacir in one night than the entire city of Clearwall had done in a lifetime. Ilahna did not trust her, but at least she was a visible and singular threat.

And for the first time since that dream-like night in front of the temple's courtyard—Jacir did not have to hide. Ilahna did not have to muffle his whispers in the night or stay partially awake to listen for boot steps on the cobblestones outside.

Ilahna lay unmoving on a worn pallet within the ancient sewers and stared at the damp, vaulted ceiling. The sound of Jorthee's screams had faded, as had the anger and the fear. Now she only felt numb. Empty. Every part of her ached, and yet she was out of tears or even thoughts. So, she only stared at nothing, listening to the soft sound of Jacir's breathing that was only occasionally punctuated by hiccups left over from his sobs. No poems or witch words or whimpers. Just the sound of a child momentarily unplagued by demons and doors that couldn't be closed again. It was the most beautiful sound that Ilahna had ever heard, rivaling even Eitan's singing.

At the thought of Eitan, a deep pain cut across Ilahna's heart and, in that moment—just as she had the day she'd seen the line of trees above the ramparts—Ilahna longed for freedom. She did not know if she wanted it from this woman that spoke of magic and filled Jacir's head with things that would get him killed. But she also wondered if maybe there were places in the world where knowing and dying didn't have to go hand in hand. Where maybe they could live a life not controlled by fear.

The fires lit by words are stronger and brighter than anything the Proclaimers have ever built.

Ilahna wanted to do as Jorthee had asked of her. She wanted to make a world where people could at least learn of the past for themselves rather than only run from it. Rather than let someone else tell them what it means or how they should react. But she didn't know how. She didn't know where to begin. Because anyone could lie to her as easily as the Proclaimers had, and she still had no way of knowing how much was truth and how much was fabrication.

But you know what is truth and what is not. You are Ilahna Harkins, the Keeper of Truth. There was a sudden flash of the unmarred temple and its deep carved symbols.

Library.

Illindria.

For the briefest moment Ilahna wished that she had been the one to open the door as she stared across the courtyard at a temple that was not a temple. She wished that she had been brave enough to look beyond those frightening images—that she might learn something more than what was fed to her through insincere smiles and smoldering pyres.

The door she'd kept closed for years opened a fraction of an inch at this fleeting thought, and Ilahna slammed it shut again.

No. Jacir traveled between the worlds constantly, and he would have been killed years before if someone planted firmly on this side had not been watching him all the while. She'd willingly let him pass through it last night and all of her worst fears had come to pass. *Never again.* As much as Ilahna wanted to be brave, she could not let herself get lost in… whatever world was hidden beyond that doorway. Not for truth. Not for freedom. Nothing was more important than Jacir.

Ilahna thought that they were possibly out of the reach of the Proclaimers' ears and eyes now. But there were dozens of people who must have whispered under their breath in the comfort of their own kitchens, far from the unblinking watch of the Proclaimers' rule, and still found themselves lashed to the stake come sundown. As much as Ilahna wished they were safe—she could not be certain. She had to remain vigilant.

She would protect Jacir with her life. Now and forever.

But you can still learn about views besides the Proclaimers' without opening the door.

Ilahna didn't know if that last thought was one that drifted from the keyhole of the grand door behind her mind, or if it was a quiet whisper of hope from her own heart.

The Faoii must have noticed something different in Ilahna's bearing the next morning, because she peered at her curiously for a minute before tossing a hard ration across the campfire.

"You look like you've made a decision about something important, girl. What is it?"

Ilahna took a deep breath to steady herself and looked the Faoii in the eye. "You know more about the world than what the Proclaimers teach. You might have learned it through magic and evil. You might be one of the Betrayer's followers and are the reason we're in this rathole of a life now. But you still know more than we do. I want you to tell me."

The woman cocked her head slightly, her lips pulled tightly together in a frown. But Ilahna thought she saw the faintest hint of an amused twinkle in her grey eyes.

"You recognize that your Proclaimers have only shown you a fraction of the Tapestry. A hastily cut section that paints a very specific picture. And you want to see other pieces of it? Even if it shreds the tattered shawl you've wrapped around yourself so carefully?"

Ilahna took a deep breath. "Yes. Your part might not be whole, either. Or even true. But I at least want to know what else is out there, without having to look upon the… Tapestry thing that Jacir is always talking about. I want to know what else is possible, but I want to stay on this side of the door."

The woman smiled briefly.

"No."

Ilahna's mouth dropped open. "No? What do you mean, no?"

"No. You want to learn, but I will not teach you."

"Why not?"

"Take your pick. Maybe it's because I don't trust you. Maybe it's because I don't like you. Or maybe it's because your motives are tarnished. You don't want to learn so that you may view the world and its intricate weaves with an open mind. You want me to tell you stories so that you may take what strands suit you and weave your own jagged mural. It will be no better or worse than that which the Proclaimers have given you, and I will not waste my time or breath so that one more section of an already mangled history can pass between insincere lips. You have enough to go on that you're at least questioning what you've been taught. That's enough for someone like you."

"Someone like me? Someone like *me?* You don't even know me!" The Faoii shrugged and laced her tall boot.

"I've known many like you. Someone who is willing to demolish entire forests in the name of claiming a single tree. Who find the pieces of stories that are relevant to their interests and throw the rest to the wayside. You wish to tell yourself that you know more than the guileless sheep that drift around you, but you are only led as easily as they are—if but by your own weak and poorly-conceived preconceptions. I will not give you more ammunition with which to shred whatever tale you've created for yourself within that hard head of yours."

Ilahna stood with her mouth open, dumbfounded. Finally, she recovered. "Then why are you even here? Why did you bring us here?"

"I already told you. Your brother called to me, and I was compelled to obey. I will have to train him to at least control what he has before I can live in peace as far away from both of you as possible." Ilahna's heart sank a little.

"You really don't care about us at all, do you?" The Faoii didn't even look up.

"No. But if it helps you, then realize that the man lashed to the stake last night did. I heard it in his screams. He had high hopes for you. And if it makes you feel better, then believe that I do plan to train you enough so that you *might* live long enough to *possibly* live up to those high hopes."

Ilahna opened her mouth to reply, but the Faoii raised her hand to stop her. "This conversation is over. Eat your ration and be quiet for a time. The coming days will be hard enough without you prattling on so incessantly."

20

Ali swung her wooden sword against the tree. Hard. It cracked against the bark, and she changed stances. Again, she swung. Again, it hit its mark firmly. Ali paused, leaning on her knees, panting. She would never be a Faoii, but the years since her last dismissal had not been spent idly. She still trained by herself. She still followed all the codes and lore she knew, though now it was more out of defiance than belief. Someday she would prove to the Order that they had been wrong. Magic or no magic, she *was* worthy.

A sudden shout from the other side of the house caught her attention, and she followed her father's angry protests, sword in hand. "This is our home!" he yelled. "Our family has lived here for generations! You can't just force us out of it!"

The voice that answered her father's outcry sent a chill down Ali's spine—it was so filled with power and firm inflexibility. She moved around the edge of the house with growing dread. A Faoii stood on the porch, her bronze breastplate catching the sunlight.

"The Monastery of the Horned Helm is growing rapidly, Citizen. This land is needed. You will be fairly compensated for your trouble, and a suitable plot of good soil has been chosen for you. You will still be under the protection of the Monastery. But you have until the first falling of leaves to relocate."

"What about the harvest?" Ali's mother cried, wringing her hands from the doorway.

"One of our unascended will complete the harvest and deliver your gains to your new abode. The Faoii are not unreasonable."

Ali released a dark laugh without realizing it, and the Faoii turned towards her. Ali opened her mouth to speak, but her father cut her off.

"Ali. Get in the house."

Ali did, giving the Faoii a long, hard glare as she passed. The Faoii's hand twitched towards her fantoii hilt, but she did not draw it. Instead, the warrior only squared her shoulders, and Ali *felt* the power rolling off her in waves.

Any normal person would be afraid. Ali could feel the terror in her mother's eyes. Watched her father draw back a pace. But Ali only squared her own shoulders, not breaking eye contact as she passed with even, measured steps. There was no fear in her, and the Faoii must have felt it, because the look in her eyes changed from audacity to… surprise.

"Ali. House. Now," Ali's father snapped, regaining control. Ali broke eye contact with the Faoii and entered without argument. Her mother followed, guiding the way towards the kitchen.

"First leaf fall, Citizen. An unascended will be back in the next several days with a map and gold for your relocation. Farewell."

Ali's father closed the door without replying. Once the door was firmly shut, he let his shoulders droop as he leaned against it. Ali's mother had buried her face in her hands.

"Danther. What will we do? This is our home."

"I know. But there's nothing to be done about it. They're moving the others, too. Everyone got the same raw deal. But we're not without hope. We'll move to the new plot. Start over. They're giving us enough gold to make it as easy a transition as possible, I guess."

"They can't do this, can they? Force us out of the home your ancestors built?" Danther sighed, looking older than he had a few moments before.

"Who's going to stop them?" he mumbled from the crook of his arm.

Ali looked at the practice sword in her hands. A sudden, burning hatred rose in her, and she pictured swinging it against the Faoii's smug face. But she knew the wooden sword was no more effective against a Faoii breastplate and ivy helm than her mother's broom would be. It was not enough. It would never be enough.

With angry, stomping steps, she retreated to her bedroom, stopping at the doorframe with her childhood heights carved into it. Her father's were there, too. And her grandmother's. Those would be gone, soon. Destroyed so the Faoii could have their space. Their iron swords. Their practice grounds.

Ali flung her wooden practice blade onto her bed and reached for the dagger she often used for her chores around the farm. With a quick and violent flick, she cut off the braid she'd been growing her entire life. Her first haircut. She watched wisps of hair drift to the floor, the tight weave loosening in its tumble.

She had grown that braid to prove she was worthy of the Faoii. But today, she didn't think the Faoii were worthy of her.

21

Ilahna panted, hands on her knees. Her blade lay in the putrid puddle at her feet.

"Pick it up. Again."

"Why are you doing this?"

"You're the one who tried to turn back and die for a fantoii. Some part of you wanted to use it. And you're foolish enough to try and raise it against those who are better trained than you someday. I won't let you die the moment I walk away because you're too dumb to see how unprepared you are. Do you see anyone else who is going to teach you? Pick it up!"

"What if I don't want to learn it?"

"Then don't. Walk away now. I tried to keep you alive. It is not my burden should you turn that away. I intervened the one time.

There will not be a second." The Faoii said the last part vehemently, casting a hate-filled glance in Jacir's direction.

On the other side of the cavern, Jacir sat motionless, watching Ilahna with intent eyes. Ilahna shuddered.

"Jacir. You don't have to watch this."

"He does. Who else is going to protect him when you fall?"

"Shut up! I'm not going to fall!"

"You will if you don't pick that blade up again."

Tears stung Ilahna's eyes, borne of fury and hatred for this stranger. "If you really care about his well-being, you'd take him as far away from here as you can!" Ilahna brought her blade up again, shaking it at the woman angrily.

"Foolish girl. You think the Proclaimers are only in Clearwall? You think he'd be safe anywhere else with a sister who doesn't even know how to fight peasants?" The Faoii brought her own blade down towards Ilahna's shoulder, and Ilahna jumped back a step.

"What do *you* know about him being safe? You've never been around his entire life! He begged you to come! And you never did! You only cared because he overpowered you!" Ilahna swept upward with her blade. The other woman parried easily.

"I was there when it mattered. Or have you forgotten?"

"I haven't forgotten that you talk about protecting him and about him having things to do, but we stay in this putrid sewer in the center of the worst city in the world! What good are you doing for him?"

"But, Ilahna. I'm learning so much!"

Ilahna stumbled at Jacir's sudden voice, and the Faoii knocked her blade from her hand. She barely noticed.

"You're learning? What?"

"Everything you refuse to." The Faoii kicked Ilahna in the chest, hard, and she fell on her back into the muck. "For every day we stay here your brother learns about the world and all within it—all that has ever been in it. He learns about the wars won and lost, the stories told and erased. He learns about where he's come from so he can decide where he wants to go. You just focus on where you are and wish it was something different."

Ilahna stared at Jacir as his eyes unfocused again, no longer watching them fight. She could almost imagine the door he was traveling through to see whatever the Faoii was talking about.

"The door?" She shuddered. "You're having him go through the door?"

"Of course. How else is he supposed to learn? It's not as though you're figuring out the world while you lie there in the mud. Hiding from everything beyond the walls you know."

"It's not that. I just want to make sure that I'm focusing on what's real."

"What makes you think that the things he sees aren't real?" The Faoii stepped up to Ilahna, towering over her with one hand on her hip. Ilahna shook her head.

"That's not what I mean. I know that when he goes to… wherever he goes, he's not here. Not really. He can't see the things right in front of him. I need to stay here. I don't want to miss anything that comes when he's looking at things that no one else can see. I want to be here. For him. To protect him." It was true, but another, deeper part of her knew it was because she was afraid of what waited on the other side.

The Faoii snorted. "Well, you're doing a fine job of learning how to do that, aren't you?"

Ilahna narrowed her eyes and rose to her feet. She picked up her sword again.

Ilahna lost track of how long they'd stayed in the sewers. Time and again she'd made her way to the surface and crept to the smithy where Eitan still waited, but it was always surrounded by posted Proclaimers, and she was never able to make it close enough to even sound a birdcall. Her heart ached that her last words to Eitan had been an unintentional lie. *We'll be back before the next bell.* But the posted guards meant he was still home. Still being watched, obviously, but still safe. And that was something.

I'll come back for you. As soon as I can. I promise.

She hoped she'd be able to keep this promise better than the last one.

Weeks passed, and slowly Ilahna began to trust the woman that had saved their lives. The Faoii was never kind, but Ilahna never had a reason to believe she was dishonest, either. And, while she was never brave enough to prop open the door that Jacir went back and forth through constantly, she kept trying to ask the woman about things she'd never known to question before. At first it seemed useless, but eventually, the Faoii started to respond.

"You said that the Proclaimers are everywhere. But they say that everything outside of Clearwall is just savage wastelands and the few farms under their protection. They send soldiers out to protect us from barbaric invaders. What's really out there?"

The woman peered at Ilahna as she stirred the ashes of the fire. "You could go through that door you've barricaded so thoroughly and find out yourself," she said.

"Please. Just tell me."

The Faoii leaned back and considered her answer. "Poor people, mostly. Peasants that are starved for sustenance. Shades that have no purpose and no future, and no way to attain either of those things. They come to places like Clearwall sometimes because their own homes have been decimated by soldiers or bandits. They seek a better life. They have no way of knowing that the cities they seek sanctuary in have already painted them in dark lies of 'otherness.' That, even if they find a way to enter the gates, their neighbors would turn them in to the Proclaimers out of fear and bitterness within a fortnight.

"Your Proclaimers are very good at painting others in shades of 'otherness.' Separating people with words like 'us' and 'them.' Most people in Clearwall forget that people are just people. Not Faoii. Not Danhaid. Just people."

"Danhaid? You mean the nomads?" The Faoii nodded, and Ilahna moved a little closer. "Do you consider them people? Like the rest of us, I mean? The Proclaimers say the Danhaid would burn the city to the ground if they ever got close enough. That we're lucky the Proclaimers keep them at bay and don't let us out. But they also say the Danhaid aren't even capable of speech. Just violent warmongers."

"Hardly. The Danhaid had a beautiful way of speaking. It sounded like flowers blooming and rivers running over rocks. It was… poetic. And sometimes it reminded you of the stars."

"Was?"

"There are none left. Your Proclaimers only say that the Danhaid still prowl the lands outside Clearwall so that your people are constantly afraid. Scared people are easy to control. But it is only lies. There were less than a hundred Danhaid left during the Faoii-Croeli War—the Godfell War, as you call it. They were rounded up with the Faoii and Croeli and killed as they were."

"Why do you separate them like that? The witches?" Ilahna asked quietly, watching the woman's face in the firelight.

The woman laughed softly. A cold, mirthless laugh. "There was a time when you could be killed for thinking they were one and the same."

22

Ilahna crept back into the sewers, ill at ease. The Proclaimers still surrounded Eitan's home, not giving up. She thought she and Jacir would be able to leave the sewers by now. She'd hoped that their lives could return to some semblance of normal.

But then... Ilahna didn't want to go back to "normal." Normal was what led to this terrible experience in the first place. "Normal" wasn't good enough.

She stood silently in the doorway of the long-forgotten barracks, watching Jacir sleep, his lips moving in quiet, magical murmurs. While she still did not want to see for herself what was on the other side of the door, she thought that now, maybe, she wanted to protect its open portal for any others that thought differently. And she wanted to protect those above who might someday choose to go through of their own volition, or who couldn't control when they did. There had to be others like Jacir in the world, and they shouldn't be afraid of their own thoughts. Of their own abilities. It wasn't right. No one should be afraid of who they were.

Clearwall was a casket. There was no way to learn things other than what the Proclaimers preached from their iron pulpits, rapping their gauntleted fists against the metal as they spoke. There was no way for the people of Clearwall to know of the stories that came from the Godfell War, for even the verbal retellings of old stories only came in hushed whispers and usually ended at the burning of a stake. There was no way for anyone to know what lay beyond the walls, to know that the Danhaid were dead but had once been beautiful. To know that the "all-mighty" Proclaimers dined on the offerings that came off the backs of those who suffered, not from forgotten Gods.

Seething at the piled lies and generations of fearmongering—at a hatred built up against people that could not even control what they had—Ilahna left her brother's sleeping form and crept into the central chamber of their little camp.

She was not sure the Faoii ever slept. The old woman was crouched before the fire, staring with unfocused eyes into the flames. Ilahna waited a moment, then cleared her throat before approaching. The Faoii did not even look up as she spoke. "What is it, girl?"

"I have more questions for you, if you would answer them."

The Faoii gave the slightest smile and rose from her crouch, rolling her neck as she turned to face Ilahna.

"More questions about who I am and what I want? Trying to decide if I'm a threat to your brother?" Ilahna shook her head.

"Not exactly. I… I want to know more about the past. The real past."

The Faoii raised an eyebrow and crossed her arms, shifting her weight to one hip. For a moment, she looked like she was going to object or make fun of Ilahna again, but something in her expression changed, and she nodded.

"Very well." She motioned to the fire and they both sat. "What do you want to know?"

Ilahna licked her lips. "What makes a Faoii? How do you become one?"

"Through training. And faith." The answer was immediate and sure. "Faoii are—were—trained from very young ages to be protectors and harbingers. It was a hard and dangerous life even before the Proclaimers rose to power. But it was not without its rewards."

"But what about the ones that can…see things? The ones like Jacir? Could they all do that? Or just some?" The woman was silent for a moment.

"Only some. We called them Weavers. Faoii that could see the Eternal Tapestry and its many strands—who could look upon the past and future and guide our entire Order with what they saw in the threads. It was considered a very rare and wonderful gift."

"The ones who have this… gift. Where did they get it?"

The Faoii rubbed at her cheekbone, thinking. "I have tried many times to find that out. I watched the Tapestry for many years looking for a pattern. Sometimes it follows families, lines of Weavers across centuries, like my mother and her mother before her. Other times, it grows out of nothing—like dandelions in barren fields. Little miracles."

"Which is Jacir? Do you know?" Ilahna unconsciously leaned forward, her heartbeat picking up speed.

The woman smirked a tiny bit at her excitement. "Do you really want to know?"

"Yes! Of course!"

The next question was colored with something like mirth and a deep, brooding pain.

"Why?"

The way it came from the woman's dark lips made Ilahna pause, and she knew she couldn't answer flippantly. Whatever she said would have to be the truth—even Jorthee wouldn't have been able to escape this woman's Sight. There could be no false-facing here. But she wasn't even sure if she knew what the truth was.

Ilahna thought for a long time, and the woman waited patiently, watching the young girl with steady, steely eyes. After several minutes of self-reflection, Ilahna took a deep breath.

"Because… because whatever you tell me would help me understand our purpose. If Jacir and I are from a line of magic, then I want to do right by those who came before me, even if I never knew them. If they helped to ruin the world, I want to atone for that. Fix it. If they were good, then I want to uphold whatever it was they stood for. And if Jacir is a miracle… well, there has to be a reason he's like that, right? There must be someone or something out there that decided he was important enough to have that gift. If he has a destiny, then I want to help him find it. I want to give people a reason to believe…to believe in magic again." The words caught in her throat a little, the word "magic" stinging like a wasp above her tongue. On reflex, she looked around for hidden Proclaimers in the dark, suddenly very afraid. The Faoii frowned and threw a twig into the fire.

"So, you want to know your own history so you have an excuse to honor either forgotten heroes or ancient Gods? Is that all the ambition you have, girl? To uphold another's wishes? Why not just live and act for yourself?" Ilahna wanted to take offense at the Faoii's tone, but it seemed like too much effort. For once in her life, she didn't want everything to have to be a fight.

"Because, for once… for once I want to be part of something bigger than myself. I want to belong somewhere. Be something. If I know how we got here, I might be able to figure out where I fit in." The Faoii's eyes softened a shade.

"Listen to me, child. You do not need to know your place in the Tapestry to be something grand. You can be grand and weave your own design in its threads whenever you choose. You could be part of something bigger than yourself on any day, regardless of those who came before you. You should not wait to be given a purpose."

Ilahna chewed on that for a long time.

"How do I know if I'm making the wrong choices?" she finally whispered. "If I work to become something greater than I am and ruin the world rather than fixing it?"

A deep pain flooded the woman's eyes, but she masked it quickly. "If you ask that too often, you'd never do anything at all." It sounded like something Jorthee would say, and Ilahna was momentarily overcome with a deep longing in her heart. After a moment, she tried again.

"But if you don't ask it often enough your choices could affect the lives of a million people down the road and you'd never even know it! Just like.... Just like they did." The old Faoii frowned, studying the girl's face.

"You're speaking of the Faoii-Croeli War. Of the warriors that fought to free themselves from Illindria's chains."

Something bubbled up inside Ilahna as she considered the arrogance of the statement. The selfishness. At the life she and so many others had been forced to live because of the actions of those that came before. "Free themselves? *Free themselves?* They *killed* the Gods! They ruined any chance the future had of blessings or a pleasant existence! Those Faoii had the power to see more than we could ever see. They were better off than we could ever be! And they ruined everything, anyway! We are still suffering from that war. We might *always* suffer for that war. There are millions of people out there who will never live without fear, who will never be allowed to dream or wonder—and it's because the Faoii witches tried to change the world for themselves instead of wondering what might happen to those of us living in the aftermath!" She flung her arm up to point at Clearwall's streets above her head. "Those people deserve more than that. The Faoii took everything from them!"

The Faoii met Ilahna's anger with a cool dejectedness. "You cannot always blame those that came before for the way things are now. Not while you and others like you hide in darkness and lies, sure that nothing can be done except complain about what came before." She gestured above their heads, as well. "There are enough downtrodden townsfolk out there to build an army with, and you think you're the only one who thinks as you do? That you can't build something greater than what you are from that?"

Ilahna snorted. "Build something? No one else wants to *do* anything. They'd rather cower and be herded like cattle. And those few that do stick out and try to be more than what they've been told to be..." She thought about Jorthee's story of the children in the school. An image of her uncle's bloodied face flashed across her mind and she fell silent.

The Faoii shrugged. "Then why not join the Proclaimers? They have a shared goal—a brotherhood that stands united against the forces of darkness. They hate the Faoii as much as you do. Surely that would give you the purpose you seek."

Ilahna spit on the ground. "The Faoii might have gotten us into this mess, but the Proclaimers keep us here. They make everyone afraid of everyone else. They kill innocent people for symbols found under paint or wearing their hair in a braid too often. I can't follow such monsters, no matter what type of oaths they make us swear."

The woman smiled from below hooded eyelids. "I knew of a man, long ago, who said something very similar."

Ilahna leaned back, the anger and intensity of their previous discourse fading. "Was he like you? A witch?" The Faoii did not seem to take offense to the word.

"Not at all. In fact, he was a common soldier—an oddity in the Faoii-Croeli War. Of all those who clashed, he was not called upon to fight by Gods or kings. He wasn't even a general. Just a city guard with a good heart." She leaned forward, her voice still soft.

"He was everything that you could be but have not sought. He never felt like he had a higher purpose, never sought to fill the roles that others offered him. He just wanted to do the right thing. For his country, for his friends. And for that, he was a better person than most of those whose names were written in the history books before they were destroyed. But history doesn't even remember his name."

"How do you know about him, then?"

The Faoii shrugged. "There were many stories that were passed down orally before the Proclaimers cut out the tongues of those whose stories did not suit them. Now you know his tale. A sliver of a girl to carry on a sliver of history."

Ilahna thought about the young soldier for a long time, fighting battles that he believed in without being told to. Changing the world for no other reason than that he wanted to try.

"Do you know his name?" she finally whispered.

"Emery. Emery Harkins."

Ilahna tried to stifle a laugh, barely able to choke it down. The Faoii gave her an odd look.

"Why do you respond this way?"

"Because all the Harkins I've ever known were nobodies bred from nobodies. At least one of them tried to be more than that. And he almost succeeded. But then his story was lost, anyway."

"Not lost completely. Now you have it. What you do with it is up to you."

Ilahna stared into the fire, watching a ball of silk strand moss unravel and spread across the floor as she thought about the unknown soldier that might not even have existed. A nearly-nameless part of history. And yet… and yet she wished she were strong enough to do good in the world purely for the fact that the world needed good people. She wished she wasn't so afraid.

At least one Harkins in the world tried to be more than they were. I wish I was one, too.

Finally, Ilahna took a deep and shuddering breath, and something clicked into place behind her eyelids. The Faoii raised an eyebrow.

"You've come to some sort of conclusion."

Ilahna nodded, trying to put her thoughts into words. "If the Proclaimers and their Old Gods kill people for having power they didn't ask for… People like Jacir… Then risking their wrath and using that magic is the darkest betrayal a mortal can commit." Ilahna's heart hardened further against the Proclaimers as she spoke, but deep down, a stronger truth welled up within her, filling all the cracks and spaces in her soul. "…But if that's true, then maybe those are the types of Gods that *need* to be betrayed."

The words, though whispered, echoed through the cavern, and from across space and time, Ilahna knew the Betrayer had said the same thing, once. Maybe not in so many words. Maybe not with words at all.

But for the first time in her life, Ilahna thought she understood why a mortal would want to kill a God.

The Faoii stared at Ilahna from across the fire, her eyes calculating.

"You have more secrets than what you hide for your brother." It was not framed as a question. "You know things you're not supposed to know."

You are Ilahna Harkins. Keeper of Truth.

Ilahna swallowed hard. "I… I don't know. Maybe. Sometimes I suspect things. I think things I shouldn't think. But I don't know if they're true or not. There's no way to know the truth anymore."

So much of the truth was in the past. And so much of that had been lost to the people of Clearwall. Ilahna wasn't sure she wanted to learn all the untold secrets of their world from a woman that treated everyone and everything—especially her—with such disdain. But something in the Faoii's eyes when she talked about the past pulled at something deep within Ilahna's heart. Something that she wanted to bring to the surface, but didn't know how.

"Faoii." Ilahna finally whispered, bowing her head slightly. "I know you do not like me. I know I have not been the pupil you wish I was. But... please... I think I need your help. I don't want to keep secrets from Jacir anymore. Or from myself."

The woman poked at the fire, her face grim. Ilahna tried again. "Please, Faoii. I don't know why I hear whispers in my mind or words that aren't my own. I don't know what it means. I don't know anything at all except that the truth is important. Not just for me and Jacir. But for everyone. And sometimes my heart pulls me forward so hard it hurts. But no one else is searching for the answers to what we are. Of where we come from."

Ilahna felt tears in her eyes. A demanding pulse from deep within her soul screamed to know the truth about things she'd never questioned. It nearly deafened her. For a moment she thought she would go mad with the tempest that swirled inside her. She squeezed her hands against her thighs so hard she felt her nails cut into her skin. She could no longer see the fire or hear Jacir's gentle snores. Instead, all she could comprehend was the massive stone door that she had barricaded over and over again, groaning and swelling as something on the other side tried to force its way out.

The truth was there, behind that door, but Ilahna still did not want to open it. Her heart told her that the truth was at her fingertips and that she needed to know it, but Ilahna would not—could not—reach for the handles that called to her. There had to be another way. There had to be something she could do to ease these cries.

"Please, Faoii," she whispered again, though she could not hear her own voice amidst the screeches of the winds behind the stone slab that dominated her vision, looming over her until there was nothing else. She couldn't hold it back. She couldn't—.

Suddenly, everything stilled at once. Ilahna opened her eyes, and the Faoii was in front of her, two dark hands on either side of her face. Ilahna realized that her cheeks were wet with tears.

"You have power in you too, girl. It's a shame that you hide from it so. But, I suppose I understand. Your heart knows that the truth of what we are is borne of blood and misery. It wants the truth, but understands enough to fear it."

The Faoii returned to her side of the fire and pulled a small packet from her cloak. She poured its contents into a kettle and set it above the flames. It was not until after the tea had brewed and she and Ilahna both held small tin cups that she spoke again.

"The Faoii-Croeli War, or the Godfell War as you call it, was very difficult on people. The destruction of Illindria shifted power in ways that no one could foresee, and those that had grown powerful in the past were suddenly just… ordinary, while those that had once had nothing could now determine their own fates for the first time. Illindria no longer watched the Weave, no longer controlled events on a grand scale. The Croeli were welcomed by some and shunned by others. But overall, the people tried to work together to create something better than what they had before. Their lives were no longer dictated by someone else. They wanted to build something grand of their own volition.

"People worked hard for a while. They found joy and strength in guiding their own futures. Some fought against the change, but eventually they fell into the shadows, and people prevailed. Not Gods. Not Weavers or Faoii or witches. Regular people. All people. Together."

The Faoii's voice turned bitter. "But then things started getting difficult. New generations were given everything by parents that had grown up with nothing. They became greedy and entitled. Took what their parents offered and simply assumed that that was how things had always been. Soon, none alive remembered what it was like under Illindria's reign. Children that had never known hunger or work were suddenly the only ones left to move things forward. They were forced to take jobs, but no longer had the skills. The economy shattered in the hands of the lazy. Instead of blaming themselves, though, people blamed the lack of deities. It was too hard without someone giving them everything."

Ilahna thought about all the times she had stolen from a merchant without care. How she had convinced herself that someone unable to protect his own goods did not deserve to have them. She thought about how the people of Clearwall turned on each other so easily, focused only on their own little lives and tiny fistfuls of grain or fish, and never about those who lived next door in the same circumstances. How it was easier to turn someone into the Proclaimers and call them a witch than see them as a person.

"How do we fix it?" she whispered. The Faoii looked across the fire, and for a moment Ilahna thought the woman could see into her soul.

"What does your heart tell you?" she asked.

Ilahna focused inward onto that little voice that often spoke so clearly when everything else was jumbled and chaotic. It rang out to her more quickly than she expected. "I think it all begins with trying to help people move forward, instead of trying to reclaim a past that never truly existed."

The Faoii turned the corners of her lips up in the faintest hint of a smile. "Maybe you are smarter than you seem, girl."

Ilahna was about to respond when Jacir's startled cry shattered the silence. His wail was ear-piercing and tortured, and it dug icy tendrils into Ilahna's heart.

Ilahna jumped to her feet and charged down the twisting path, barely registering as the Faoii followed behind. When she arrived, Jacir was rocking on his pallet, knees to his chest as he tried to stifle his tears.

"Oh, Jacir," Ilahna whispered, sitting beside him, and hugging him close. "What happened? Was it a dream?"

"I hope so. Oh, Ilahna!" His voice rose to a wail as he buried his face in her shoulder. "It was so dark. There was so much pain in the air. Who could do that to people?"

Ilahna pet his hair softly. "It's okay, Jacir. It was just a dream. It's okay."

"Was it?" he sobbed. "I hate not knowing what's dreams and what's real, Ilahna. I hate it!"

"All of it is real. Just in different perceptions." The Faoii woman stepped from the darkness and knelt in front of Jacir. "What did you see?"

Jacir swallowed and pulled away from Ilahna a little, his eyes red. "Eitan. They have him. They're looking for us, and they think he knows where we are. So they took him! And now they're hurting him!"

Ilahna's heart stopped, then thundered so loudly she almost couldn't hear Jacir's cries.

"No," she whispered. "No. I was just at the smithy. The Proclaimers are still watching it. Watching him."

Or are they just watching for us? Waiting for us to return while they torture Eitan?

Ilahna thought she was going to be sick. Her head spun and tilted with a single, repeated phrase. The Proclaimers had Eitan. The Proclaimers *had Eitan.*

The Proclaimers had Eitan!

She was already marching back towards the sewer exit before her mind could catch up with her feet. Jacir trotted after her, pulling on her arm. "Wait, Ilahna! Stop!"

Ilahna shook him off, but the Faoii's velvety iron voice caused her to pause. "Running out of here to get yourself killed isn't going to help anything. Use your head, girl." Apparently, the kind Faoii that Ilahna had been speaking to only minutes before was gone. But so be it.

"They have Eitan. He's never done anything wrong in his entire life. He's watched us and protected us and been there for us through everything. And they're hurting him because of us.

Because of *me*." Ilahna clenched her fists at her sides. "I have to help him. *We* have to help him."

Ilahna's hatred was too deep for even tears. The burning in her soul transcended fury. "I will *not* lose another friend to the pyres. Never again. This ends here."

The Faoii looked her over carefully, reading something in her face. "You are going to do this no matter what I say, aren't you, girl?"

"Yes."

The Faoii sighed. "There are things you need to learn, still. I suppose this will be as good an opportunity as any other. Let's create a plan so you don't get that fool head of yours knocked off the moment you step outside."

23

Ali stared out across the barren field. The crops hadn't come in. Again. Her father couldn't understand it. The soil seemed good. The rains had come and gone. But the fields remained lifeless and barren, despite his magic and patience. The first year had seemed understandable. It was a new plot. Who knows what could have gone wrong before they'd been there? But the second year? The third? Their family was beyond just "good" at farming. Generations of Danther's ancestors had coaxed life from seemingly barren soil. They knew what they were doing. And when knowledge wasn't enough, they had that magic knack that Ali had, until now, taken for granted as nearly-useless. But things were different now.

The Faoii had been no help when Ali had accompanied her father to the Monastery last summer. The Order had agreed to send an unascended out with the farmers, and Ali's childhood friend, Calari, had spent several weeks with them trying to coax life back into the earth. But even she could not find anything wrong with the soil.

"The Faoii cheated us, Calari. They must have." Ali said one night, pacing angrily in front of her bed. Calari put aside her polished breastplate.

"The Faoii do not 'cheat' those that they protect, Ali." She sighed at Ali's angry snarl and stood up, standing in front of her pacing friend. "Ali, I know that you still feel betrayed by the Order. Is that why you keep your hair so short, now?" She reached out to Ali's pixie cut, but Ali jerked her head out of the way. Calari let her hand drop.

"I don't know what's going on with the soil here, but I want to help. No one knows this, but the Monastery of the Broken Shackles will be expanding soon. I can help your family secure a good plot of land with established fields that have supported several generations of farmers. The current owners are aging and have no heirs—"

"I don't want your help!" Ali snapped. Calari looked hurt and gazed at the floor. Ali sucked in a breath before sitting down next to her oldest companion.

"I'm sorry, Calari. I don't know why I said that. I'll ask Father what he wants to do and send a letter to the Monastery after we have a chance to think about it. Okay?"

Calari smiled and put one arm around Ali's shoulders. "We'll figure it out, Ali. Don't worry."

The next day, after Calari had left, Ali told her father about the offer. He shook his head sadly in response.

"No, Ali. No more moving. We will not keep replanting ourselves at the demand of Faoii."

"But, Danther, what will we do if not move?" Ali's mother's lip trembled as she looked to her husband for guidance. Danther only looked defeated.

"I don't know."

Ali's heart clenched and she left her parents staring dejectedly at the kitchen table, looking lost and afraid. On impulse, she went to her mother's sewing room, filled with homemade thread that glowed with its own light. She grunted as she dragged out her mother's great cedar chest and began sifting through it.

"Ali, dear. What are you doing?" her mother whispered from the doorway, wiping her eyes.

Ali didn't answer and kept searching, piling the chest's contents on either side of her. Finally, she dug out a small wooden triangle with a clockwise spiral in its middle. She held it up to her face, her soul seeking the warmth and hope her ancestors had doubtlessly woven into it upon its creation. But there was nothing. The symbol was dead and lifeless in her hands—nothing but dusty wood and brittle string.

Burying the sense of disappointment, she lifted it gingerly, anyway, brushed past her mother, and brought it out to the living room. With careful, deliberate movements, she hung it in the window next to the door.

"The Fallen Goddess? Why, Daughter?" Danther asked quietly, staring at the little ornament.

"Why not?"

"But...There are no Gods left, Ali. Surely this is no answer." Her parents stood behind her pensively, but neither tried to remove the bauble from where Ali had placed it.

Ali turned towards her parents, her back straight, her eyes blazing. "Maybe not. But our ancestors built a farm and family out of nothing. They thrived when so many others failed. And through it all, they hung one of these in the window. Maybe there are no Gods left. But only the Faoii tell us that. One single Faoii claimed to kill a God. If they are going to take everything from us, then maybe we can't stop them. But...maybe this is something we can take back. Something we don't have to give up." Ali's mother looked imploringly at her husband.

"What could it hurt, Danther?"

For a long moment, Danther stared at the symbol one of his ancestors had so lovingly created in forgotten days. Ali saw the hint of nostalgia on his face—memories of seeing the decoration in his youth. The faintest twitch of a smile brought up the side of his mouth.

"Nothing. Nothing at all."

Ali had no idea in the moment what her small act of defiance would spark. But as the little symbol caught the sunlight between the edges of its spiral, something deep and unrecognizable welled up within her. She held the swell of power to her chest, knowing that it was not borne of worship, but of defiance. The willingness to stand against what was unjust. And she was determined to help it grow for as long as it took.

24

As much as Ilahna wanted to tear down the walls of the temple in the middle of the square and force the Proclaimers to tell her where they were keeping Eitan, she knew it wasn't possible. The temple was heavily guarded, and while people had been welcomed inside during her youth, now only the Proclaimers were allowed to even climb the front steps.

Furthermore, she didn't know where they were actually keeping the blacksmith. Were there cells in the temple? Somewhere below ground? In the bell tower with the great iron bells that so often haunted her dreams? She wasn't even sure they were in the temple proper or if prisoners were moved somewhere else. So many people were arrested or simply disappeared every day. Was there enough room for them all within that towering building and its mutilated façade? She paced the sewers agitatedly in frustration and worry.

"Stop pacing, girl. You're giving me a headache." The Faoii's words cut through Ilahna's thoughts, and she spun to face the old woman kneeling in front of Jacir. "If you are not going to open the door to follow your brother through, then kindly stop being a distraction as he learns things beyond your shortsightedness."

Ilahna scowled at the Faoii's biting words but stopped pacing.

"It's okay, Lana. Don't be scared." Jacir whispered. "I think we can find him."

Jacir didn't open his eyes as he spoke, his voice drifting. His brow was creased with concentration, his pale skin waxy in the firelight. The Faoii redirected her attention to the boy.

"Don't focus on her, Faoli. Look for your friend. Focus on the eye you so often use to see the Weave. You have the innate ability; we need but harness it." Jacir frowned, the creases on his forehead deepening under a shine of fresh sweat.

"Look at him." Ilahna cried, clenching her fist. "It's hurting him! Isn't this something you can do, with all your supposed power?" Ilahna's voice was cold, but the Faoii's gaze was downright icy as she turned towards her again.

"I don't know who we're looking for, do I, girl? And even if I did, it is the young Faoli's turn to learn how to do such things himself. We can't all just pace back and forth and wait for others to do the work we want to see accomplished."

Ilahna opened her mouth to reply, but the Faoii had already turned back to Jacir, their conversation evidently finished. "This is the first step, young Faoli. Someday, should you choose, you may guide your mind's eye willfully to all the places you desire to see. But for now, you need only follow the current where it goes. Breathe deeply and let your mind wander as it does in dreams."

"What if I can't find him?"

"You will. We may take all the time you need. But your unconscious mind was able to call to me, a stranger, across the threads. It will pull towards him with ease." She reached out and rubbed at Jacir's temples. "When you see your friend, you need only look for closer details. The walls. The air. The smell if you can. There is no need to bend the Weave to fit your desires. Only ride its strands to where they'll take you and tell us what you see."

Ilahna took a few steps closer. "Wouldn't it be easier to follow them purposefully to wherever Eitan is?" she asked.

The Faoii shot Ilahna an angry glare and did not reply. For a moment it looked like Jacir was going to answer Ilahna when the Faoii didn't, but his face relaxed again as the old woman thumped him on the forehead.

"Ignore her. Concentrate. Follow the stream wherever it goes. We can discuss other rivers later."

Ilahna lost track of the time as she watched her brother travel to places she could not go. His frail body tensed up as he pried at a door that had always opened of its own accord before. But, then, suddenly, his face and body went lax, and his mouth began to move with barely perceptible words. "There are trees outside the walls. They get pushed further and further back each year, and the deer have to recede deeper into the forest to remain in cover. There are old stone buildings hidden, there, too. A fox family lives where a woman once kept her brooms."

The Faoii nodded and resumed massaging his temples. "Good. Look for the flow of a river that leads closer to home. Follow the current towards Clearwall."

Jacir was silent for a few minutes, but suddenly the light on his face changed, and he spoke again. "Farms spread across the countryside. They're backed up almost to the new wall being constructed around the farthest outreaches of the Maze. It is bigger than the original one, the wall that once outlined Clearwall but now separates the rich districts from the poor. So much has changed. So many new buildings. These families that once lived so far away from civilization wonder at the city in their backyard. You need a special writ to enter and exit Clearwall now. The King has not been seen in days. Proclaimer Tosleh says that it is for the protection of everyone, but one mother wonders how they will make new clothes for the children this winter, since the Proclaimers have forbidden them from raising their own sheep. They had to focus on chickens now, by order of the King. And how the children are growing tired of eggs."

"I remember those days," the Faoii murmured. "Everyone knew the tides were changing. But the steps were small. Little moves that make sense in the moment, until you look around and realize you no longer recognize where you are." She whispered to Jacir again. "Closer, still. You are doing well, Faoli."

"Wait. He's seeing the past?" Ilahna asked, momentarily forgetting about her brother's concentration. The Faoii glared.

"Eternal Blade, girl. Be silent!" There was a rush of power at the words, and in that moment Ilahna understood what it meant to have the power of a Faoii, her entire body trembling at the force. She sat down obediently, her lips pressed together.

Luckily, Jacir seemed unperturbed. "This was a battle keep. The Clearwall family staved off a thousand soldiers between the rivers. They built a city out of the survivors. Sections fell and were rebuilt and changed and shifted over centuries. Stone changed for glass. Blood-worn battlements covered by tapestries. There are… so many faces. Voices. So many people have been here. Are here."

Jacir began to shake, and Ilahna immediately went to try and comfort him, but was stopped by another sharp glare from the Faoii. "Let them pass easily. Don't focus on any but what you want to see. Let them roll over you like waves on a beach, Faoli." Jacir's face relaxed.

"I have never seen a beach. There is one, far to the west. Small creatures crawl out of it, sunning themselves on the sand, laying eggs and exploring things no longer touched by man."

"Focus, Faoli. Clearwall."

Jacir went lax again and did not say anything for a long time, though Ilahna saw his eyes moving beneath their lids. Eventually he smiled. "Ilahna just jumped onto the roof before running away. Eitan yells funny things at her and looks angry, shaking a fist in her direction, but when he goes inside he smiles until his face hurts. He's using scraps from the smithy to forge a ring."

Ilahna's heart thumped in her chest and her face flushed.

A ring.

Eitan wanted to make her a ring.

Ilahna wanted to imagine all the possible futures they might have together. The dreams and lives that might come on a horizon she couldn't yet see. The details were unimportant, but at the center of all of it was something wonderful: Eitan holding her hand while she wore a ring he'd made of iron scraps and love.

But Ilahna could only conjure up thoughts of the pyre. Of the Proclaimers beating Eitan until his face was as bloody and swollen as Jorthee's had been. Of his sweet, beautiful song being replaced by screams as the flames rose higher. Her stomach twisted and she thought she might be sick.

None of it would mean anything at all if they couldn't find him. If she couldn't save him.

"You are very close now, child. Come a little further," the Faoii whispered to Jacir.

Again Jacir's face went lax as he followed the threads. A few moments passed before he whispered, "I found him."

"Good. What do you see, Faoli?"

"The walls are old and stone. It smells wet. They are rough and dark and stained black in many places by thousands of torches in the same place. The sconces do not have the designs of the temple or the Proclaimers or the Gods."

"What do they have?"

"A crown over a river with a star."

"That is the crest of Clearwall. Very well, Faoli, you may return."

Jacir opened his eyes and smiled a relieved smile before slumping sideways with an exhausted sigh.

"Jacir? What's wrong?"

"Calm down, girl. He is only sleeping. He has worked many muscles that he hasn't used before." The Faoii considered for a moment, looking at the young boy. "I expected this process to take days or weeks. I have never seen a Weaver learn to traverse the Tapestry so quickly. I never would have imagined so much power could be in the hands of a child."

Ilahna made sure that Jacir was comfortable and wrapped a blanket around his snoring frame. "But we know where Eitan is? We can go save him now?"

"Wait until your brother awakens. It is possible that we will need him. And, even if you were capable of saving your young love on your own, I doubt you would be willing to leave your brother behind?"

Ilahna thought about it for a moment before shaking her head. She needed to go help Eitan. Every minute he stayed under the ruthless fist of the Proclaimers was one too many. But she could not do it alone.

She took leaden steps towards the fire, her heart still pulling her towards the ladder that would lead her to Eitan. To love and fantasies and a future she'd often dreamed of but never guessed he'd wanted to share.

Please hold on. Soon, Eitan. I promise. Hold on a little longer.

I'm coming.

25

The night didn't seem dark enough or the Maze twisted enough when Ilahna, Jacir, and the Faoii inched from the sewers and onto the streets of Clearwall. Ilahna had made several sojourns out into the streets to check on Eitan before this, but she'd always gone alone. Now, as the three of them crept across the roofs, Ilahna was more aware of every brush of their feet against cracked tiles. Every creaking board that groaned beneath their weight. Every flutter of wings as they surprised pigeons from their roosts.

She could feel the apprehension rolling off of Jacir in waves. It fed into her own fear, too, and the siblings jumped in unison each time they heard booted feet on the streets below or imagined the sound of a Proclaimer drawing their sword.

The Faoii, however, seemed unperturbed, and she bounded forward, silent and graceful as she led them towards the rocky cliffs at the far end of Clearwall. The urchins had never been this close to the inner wall that surrounded the rich districts pressed up against the bluff that supported Clearwall Keep. The buildings were old but sturdy—far cries from the ancient tannery that Jorthee and the urchins had called home.

"Faoii, the temple is in the other direction. Towards the lower markets. Where are we going?" Ilahna whispered as they crouched behind a well-kept chimney, while an armored Proclaimer passed on the street below.

"The sconces our young Faoli described bear the crest of Clearwall. The crown above the Twilight River." She paused at Ilahna's quizzical face. "The Starlit River then. Such an unnecessary change," she huffed under her breath. "The library-" Another exasperated sigh as the Faoii rolled her eyes. "The *temple* doesn't bear that crest inside. Their sconces have an inverted triangle with a clockwise spiral."

"You've been inside the temple?" Ilahna whispered, almost too loudly. Below, the Proclaimer stopped, looked around, and continued. The Faoii shot Ilahna a hard glance.

"Hush now. I need to concentrate."

For a moment the Faoii's gaze went far away, as she peered over a landscape Ilahna couldn't see. Jacir exhaled slowly, amazed.

"You control it so easily. Can I learn to do that someday?"

The Faoii frowned. "Perhaps. Following the natural flow of the strands is not difficult, and you have already mastered the first steps."

"Will I be able to travel physically across all of it, like you used to?"

"No." The answer was immediate and cold.

Jacir looked disappointed. "Why not?"

The Faoii softened a little. "The way has been lost now. There was a cursed plant, once, that offered dark powers in the guise of gifts." She caught Jacir's dismayed expression. "I assure you, young Faoli, that you do not want the burden that would have come with its use. You use the Sight well enough without that pain."

"What plant was it?" Ilahna asked before she could stop herself.

Before the Faoii could reply, Jacir's lips moved in a breezy whisper that made Ilana's skin crawl.

"Tonicloran."

The Faoii shuddered. "It is best not to even think of it, Faoli. The world is better now that it is gone." She looked over the roofs again, and her eyes focused on something familiar. "Come, children. I know the way."

They followed the Faoii through a twisted path across buildings that did not crumble under their footfalls. And, as they neared the cliff that supported the jewel of Clearwall, Ilahna could not hide her amazement.

It was unlikely that any of the Maze urchins had ever seen Clearwall Keep up close before. While Ilahna had long admired it from the lower, cracked and paltry establishments of the Maze, she had not realized how truly grand it was, even from within Clearwall's inner gates. The ornamentation that adorned its stately towers and high-glassed windows glittered in the torchlight, reflecting the moon and the gleam of the Starlit River. Even the grand temple did not have so much glistening gold and wrought silver around its towering pulpits and crystal chandeliers. Ilahna looked down at Jacir's shabby boots as they ran across the rooftops. Even the broken tusk of one of Clearwall Keep's snarling gargoyles would be worth more than all the money they had ever had. It could keep Jacir warm and fed for years.

A dark rage filled Ilahna as she pushed herself harder. She wanted to scale the inner wall that surrounded Clearwall Keep. She wanted to break a guard's nose on the shiny banisters she would never have been allowed to even glimpse, were it not for this Faoii who deigned show her more than what she'd ever dream of. She wanted to tear the jewels from the walls and shove them down a Proclaimer's throat until he gagged beneath their weight. Her entire life, she had dreamt of the day she might, even for a moment, see the finery inside the palace on the top of the mighty cliff that rose above the Maze. She had prayed to every God the Proclaimers spoke of that someday it might be so.

And now the Proclaimers with their honey-words and venomous tongues were keeping someone inside those walls that meant more to her than any of it. She would happily burn it all to the ground to retrieve him.

But the Faoii did not bring them to the parapets. Did not scale them with that sure step that didn't quite seem to hit the slanted roofs and stone walls the way that Jacir's and Ilahna's did. Instead, she stopped quite a distance from the inner gates, peering over countless buildings that spread out in all directions.

As they watched, the woman's grey eyes unfocused as she stared out across the city. Jacir reached out and just barely touched her dark hand, and his eyes dimmed as well. His lips began to move. "It's the taxes pantry. It leads to the tax collector's office. That's where I left the cart… I know it's not fitting for a Faoii, but I didn't know another route." Ilahna frowned. The voice was still not Jacir's, but she felt like she recognized it. It almost reminded her of Jorthee, but even that didn't seem right.

"There." Both Jacir and the Faoii alighted on the same building, and Ilahna forgot about the voice that reached her from across the ages as the others came back to themselves simultaneously.

"A home, now. I wonder if they bricked up the passageway?" The Faoii whispered, seemingly to herself. Jacir answered anyway, smiling at the thought of helping.

"Do you want me to try and see from here? I'm getting better at controlling what I look at."

"No." The Faoii's answer was immediate and jarring. She paused and tried again, her voice softer. "No, Faoli. You've stared at the Great Tapestry enough for now. It is too easy to become dependent on it. And once you feel you cannot survive without it, it is so easy to become tangled in the strands."

"Is that why you try not to do it anymore?"

Jacir's question seemed so soft, so innocent, but Ilahna saw the woman's back stiffen and her hand tremble at his words. Her fingers clenched into a tight fist as she exhaled. For a moment, the air charged with electricity, and Ilahna felt true fear as a deep, dark anger rolled off the Faoii in waves. Jacir shrank back immediately, but the sudden fear she saw in her brother's face only made Ilahna bristle. Ignoring her own terror, she moved to stand between them.

"Faoii, I don't know what Jacir just woke up in you, but I need you to unclench your fist. If you try to strike him, you will have to go through me." She put a hand on her fantoii's hilt.

The Faoii seemed startled to see her, and she jumped a bit to suddenly find herself face-to-face with Ilahna. Then, when she at last seemed to comprehend what was happening, her eyes flitted to Ilahna's hand on her sword hilt, and she released a grim chuckle.

"Look at you, girl. Maybe you really are worthy of being the young Faoli's protector." She turned to Jacir and Ilahna took a tentative step back.

"We can move forward without depending on magic and things that call to creatures we don't want to awaken. Anything in the world can be a crutch to lean on or a hole to fall into. You have other, more mundane skills. Use them. Look at the house. Tell me what you see."

Jacir looked. "It's old…" His eyes faded slightly. "It has housed noblemen and their wives. Two brothers. A widow once. The door used to be red. Men and farmers brought money and crops here at the end of the season. There was a tree out front, long ago. Before it was even built. Before it was a city."

The Faoii frowned and thumped him on the forehead. "You remind me of a discussion I had once, long ago. No, little Faoli. Don't use the Sight. Use your eyes. What do you *see*?"

Ilahna frowned and focused on the house, too. "There are no footprints in the mud."

"Very good, girl. You're cleverer than you look. What else?"

Ilahna glared at the Faoii, but looked again. "The windows are frosted on the inside, too. So, there hasn't been a fire there, even though it's been cold the last several nights."

"And what, then, might this mean?"

"The house is empty," Jacir piped up. "No one has lived there this season." The Faoii nodded.

"There are many skills in the universe. Don't let some starve while others are glutted. You never know when uncontrollable forces will try to hobble you." She stood. "Move quietly, children. Let us see what buried treasure they might have left behind."

26

Ilahna had broken into many buildings in her lifetime. It wasn't something she was ashamed or proud of—it was simply how she and Jacir had survived for too many years. But she took pride in the skill now as she smirked at the Faoii, laying a hand on the old woman's wrist. "Wait. I have a better idea."

The Faoii frowned and pulled her hand away, still clutching the rock she had been preparing to use on a back window. Ilahna couldn't help but grin a little bit more as she removed her lockpicks from her trinket belt and silently went to work on the door.

Ilahna had never really needed the lockpicks. Most of the houses in the Maze did not sport actual locks, and instead were only secured by simple latches or the general belief that mazers had nothing of value to steal. But she had seen one of the other urchins, Gavin, boast about his skill with the little tool set, and she'd watched him pop open a flimsy lock on a crate once just to prove he could. She had no reason for such a toy—but she'd wanted it.

Gavin had no use for her regular trades, however, and reveled in the joy that came from taking everything from someone with big bets and bigger deceits. It had taken months of pretending to lose at Kings and Witches (and dozens of small, insignificant bets) to finally draw the other urchin into putting up his crafty lockpicks. Ilahna had put forward her favorite dagger, and (after having won every game beforehand) young Gavin had thought it would be an easy win. A tax on Ilahna's poor skills and stupidity for continuing.

All her lies had finally paid off, though, and she still felt a thrill of pride as she remembered Gavin's look of shock and betrayal as she pulled the knife and lockpicks to her, smiling gleefully. Now, she felt the same surge of pride and elation as she saw the Faoii's eyebrows lift in surprise as she dropped her little stone. Ilahna did her best to mask her smile at the door's sure *click*.

"All done," she said smoothly as she straightened again. She pushed open the door and tried not to look too smug as she watched the Faoii advance.

"Your false-facing needs work. But I suppose you have earned that cocky gleam in your eye, Ilahna."

Ilahna's smirk spread into an actual grin at the Faoii's use of her name. She couldn't help it. But as they entered the dark and dusty room that had hosted dozens of lives only she was unable to see, her smile faded. Eitan was still locked away somewhere. And this dirty room that had fallen into disrepair long before did not seem to hold him.

"What are we looking for?"

The Faoii paced the ground, her footfalls muffled by the carpet laid on the floor. Moldy and grimy as it was, Ilahna felt a pain in her chest at the sight of it. There was more luxury in this room than she and Jacir had ever known, ignored and forgotten for an untold number of years.

The Faoii's boot hit something hard, and she used a dagger to slit the carpet with a single, clean motion. With a strength that surprised Ilahna despite everything, the Faoii ripped the rug up with her bare hands, revealing a closed trapdoor in the floor. She used the dagger to pry it open, and Ilahna stared into the inky blackness below the abandoned house.

"Who goes first?" Jacir whispered uncertainly. Ilahna heard the tremble in his voice and smiled, ruffling his hair.

"Don't worry. I'll go. Hand me the light."

Jacir passed Ilahna the torch the Faoii had had them shove in his bag, and Ilahna lit it with the flint from her trinket belt. She held it towards the exposed hole for a moment, but there was nothing to see except for the stone floor a fair way down. A chill crept up from the opening.

Ilahna took a deep breath, but then offered Jacir another smile as she carefully placed her foot on the first rung of the ancient wooden ladder. It held.

Slowly, carefully, Ilahna stepped down, rung by rung, testing her weight, being sure of her balance. Braced for anything.

It still came as a surprise when one of the wooden slats snapped under her booted foot. Ilahna held on tightly, but the sudden, full weight on the upper rung was too much, and it broke beneath her clutching fingers. Ilahna didn't even have time to flail. There was only Jacir's surprised face and a sharp impact as her back hit stone. The torch went flying in a different direction, its circle of light illuminating the stone wall a few strides away.

Ilahna only had time to be thankful that it didn't go out as she tried to suck the air back into her lungs and convince her mind that she was okay. Finally, her brain decided that she wasn't dying, and her stunned limbs began to respond to her commands.

A stream of vibrant curse words spilled from Ilahna as she rolled over and forced herself to her feet. Nothing appeared to be broken, and she angrily snatched the torch from the floor. There was a laugh from overhead.

"It seems she's fine, young Faoli. You may breathe again."

Ilahna looked up to Jacir's terrified expression and tried to reassure him.

"Yeah. Yeah, I'm fine, Jacir. Don't worry about me."

She could see Jacir relax a little in the gloom, and she used the torch to look around the newfound cellar. There was nothing except for a long stretch of tunnel leading in the direction of Clearwall Keep.

"We've come this far. Might as well keep going." Ilahna set her torch down carefully and stretched up her arms. "Jump, Jacir. I'll catch you."

Jacir buckled at the idea. He trembled as he moved closer to the hole on hands and knees. "But…It's so far, Lana."

"What? Are you kidding? Come on, Jace. You've jumped off roofs higher than this."

"Not that kind of far. If we start down this path… there's no going back." In the wan torchlight, Ilahna could see that Jacir's eyes were distant, unfocused. But still terrified.

"We can get back up, even with the broken ladder. Or we'll find another way out. It'll be okay." Ilahna looked at the crumbling pieces of wood and stone beneath the trapdoor. She'd scaled worse things before. But still Jacir did not come.

"What do you see, Faoli?" the Faoii asked.

"Everything is changing. Minute by minute. There are so many paths from here."

The Faoii nodded. "I have been in your shoes, young Weaver. We are at a crossroads. Where we go from here might very well determine the course of Clearwall and Imeriel's story for years to come. It might affect thousands of lives. Do you wish to continue?" Jacir stared into the distance for a long moment.

"There are too many threads. Too much to see. Any choice we make—it changes everything!" His body convulsed once and Ilahna's mouth went dry.

"Jacir! Jacir! It's okay!" Still Jacir shook, his eyes darting across a million scenarios she couldn't see. "Faoii! Snap him out of it!"

The Faoii shook Jacir, but still his eyes roved over the darkness, his body stiff and straining. The Faoii's eyes glazed when she touched the young boy, but she pulled away violently, shaking her head. "A decision must be made if you want to set the course, girl. He is in no state to decide the fate of thousands, and it is burying him. You are unburdened by the Weave. Choose!" Her voice cut across the din, sharpened by the faintest hint of fear.

Ilahna didn't want to be in charge of a thousand lives. Especially when she couldn't see the outcomes. She didn't want to be the one to make such great decisions.

It would not be difficult to rescale that wall. Go back to the sewers or the tannery or somewhere else. Melt into the background of Clearwall until the end of her days. Keep Jacir from all of this. That would be the easiest choice. The safest.

Jacir and the Faoii could see so much more than her. Shouldn't they be the ones to decide…?

But then she thought of Eitan and her heart hardened. She didn't have to see all the possible futures to know the one she wanted to fight for. She could not leave him here.

Ilahna set her mouth into a grim line and planted her feet as she made her decision.

"Jump, Jacir. I'll catch you."

The path set, Jacir's face untwisted from its scowl immediately, and he sagged with a relieved sigh. After a moment, Ilahna repeated her decision. "Come on, Jacir. We're going to save Eitan. We're going to find a future that's better than our past. Jump down. I'll catch you."

Jacir actually smiled as he jumped.

27

Ilahna couldn't tell if seconds had passed since they entered the tunnel or if it had been years, but they finally reached an iron ladder leading upwards. Relieved to be free of the stifling darkness, Ilahna ascended quickly. They had made it into Clearwall Keep—somewhere no mazer had dared to tread before. She tried to imagine the riches that would lie beyond this forgotten door. Of the splendor. But the only treasure she could conjure were pictures of Eitan, knowing that he was above them. Somewhere.

Hold on, Eitan. We're almost there.

She pressed the trapdoor with her hand. Then frowned and repositioned, shoving up with her shoulder.

Nothing.

Ilahna's heart fell into her stomach. She had not considered that the door might be blocked from this side, too. But of course it would be. It was obvious that the 'overstock pantry' had not been used for many years. She cast a nearly frightened look at the Faoii, who only settled her weight on one hip and crossed her arms in response.

"Are you going to ask for help every time you reach an obstacle, girl? How are you ever going to become more than you are if a few ancient slats can stop you?"

Ilahna narrowed her eyes and inhaled through her nose. She hated the Faoii, sometimes. But she hated how right she was more.

With a sharp exhale, Ilahna rammed her shoulder upward with all her strength. The boards above her moved an inch before slamming down again. She bent her knees and rammed upwards again, throwing her entire body weight against the trapdoor. Something banged hard above her head, and there was a crashing sound. Below her, the Faoii pursed her lips and drew her fantoii.

Ilahna's cheeks reddened as she waited for the sound of footsteps above. The sound of an alarm. But there was nothing. Only her heartbeat in her ears.

Ilahna straightened slowly and pushed on the trapdoor again, more carefully this time. It resisted a little, but finally yielded. She climbed the ladder with tense muscles, still expecting an attack at any moment.

The storage room she found herself in was dark and musty. Puffs of ancient dust sprouted beneath her hands as she pulled her way up and reached down to assist Jacir. A heavy, though rotting, bookshelf lay toppled to one side of the trapdoor, its shelves newly broken and layers of dust shaken loose by her antics. Jacir sneezed as he stood up, then quickly tried to stifle the sound, but was too late.

Still no one came.

"Maybe some sort of deity still watches us after all" the Faoii whispered as she crept towards the door on the other side of the room. "Come quickly, children."

Posed to fight, the Faoii used one hand to open the door a crack. Ilahna held her breath as the Faoii peered through the crevice.

Finally, a shocked whisper from the Faoii's dark lips: "What has happened here?"

The small group opened the door completely and stepped into one of the corridors of Clearwall Keep. Dust and grime covered the once-noble rugs and fixtures that adorned the hallway. A quiet, wistful breeze echoed from further within.

"Maybe they just don't use this hallway anymore," Jacir whispered without heart. Ilahna tried to smile for him, but the foreboding in her soul leaked through, and Jacir didn't return the gesture.

Silently, they crept their way to the end of the hallway and peered around a corner into the main corridor of Clearwall Keep. The skeletal remains of a grand chandelier hung limply from the center of the room, its spiderwebs giving a ghostly feel to the now-glassless fixtures and ancient, melted candles. The grand staircase that rose on either side of the room stood as a silent monolith to a kingdom that had fallen with no one aware of its passing.

"Where is the king? King Lucius Clearwall VII reigns. We have seen his edicts. We have followed his laws." Ilahna's whisper snaked through the tomb-like hall.

"Have you?" The Faoii made more of a statement than a question, implication in her voice. She idly kicked the remnants of a crumbled banister at her feet.

"The Proclaimers… Have we ever been under any thumb but theirs?"

"I have learned over the years that kings are so often merely puppets. Yours, if he ever truly lived and was not simply a name on the Proclaimers' lips, was not the first. Not even the first in Clearwall."

"It doesn't matter," Ilahna hissed. "It wasn't a king that took Eitan. The Proclaimers reign and maybe we always knew it. But they have Eitan, and we need to get him back." The Faoii didn't respond and motioned them forward.

The dark stairway leading downwards into darkness that the Faoii at last led them to seemed in less disrepair than the other parts of the keep. The dust on each step was less obvious, and even a few relatively recent footprints made their marks on the stone slabs. They still seemed old, having earned a layer of new dust that was slightly lighter than the caked grime that the rest of the keep sported, but it made Ilahna nervous, nonetheless.

"Why would he be here? It looks like no one has come this way for a long time."

"This keep has become a place of secrets," the Faoii whispered. "It seems there might be many."

They descended the staircase carefully, but the sounds of their feet still seemed deafening in the silence of the echoing chamber. Finally, the little group reached a room filled with mildew-covered cells and barred doors that hung lopsidedly on rusted hinges. Water dripped somewhere nearby.

"This isn't right. Eitan isn't here."

"Shh. Listen."

Ilahna did. At first there was nothing. Just the whistle of wind through empty halls. But, finally, a faint and desperate moan. The far-off jangle of chains against stone. Barely picked up on a chilled breeze through chambers that hadn't been seen by the eyes of man in years, the sounds made Ilahna shiver.

"If it's the Proclaimers, we shouldn't be able to hear them. The temple is too far away."

"Then walk lightly, girl. Who knows what we'll find?"

28

Buried secrets are always the ones that people want uncovered the least. And as Ilahna and the others traversed silently through the corridors beneath Clearwall Keep, she wondered at how she'd come to be walking through the entombed secrets of the Proclamatic Order. It would not be so difficult for them to bury her and Jacir here, too. Away from the light of day. Away even from the pyres, whose publicity proclaimed slights against the reigning temple both real and imagined. But the things they were looking for were darker than even the ashes of those consigned to the flames. There would be no public death if they were caught here. Too many secrets would be drawn into the light along with their screaming bodies.

This is what happens to all the people who actually are a threat to the Proclaimers. Whose cries from the pyre might elicit more than shouts of triumph from the mob. These are the ones that still have information the Proclaimers want, or minds they can break and reform into new recruits. The people whose torture serves a greater purpose than their death would.

Ilahna should have realized that the number of people that had disappeared from Clearwall's streets had far outnumbered the pyres built in front of the temple. It was easy to forget the faces of neighbors and urchins that you saw sometimes in the market square. But everyone was so afraid of everyone else, now. The Proclaimers had convinced the entire city that every neighbor could be a witch. A traitor. Every whisper could be a spell. So you saw only faces, not people. And, even if you got used to and recognized the same faces every day, without that hint of humanity that the people of Clearwall had forgotten how to see from behind their eyes, the faces could so easily disappear. Just one less gaze in a sea of people who looked at each other with equal distrust, quickly replaced by a hundred other equal gazes. Ilahna wondered now how many people she'd passed every day without recognition, and then was unaware of when they were gone.

It started when they made us something less than human. Dogs are easy to bring into places like this. No one notices when there are less dogs on the street. In fact, they rejoice.

It wasn't that long ago when the only thing Ilahna cared about was making sure Jacir could eat that week. That maybe she could steal another blanket. And it never mattered to her that the people she stole from were probably struggling as badly as she was. They were just faces. Just forms in a sea that didn't matter to her. The witches on the pyres were just screams.

The moans and pained cries from the long, dark tunnels were growing stronger. Closer. Ilahna was barely able to make out the walls on the far edges of her torch, but what she did see told her that these caverns and tunnels were newer than the dusty, crumbling stairs and ancient wrought-iron cells that they had first encountered in the jail below Clearwall Keep.

She didn't know how long ago the Proclaimers had bridged the gap between the monarchy and the temple, but for some reason it did not surprise her that they'd filled the space with torture chambers and mass graves.

Footsteps from the corridor ahead of them made them freeze. Quickly, Ilahna put out the frail light of their torch, pushing Jacir against the wall in the now-dark hallway. She felt more than saw the Faoii draw her sword across the corridor.

Two pairs of booted feet clanged against the worn stones in the passageway up ahead. The steady step and the sound of scabbards against breastplates in stride was unmistakable. Proclaimers.

But, as Ilahna pressed herself against the wall and tried to control her breathing, she realized there was something different about these foot soldiers. Their movements were in formation, their stride long-since trained into their bodies by muscle memory alone—but gone was the stoicism and pressed lips of displeasure and a haughty surety of one's station. Here, in this place where none could see them and those who did were never seen by others, the Proclaimers were something else entirely.

They were human. Just… regular people. Talking to each other with hand gestures and the occasional laugh. Ilahna had always known in a logical sense that the Proclaimers were simply human, but the ceremony and propaganda that surrounded them had always made them seem like something much more than mere mortals. Seeing them now—a man and a woman, barely older than her—made her stomach twist a little. Because it was much easier to hate the Proclaimers when they were faceless behind their cowls. When you didn't have to think about them being people who truly believed in what they did.

The trio held their breath and the two Proclaimers passed by, oblivious to the dangers that lurked in the unused passageway next to them. They never even glanced towards the intruders, but it took several silent moments before Ilahna's voice crawled out of her throat.

"There will be more going forward. How will we get by them all?" Ilahna whispered, afraid to relight the torch.

The Faoii narrowed her eyes and balanced her weight on one hip.

"You tell me. This is your mission, is it not? How do you want to proceed?"

Ilahna tried to swallow her terror and resentment. Every bone in her body demanded that she turn around while they still could, but she knew Eitan was still ahead. They could not leave him. She swallowed hard before speaking. "Carefully. We sneak by if we can. We fight if we can't."

"Lana!" Jacir gasped. "We can't possibly win." Ilahna tried to give him a smile, but her heart was cold enough to make her words come out like icy shards.

"I'd rather go down fighting than end up as one of the screams echoing in these halls that no one above ever hears." She set a trembling hand on her sword hilt. "Faoii, will you take Jacir back to the surface? I know the way now."

"No!" Jacir cried, almost too loudly. He pressed a hand over his mouth to stifle the sound but continued as soon as he knew that no one had heard. "We'll get Eitan together. All of us." Ilahna was about to protest, but another tortured wail from deeper into the dungeons twisted at her heart. They did not have the time to argue. She ruffled Jacir's hair.

"Then be careful. And if something happens… if something happens, promise me you'll run, okay?"

Jacir nodded solemnly, but the Faoii frowned. "I should hope that you didn't bring us all the way here with plans of dying, girl."

"Of course not. I told you, we're going to sneak our way through, we're going to save Eitan, and we're going to sneak back out."

"Is that your entire plan? You don't want to fill out the details a little more before we start?"

"Stop arguing with me and I'll show you, witch."

The Faoii barely smiled in the darkness. "Lead on then, girl."

Slowly, carefully, Ilahna relit their torch and slipped into the hallway, keeping her weight on the balls of her feet. Jacir followed her awkwardly, but Ilahna had faith in his abilities. Jacir had only gotten this far in life by staying unseen. His mind had betrayed them before, but his body never had. Behind him, the Faoii oozed into the hallway, shifting like the shadows in the firelight.

Sounds seeped towards them through the dark tunnels, and Ilahna shivered as they began to form into recognizable echoes. Whispered prayers and oaths. Chants. Sometimes conversations or even laughter. All the sounds that Ilahna had learned to associate with the temple in the square. The sounds of the secret world of the Proclaimers, hidden deep beneath the heart of Clearwall.

But, deeper than the prayers and oaths and chants, there was something darker. Something muffled under the strong incense and suffocating propriety of the Proclamatic Order of Truth. And Ilahna realized that it, too, reminded her of the temple and prayers she and Jacir had seen the Proclaimers give from their iron pulpits. Deep, buried cries of pain. Moans. Sobs. Fear. Heartache. The stench of piss and dreck. The coppery taste of blood. The sickly-sweet smell of untreated infection. Death.

Now that Ilahna was aware of it, her eyes watered and stung at all the sensations that had been so thinly veiled before. Part of her knew that she never literally sensed these things in the temples or next to the Proclaimers—but she also felt she had always known it was there, barely obscured by their heavy spices and sweet smiles. Their pristine white cloaks and breastplates that gleamed so prettily in the firelight.

Ilahna thought she was going to vomit.

"What's wrong, Lana?" Jacir whispered, and Ilahna realized she had stopped walking, bent over at the waist and clutching the wall for support. She tried to breathe past the saliva in her mouth.

"Don't you smell it?" she finally ground out.

"I don't smell anything." Jacir frowned at her, and she could visibly see his face slacken a bit as he pried at the edges of the unseen door.

"Don't!" she hissed, but too late. Suddenly all the emotions she had only barely touched upon flooded Jacir, and she watched him pale, droplets of sweat beading his brow before he stumbled to the wall and retched. Ilahna sighed and eased towards him, rubbing his back.

"It's so dark. It's so deep. There are so many pits filled with bodies here. So much death. How does no one else see it? The world is rotting from within. And no one sees." Jacir was crying and Ilahna tried to comfort him, still casting wary glances in all directions. They could not afford to stop here. Not now. Not at the heart of the rotting corpse that Clearwall had become.

"We'll make them see, Jacir. Some way or another. We'll fix this."

Jacir's stomach heaved again, though nothing came up, and he stood, trembling against the wall for another minute before finally straightening. "We have to keep going."

The Faoii crouched at the end of the hallway, her blade unsheathed. She watched the passageways with a trained eye, prepared to pounce on any unlucky soul that rounded the corner. She glanced back at them, but there was no irritation in her eyes, like Ilahna had expected. Something clicked as Ilahna looked at the woman's steady grey eyes.

"You knew that coming down here would awaken… whatever that was in us. You knew we couldn't hide from what we knew if we went to the center of all of it."

The Faoii did not deny the accusation. "You had to see. I did not know what would awaken in you and what would not. But if someone can look at the heart of evil and not have something change inside of them, a kernel of rage or an unquenchable thirst to fight back, then that evil is already too deep to be carved back out. You would have not survived in this world without that spark, and I will not be the tool of such dark tendrils ever again. This would have ended here, and all three of us would be free."

Ilahna was caught off guard by how callously the Faoii said this but could not bring herself to argue. If she had been untouched by all this darkness at the heart of their world, then she was not sure she'd want to live on with such a deadness inside her.

As they continued down the corridor, muscles tight and heartbeats in their ears, Ilahna lost count of how many times they had to press themselves into dark alcoves and shadowy areas at the sound of booted feet. Finally, they'd given up on their torch, afraid of casting warning glares off the stone without knowing who or what was around the corner. They inched along the corridors with searching footsteps, having nothing but instinct and straining ears to rely on.

The screams of pain and wails of despair echoed louder, and Ilahna once again bit back bile at the thought that those disheartened, tortured cries might be coming from Eitan.

We're coming. Please hold on.

But then, riding beneath the blackened waves of horror, came another sound. A sound she'd heard a thousand times before. A sound that lifted her heart and made the darkness and death around her slightly less oppressive. For a moment Ilahna couldn't believe it, but once she'd grasped that sweet echo, there was no denying in her heart what it was.

Eitan was singing.

Ilahna's heart clenched. Even here, in this dungeon of despair and horror, Eitan still found the strength to sing. She thought back to how many times she had listened to his voice rise over the sound of his hammer, how comforting it had always been. But even in her strongest memories, nothing about Eitan's voice could have prepared her for what she heard drifting through the ghostly cacophony of death and despair that surrounded them now.

Eitan's song was so different than the monotonous, droning chants of the Proclaimers and the solemn-sounding prayers. It was shaky and weak, but it was still more powerful than anything that seeped from between the Proclaimers' lips. It felt like the way the air smells before a storm. Like the static buildup right before a shock. Ilahna could *feel* the power riding through Eitan's shaky notes as they drifted through the darkened corridors. It strengthened her heart. It brought her courage. Somewhere in the darkness, the Faoii released a sort of sigh.

"I have not heard battle magic for years. I had forgotten how strong it could be."

Ilahna's first instinct was to withdraw at the words. The fear of magic and the unspeakable horrors that came with it still persisted. But as she listened to the song that rose above the darker sounds of the catacombs, her fear dissipated like tattered ribbons in a breeze. Her strides were strong and confident as she rounded another corner, following the radiant tune further into the tomb.

The ground here was clear of dust, the passing of feet day after day evident. Though it was not as well-trod as the streets or the temple, Ilahna did not doubt that this dungeon was a large part of the Proclamatic Order, and that it was used much more frequently than she had hoped. The dingy tunnels were lit by sconces bearing the crest of Clearwall, and Ilahna wondered why the Proclaimers had adopted these twisting corridors so far below Clearwall Keep and not a lair closer to the surface.

As if in answer to her internal thoughts, a sudden, earth-shattering scream ground Ilahna's eardrums and put all her hair on end. She had never heard such a sound of pain before. Not even from the pyres. Her skin crawled.

Such terrible cries would doubtlessly filter their way up to the streets if built below the temple proper, a dark secret even the lowliest scum of Clearwall could not ignore. Of course the Proclaimers had used the rocky cliff face beneath Clearwall Keep that the rest of the town could not touch. The screams and despair needed to be separated from the people of Clearwall by stone and air and a willful ignorance.

Ilahna led the others at a snail's treacherously slow pace past rows of barred cells with stone floors stained by unknown fluids, the stench of death and despair clogging their nostrils. A few of the wretched cells held hunched, broken people that did not even look up at their passing. But as they got closer to the sound of Eitan's singing, the captives around them began to stir more often. Began to raise their heads. The faint hint of hope in their eyes was dulled, but it seemed to brighten as the song continued. They opened parched and bleeding lips to speak as the trio moved forward, and soon Ilahna could no longer meet their eyes. Could not bear to see the hope there. Because she knew she could not save all of them.

This isn't right! None of this is right!

Ilahna screamed internally as she looked at all the people around her—all the lies and lives that had been buried in the darkness. She *needed* people to know the truth of what had become of Clearwall. If she could not free them, she had to do something. She *needed* their stories to be told.

You are Ilahna Harkins, Keeper of Truth.

Clearwall needed to know what was happening beneath the Keep. The only way that these people's stories could truly be spoken was if they were allowed to tell them. And the Proclaimers had locked their tongues and hearts beneath the cliffs of Clearwall Keep to make sure that could never happen.

They deserve better than this. We all deserve better than this.

The leaden rock of power she'd experienced before was heavy and pulsing in Ilahna's gut as she put her head down and pressed forward, trembling at the lies that the Proclaimers had leaked through their wide smiles. Ilahna knew that Jacir or the Faoii was saying something behind her, but she couldn't focus on anything besides the blurring in her eyes and the screams around her, only a few of which were from the prisoners who barely had voices to cry. Instead, she felt the crushing weight of all the lies and hidden motives that had bled into the rocks that swirled around Ilahna's head, deafening her, blinding her…

Ilahna wanted to scream but felt if she opened her mouth she would drown. Her knees nearly buckled as she was suffocated by the darkness of the Proclaimers' tombs. There was no escaping. The truth was too far buried.

This time it was Eitan's song that pulled her through the clamor.

Ilahna focused on the blacksmith's sweet melody, slowly coming back to herself. Jacir and the Faoii were next to her, but she did not hear their frantic whispers. Instead, the cries of pain and terror that still echoed from the shadows of her mind tore at her heart. At her throat. She wanted to claw out the eyes of the Proclaimers who could cause such pain and then walk through the streets above with such an air of superiority. She wanted to burn this entire terrible place until it was nothing but rubble and twisted bars of iron.

But still Eitan's calming voice carried forward, punctuated sporadically by pained groans or screams, and Ilahna forced herself to focus on the life she could save rather than the ones she wanted to destroy.

I just think that the people of Clearwall deserve leaders that focus more on life than death. Wasn't that what she'd told Jorthee?

Ilahna centered herself, forcing her shaking hands to still and followed the song gain. She couldn't understand how Eitan could be subjected to such torture and still have the will to sing.

The Proclaimer tasked to Eitan apparently felt the same way, because Eitan's song was stopped again with a pained gasp of air and the sound of metal hitting meat.

"We'll see how long you think you can keep singing, boy. But in the end, the last breath you use will be to tell us where the girl and her brother are."

Eitan coughed, and Ilahna heard liquid splatter against the floor. She was certain he would stop singing, then. How could he not? But the notes started again, raspy and uneven, but there. Another sound of a gauntlet hitting flesh. Another gasping pause. Another shaky start.

The icy crystal of pulsing rage inside Ilahna hardened, though its screaming shades did not threaten her any longer in the light of Eitan's calming song. Instead, it became a jagged lance of purpose as she focused on the truth directly in front of her: Eitan had never done anything to deserve this. He was the greatest man she knew, and now he was paying the price for a crime he'd never committed.

It should have been her in this place of death and steel. It should never have come to this. For anyone.

Ilahna didn't even realize that her blade was in her hand. She didn't hear whatever the Faoii behind her whispered as she suddenly lurched forward on legs that didn't feel like hers. She didn't know what she would do, but she couldn't hear anything other than the blood rushing in her ears and Eitan's melody that persisted despite everything else. Her wobbly legs strengthened, and she sprinted, cold and silent and like a shadow. She barely had a chance to take in the room she found herself in, with its metal table and chains and bloody instruments laid out haphazardly on a small brazier.

Ilahna had only a moment to see a Proclaimer's broad back and bright breastplate reflecting the torchlight, shiny in its self-proclaimed righteousness. She had only a moment to smell the blood and urine and burning flesh. Only a moment to see the Proclaimer begin to turn at her presence, blood-covered gauntleted hand still raised in a fist. He'd removed his helmet in the oppressive heat of the brazier, sweat beading on his high forehead despite the chill of the catacombs. That was all she saw of him, though. She did not even recognize this man as human. Maybe he wasn't, anymore. But Ilahna's fingers tightened around the hilt of her blade, and she swung it like it had always been there, attached to the end of her arm. It curved up, past the protruding edge of his pauldron, biting into the fleshy area below his jawline, the tip catching the soft spot under his chin. There was a look of shock in the Proclaimer's eyes, a half-hearted attempt to bring his arm up to block or attack, and then only a wet gurgle and two faltering steps towards her. Blood sizzled on the brazier as he fell.

It took a moment before the rage of disgust and hatred eased enough for Ilahna to hear again. Her hand was trembling and her blade tumbled to the ground as she stared at the dead Proclaimer and the growing pool of blood. Behind her, Jacir's squeaking voice uttered a quivering question she couldn't hear. She felt the Faoii's presence behind her, felt strengthened by the sudden weight of the hand on her shoulder.

"I would have done it for you, impetuous girl." But there was no malice in the voice. Ilahna shook her head.

"I had to do it myself."

The Faoii seemed to understand and removed her hand, stepping away. Ilahna realized that the singing had stopped.

"Ilahna?" The voice was weak. Barely above a whisper. "Is that really you? You're alive. I can't believe…" The rest of the words were drowned out by a wet cough.

Eitan.

Ilahna broke free from her sickening reverie and looked into Eitan's pain-glazed eyes. There was terror there. And relief. A twinkle that she'd feared would be lost. She thought she would have died if that had faded.

She tried to smile for him, but felt it was probably more terrible than comforting. "Eitan. I'm here. We're going to get you out of here."

It didn't take long for Ilahna to undo the strap on Eitan's wrist. He tried to help her with the other one, but his fingers only brushed the leather, useless. She undid that one too and moved his arm over her shoulder as he suddenly toppled and nearly fell.

Eitan had worked his entire life in the smithy. He was made of muscle and laughter, and for a moment Ilahna thought she wouldn't be able to keep him upright, but she steeled her legs and let him lean into her.

"I'm here, Eitan. I'm here. I'm sorry. I'm so sorry for everything. But I'm here now."

"Ilahna..." Eitan tried to stand straight. Tried to brush the curls out of her face with his free hand. "Ilahna... I love you."

Ilahna let out a sobbing sort of laugh. "Eitan, you're the least romantic person I know, saying something like that here." But her heart fluttered in her chest and she felt stronger as she pulled him against her. "I love you, too. And I'll always come for you, okay? I promise. I'll never lose you again." At the door, Jacir glanced around nervously.

"Ilahna. We have to go."

"We're ready."

It had taken luck, silence, and more than one dash across barely-illuminated halls to get here. With their wounded friend in tow, Ilahna wasn't sure how they were going to get out again. But she knew they had to try. She readjusted Eitan's weight on her shoulders and made sure she had enough range of movement to reach her resheathed blade. "Okay, we can do this." She looked all three of her companions in the eyes and put more conviction into the phrase. "We can do this."

They edged into the hall, one after the other, Eitan breathing heavily in Ilahna's ear. Ilahna worried about the blacksmith's capabilities, but he kept his feet moving and stifled the pained gasps she could feel in the tremors of his body. Ilahna whispered quiet encouragement to him and silently cursed the people who could do this to an innocent man.

It was by sheer luck that no one stopped them as they moved back to the crumbling stairway beneath Clearwall Keep. It was easier this time, since they knew the route and which passageways had been left mostly undisturbed. But even with the short, hobbling walk down abandoned corridors, Ilahna could feel Eitan's trembling and exhausted body next to her. By the time they reached the stairs, he was barely standing on his own. Ilahna looked up at the stone steps that rose into darkness. Next to her, Eitan didn't even raise his head, blood seeping sluggishly from a dozen different wounds.

"Jacir, grab his other arm," Ilahna instructed. Behind her, the Faoii kept a hand on her blade, watching for trouble, but apparently content to let the two children bear the weight of this encounter. Ilahna didn't care. This wasn't the Faoii's fight. Or her friend. She'd get Eitan out of here with or without a blighted witch's help.

Those stairs might as well have reached the top of the outer wall. Or the moon. It took what felt like ages for Ilahna and Jacir to surmount them, dragging Eitan's near-lifeless body between them. But Ilahna refused to stop to rest. Refused to give up hope. "Hold on, Eitan. We'll get you somewhere safe. I'm so sorry we did this to you. Just hold on. We'll make it right. We'll make it right."

Finally, Ilahna's shaking foot hit the last landing, her heel breaking the already-crumbling tile there.

"Where…are…we?" Ilahna almost didn't hear Eitan's words over his struggling breaths. She glanced behind them at the trail of blood droplets they'd left in their wake. If they didn't do something soon, all of this would be for naught, anyway.

"We're at Clearwall Keep. Don't worry. We're going to get you out of here."

"We… have to tell…the king." Eitan's voice was stronger now, and he tried to straighten under her arm. Ilahna shook her head as she pulled him forward.

"There is no king. Only the Proclaimers. And they're going to find us soon."

Eitan sagged, and he released a desolate moan. Ilahna's heart broke a little at the sound. She wasn't sure exactly what Eitan wanted to tell King Lucius VII, but she felt the despair roll off him in waves as he grappled with the fact that no such person existed.

They stopped to rest in the long, cold tunnel that had once been an overstock pantry between Clearwall Keep and the tax collector's office. Sure that they were safely deposited, the Faoii went back up the trapdoor with quick, silent footfalls to clear away some of the blood trail they'd left behind. Eitan was shivering as Ilahna tried to bandage the wounds on his blood-streaked chest with strips of her worn tunic.

By the time the Faoii returned and Eitan felt strong enough to continue, Ilahna had lost track of time. But she had not heard any of the Proclaimers' booted feet in the vacant halls above. If they had ever known of this route into Clearwall Keep, that knowledge had evidently been forgotten.

It was not a long climb up the ladder beneath the abandoned home at the end of the tunnel, even with the broken rungs that Ilahna had fallen from on the way down. But the short distance felt like miles as Ilahna followed close behind Eitan, her breath catching every time his weak grip almost failed.

Eitan did not complain, only set his jaw and pushed onward, humming under his breath as he forced his tired body higher. Ilahna watched the bulging muscles work in arms that had swung a hammer his entire life, the sinew of his back cording like rope. Even in his exhaustion, the blacksmith was able to pull himself up out of the ground without incident.

The abandoned home from days gone by was quiet. None of the dust had been disturbed, and Ilahna felt the grip on her heart loosen a little bit. The Maze was close. The Proclaimers didn't know the Maze like she and Jacir did. Those twisting streets of stone and rot that had protected generations of degenerates and forlorn. Those streets that had been her playground and her refuge all her life. If they could make it to the Maze, they could make it to the sewers. They would be safe until Eitan could heal. Until they could decide what to do next.

But the Maze was a long way off. The little group kept to alleyways and the dark crevices of Clearwall, but there was no escaping the feeling of eyes all around. The sense of being exposed. In the light of the moon, everything was made of shifting shadows and uncertainty, and without being able to utilize the roofs, Ilahna felt cornered. Vulnerable. And there was a twinge on the back of her neck she couldn't dismiss. A quiet whisper that the shadows were moving just a little too erratically—that someone was darting around corners just out of her peripheral vision. She repositioned Eitan's arm and kept going, telling herself it was only the urchins of Clearwall, watching a spectacle in the dark.

But the mazers never venture this far out, do they?

Ilahna shook the thought away. They were close enough. They could see the second wall that led to the Maze. It had been constructed during a plague that had wiped out much of Clearwall before the Proclaimers had come into power. They'd quarantined the infected behind the stone, and many families had never been able to return. Though the plague had long since run its course, everyone still saw the mazers as undesirables. But that was about to work in their favor. They could get lost there. They could survive there. Just a little further.

"Hold on, Eitan. We're almost there." Ilahna glanced over to see if he would respond, but a glint in the street caught her eye instead. Then another. A blade here. A breastplate there. The sudden sound of footfalls on stone. Jacir heard it too and froze. Behind them the Faoii released a soft curse and drew her blade as a ring of Proclaimers marched out of the shadows around them. Ilahna saw half a dozen escape routes in grates and low-hanging eaves, but she could not leave Eitan behind.

"Jacir! Run!" she yelled even as the Proclaimers tightened their circle, but Jacir didn't move, clenching both hands and standing next to his sister with grim determination.

"No, Ilahna. I want to stay with you."

Ilahna's eyes roved over the guards. She looked for an escape, and upon finding none, drew her blade. But they were trapped.

Madame Elise stepped from the ring, her sword and breastplate glinting in the moonlight. Her armor was only slightly less menacing than her smile.

"Good evening, children. I had wondered where you'd gone. It is high time you answered for your crimes."

29

The little symbol of the Fallen Goddess had been in the window for several months, and while the crops had not improved, Ali's family had been able to make a tidy sum in a very unexpected way.

"Are you the one that makes the symbols of…of the Old Gods?" The seamstress on their porch wrung her hands and looked around nervously despite Ali's mother's kind smile. "The ones that shine with their own light?" Word had spread of a resurgence of the Old Ways, and rural families whose bequeathed superstitions had never quite died had begun requesting the little charms on a regular basis, traveling from distant farms and homesteads to purchase the trinkets out of nostalgia and curiosity.

Most customers chuckled and said that they didn't believe anything would actually come of these old rituals, but Ali felt a humming sensation beneath the trilling laughter. There was an undercurrent in the shrill hitch of their voices—a thinly-veiled trickle of hope stemming from a well that was deeper than any of the small comforts they could find in their newly built homes and replanted lives.

"Yes. What can I help you with?" Ali's mother asked, still smiling.

"Do you have something I can sew into the hem of my dress?"

Ali helped her mother construct a smaller variation of the triangle and its clockwise spiral. The Faoii might have been unhappy with the crafted reminders of a Goddess they no longer spoke of in the monasteries, but there was nothing the Order could truly do about them. These objects were just trinkets. Declaring them as anything else would be to declare their power and forbidding them would be to show fear of woven baubles. So, the Faoii never protested.

And Ali slowly began to believe in the power of the Old Gods.

30

Ilahna had expected Madame Elise and the Proclaimers to take them back the way they'd come. Back through that decrepit castle and all its lies and hidden secrets. Back to those torture racks and bloody catacombs far beneath Clearwall's crumbling streets. But instead, they were herded in the opposite direction. Towards the temple. Ilahna shuddered, unable to verbalize why, but knowing with all her heart that this fate was much, much worse.

By the time they reached the courtyard at the base of the temple's grand steps, a large crowd had already been drawn by the Proclaimers' cries through the darkened streets of Clearwall. The sleepy-eyed citizens winced at Ilahna and the others through their hastily-gathered torches.

"Citizens of Clearwall! Thank the mighty Old Gods that they have drawn out the darkest amongst us! See the last of the Faoii of old and her wicked followers!" Madame Elise took one of the torches and shoved it close to Ilahna's face, illuminating the smudged skin and tangled curls. A few women in the crowd gasped at her youthfulness. Madame Elise's eyes were nearly as cold as her voice. "Hold closely your progeny! For one never knows what wickedness might creep in the dark crevices of Clearwall!"

The Proclaimer's words prickled Ilahna's skin and she barely heard the din and murmurs raised by the ever-growing crowd. Her heart was on fire. *Lies. It is all lies.*

Ilahna felt that stone of contempt and rage in her soul reform, and this time she did not try to bury it. The pyre was coming. She doubted she could escape it, and even as a lump lodged in her throat in terror of the flames, that rock of anger and disdain in the pit of her stomach that flared to life in the face of the Proclaimer's lies was bigger. Brighter. If they were going to die, she wanted to die knowing that she'd tried to spread truth rather than fear.

Her entire body shaking, Ilahna took a step forward, still supporting Eitan at her side. She nearly stepped into the flame of Elise's torch, and she felt it burn her nose, but she didn't care. The fire flickered as the indignation rose within her, screaming for freedom. *It wasn't right. None of this is right.*

"Enough lies, Proclaimer!" The screeching words were out of Ilahna's mouth before she even realized what she was going to say. But she needed the world to know. The truth *needed* to be heard. "You accuse *us* of secrets and wickedness? We have seen your halls beneath Clearwall Keep, Madame Elise. Your corridors of blood and torture. You have these people's families! Their children and spouses! Bound in chains below the empty keep!"

"Silence!" Madame Elise's eyes sparked as she rounded on Ilahna, whisking the torch away and using her opposite fist to backhand the girl hard enough to crack her cheekbone. Ilahna felt her eye swell closed immediately, and Eitan tumbled from her grasp. She had just enough time to see him stand shakily before Madame Elise demanded her attention again. "Silence," the Proclaimer repeated. "Do not wave your forked tongue at me, filthy child. No one here will believe the lies of Faoii."

And Ilahna realized that she had said "us." That she had grouped herself with all the Faoii witches in a single sentence. There was no coming back from that. No possible redemption or begging for retraining in the temple. The other people in the courtyard had heard it, too, and their rage and clamoring grew as more torches were lit. Angry, heaving bodies piled closer to the small, weary group huddled in the square.

Jacir took Ilahna's hand and trembled a little beside her, and for a moment her heart fell when she realized that he had been right as he'd watched her descend the ladder into darkness. There was no going back. But, as the fleeting faces of those locked beneath the keep flitted across her mind, she realized that it was better this way. She didn't want to go back to how things had been that morning. Never again. Eitan took her other hand, and it was warm and gentle and comforting. He hummed something under his breath—the tiniest hint of a love song—and it gave her strength.

As she stood there, hand in and hand with the two most important people in her life, Ilahna thought that she should be afraid. Ashamed of what she had done to bring them all here. But as she saw the triumph in Madame Elise's eyes, watched the bloodlust grow in a people who only knew how to hate, the crystal in her soul hardened and pulsated.

So be it. Time for Clearwall to know the truth.

"I demand to be judged by King Lucius Clearwall VII! Let he that protects Clearwall be the judge of the last of Her greatest enemies!" Ilahna took that gem of truth and screaming fury and drew it up with those words that shot from her mouth towards Madame Elise with all the strength she could muster. The command hurtled across the courtyard like a gale, flickering the torchlight and silencing the sudden clamor of townsfolk. In the sudden, deathly quiet, Ilahna repeated the command in a much lower tone that slid through the silence with ease. "I demand to be judged by the King," she repeated. "It should not be a problem if he still reigns. Is that not correct, Madame Elise?"

Madame Elise could not deny the show of force that had just erupted from the young girl in front of her, nor could she deny that everyone around her had felt the display of power, as well. And Ilahna knew the people had *felt* the truth in her words.

It was different this time. It had to be different this time. The Proclaimers had often used the rumors and belief of witches to their advantage, but none of Clearwall's citizens had ever actually seen someone who could potentially best them. For a moment there was a calculating hatred behind Elise's eyes. Almost immediately, however, it dissolved into something far more sinister, and she smiled.

"So be it. Children of Truth, take them to Clearwall Keep. His Majesty will judge them from the Starlit Throne."

"No!" Ilahna screamed, and the gale that exploded forth with her cry crashed into the Proclaimers, pausing them in their advance. "The people of Clearwall need to know the truth! They *deserve* the truth!" She turned to the crowd, raising her voice even louder. "Do you not think you deserve more than the mangled bits of watered-down history that they feed to you like gruel? Do you not want to see for yourself if the truth is real or not? I promise you, Clearwall: There is no one on the Starlit Throne! The keep is empty. And history is so much more and less than you've been told." The words soaked into the crowd, and the people squirmed uncertainly. Madame Elise tried to wrest back control.

"These are the lies of a Faoii! The tongue is the first step to the pyre! By listening to the young witch, all of you are walking closer to the cliff that will lead to the doom of your families and all of Imeriel! In the name of King Lucius VII, I call for the death of these witches! Cleanse Clearwall of their lies!"

It was the word "lies" that did it. The people of Clearwall could tell it did not sound the same coming from Elise's mouth as it had from Ilahna's, and for the first time they did not immediately move in response to Elise's order. They did not surge forward in a tidal wave of fanatic hatred and thoughts of fire as they always had before.

"But… what if she is right?" Someone far in the back whispered just a little too loudly, and there was a ripple of surprised gasps and angry grunts of dismay. On any other night, the dissenter would have been lashed to a stake alongside the others. But something in Ilahna's voice had made them pause. Made them see the faintest glimmer of truth in the dark web the Proclaimers had woven.

Madame Elise bristled at the question, but her voice was slightly less sure as she ordered the naysayer to be brought forth. The command rang out against the mob, but no one moved, and even Elise's guards fidgeted uncertainly in the silence.

Madame Elise's face paled, then reddened with rage. She spun on Ilahna again, but the urchin didn't flinch as Jacir and Eitan squeezed her hands.

"Tell them," Jacir whispered. "Tell them the truth."

"We're behind you, girl."

Ilahna glanced behind her towards the Faoii. Something ancient and wonderful glinted in the woman's suddenly green eyes as she gathered a low, long-forgotten warsong in her throat. The Faoii's voice was worn and cracked with age, and for a moment Ilahna thought she would falter, though she had no idea why the thought panicked her so. Eitan picked up on it, too, and, with another squeeze of Ilahna's hand, lent his voice to the Faoii's. His smooth tenor thrummed in the air, low and rumbling and strong, and it drowned out whatever shrill cry Madame Elise might have released if her mouth had not dropped open in surprise. For a moment Ilahna was equally surprised at his boldness, but she understood. As much as Eitan had been trained to fear the Faoii and their magics, he had now learned to fear the Proclaimers and their catacombs more.

"Tell them, Lana. Tell them the truth." Jacir repeated. "They'll listen to you."

Ilahna swallowed once before speaking with all the courage she could muster. "We have been to your Keep, Proclaimer. It is built on top of secrets, lies, and the crumbling remains of the Starlit Throne. Your Proclamatic Order has slit the heart and spilled the lifeblood of Clearwall." Ilahna's voice was hard and cold, and it rode across the crowd on Eitan and the Faoii's rising song.

"Lies!" Madame Elise screamed. "It is all lies!" She reached for her sword, but before her hand could touch the hilt, Jacir flung his arms into the air. A torrent of wind flew up, stirring the ashes that perpetually covered the temple square.

Even Ilahna wasn't prepared for what came next as terrible, ghostly tapestries appeared around the courtyard, depicting perfect, spectral displays of the horror and sorrow they'd seen in the catacombs. The crowd gasped at the broken, tattered ruins of Clearwall Keep. The shattered remains of a once-grand throne. The howling, desperate faces that peered out from barred cages barely larger than their bony frames. The Proclaimers with their whips and chains. The sunken faces of Clearwall's lost.

The wind howled in Ilahna's ears as she glared at Madame Elise through her tears of rage and hatred. "This is how the Proclaimers have protected Clearwall, Madame Elise! You've buried all you could, but no grave is deep enough to hide the truth of what you've done here."

Some of the people of Clearwall let out yelps of terror and made quick anti-evil signs with their hands, but Jacir pushed harder, pulling pictures and threads through the great stone door as his dark images spun around the square. As the citizens watched years' worth of images depicting souls whose deaths had been buried in the Tapestry's Eternal Weave unravel across the courtyard, their fearful cries were replaced with shouts of protest and recognition.

Ilahna had always known what tied everyone in Clearwall together: everyone had lost someone. And Jacir could look through that door and see them all.

Finally, the flickering tapestries faded and Ilahna found herself staring at two eyes that brimmed with hatred.

"How did you do that?" Madame Elise hissed, rounding on Jacir. Jacir stood, his back straight, seemingly taller than he had been a moment before. His hand once again clutched Ilahna's tightly.

Madame Elise didn't seem to notice the rising clamor of the mob around her as they yelled for justice and the whereabouts of their lost loved ones. The Proclaimers weren't focused on Ilahna and the others at all now, staggering a little in an attempt to hold the rising mob at bay, but Madame Elise ignored them all, her rage rolling off her in burning waves.

"That was the Great Tapestry!" she screeched at Jacir. "The domain of the Gods! How did you see it? What have you done?" Maddened beyond reason, the First Proclaimer reached for Jacir with one clawed hand, and Ilahna forcefully shoved her back, drawing her fantoii.

Around them, the mob was growing larger, angrier, screaming demands to see the king. To see the tunnels beneath the keep. To see their lost loved ones. Ilahna used their anger to steel herself as she squared her shoulders and raised her blade to face the First Proclaimer head-on. Behind her, the war song grew louder.

As the clamor around them raised in pitch, the madness in Madame Elise's eyes finally dimmed a bit as she realized what was happening. She tried to regain control.

"They are witches! Faoii! Burn them all! For the safety and light of Clearwall!" But her voice wasn't enough to cut through the cries of the mob or the Faoii song that twisted through everything. Ilahna felt for it in the air and let her voice carry across it.

"We are many things, Proclaimer." The words streaked through the mob, and the people trembled in its wake as Ilahna raised her blade to the Proclaimer's chest. "But we are not witches. And we are not afraid."

The unseen dam that held back the angry, desperate mob of Clearwall broke suddenly, and the crowd surged forward. The Proclaimers held their ground, and the courtyard was quickly filled with the clash of metal against wood and screams of rage and triumph.

Ilahna didn't know if the citizens were fighting the Proclaimers or each other, and she didn't want to wait to find out. Madame Elise made another move for Jacir, but an angry man dressed in tattered clothing rushed her, and she was forced to focus on him, instead. Ilahna parried a glancing blow and shoved Jacir behind her as the mob grew around them.

Ilahna was prepared with her entire being to make good on her words to the people of Clearwall. To make her stand here and now. But as she parried another blow from a different body in the fray, Jacir's sudden cry gave her pause.

"Ilahna! Don't let her draw her sword!"

It took Ilahna a minute too long to realize who Jacir was talking about, and by the time she finally located Madame Elise in the crowd, the Proclaimer already had her hand on her sword's hilt. A chill ran through Ilahna, making her arms feel like lead. She knew she wouldn't be able to respond in time to stop the First Proclaimer's draw.

It's over. It just started, and it's over.

But just as the thought had formed, Ilahna caught the flash of a long, white braid. The Faoii burst from the crowd, releasing a chilling warcry as she tackled the Proclaimer with all her might. The two fell in an undignified heap, lost into the mob of shoving bodies.

Free of the bindings that had held her, Ilahna swiped upward just in time to block another swing and forcefully shoved the newest attacker into the waiting arms of scrambling fighters.

"Ilahna! We need to get out of here!" Eitan's voice was filled with urgency, and Ilahna didn't argue.

"Please tell me you can run," she begged, ducking under a flying torch.

Eitan nodded grimly. "I'll make it."

"*We need to go! It's coming!*" Jacir screamed.

Ilahna made a break for a hole in the crowd, scarcely escaping the melee with the others still behind her. From somewhere in the crowd, the Faoii disengaged, as well, and matched their pace.

They'd barely made it out of the courtyard when, behind them, the sounds of fighting abruptly stopped. The resulting silence was eerie and definite.

Ilahna didn't want to know what Jacir had seen or what had happened in the temple square that they were rapidly leaving behind. Instead, she pumped her legs harder, seeking a safety that would never be guaranteed in Clearwall.

31

They ran.

Ilahna pushed her protesting legs harder as she darted across the cobblestones and through the twisted corridors of the Maze. There were few people out in the dead of night, and those who were awake were doubtlessly in the temple square after having been summoned by the Proclaimers' orders.

But thieves and vagabonds always inhabited the Clearwall, and Ilahna was so focused on what lay behind them that she was not concentrating on the everyday dangers of the Maze.

She should have been prepared for the single, desperate mazer crouching around a sharp corner, lurking at the sound of soft-booted feet in the night. But the lurker could not have been prepared for another urchin—why would a mazer take to streets rather than the rooftops?—and his ambush failed as Ilahna saw him just before he pounced. She slid forward at the sight of him, catching him in the calf with her heel. The two mazers ended as a jumbled heap on the Maze floor, Ilahna breaking the silence with a string of curses.

"Get out of here! I don't have time for your nonsense!" she screeched at the cloaked figure. The man started to scramble away, and Ilahna's hand instinctually went to her belt pouch. The strings had been loosened, and Ilahna was momentarily impressed at the other man's skill. But a few coins were the least of her worries, and Ilahna pulled the string of her belt pouch shut as she rolled to her feet.

"Hey! Stop!" Eitan yelled, but the shadow was already scurrying down the alley.

"It doesn't matter. Come on." Ilahna said, leading them further into the Maze. The collision had already been forgotten by the time they turned the next corner.

It seemed like an impossibly long sprint without the aid of roofs and walls, but soon Ilahna and the others had left the Clearwall mob far behind, with nothing denoting their passage except for the alarm bells that echoed hollowly through the night. Then, even those were finally stifled by the dingy sewer walls as the group finally reached their haven.

Eitan was pale and shaky as he finally slumped against the damp wall of the sewer, breathing heavily, several of his wounds seeping blood again. But he tried to offer Ilahna a smile as she crouched in front of him.

"You're amazing, Ilahna. I don't know if I ever told you that before." Ilahna smiled softly and offered him her waterskin. He took a long pull from it and motioned to her belt pouch. "Are you okay? Did he get anything?"

"You're asking if *I'm* okay?" she chuckled as she checked her trinket belt for anything missing. Nothing was, and she carefully opened the drawstring pouch to see if any of her few coins had disappeared. Instead, she found a small bundle carefully wrapped in moss nestled on top of the coins. Eitan whistled low.

"Good thing there wasn't any flint in your pouch. Who'd go to that much trouble to give you silk strand?"

"I don't know," Ilahna replied as she carefully unwrapped the parcel. She gasped at the treasure in her hand as the moss fell away. "It's an egg." She finally responded, surprised. "A hollowed egg."

"Open it!" Jacir said excitedly. For as long as Ilahna could remember he'd been intrigued by Clearwall's hidden message system, and Ilahna ruffled his hair before handing him the fragile trinket.

"You go ahead, Jacir. Carefully. We don't know what's inside."

Gently, Jacir cracked the egg on the stone floor and pulled the shell apart with his thumbs. A rolled piece of thin cloth, almost light enough to be considered parchment, fluttered to the ground. Jacir handed it to Ilahna proudly.

Ilahna unraveled the cloth to reveal a stitched image. Something about the small, rounded house and its almost-comically tall chimney was familiar to her, but she couldn't place it. A moon drawn at the top and the sun at the bottom were equally perplexing, but there was no doubt that the solitary human figure with its curly, fiery red hair was supposed to be her.

"What is it?" Jacir asked, hopping from foot to foot in anticipation.

"A drawing. Of me." Ilahna rose and licked her lips, her fingers trembling. She thought that she was a talented thief, but the stranger's abilities were awe-inspiring in comparison.

Jacir stood on tip-toe to look at the cloth in her hands. "I know that place!" he squeaked. "That's the big oven outside the burnt-down bakery."

Ilahna looked at the drawing again, and it clicked. Now she recognized the wide mouth and the towering stack that had been untouched when the bakery itself fell in a heap of charred remains, after the baker had stupidly used silk strand moss in the inner kiln. The oven was no longer used as it was designed for, but instead stood as a stone monument to older days.

"I think you're right," Ilahna said, ruffling Jacir's hair again in appreciation. "So… The stone oven. I know where that is. And the moon at the top with the sun underneath must be… an indication of time?" Ilahna said it like a question, but as soon as the words were out of her mouth, she knew she was right. "Halfway through the night."

"Do you want us to come with you?" Jacir asked.

Ilahna considered. "It only shows me," she replied. "I don't know who they are or what they want, but I'm fastest on my own, anyway. Plus, I need you to stay here with Eitan." She caught Jacir's look of uncertainty and tried to assuage his fears by giving him the rolled piece of cloth and a bright smile. "Don't worry about me. There hasn't been a guard that could keep up with me yet, has there?" Jacir's grin was a little less sure as he shook his head.

"Don't worry," she repeated. "I'll be fine. I want to know who this person is, and what he wants."

"It could be a trap." Eitan's voice was heavy with pain and exhaustion. Ilahna could see the harsh lines in his face, watched the heavy droop of his eyelids and quivering inhales in his chest. And still he pushed through to reach toward her cheek. "Please be careful, Ilahna."

Ilahna pressed her cheek into his palm. "It's past midnight now, anyway. I won't be able to go until tomorrow. Let's worry about you right now." Ilahna draped Eitan's arm across her shoulders and helped him hobble to her worn pallet. He collapsed into it, asleep before she'd even released his arm.

When she turned back around, Jacir was still holding the cloth, staring unfocused at several symbols painted on the back side. The Faoii studied it for a moment over his shoulder, and her eyes darkened two shades before she snatched the cloth from Jacir's hand and flung it into the fire. Its edges curled before it caught and turned to ash.

Ilahna began to protest, but the Faoii was already stalking out of the sewers, the muscles in her back tensed like coiled ropes. Ilahna watched her go, but didn't try to follow. Instead, she went to Jacir, gently holding his hands. "Jacir? What did it say?"

His voice came from far away, but the word made her heart speed up and a fire rise in her belly.

"Revolution."

32

Ilahna blew into her hands in an attempt to warm them as she crouched in the crumbling remains of the once-grand bakery. She didn't know why no one had ever built over the old foundation, especially seeing as how Clearwall was already crowding people out from between the walls and into smaller and smaller abodes. She supposed it was possible that the land was still owned by someone, though they would have to be of considerable rank or power to keep the Proclaimers from simply taking the land out from under them.

Why are you thinking about this?

Ilahna wasn't sure if she was more nervous or excited. She had brought her sword with her as a precaution, had crept into the shadows of the crumbling walls well ahead of the appointed time so that she could see who the summons had come from and act accordingly. But now it was nearing midnight, and no one had appeared.

Ilahna was beginning to think that she was the butt of some unknown joke and was moving to leave when one of the shadows behind her detached itself from the others and slunk towards her in the darkness. She had just enough time and awareness to spin towards it, blade outstretched, before the moon appeared from behind the clouds and illuminated the stranger.

A tall, thin man in a hooded cloak raised his hands in a placating gesture as he took a cautious step towards her.

"I'm impressed, Miss Ilahna. You're quite sneaky."

"Apparently not sneaky enough. How'd you get behind me? Are you the one that gave me the message?"

The man shook his head. "My name is Tanner. And I'm just one of many. We space out our travels into town, lest one of us be recognized. The man that ran into you last night took a very big risk getting you that message. He'll be laying low for a long time now."

"If you don't trust me, then why are we here?"

The stranger shrugged one shoulder. "I think you misunderstand. It's not that we don't trust you. We have no idea who else might have been watching. While we're all very good at remaining hidden, we still have to take every possible precaution to protect ourselves until the time is right."

Ilahna eyed the man. He sported a cutlass and a leather jerkin under his dark cloak. Neither was legal to make or wear in Clearwall. "Right for what?"

The man gave her a surprisingly kind smile. "That's not up to me. I just follow orders. And tonight my orders are to bring you to the one who gives them. If you're willing."

"And if I'm not?"

The smile faded a tiny bit. "Then I leave you here and we don't make contact again. You're good, but it's unlikely you'll be able to find us on your own. This was just an offer for parley. We won't ask you to meet with us again if you choose to leave now." He paused, looking her in the eye. "But you showed up. So, I think, deep down, you want to know."

Ilahna's stomach and heart screamed at her in the affirmative, but she tried to mask her thrill as well as she could. Instead, she sighed in exasperation and rolled her eyes.

"You're really good at answering questions without actually saying anything at all."

Tanner laughed. "That's kind of my job until you decide for sure whether you're going to come or not. Thanks for noticing."

Ilahna almost smiled, but caught herself. "Take off your hood," she demanded, instead.

He did so without question, and she saw his tanned face and wheat-colored beard clearly. His hazel eyes twinkled a bit in the moonlight.

"If you decide not to come with me, it's not like you're ever going to see my face after tonight, anyway. Is that enough? Have you made your decision?"

Ilahna's heart had already made up its mind, and her mouth followed almost before she realized what it was saying. "Fine, Tanner. I'll follow you to Gods-know-where in this blasted city. Lead on."

Tanner's eyes creased at the corners as he grinned and bowed. "On the contrary, Miss Ilahna. You're about to see life outside of Clearwall."

Ilahna thought he was making a joke. No one was allowed to just...leave Clearwall. Even the trade caravans were closely watched, their inventory and wagons thoroughly searched before entering or exiting the gates. The few people that she knew of that had tried to leave Clearwall hidden in barrels or clinging to axles had been promptly found and burnt at the stake, traitors to the Crown. What this man said was impossible.

But Tanner only grinned wider and pulled his hood back on. He kept to the shadows and motioned for her to follow, until they had crept out of the old bakery's protective embrace. Past the torched remains of the old porch where the baker had once displayed his goods to cool. Past the charred logs and fallen beams. Into the shadow of the stone oven that still stood, tall and strong and unblemished by time, with only a destroyed triangular symbol carved into its stack to acknowledge that things had once been different.

Tanner climbed carefully into the ancient kiln and knelt for a moment. Ilahna watched, confused. Then, there was an almost inaudible *click* and a panel in the stone floor shifted. Tanner winked as he lifted it, proudly displaying the tunnel below. Ilahna's mouth went dry and her heart sped up.

There was a way out of Clearwall.

Still not sure where they were going, even less sure of who they would meet when they got there...Ilahna didn't care. She didn't hesitate as she climbed down into the sloping passageway beneath the oven. Behind her, Tanner produced a candle that barely lit the earthy walls on either side.

"There. You see? Welcome to the revolution, Miss Ilahna. Everyone is very excited to meet you."

Ilahna had never seen such a long tunnel before, and the surrounding smell of earth made the air seem thicker than that in the sewers or abandoned pantry. It felt nearly oppressive, but Ilahna reminded herself that she'd once felt the same way about crawling through tight spaces as a thief and about the rats scuttling in the sewers. Determinedly, she fought past the sudden claustrophobia and forced herself forward as Tanner led her through the hidden door and into the darkness of the soil.

They traveled further than Ilahna had ever gone in a straight line. She did not even think it was possible to move in one direction for so long without walking off the edge of the earth. Even when she crossed the rooftops of Clearwall, she had never been able to cross such a span of earth and time without changing direction. The walls were always in the way. And beyond them, the cliffs or rivers. She closed her eyes as they walked, trying to orient herself. It was not so difficult since they were still facing the same direction they had been in the oven.

The trees. Ilahna's thoughts darted back to the fine line of green she had seen on the horizon so long ago. *We are going to the trees.*

Her heart was momentarily overtaken by the idea of bringing Jacir here. Of showing him the things he had only seen from behind a door that no one else could breach. To remind him of his own sanity in the days where she saw him questioning it with eyes that were too old for his tiny frame. Hope lay at the end of this uninterrupted line of earth, and not just hope of allies or plans or revolutions.

The reminder that others were waiting for her at the end of this tunnel, and that no one else knew where she was, sobered Ilahna quickly. Trees or not, she had to find out what these people wanted. Who they were. Whether or not they were a danger. To her, to Eitan. To Jacir. Resolutely, Ilahna squared her shoulders and reopened her eyes. She never thought that she would find answers under trees.

Tanner's candle had almost burnt to a nub when Ilahna noticed a change in their surroundings. The hard-packed earth became less symmetrical. Began to slope in some areas as great, twisting roots snaked their way through the soil to create irregular, living archways in the dirt. Ilahna laid her hand on the rough bark of a root that was thicker than her arm. She could almost feel it pulse with life beneath her palm, and Ilahna found herself wondering if she had ever been surrounded by the living before. Did the people of Clearwall count? She didn't think so.

"You must go through a lot of candles," she joked, trying to tear herself free from the disconcerting thoughts. Tanner gave her a quizzical look, and she gestured to what was left of the candle in his hand. He shrugged.

"Normally, we don't use them. The path is straight. Why waste the resources when you know the way?"

Ilahna pondered that for a moment and followed him again, breathing in the scent of earth. She had known dirt before. She had planted and gardened for nobles in exchange for coin when she was young. She had scrubbed it from her skin. But this was different. She nearly trembled with how different it was.

Finally, Tanner stopped at a ladder placed against the worn earth wall. Ilahna climbed it deftly, nearly bumping her head on the rough-hewn roof that barely peaked above her at its top. She ran her fingers over this wood, too, indifferent to the splinter it left in her palm. There was no soil in this part of the tunnel. No carving or signs of human adaptation. Only the gracefully-curving boughs that reached upwards to an open sky.

So enthralled by being in the living heartbeat of such a majestic plant, Ilahna almost didn't notice the door that had been carefully grafted into the living wood. With a nod from Tanner, she carefully pushed it open.

Trees. More trees than Ilahna had ever dreamed there could be. The scent of the forest was ripe and clean and stung her nose with how strong it was. The ground was a carpet of brown needles and soft moss. And the trees stretched so far in every direction, she could not see the ridgeline she knew was there.

Ilahna took a minute to pull herself from her amazement and centered herself. She knew which way they had come from, and she turned in that direction to peer towards Clearwall. It did seem the forest was thinner there, but there was no sign of the great walls that surrounded and separated the citizens. Only a hazy cloud of smoke that hung over Clearwall in a smoggy covering, lit from beneath by the fires and the Proclaimers' ever-burning pyres and torches.

The Proclaimers. Ilahna gulped down her awe and remembered why she was here. She turned towards Tanner and nodded. He gave her a kind smile and led her deeper into the forest, weaving through the trees with a practiced certainty. Ilahna followed, still brushing her hands over the bark of the surrounding trunks and testing her weight on the earthen floor that gave a little with each step. She tried to mask her amazement, however, as they suddenly broke through the trees and into a natural clearing. There were several low fires and scattered sleeping rolls, but her attention was captured by a broad-shouldered man that stood at their approach. He had a sword in his hand.

"Who is there?" the man rumbled, his sharp eyes scanning the ridgeline.

"It's just me, Your Highness. I brought the young girl that escaped the old man's pyre all those weeks ago. The Proclaimers didn't get her, after all."

Ilahna frowned uncertainly. *Highness?*

The man resheathed his sword and approached them with a long gait. He was tall and broad-shouldered, with a strong jawline and piercing grey eyes. His black hair was a little longer than Ilahna expected from someone who claimed to be nobility, the whiskers on his chin unshaven, though not uncomely. His bearing was straight and proud, though there was a glimmer in his eyes that made Ilahna think he was kind and prone to laughter. He was dressed in a simple peasant's tunic that had no patches, and his breeches and boots were of nicer quality than anything she had ever owned.

As he approached, Tanner bowed at the waist, and after a second's hesitation, Ilahna did so, too. The approaching figure laughed.

"You bow so readily, girl. Do you know me? Recognize me?"

Ilahna looked up into his face again, without straightening her back. She shook her head.

"No, sir. But I am an urchin of Clearwall. And I learned a long time ago not to draw the ire of someone who thinks they're more important than me."

It was a dangerous thing to say, but these people had called Ilahna to them. Now she would find out why. She forced some steel into her spine and stood straight without breaking eye contact.

Much to her surprise, the stranger laughed again. "We all had to learn the same. The Proclaimers are a dangerous and cruel master." He bowed his head and brought a hand to his chest. "I am Aurelius of Clearwall, illegitimate son of King Lucius VII. Heir to the Starlit Throne. Normally we would introduce a prospective candidate to the revolution more slowly than this, but we recognize that your brother will look for you if you do not return soon."

Ilahna's eyes widened and her fingers flicked towards her sword hilt on reflex. Aurelius saw it and raised one hand. "You were the first person to ever scale the wall, Ilahna Harkins. We have been watching you for a very long time. And I promise, if we'd ever wanted to hurt you or young Jacir, we could have done so. Neither of you are in danger." The tension in Ilahna's shoulders did not ease.

"If you say so, your *majesty.*" She bit back the sarcasm that dripped from the last word a little too late, suddenly mindful of the gleaming sword at the man's hip. Aurelius didn't move, but a quiet, feminine trill of laughter broke the sudden tension.

"Oh, she is a biting one, isn't she? She must drive the Proclaimers absolutely mad." Ilahna straightened to see a small, moon-faced woman approach. Her hair had the same silvery sheen as the Proclaimer's breastplates and her eyes looked like liquid drops of turquoise. The young woman gave a sweet, understated smile at Ilahna's gaze. "You should ask her what's really on her mind, Your Highness."

Aurelius glanced behind him, then beckoned the woman forward. "Ah. This is Lucinda, my advisor. She has an eye for seeing what people don't mean to show, and I trust her judgement implicitly. Very well. Tell me what you want to say." Ilahna gulped down her uncertainty, her gaze still caught in the mesmerizing turquoise eyes.

"Okay," she finally said, refocusing on Aurelius. "Okay, fine. I think it's preposterous that you introduce yourself like that. Even if you are the heir to Starlit throne—which I have no reason to believe—that's a big claim to make. There's no way to prove it. Clearwall Keep is empty, apparently abandoned. No one has seen the King with their own two eyes in… I don't even know how long. So even if you were an exact copy of His Majesty, no one would be able to verify it. Anything you present as proof will be quickly and effortless discredited by the Proclaimers, and you will be burnt at the stake along with all that follow you. If you plan on bringing these claims of heirship to Clearwall, I don't think you'll make it very far before you're silenced." She took a deep breath.

"It's just… dumb. You should probably work on something better if you're trying to wrest Clearwall from the Proclamatic Order of Truth."

Aurelius smiled a tiny bit as he studied Ilahna. After a moment, he nodded.

"You don't skirt around the truth, do you? I should have known you wouldn't be meek, urchin or not. But you're right. In everything you've said. And we have already considered all of it." He motioned her to follow him and started making his way to the fires in the camp. "We know there's no way to take Clearwall back without a fight that the Proclaimers do not intend to lose. But Clearwall *does* need to be retaken by someone who will listen to the actual people and not long-dead Gods. And those people need to feel safe, no matter what abilities or traits they're born with. As King of Clearwall, I intend to set that right."

Aurelius' words sparked with truth, and Ilahna's uncertainty fizzled as a thrill of hope surged through her. She could almost picture the Clearwall he promised—and it was the one that she'd imagined for Jacir nearly all his life. She'd thought she was the only person to believe in it. She'd thought that everyone else would be too afraid to look towards that future with anything less than hatred. But here, in a man that might or might not have a legitimate claim to the seat of power in Clearwall, was hope of something better than even her brightest fantasies. It would be difficult to get there. It would be bloody and painful as they upheaved everything that Clearwall had become.

But sometimes you must rebreak a bone if you want it to heal properly.

Ilahna smiled at Aurelius, her face warmed by the firelight. "Honestly, sir? If you're trying to bring that kind of order to

Clearwall, then I don't think I care if you're a legitimate heir or not."

Aurelius put a thick hand on Ilahna's shoulder. "I assure you, I am Lucius' son. And that legitimacy will help us where hope alone will not. The people of Clearwall crave a new order. We just need to help them all realize that there is a change on the horizon. And that the Proclaimers *will* relinquish their hold, one way or another."

Ilahna made her decision with a rashness that would have disappointed the Faoii. But she knew that Jorthee would have understood, and that strengthened her resolve.

"I want to help."

"I thought you might." Lucinda's bright smile reminded Ilahna of the moon on a clear winter night, bright and gorgeous. "We chose to seek you out after what happened with your brother at the pyre, but we were not able to find you after you disappeared with the cloaked woman. One of our scouts acted on his own initiative after your display in the temple courtyard last night. I think that Aurelius wanted to scold him for acting with such impunity, but I am not sure either of us were actually surprised. You stir people to greatness, Ilahna Harkins. You reach the parts of people that the Proclaimers have sectioned off. And your brother… he can do more with the Tapestry than any of us thought was still possible. The resistance needs you both. For the betterment of Clearwall and her people."

"The blacksmith would also be very useful to our cause, if he is willing and if you trust him," Aurelius said. "But you must absolutely believe in his loyalty if you bring him here. We cannot lose the revolution from within the ranks."

Ilahna shook her head. "After what the Proclaimers did to him, Eitan was already trying to get to the king. It nearly crushed him when he found out there wasn't one. He'll swear to you without hesitation. I know it." Aurelius nodded and turned away.

"Then you are welcome to return to Clearwall and prepare them. Tanner will help you plan the details."

"Wait," Ilahna called, prompting the bastard king to turn back in her direction. She cleared her throat, her heart pounding in her chest. "Wait. There is one more I'd like to bring."

"If they follow you, I am sure they are worthy of our cause," Lucinda said sweetly. "If you trust them, of course."

Ilahna lowered her voice. "She is Faoii. True Faoii. Not one of the peasants the Proclaimers burn."

Aurelius' eyes widened while Lucinda's narrowed. After a moment, he spoke in gravely tones.

"That's an… interesting claim to make. Even the witches that are still left don't use that term anymore. Only the very sick or the very stupid."

"I know. But I don't think she's crazy. And I don't think she's what the Proclaimers have taught us to fear. She's teaching Jacir to better use the powers your people saw in the square last night. I need her with us. Witch or not."

Aurelius seemed to think it over for a long time. "Are you willing to bet your life on her trustworthiness?" Ilahna nodded without hesitation.

"Yes."

"Are you willing to bet the rest of ours? All of Clearwall? All of Imeriel?"

That brought Ilahna pause. And for a moment she stood, silent and uncertain.

Lucinda smiled and took a dainty step forward, placing a pale hand on Ilahna's arm. "Look deep inside yourself. There is something in you that tells you the truth even when you don't know it, isn't there? Use that."

Ilahna nodded and closed her eyes, pulling up the strand of whispers and truth from deep within her. Finally, she spoke.

"The Faoii does not harbor any ill will towards us or your people. She has her own motives for what she does, but they do not align with those of the Proclaimers. In fact, I think that she sees the Proclaimers as evil. I trust her. I don't think she'll help the resistance, exactly. But she won't stand against it, either. And she *will* help Jacir." *Even if it's because she feels like she doesn't have a choice.*

Satisfied, Aurelius nodded. "Very well. But she is under your care, Ilahna Harkins of the Maze. If the Faoii's presence causes any disruption to the camp, or brings the Proclaimers on us, it is on your head."

Ilahna nodded. "I understand." And she did. She eyed the sword on his hip and knew that people had paid for their mistakes with blood before. Aurelius put the good of his people above all else. Those who brought harm upon his people felt the price at the edge of his blade.

Aurelius crossed his arms over his chest and watched her closely for several long moments. Finally, he seemed satisfied. "Very well. Go talk to Tanner about our next steps. It is good to have you with us."

As Aurelius and Lucinda turned back to the fire, Tanner approached, grinning broadly. "That didn't go so bad, did it? The

Lady Lucinda was very sure you would be on board. Now, let's talk about getting your friends here." He walked her back to the tree and its small door.

"We try not to use the passage that often, lest it be discovered, and we've already utilized it once today. But we need you to get back to your friends before they come searching for you and lead the Proclaimers right to the oven. That would torch all of us, so there's no helping it. You've got to go back tonight. Luckily, you're sneaky. I think you'll be okay. But then you have to lay low for a while. As in, don't go anywhere near the entrance. Got it? You can return with your friends through the tunnel after the next round of scouts return to report." Tanner put one hand on the side of his temple and thought for a moment. "That's… Eleven days. Can you do that?" Ilahna nodded.

"Eleven days. Thank you, Tanner. We won't let the resistance down."

"Oh, I know. A lot of people have put their hopes in you and your brother. And after living in Clearwall their entire lives, hope is a very rare gift, indeed."

33

When Ilahna told them about the resistance in the forest and everything she had seen, Jacir and Eitan showed a mix of bubbling excitement and fear. The Faoii, however, only frowned dourly and barked at Jacir to return to his meditations. Ilahna raised a quizzical eyebrow. She'd thought the Faoii would be pleased.

There were a few provisions that they wanted to gather in the eleven days before their departure, unsure of what would be available in the forest and aware that they might not reenter Clearwall for a long time after they left her stony walls. Ilahna volunteered to go, not only because she was the best thief in the group, but because she wanted to see what the people of Clearwall were doing to thwart the Proclaimers now that Jacir had shown them the proof of what lay below Clearwall Keep. She kissed Eitan on the cheek on her way to the entrance, and he grasped her hand.

"They'll be watching my shop, but try to find tools, if you can. I won't be much help to the resistance without a set of tools. But please, Ilahna. Please, don't do anything that might get you hurt. Come back safely."

"You know me, Eitan. I'm the safest person you know." Ilahna winked as she left the sewers, an empty canvas sack in hand. She tried not to chuckle at Eitan's exasperated sigh behind her.

As Ilahna darted across rooftops and over the heads of merchants and peasants, she'd hoped to hear the clanging of weapons or the still-screaming protests of the people that had finally been shown the deceit and horrors of the Proclaimers and their lies. But as she shifted from building to building, searching for safe and easy marks to get the things she needed, Ilahna noted with dismay that the people of Clearwall had evidently been bent into submission once more. Save for a dark chill on the air and the faintest whispers she could sometimes hear just out of earshot, it seemed to Ilahna that nothing had changed at all.

Several hours later, Ilahna kicked a stone angrily as she stepped back into their little camp, her bag of stolen goods spilling gracelessly where she threw the satchel down.

"And what has you so upset now?" the Faoii asked as she poked at the fire, watching another tendril of silk strand unravel in the blaze. The others were asleep in their bedrolls, and Ilahna forced herself to breathe deeply and speak quietly for their sake.

"They're not *doing* anything."

"They're probably doing more than you do when you sleep. Jacir is exploring the Weave. The blacksmith is fixing his broken mind and body. You only snore."

Ilahna rolled her eyes but forced herself not to rise to the challenge. Instead, she sat by the fire and shook her head.

"Not them. Above. I thought that the people would fight back. Root out the Proclaimers and take back our city. But it's only been two days, and the shouts and protests have all but stopped. They're just returning to what we had before."

"What did you expect to happen when peasants go against warriors? Sticks against swords?"

"They have more than that, though. For a minute there, they had *fire*. They had strength. They had a desire, and unity and a *need*. For a minute, I thought they had enough."

The Faoii snorted and tossed the stick she was using to stir the fire against the sewer's wall.

"Everyone has that fire in them, girl. It's buried deeper in some than in others, but everyone in the world has *something* that they think is worth fighting for, deep down. Kindle it in enough people and you have an army. But the thing is, you have to kindle it deeply enough and keep it going long enough for it to spread. People like the Proclaimers have more experience dousing that flame than you have of igniting it, girl. Maybe the embers for these people will burn a little brighter now, deep in their hearts. Maybe they'll whisper a little more often or pray a little bit differently. But it's not enough for what you want. And it probably never will be."

"But if we get them to the resistance, it would spread faster. We could all keep that fire going together."

"Oh? Are you going to sneak every person out of Clearwall? Think clearly. How long before the Proclaimers notice that?"

"We can't just let people roll over and die because that's all they know how to do. We need to be able to show them that they can fight back. Teach them *how* to." The Faoii scoffed.

"You've raised your blade in battle *once*, girl. You're no commander." Ilahna was about to protest. She was better than nothing, at least. But something clicked in her brain, and her head shot up to look at the Faoii from across the fire.

"You could help us." Ilahna put some steel in her voice and forced herself to meet the woman's grey eyes. "With the resistance. Jacir and I could help to pull people into it, or at least not be so afraid of it. But you could teach people how to defend themselves from the Proclaimers. You could stop the witch burnings. Teach people not to be afraid. Like you did with me." She spoke more quickly, the words pouring from her before the other woman could be given time to interject. She didn't even notice as the Faoii's eyes darkened with each word or that she seemed to look far into a place that Ilahna couldn't see.

"You're what Clearwall needs, Faoii! People are so scared. We can't breathe or tell stories or dream anymore. But you know so much more than everyone else. Who knows? Maybe you could even—"

"NO!"

Ilahna winced from the power in the word, from the sudden spark of green in the woman's usually grey eyes, from the force of the stone floor crumbling even before the woman's dark fist rammed straight down into it. "No! I have fought my wars. I have looked and pulled and stretched and done everything I could to fix it all and *look what happened.* They burnt my friends, destroyed everything we worked for. They erased our names from the histories, blamed us for every ounce of work they had to later endure in the name of progress. We all fought until our hands and minds bled, until our hearts could hold no more sorrow and our throats could no longer utter a battlecry and *for what?* For freedom? Freedom led to economic collapse, to fanatics with torches. Barely a century had passed before the libraries were temples and the Faoii were just ashes. Everything we did. Everything we were. It's all gone."

For the briefest of moments, tears welled in the Faoii's eyes and washed away the color, but she blinked them back almost immediately. The grey orbs stilled and hardened.

"I have fought my war. I am done. Fight your own if you want to. Join this resistance that you have leaked into the others' ears like honey, but I will be no part of it. Go fight in your revolution. Your war. But be prepared for the consequences you can't yet see."

Ilahna sat in silence for a moment, looking at her hands. After a long time, she gulped her fear back down and dragged her eyes back up to meet the woman's. And she *knew.*

"You're her, aren't you? The Betrayer."

The grey eyes seemed to look right through her with their dispassionate gaze.

"Some have called me that," the Faoii whispered back.

"What about before? What did they call you then?"

The eyes refocused for a moment, and the faintest hint of green recolored the irises.

"I was Faoii-Kaiya, last of the Monastery of the Eternal Blade. But... but they used to call me Kai."

Ilahna's heart thundered in her chest and her mouth went dry. "How... how is that possible?" she finally squeaked. "The Godfell War was 200 years ago!" Kai blinked slowly at her with ancient, knowing eyes.

"187. And I assure you, girl, that I feel every single one of them deep below my bones."

With that, the Faoii, Kaiya the Betrayer, stood and walked slowly to the opening of the sewers. As Ilahna watched her, framed by the moonlight, strands of her long, white braid coming loose and moving in the breeze, she could almost see the woman who transcended time not as a warrior or as a witch...but as a person who had lived far too long and seen too much for mortal eyes to bear. And she could not help but marvel at a person who had witnessed so much and come through the other side intact.

34

It was a beautiful autumn evening when a lone man came to the door. Ali stood obediently behind her father, but she was now tall enough to see over his shoulder and look at the slender, stern-faced man, who wore a silver breastplate over long, white robes. Ali nearly gasped. She had never seen anyone like him before. Even the Faoii and Croeli looked more battle-ready than serene. In contrast, this man gave off a calming aura despite his armored torso.

"Yes?" Ali's father asked.

"Hello, Goodman. I have come about the Illindrian symbols I have seen in town. A local baker sent me here."

"Yes, of course." Ali's mother smiled broadly, moving her husband away from the door. They'd quickly learned that Danther was not much of a salesman. "Come in, come in, sir. We have several designs and materials. What are you looking for?"

The stranger stepped into the house lightly but didn't even look at the aging woman speaking to him. Instead, he met Ali's astonished gaze.

"Actually, Goodwoman, I think I have found what I've been searching for." He bowed before Ali, causing everyone in the room to freeze. Ali looked to her parents uncertainly.

The man straightened and smiled. "Madame, I am First Proclaimer Tosleh of Clearwall."

Ali gasped. Clearwall! The capitol was so far away! Even with her mother's ability to weave light into thread, to imagine that someone would travel so far for a trinket! The visitor smiled kindly at her bewilderment and lifted one of her hands to his lips. "I had heard that a Daughter of Truth was spreading words that the Faoii have tried to cover up. I have journeyed far to meet you. May I speak with you for a time?"

"Now, wait just a moment," Ali's father butted in, bristling. "I'm not going to have a stranger from nowhere talking with my daughter just because he has some fancy manners and clothes." Tosleh smiled.

"Of course not, sir. I would happily speak to all of you at once if that is preferable." Ali's father grunted his approval.

Ali and her parents gathered around their kitchen table, listening intently to the stories that Proclaimer Tosleh spun with silken words and long-forgotten dreams. Stories of ancient Gods and lush valleys and overabundant crops.

"You've noticed how things have seemed so much harder now than they were in our parents' and grandparents' times?" he asked sweetly, leaning forward with bright eyes. "How the Faoii seem to be spreading beyond their bounds while the rest of us are pushed back to the shadows of civilization, clawing for their scraps?" Ali's parents glanced toward the door and each other, but Ali leaned forward, eyes wide.

"Yes!" she nearly cried, her excitement overcoming her. "Yes! Even though they say everyone can join the ranks, now. It's all lies!" Tosleh nodded.

"The Faoii know so much more than they let on, child. They can see the Great Tapestry that ties all the world together—the domain of the Old Gods. But they hoard it jealously, only letting those within their monasteries' walls know what potential the future holds. The rest of us are left to follow their whims and orders. At the mercy of tyrants."

"That's... that's not quite right," Ali's mother squeaked. "It's... It's that the Faoii see more than us. They know more than us. The Faoii guide us with the knowledge the Weavers see." She fidgeted with her apron as she spoke.

"But how do you *know*, Mother?" Ali demanded. "Is that why they won't let even the best fighter in the region through their gates? Why they forced us from our home? How do we know anything they do is out of kindness or good will? Just because that's what they *say*?" Her mother opened her mouth to speak, but closed it again, looking down.

"She is right, Goodwoman," Tosleh replied, reaching across the table to grasp the woman's wringing fingers. "They tell us that things are better than they have ever been before, but still people find themselves homeless and lost. Still the crops do not come in. The people under the supposed protection of the monasteries suffer. And it is hardly just." He squeezed her hand. "But there is a solution. Something stronger than the Faoii and their guarded temples. Something that can overthrow their unfair rule."

"What?" Ali whispered, her eyes alight. Tosleh smiled, and his gaze bored into hers.

"The Gods for whom the Tapestry was woven. Those that could destroy everything corrupt within the Faoii-Croeli Order. They wait to take back Their thrones."

Ali's father grunted and leaned backwards, crossing his arms over his chest. "Pretty words. But even if they're true, at what cost?"

Tosleh smiled and released Ali's mother's hand to gesture before him. "Only Their freedom from under the Faoii threads that bind Them to the Weave. With faith and determination, we can return the world to how it is supposed to be. It is our right. And our duty. And I promise, Daughter—" he locked eyes with Ali again, seemingly pulling something up from the depths of her soul—"the Old Gods reward those who help Them."

Ali's father stood up abruptly, jarring those gathered at the table. "I think it's time you left," he growled. "This house does not betray the Faoii."

Tosleh did not argue or protest. He only stood gracefully and thanked them for their hospitality before gliding out the door. For a moment, Ali's parents stood in the living room, watching him walk down the road. Once he was out of sight, Danther turned to his daughter.

"Ali, go get more wood for the fire."

Ali did, but as she gathered the logs in her arms, she could not stop thinking of the visitor and his words. And as she looked across the barren field next to the log pile, a quiet thought came to her, unbidden.

All hail the Old Gods.

35

The Betrayer—*Kai. She was a person before the Proclaimers made her into something else,* Ilahna reminded herself—was not there on the eleventh morning. Eitan and Jacir checked over their supplies and Ilahna watched the Starlit River pass before the entrance to the sewers. Ilahna hoped that this was the last time they would have to hide here. She glanced around at a sewer that had apparently been so much more over the years, and idly wondered what other secrets it would harbor in the future.

The trio waited that day in a tense silence that only barely masked the buzzing undertone that comes right before a catastrophic change. Jacir hopped from foot to foot as he watched the sun set beyond the Starlit River.

"Do we wait for the witc—the woman?" Eitan asked quietly in Ilahna's ear. Ilahna shook her head.

"If she was able to find her way past the walls of Clearwall to save me and Jacir from the flames, she can find her way to wherever we go, if she wants to. She can make her own choices."

"I don't understand why she came at all if she was going to leave again before Jacir could learn…whatever it is she wanted him to learn," Eitan whispered, peering over Ilahna's shoulder at the younger boy. "He seems more… together than he used to. But even I can tell that he needs help to control his magic. And she might have been the only chance he had." Ilahna frowned for a moment, then shook her head and shrugged her satchel over her shoulder.

"I'm not even sure *she* knew why she was helping Jacir. I know she kept saying that he'd compelled her originally, but by the end it seemed like more than that. There were times when I think she wanted us to learn. To change things. Who knows why she disappeared when we finally figured out how?"

"Maybe she's just crazy." Eitan shrugged and wrapped an arm around Ilahna's waist, kissing the top of her head. "You've done amazing things without a witch's help, before. I'm right behind you no matter what."

Ilahna smiled, but the words were a bit sour in her ears. They'd forge ahead, with or without the Faoii's help, but it definitely seemed like Kaiya knew more of the world than Ilahna would ever have a chance to learn on her own. It was troubling that a woman that had lived through so much and impacted the world in so many ways would run away before stepping a foot on the path Ilahna had chosen. If Faoii-Kaiya did not think she could face this revolution, what hope did the rest of them have?

Enough. We have enough.

They had to. And one way or another, they were going to see this to the end. Ilahna kissed Eitan's hand and crouched in the mud one more time, tracing out their path in the crude map she had drawn.

"Are we ready?" she asked the others.

Eitan pulled his hood up and nodded. Next to him, Jacir flashed a quick smile and punched his fist into his hand excitedly. Together, the trio crept into the night. The sewers whistled with an aching breeze in their absence, one more ancient piece of Clearwall that held nothing but memories and old secrets.

Eitan was not nearly as skilled at traversing the Maze as the other two were, having never had to explore its many passageways and escape routes for survival. But he followed Ilahna's instructions carefully, stopping when she motioned and holding his breath when necessary. It was obvious that he was still recovering from the terrible ordeal beneath the Keep, but Eitan pressed on, regardless. The trio made it to the burned-down bakery and its secret passageway without incident.

The walk through the tunnel took even longer than it had when Ilahna had first come this way, and she was quite glad that she had stolen several large candles. But she could not be angry at their slow pace as she watched her brother take in the tunnel that spread to the horizon.

Jacir could barely contain his wonder at the massive, sturdy roots that formed the roof and tunnel walls. Time and again Ilahna and Eitan stopped as he pressed his palm against the bark, marveling at the indents the wood left in his skin. Eitan laughed out loud as the young boy's curiosity finally overtook his sense, and he licked a particularly large and twisted specimen.

"It tastes like…beets," Jacir said, his eyes wide and sparkling. "Lana! It tastes like beets!" Ilahna felt thrilled to see his joy—he looked like what she expected children used to look like, when they were allowed to just be children. Carefree and filled with wonder.

"Just wait until you see the forest," she replied, motioning her little brother forward. Jacir grinned and scampered after her and the candlelight.

"Do they change color?" he exclaimed, momentarily forgetting that they were supposed to be quiet here. "Red and orange and gold?"

"Not that I saw," Ilahna replied. "They all seemed green. And with needles rather than leaves. But maybe there are different kinds deeper within. I did not see much beyond the camp."

Jacir seemed content with this answer and kept close to Ilahna's heels as they continued the long journey past the far-off tree line.

When they finally reached the end of the tunnel, Tanner was there to greet them.

"I was afraid you'd been captured. It's good to see you all safe." He motioned the little group towards the faint light of fires in the distant clearing. "His Majesty wants to speak with you."

Eitan, who had always lived within the walls and the safety of his smithy, was less at ease than the others were. He cast fervent glances towards the tree line with every strange noise of wind, bird or patrolman that came through the creaking branches. Ilahna smiled warmly and tried to ease his discomfort by taking his hand as they sat by a fire made of real wood. He seemed slightly less troubled within the ring of light from the flames.

Aurelius and Lucinda were already there, and the bastard king made formal introductions. "I am pleased you came, blacksmith. We have much use of your skills," Aurelius declared in his rumbling voice. "We have stolen blades with your mark on them. You do good work." Eitan beamed with pride despite the sudden sound of an owl that made him jump. He recovered quickly and the others were kind enough not to laugh.

Now properly seated around one of the fires, Ilahna, Eitan, Aurelius, and Lucinda were keen to let Jacir stare in wonder from within the little circle of clearing as they spoke. Even while everyone agreed that the future would, in many ways, depend on him, for a moment they were content to let him be a child discovering nature for the first time. Ilahna and Eitan were also new to trees and the wonder that stood outside Clearwall, but they were able to put their amazement aside long enough to focus on the future. If they planned well now and moved forward with a set direction, then they would have their entire lives to explore what they'd never been allowed to see.

"Where is the other one? The Faoii?" Aurelius asked, looking between Ilahna and Eitan with narrowed eyes. Ilahna shifted her gaze to the ground.

"She's not coming," she said before adding quickly: "But it's okay. We don't need her."

Aurelius nodded, stroking his chin. "Very well. It is probably better this way. At least we understand the motives of those gathered here. She was a wild card I did not want to gamble with." Lucinda cleared her throat softly and Aurelius nodded. "Yes. Why we've invited you here. We have seen what you and your brother can do, Miss Harkins. We know that you are both capable of swaying the hearts of those in Clearwall, albeit in different ways. And there is no king or emperor in the world who may lead a nation without his people's hearts. He may rule. He may control. But he cannot lead. The people of Clearwall—our people, *my* people—have been kowtowed by fear for far too long. We need to retake the Starlit Throne and either bend the Proclaimers back to their place at her feet or break them completely. We must dig out the rot in Clearwall. And we want you to help us."

Ilahna leaned forward, grasping at Eitan's hand as she did. He squeezed softly as Aurelius continued.

"A few of the people we have here are trained with weapons, though not as well as the Proclaimers themselves. But there are children of soldiers or Proclaimer fallouts that escaped whatever pyre comes at the end of the Proclamatic Order trials. They are teaching the regular commoners how to fight as best they can. Sometimes with swords or bows, but mostly with staves until we find more blacksmiths—but they do what they can with what they have, and they do it well. Mostly because, above everything else, the people you'll find in these woods have heart. We'll have an army by the time we decide to take Clearwall head-on."

"How can we help?" Ilahna asked, almost too eagerly. Aurelius smiled at her enthusiasm and turned to Lucinda. The wispy girl looked thoughtful.

"Your strongest talent is obvious, Eitan. We need blacksmiths, and you are one of the best. Your presence in camp will boost morale more than I think even you realize, even if you don't lend your voice to the chorus." She smiled an understated smile before turning to Ilahna.

"But you, Miss Ilahna. You don't want to learn your magics, do you? The ones that manifest when you feel it is time for truths to rise?" The question did not seem like an attack, but Ilahna fidgeted uneasily. She didn't know how to explain the fear wrapped around the door she'd barricaded shut. The terror she felt when that crystal of power formed in her gut—no matter how useful it sometimes was. She swallowed hard, and Lucinda smiled. "Do not worry, Ilahna. We are trying to create a world where everyone can choose for themselves. Your brother wants to open the door. You do not. That does not make either of you any more or less useful than the other." She turned to Aurelius and whispered in his ear. After a moment, his face lit up.

"Yes, indeed! We will need people to prepare the forest. And our soldiers will need to know the lay of the city when we take back the streets." He smiled and turned back to Ilahna. "Miss Harkins, the revolution would like you to be its first cartographer."

"I don't even know what that means."

Eitan laughed and squeezed her hand. "It means you'll be making maps, Love. And why not? You know the Maze better than anyone alive."

"Not just of the Maze and Clearwall," Aurelius interjected. "I will need you to map what you can of the forest, as well. We cannot be safe if we don't know what's beyond our back door."

"I can do that!" Ilahna declared. "I know I can. I won't let you down. I promise."

"Having a map of the forest will be helpful when we search for the others." None of them had even realized that Jacir had returned to the circle, and several members of their little party jumped.

Ilahna spun to face Jacir. "What others?"

Jacir's eyes were unfocused, and he stared off to the south. "Clearwall is not ready yet. But there are pockets of those that have escaped the Proclaimers over the decades. They huddle together in little groups that can't get any bigger or the Proclaimers will find them. And if the Proclaimers find them, they'll burn them, too." He frowned for a moment, still staring at nothing, before a sudden spark lit his face. "They have magic! All of them! And none of them are ashamed of it. Isn't that beautiful?"

Everyone stared at Jacir in silence. Then, Lucinda and Aurelius shared a glance. "If I present you with a map, do you think you could mark these people's locations?" Aurelius asked slowly.

Eyes still unfocused, Jacir nodded.

"Someone find us a map of Imeriel! I don't care how outdated it is!" Aurelius yelled, and there was a scuffle in the trees. Before long, Tanner had produced one and laid it on ground before Jacir. The urchin crouched low, his fingers gliding across the painted symbols depicting rivers and roads. Every now and again his fingers would stop with a firm finality at one place or another before flitting away once more. Lucinda followed Jacir's movements and used a feather quill to mark a small portion of the places he indicated.

Eventually Jacir finished pointing out his pockets of potential allies and his eyes cleared again. He sagged a little bit and Ilahna gripped his arm. "You okay, Jace?"

"I'm fine." He smiled and straightened, his eyes fully clear now. "Can I go look for squirrels? Or eggs? Ooh! Eggs! Can you imagine how many must be out here? Trisha would be so jealous!"

"What? Eggs? Why do you—never mind. Yes. Stay close enough that I can see you." Jacir grinned and scurried into the trees.

"You baby him more than is necessary, Miss Ilahna. He is stronger than you know." Lucinda's voice was soft and kind, but the words made Ilahna bristle defensively.

"You've only just met him. Let me worry about my own family." Lucinda lifted her hands apologetically and looked back to the map, then whispered to Tanner who retreated. He returned a few minutes later with a small table. Ilahna released some of her anger and stood over the map as the others laid it out.

"Jacir pointed out a lot more places than that. Why did you pick some and not others?" Ilahna asked. Aurelius opened his mouth to reply, but Ilahna looked directly at Lucinda, and he closed it again.

Lucinda studied Ilahna with those two doleful eyes for what seemed like centuries. Ilahna frowned. "You're hiding something. What is it?" Lucinda blinked and looked down at her slipper-clad feet, almost ashamed. Around her, Ilahna noticed several of Aurelius' men inch a little closer to the circle. Aurelius waved them back.

"Go ahead, Lucinda. There are no secrets here. We have to trust each other if we are going to remake the world in a better image."

Lucinda steadied herself and looked up again. "I watched the Weave. Some know it as the Eternal Tapestry. I cannot see very far into the future of the threads; they get to be too much too quickly, and I get tangled. It is…very hard to come back. But if I know where to look, I can catch a glimpse of someone's mindset. Of their gifts. It's how I knew you would come. How I knew we could trust you. When Jacir showed me where to look, I could glimpse just enough of the people in each area to determine that they were the type of people we are looking for."

"And the ones you didn't mark? What's their story? Aren't they worth asking? Worth saving?"

Lucinda spread her hands. "We do not have time to ask all of them. You saw how many your brother indicated, and they are scattered all across Imeriel. Perhaps, with time, we will be able to reach out to every disenfranchised group throughout the country, but for now we must start somewhere. I discounted tiny groups of a hundred or less. Groups comprised of mostly the very young or the very old. I foresaw a few of the tribes speaking a language we could not learn in time. Two attacked us before we even arrived. But these here—" she motioned to the circles she had made on the map— "these are likely to join our cause."

"You mean they *will* join us, right?" Eitan put in. "You saw them agree to fight the Proclaimers?"

Lucinda spread her hands. "Perhaps. The Weave is not set in stone. Perhaps someone like Jacir could follow all of the strands and tell for sure which outcomes are more likely than others. I only acted upon what I know for certain."

Eitan looked to Aurelius. "And you're… okay with this? Depending fully on this… Tapestry? On magic? Is that the Clearwall we can expect once the Proclaimers are gone?" Ilahna felt badly for Eitan. He was trying, but it was hard to completely throw off the shackles that the Proclaimers had used to bind them all over centuries. She squeezed his hand.

"We need a world where people like Jacir can live without fear of the pyre every moment," she whispered. "We have to prove that sometimes magic can be used for good, Eitan. You never thought Jacir was evil, right?"

Eitan shook his head slowly. "No. I trust Jacir. I figured he was wrapped up in something bigger than him. I can… I can learn to trust this, too."

Aurelius nodded and put a hand on Eitan's shoulder. "That is a difficult thing to say, lad. I know how tight the Proclaimers have us all wound. But I trust Lucinda. She has never led me astray before. She will lead us all forward as surely. Do not worry." He turned to Ilahna. "You do not doubt your brother's visions?"

Ilahna shook her head. "No. Sometimes it's confusing, but as far as I can tell, everything Jacir sees and says is true."

Lucinda nodded. "You would be the one to know. But even I can tell that the young master can see further and more clearly than I can, with much more accuracy and control. I think your brother is much more powerful than he realizes. He will lead us to great places."

Ilahna watched her brother climb the trees circling the camp and wished he didn't have to lead them anywhere. *Children should be allowed to be children.* But as she thought of all the other urchins they had known in Clearwall, she knew that that hadn't been true for a long time.

Maybe a Clearwall under Aurelius' reign would make it true again.

Ilahna hoped so.

36

Ilahna and Jacir had done well as mazers, but nothing in the Maze had prepared them for the absolute freedom the forest offered. While Ilahna spent most of the days meticulously drawing out the jagged Maze on thick squares of cloth and Jacir trained with Lucinda deeper in the trees, the urchins spent every spare moment they could leaping from bough to bough, laughing and screaming into the wind. Years of roof-running had given them impeccable balance on slanted beams and uneven overhangs, which translated well to branches and spurs. But roofs had never offered them the absolute freedom they found here.

The forest became Ilahna and Jacir's playground, and for the first time in their lives they felt they could race and explore without worrying about catching an arrow in the side or falling into a trap laid by a jaded merchant. In the long hours of daylight, Ilahna and Jacir roamed the canopy, laughing as they delved further and deeper into a forest that seemed to go on forever in every direction. The deeper they went, the more types of trees they found, their branches spreading and twisting in a tangled array of bark and moss, and Ilahna would mark the different terrain on makeshift maps of rough canvas, awed by the variety outside of Clearwall with each new plant they found or animal they spotted.

"You know," Ilahna said one evening as she and Jacir sat on a branch and watched the beginning twinkles of stars dotting the sky. "We could keep going. We could go on forever and no one could stop us or find us. We can be free of Clearwall. Of the Proclaimers. Of… whatever everyone wants from you. Everything. Just you and me and Eitan. We could make a new life. Together." She turned to Jacir, watching his silhouette in the fading light. She was happy to have a place here. A purpose. She wanted to see the Proclaimers fall. But it would be dangerous, and her brother's safety and happiness were more important to her than any of those other things. "If you want to, Jace. We could do it."

Jacir thought for a long moment. "No thanks," he finally said quietly, still staring at the stars. "It'd be nice… but I don't think we'd like being free when everyone we've ever known is still trapped. And the Proclaimers… they reach so far. I don't think we can run from this." He turned to look Ilahna in the face. "And if we can… I don't think I want to."

Ilahna stared at her brother, and in the darkness he seemed taller. His shoulders seemed broader, his face longer. He seemed older than the scrawny, gawky brother she'd had a moment before. But she nodded.

"I guess that's what makes you you, Jacir. Come on. Let's get back before it's too dark to see."

"Just a little longer? Please? I know I can get us back. Even in the dark." He leaned back on the branch and stared at the sky.

Ilahna believed him. She nodded and turned her attention back to the ever-increasing glow of stars. They sat there, in the fading light, savoring the momentary peace while it lasted.

37

Ilahna woke to the sound of singing. She rolled over groggily and pushed open the flap of her tent. It still felt odd not to share a bed with her little brother, but now they'd grown past such things. And, in an encampment filled with soldiers, she felt he was safe enough.

The camp was already busy as the revolutionists filled their cups and bowls with gruel and hard biscuits before sitting around the camp's scattered fires. Ilahna appreciated these early mornings as everyone enjoyed a shared camaraderie before beginning the more strenuous tasks that were to come with the dawn. She especially liked days like this. Days when the entire camp sang.

Weeks had passed, and Ilahna still smiled at these spontaneous choirs. Originally, they'd started in the evenings when everyone returned to the campfires. It wasn't planned, in the beginning, but Eitan was almost always at his anvil in the last few minutes before dusk, finishing up a sword or breastplate. And as he worked, he sang.

Ilahna had always known that Eitan's songs pulled on heartstrings and inspired hope, courage, and strength. But those truths were magnified a hundredfold when others joined in the chorus. And now, on some early mornings or dusky evenings, the camp would sing. Together. One more thing that tied them all together in a world that had worked so hard to separate everyone. Ilahna grinned and raised her own voice in song as she exited her tent. Eitan stopped singing long enough to kiss her deeply in the early morning sunlight.

After breakfast, Ilahna went to find Jacir, already sure of where he'd be. Lucinda's trainings were kinder than Kai's had been, and, while Lucinda was not as natural at navigating the Weave as Jacir was, she had had more time to learn teachable techniques. Ilahna leapt from branch to branch until she found the two Weavers sitting in a little glade a short distance from the regular camp. Jacir seemed at peace, and Lucinda talked to him quietly as they sat, facing each other, their eyes closed.

Ilahna approved of this new training. Kai had shoved Jacir through that frightening door roughly, scratching the edges of his mind on its rough-hewn surface. Lucinda, in contrast, seemed to whisper him through. "Think of what you want to see, Jacir. Picture the door cracking. A piece of light breaking through here and there. Look through these cracks. Follow what you see without worrying about all the other parts still trapped behind the stone. Do you see the Weave? Can you pull at a single thread?"

"Yes." Jacir whispered from far away. "But I can pull more at the door, too. It is all right there. I just have to pry at it."

"Not now, Jacir. We are working on honing what we see. Not drowning in all the threads. We want you to be able to control what patterns you look for, rather than having your mind wrapped up in all of it without your direction."

"But only seeing the things we want to see and nothing else is dangerous, too. That's what the Proclaimers do. That's how we got to where we are now. I'd rather learn how to see everything, even if it's scary. Even if it hurts. Is that not better for us? For Clearwall?"

Lucinda considered this in silence. She opened her mouth and seemed about to respond when there was a sharp whistle from the trees closer to camp. Ilahna smiled broadly at the sound and leapt into the glade. "More are arriving!" she cried, making both Lucinda and Jacir jump. She took Jacir's hand and they took to the trees, excited to see the newest additions to the ever-growing resistance.

Aurelius had sent people out to the locations dictated by Jacir and Lucinda almost immediately, and his scouts and honorary diplomats had slowly begun to trickle back to camp over the last several weeks. Some came alone, apologizing profusely for their failure. Others, however, eventually straggled back from deeper in the forest, flocked by ragtag bands of uncertain peasants or, on occasion, groups of tattooed, armed warriors. When Ilahna asked why they'd come from the wrong direction, the scouts seemed amused. "The Proclaimers watch the roads. But no one watches the forests." Even as they recruited, the revolutionists still held their security and anonymity as the highest priorities.

This newest group of arrivals were simple folk, dressed in furs that Ilahna did not recognize, carrying carefully packed pots and woven baskets filled with personal belongings on their backs. Ilahna and Jacir did what they could to help the new arrivals to food and water, offering their bedrolls to those who shook with exhaustion. The strangers seemed grateful and kind, bobbing their heads in thanks over and over, offering the resistance members beaded bracelets and small metal carvings in gratitude. It took a lot of pleasant words and discussions before the resistance was able to convince the travelers that they weren't asking for trinkets or payment. Only support. And the role they'd play in that support was up to Aurelius.

After they'd done all they could, Ilahna and Jacir sat together on one of the branches overlooking the camp. Watching Aurelius settle new recruits was always a fascinating experience.

First, Aurelius would travel through the camp, Lucinda at his side, and speak to each newcomer in kind tones. Not just their leaders. Every person. He listened to their stories with rapt attention, asking questions and conferring with Lucinda for advice. Then, he would assign each recruit to a sort of team, creating large groups of varied members and purposes, mixing new members with veterans. Ilahna and Jacir had tried on many occasions to figure out what, exactly, his goals were, and today Ilahna hopped down from the tree as he passed.

"Aurelius," she ventured before he could move on to a new group. "Why don't you keep new recruits with their own people? They already have a bond with their families and friends. We fight harder for those we love, you know?"

"But we do not want still more groups of 'us' and 'them,' Miss Harkins," Aurelius replied. "We have lived for long enough without caring for those who do not look and act exactly as we do." He moved on to speak with someone else, but Ilahna caught Lucinda's arm.

"There's more to it, isn't there?" she asked the wisp-like woman. Lucinda smiled.

"Of course. But I am needed. Ask--" she pondered for a moment, looking over the crowd. "That one. She will tell you." Lucinda hurried off to follow Aurelius, and Ilahna frowned for a moment before approaching the fur-cloaked woman she'd indicated.

"Hello," Ilahna said carefully, smiling at the deeply suntanned woman, who was shaking out a blanket. The newcomer looked up.

"Hello. Can I help you?"

"I watched your group arrive. I'm glad you're here," Ilahna said awkwardly.

The woman smiled despite the urchin's obvious discomfort. "I am too, dear. We did not think there was anyone other than Proclaimers this close to the cities. Rumors said that everyone behind the walls had been burnt at the stake already. When your scouts said you were raising an army to take back the walls and reopen trade, we were happy to pledge ourselves to the new king. We grow tired of hiding. Living in fear."

Ilahna fidgeted again. "I saw that you spoke to His Majesty. He seems to be talking to all of the newcomers that come here."

The woman nodded and refolded her blanket. "Of course. It is good for a leader to know what his followers are capable of. He is learning of our gifts and then placing us where we can do the most good." She put the blanket down and pulled a tin pot from her sack, cleaning it with the hem of her dress. "He's a strong strategist, though I feel that the small girl who travels with him is most of the power behind the plan. She seems to know who will work well together and who will not. She might understand many of the people's gifts better than they do."

Ilahna pressed a little more, surprised at the woman's open honesty. "Gifts?"

The woman looked at Ilahna like she'd asked her to describe a rock. "Well...yes. We all have gifts. Is it not the same here? Do the walls block the magic?"

Ilahna shook her head. "I don't know. I think that a lot of people might have magic, but everyone is afraid to say so. Lots of people have been burnt for being witches. I've... I've never heard it talked about so openly."

The woman sniffed and put the pot on top of the blanket. Then, she sat on the ground with her legs folded beneath her. "That's a sad existence. Maybe the rumors about the cities weren't so far from true, after all."

"But you all have magic? Really?" Ilahna must have sounded eager, because the woman smiled.

"Sit next to me, dear." They sat together, watching the others unpack and Aurelius moving from person to person, asking questions and giving orders. After a while, the woman spoke again.

"Some of our gifts are stronger than others. Some are very subtle or take longer to manifest completely. But everyone has something." She motioned to two men across the way. "Arati there, for example, can tell us that it's going to rain three days before the clouds gather. And his brother can ease someone's pain or stop a baby from crying even when no one else can figure out what's wrong. He's very handy as our doctor, though he's never been taught anything and it's almost impossible for him to teach someone else. Magic is often that way; gifts skipping generations or cropping up in the most unexpected places." She smiled, her eyes twinkling. "So, we have to keep the oral traditions going, too, so the next generations can continue if they're not blessed the same way we are."

Ilahna watched the two men across the way as the woman told her more about the abilities she'd seen and the lives her people had lived, far to the east. Ilahna could almost picture every person she described, could almost watch them discover and hone their abilities, learning from others and from themselves. This tribe was so open about their magics. So carefree. And, whether small or large, no one tried to hide what they could do. No one was ashamed or afraid of their neighbors. They lived in a world where open communication had taught people to embrace themselves and each other. And then, when something wonderful manifested itself, they celebrated the ability rather than fearing or hiding it.

Ilahna wondered how different Jacir's life would have been in a world like that. And how many in Clearwall had lived and died without ever knowing it was possible.

They sat on the forest floor for a long time, and the woman's words were so enthralling, so vivid, that Ilahna was still being transported far away from the little camp when she realized that the other woman had stopped speaking. Ilahna coughed awkwardly at the silence. "What about you?" she finally asked.

The woman smiled. "I am Risala. I tell stories. I carry our history within me and will pass it onto the next generation.

Hopefully, they will have one as capable of remembering every word, lest some of it will be lost. And without history anchoring us, we really don't have anything at all, do we? We are just boats adrift at sea."

Ilahna nodded slowly, though she had no idea what a sea was. "What if we learned to use the symbols again? The ones people used to draw? Wouldn't that be easier than hoping someone else can carry on the oral tradition as you can?"

Risala closed her eyes and nodded to herself. "There was one in our tribe when I was a little girl. He knew some of the symbols. Could draw a few of the words in the sand. 'Hello' was his favorite." She smiled. "I have not forgotten what he taught me, and I will teach the symbols to my protégé when the time comes. Perhaps the next generation will build on the scraps of what the past left behind."

Ilahna closed her eyes and leaned backwards next to Risala the storyteller, feeling the sun on her face. "Tell me what you think it will be like. If we succeed, I mean. If we find a way to change everything."

She heard Risala chuckle next to her. "I tell of the past, child. Not the future. There are soothsayers who can tell you what you want to know."

"They'll tell me what they see in the Weave. And that's always changing. I want to hear what you think." Risala thought for a long moment.

"It may not have truth to it, dear."

"No. But it will have hope. And that's important, too."

Risala didn't say anything, but Ilahna could almost feel her smile. Then, the two sat together under the warmth of the sun, painting stories of what they hoped to build from the ashes of Clearwall.

38

Ilahna found herself drawn to the people who made it to their camp in the forest. She could feel the uncertainty in some of them. Old grudges and distrust held across generations. And she felt a sense of purpose as she helped people reach deep within themselves to put aside the negative things that caused needless dissention. Above all, Ilahna wanted to help spread a cohesion. A sense of unity. That abstract concept she'd been craving for a lifetime.

So, she moved between the groups, helping to share the people's stories and kindle their desires to grow and learn for the greater good of the resistance. As the groups of people drew closer, connected by invisible strands of silk made from a desire to be more than they were, the revolutionists swapped stories and skills. They learned new crafts and found others that could help them or that they could help. They traded experiences and learned from each other. And, slowly, glimpses of the coming world they would make together began to take shape.

It did not take long before there were clusters of healers, sharing stories and bits of knowledge they had gleaned without any book or trainer. Tailors who discussed how to layer for different seasons and with different materials when sheep were scarce. Cooks who shared recipes with ingredients Ilahna had never heard of, and people who seemed able to find such ingredients in even the most difficult terrain. Smiths who swapped techniques for stronger blades or faster arrows.

More than anyone else, Ilahna liked to watch the people who could see the Tapestry. Prophets and seers gathered in the glade, sharing the burden of the future and the path, offering new and seldom-tread routes across the Weave. So often they talked about tricks that kept someone from getting lost in the strands. And, all the while, the group watched the Tapestry together, trying to decipher the way that would lead them forward.

It was eerie to watch a dozen people stare, unblinking and with unfocused eyes, at nothing. Ilahna never knew what, exactly, they searched for, but her heart would often clamp fearfully when the group would jerk simultaneously from their reverie, shaking and pale. The first time it had happened, Ilahna had run to Jacir, begging to know if he was okay.

"I'm fine, Ilahna. We just… went down a path that did not end well. It's very easy to see darkness when you look at the future. Sometimes it gets so dark so quickly that we can't see past it. So we have to come back and try again." He frowned, looking over the others around them. He picked out a young man who seemed less affected than the others. "Go tell Aurelius what we saw. He has the gift of strategy. He might have some insight on what we can do. Don't tell anyone else. It will just panic them." The man nodded and trotted into the trees.

Ilahna stared at her brother in awe. He had grown so much in such a short amount of time. But as a woman next to her suddenly vomited, still crying at whatever they'd seen across the Weave, Ilahna was once more grateful she had never opened the door to peek at what was beyond its foreboding portal.

"How can we keep looking at what's to come?" the woman screamed. "How do we look at what's coming when there's no way to change it?" She fell to the ground, still sobbing. Jacir looked at her sadly.

"Marisal, take her back to the camp. See if someone… see if someone can help her forget." Another seer nodded and guided the sobbing woman away. Jacir watched them go before he returned to his spot at the edge of the stream. "I'm going to look for other paths on the Weave," he called to the others that were still gathered there, shaky and uncertain. "The rest of you, return to camp. Gather your strength. Do not look upon the strands for now." Then his eyes unfocused and he dove back into the Tapestry.

And so it went. Jacir found an alternative path across the future that day and many others that came afterward. No matter what the other seers saw in the Weave, completely sure that nothing else could be done and that their revolution was doomed, Jacir was always willing to look just one more time. Search for one more path.

Ilahna lost track of how many times he stayed there by the stream long after the others had given up for the day, sobbing at what they had seen in the threads, curling in their bedrolls and praying to Gods that might or might not hear. But Jacir never seemed to give up, and eventually his face would light up and he would approach Aurelius with a plan the others had not seen. Had not even looked for. Had not believed would be possible.

One day even Aurelius could not hide his amusement at Jacir's newest revelation after nearly two days of staring at the Tapestry alone.

"Genius!" The bastard king roared. "This will stop the Battle at the Fell and a dozen others before the Proclaimers even think to start them!" Still boisterous at Jacir's unexpected success, Aurelius called over a scout and began giving enthusiastic instructions. Jacir jogged over to where Ilahna and Eitan were sitting. Eitan handed him a bowl of stew.

"What did you do?" Ilahna asked her brother, unable to contain her curiosity.

"There's someone in the mines who will be sympathetic to our cause once we reach him. He's going to tamper with the ore. New swords and repairs that the Proclaimers make won't hold correctly."

Eitan whistled low. "That's clever, Jacir. But it won' take them long to figure out the ore is bad."

"Yeah. But when they begin to suspect the iron, we'll start sending silk strand moss to tamper the coal. It will burn too hot and fast, and their iron will be brittle or soft. They'll overcome it eventually, in any of a hundred ways. But the fight… the Battle at Three Forks, where almost everyone died on all the other threads, and the Battle of the Fell, where Aurelius…" He trailed off, shaking his head, his face suddenly pale. Ilahna put a hand on his shoulder and Jacir smiled. "It doesn't matter because those fights won't happen now. We found a way past it."

Ilahna smiled, but her heart clenched at how worn he looked. "*You* found a way past it, Jacir. Just you."

Ilahna had always been proud of her brother, but a new level of amazement surged through her now. With one whispered suggestion, Jacir had just saved their entire revolution—and no one outside their little circle would ever know. But that didn't bother Jacir at all, because somewhere her little brother had learned to care more about the people than the praise.

Ilahna couldn't see the Weave. She didn't want to see the Weave. But in that moment, she thought the future had never looked brighter.

39

Kaiya woke to a familiar pull that filled her with both a longing and a deep hatred. Like a ghost's fingertips across her temples, she could feel the ancient, crumbling door of the Goddess' Hall open.

"No. Not Illindria's Hall," she mumbled to herself. "Just the Tapestry's."

The thought of someone disturbing the ancient chambers unsettled her. While many people could still see the Tapestry—despite generations of totalitarian regimes trying to track down anyone who posed such a risk—Kai had not thought anyone else was still capable of opening that crumbling door. No one else should have been able to walk within those cursed halls. Even she had locked herself out of them decades before. But, despite her best efforts, some part of her still dwelt there, staring at the Tapestry she could never truly escape. And that part of her was not alone.

Kai's entire body shook as she strained to keep from following the stranger into the Tapestry's great abyss. But she could not. As much as she loathed it and all it had given and taken away, the Tapestry was her ward. She could not stand idly by while a stranger physically plucked at the threads, no matter how much she desired to. As long as another Weaver—a true Weaver that had survived the rite—roamed Imeriel, she was not free.

But why now?

Kaiya didn't know. She didn't want to know. She didn't want to be pulled back to that hallway she thought she had permanently sealed. She could not look at the Tapestry again. Never again.

But she felt the doors open wider. She felt a breeze ripple the Eternal Weave as it wove itself around the limitless halls. She heard feet that were not hers step across the nonexistent stones. Everything she had worked to do would be undone. The Tapestry and its poisoned spawn could not be released upon the world again. She would not allow it.

Kaiya forced her body to stop shaking. She might not be strong enough to gaze at the Tapestry of her own volition, anymore. She might not be willing to face those halls. But even the brain-dead Croeli in her ancient war had been able to push themselves into the streams and cross to a different shore without truly stepping on the brittle stones within those chambers. She could follow the wake of the intruder who dared to cross her pool. She was still strong enough for that. She had to be.

With unsteady steps, Kaiya rose and belted on her fantoii. Acid pooled in her throat and the pit of her stomach, but she forced her body to the place where a sliver of her mind always remained, following the receding footsteps of her unknown foe past the doors that led to oblivion. She did not know where she would land, but as long as it was not before the Tapestry, she did not care.

She had done this before, long ago. It was once so easy. It almost surprised her that she'd forgotten.

"*Blinking*," she mumbled, unaware of her own voice. "We used to call this *blinking*."

40

As Aurelius continued to send out his scouts to the distant pockets of potential allies, the revolution in the woods grew. Most of the diplomatic missions towards the far-off reaches of the continent were successful, and bands of people who had tried to escape the Proclaimers and their ruthless judgements made their way to the forest and its hidden resistance.

As Ilahna met more of these outcasts and "undesirables," she realized how deep the Proclaimers' tendrils had crawled across the land, burning everything in its path like silk strand moss. Dozens of towns and cities had been occupied over the years until every settlement within easy travel of Clearwall had fallen under Proclamatic rule.

"How? I see how they took over Clearwall. But how could they take over so many others?" Ilahna asked Risala over dinner one evening, her voice nearly drowned out by the song the other revolutionists belted out around them.

"It started slowly," Risala replied. "A single Proclaimer bringing positive news from the capitol. Speaking his 'truths.' Placing enough hidden followers in the crowd to boost his words and drown out the dissenters. Praising the ways of the Old Gods and passing out trinkets to those who stayed long enough to hear his words." The storyteller looked sad as she moved a potato around her bowl. "The speeches and so-called 'Children of Truth' were easy enough to ignore in the beginning. But those that ignored the silliness of it were passive and did not stop or stand up to those who did begin to believe. No one silenced the fanatics who eventually began shouting for a resurgence of the old ways. By the time those who didn't think the Proclaimers could ever come to power realized that it was actually possible, it was too late. They were surrounded by the heretics and fanatics, separated from the others who were sane. And when they yelled from their pockets of rationality, trying to stop the pyres with words alone, it was all too easy for those in power to cut out their tongues and throw them into the flames.

"It took time, of course. But the Proclaimers are careful. They kept those who disagreed with them separated and scared. And eventually it got to the point that if you tried to run, they were already there, blocking your escape."

Ilahna shuddered and was about to respond when a commotion to one side of the camp caused her and the singing soldiers to stop. Shrill, piercing whistles of alarm sounded from deeper within the forest.

"She's already through the trees!" someone yelled in the distance.

Everyone was on their feet immediately, reaching for swords and bows. Noncombatants were herded towards the safety of the tents. Ilahna and a few others took to the trees for a better vantage point.

No one expected it when a hunched, old woman wandered into their camp. Ilahna used branches to get closer, bow in hand, though even she wasn't sure if the weapon would help her. She'd gone hunting with a few of the other revolutionists several weeks before and had discovered she was abysmal with the bow. But it was better than nothing, and while the woman did not seem dangerous, several of the seers, specifically, seemed wary about her presence. Ilahna climbed another branch higher, maneuvering behind Aurelius and Lucinda.

"I cannot read her." Lucinda whispered, her voice barely reaching Ilahna's ear. "It's like she's not even there." The statement made Ilahna feel cold.

"Who are you?" Aurelius called out, his voice booming in a manner he had not used in the camp before. "Tell me your name." The command sounded like a gong, and even Ilahna felt compelled to answer it. A few people in the crowd did, yelling out their names before slamming their hands over their mouths with embarrassed glances. The old woman, however, did not respond, and only took another step forward until she was barely more than an arm's length away from Aurelius' table. She tossed a single twisted vine onto it, its broad, flat leaves stark against the wood.

Several of the seers backed up a pace, as though it were a snake ready to strike.

The old woman did not speak very loudly, but her voice had a power behind it, drawing everyone closer to her every word. "I do not know which of you called to me across the Weave, begging for a secret weapon. For knowledge. But I was compelled, and thus I come. You ask for something to stand against First Proclaimer Elise? This is it."

Aurelius reached out to pick up the plant, but Lucinda pulled back his hand urgently. He glanced at her and frowned at the fevered shaking of her head before laying both of his palms on the table, shoulders tense. He stared at the old woman across from him. "What is it?"

"It is the last sprig of tonicloran. It is the most powerful and most dangerous plant in the world, and might very well be the weapon you've been praying for. There is enough left for one tincture. Be careful of whom you decide is worthy of it. They will see more than they can believe, and the walls of the world will fall before them. They will learn to bend the world and will of the earth and its inhabitants like willows. But if given to the wrong person, it will be wasted on the world's most painful death. And none other will be allowed to try and follow." The old woman bowed. "I give it to you, oh Bastard King of Clearwall. Now release me."

Something about the woman's words and manner made Ilahna's skin crawl, and she remembered what the Faoii had said about Jacir's summons in his sleep. She looked at him, and the surprise on his pale face was obvious.

"I didn't mean to," he whispered.

Ilahna was about to reply, but a sudden, piercing scream cut through the trees like icy arrows, pulling their attention back to the clearing.

"You cannot!" The cry was penetrating, filled with more power than even the old woman's voice had been. Ilahna nearly fell from her perch as she tried to see where it came from, bow at the ready. The gloom was nearly absolute, and at first she could not make out the figure in the darkness. But then she saw the eyes, colored a beautiful jade green, and knew who had come. The Betrayer stepped into the firelight, drawing her fantoii with one hand.

"I am Faoii-Kaiya, last of the Monastery of the Eternal Blade. The Tapestry is my ward, and the tonicloran my bane. I swore on the braid of my wife that I would not allow it to poison this land again. I destroyed all of it. I searched the Tapestry for its existence and burned every stalk that remained. The world was free of it. So, where did you get it, unnamed Weaver?"

The old woman released a wry laugh as she turned back to Kaiya. Her back straightened a tiny bit in the presence of the Faoii. "The Tapestry's threads are indeed cruel that I should find you now, Faoii-Kaiya of the Eternal Blade. In another life, I swore myself to be your end. But now we meet at last, when I have been called to strike down a foe worse even than you by someone stronger than even you were in your prime. Such cruel threads, indeed." The old woman's eyes narrowed as she took a step towards Kaiya, her shoulders shaking. "How dare you return now, after all of these years? The ascended told me that someday you would return to wreck the world anew, but that was in a different lifetime. Before the Proclaimers came. The world has forgotten you. Was better with you forgotten. When all we had left was our rage to sustain us. And yet here you stand, trying to once again stop others from improving the world. Trying once again to place yourself above those that could crush you with a thought."

The new woman jerked her sword from its sheath, nearly screaming at Kaiya. "How dare you reappear now! How dare you come when the Proclaimers may at last be stopped! To cheat Imeriel out of her future yet again! Tell me, *Betrayer*, was it the tonicloran that drew you from your hiding to follow me through the Tapestry's halls?"

Kaiya did not lower her blade. "I ask you again. Where did you get the tonicloran? Who are you that would try to reintroduce that terror to this world?"

The old woman's eyes flashed with an ancient pride. "I am Faoii-Calari, last of the Monastery of the Horned Helm. Once I swore to be your destroyer, Betrayer. Now I am called by someone greater than you to be something more than what I was. I bring the secret that will topple First Proclaimer Elise."

"Not with that. If you bring tonicloran back into the world, there will be no stopping it." Kaiya took several careful steps towards Calari. "You know the prices that one must pay for that plant. No victory is worth that cost."

The old woman's smile was malicious as she mirrored Kaiya's steps in the opposite direction. "On the contrary, Betrayer. This victory is more than I could have ever hoped for. Elise's downfall will be a blessing, but yours will be on par with miracles." She straightened again, and Ilahna realized that she was not hunched at all, though her long, white hair did seem to be authentic. "Take the tonicloran if you want it, Your Majesty. It truly will be Elise's end. But leave the Betrayer to us."

"Us?" Ilahna dropped from the tree, abandoning the bow and drawing her fantoii instead. She moved to stand next to Kai, but Eitan stopped her with a firm hand on her shoulder.

"This isn't our fight, Ilahna. Let the two witches kill each other and be done with it." But as more shadowy men and women began to step from the shadows of the trees, Jacir jumped down next to them.

"There's too many of them! Lana! We can't let them kill Kai! We need her!"

Ilahna shrugged off Eitan's hand and fell into stance, but the shadowy invaders were already swarming towards Kaiya with an eerie silence.

That silence was quickly broken as Kaiya raised her fantoii with a shrill warcry, and Ilahna was nearly staggered by the sword's accompanying song. But it also filled her with strength to face their enemies in battle without fear. She raised her own fantoii in response, momentarily disappointed that hers did not scream with a similar fervor. But she still could. She released a barbaric yell and rushed at the nearest raider.

Ilahna had never actually fought a trained foe before. Until now, her victories outside the practice ring had always been balanced on the element of surprise. So, as the invading woman turned towards her, easily parrying Ilahna's imperfect swing, Ilahna was unsure of what to do. She staggered, barely bringing her blade back up in time to block a sweeping strike. She hopped back against another. And another. Steadily being pushed back even as she heard Jacir yell to Aurelius. Aurelius' resounding boom of attack bolstered Ilahna as she barely evaded yet another twirling swing.

You have to get on the offensive. You have to do something. Ilahna's terrified mind tried to scream at her, but she could see no openings. No hope. She backed up another step even as other warriors swarmed around her, moving to drive off the shadowy attackers at Aurelius' command.

Then, suddenly, the ground was no longer beneath her feet. Ilahna felt herself falling backwards even before she could really acknowledge what was happening.

This is it. This is how you die.

The warrior in front of her saw it, too, and her eyes lit up at the surety of her imminent victory.

The glint died quickly, though, as Eitan's hammer caved in the side of the stranger's head. The woman's brain splattered against the trees, and then there was only Eitan's face in front of Ilahna as she gasped for breath.

"Ilahna? Are you okay? Talk to me!" Ilahna gulped and nodded. Eitan's face flooded with relief. "Stay down, Ilahna," he said firmly. "Let the other warriors deal with this."

From across the passage of time, Ilahna remembered the conversation she had had with Kai in the sewers.

"Who else is going to protect him should you fall?"

"Shut up! I'm not going to fall!"

"You will if you don't pick that blade up again."

Ilahna shook her head and stood back up. She knew she could do this. She had to. Determinedly, she bent down and picked up her fantoii again.

"No. We're part of this, Eitan. We need to act like it." A new thought occurred to her, and she looked him in the eye. "Eitan. I need you to sing."

"What?" He looked at her like she'd sprouted feathers, and Ilahna eyed another advancing foe over his shoulder.

"We don't have time, Eitan! Sing! We all have something! Don't fear it. Don't question it. Be who you're supposed to be and help us! Sing!" She leapt around his baffled frame and raised her blade to block the sword aimed at the back of Eitan's head. The attacking warrior gave a surprised yelp as Ilahna used the surprise to push her advantage. She swung again, fighting down the uncertainty and fear that had almost been the end of her a moment before. Around her, Aurelius' revolutionists were pressing forward, too, making their way to the mob of clashing steel at the center of the fray.

Kaiya was there, holding off a handful of fighters all on her own, sliding between blades and shifting into shadows with an eerie grace. The singing of her blade was inspiring. But Ilahna knew they needed more. "Eitan!" she screeched. "Stop standing there! Sing, damn it!"

Eitan finally seemed to shake off his uncertainty and raised his voice to sound over the clamor. The song that lifted from beneath his lips was old, from a place deep beneath the forest at their feet. It didn't say anything of Gods or prayers or the things that the Proclaimers demanded should be put into songs. Instead, it was a song of strength and courage as a group of warriors fought side by side to protect each other. It was something they'd all sung more than once around the evening meal, and as Ilahna listened, suddenly the things she'd learned in the sewers beneath Kaiya's watchful eye began to make sense. Her stance shifted, and it was easier to calculate her movements before she made them. All the things the Faoii had tried to impart to her finally clicked into place. She nearly laughed at the power of it.

The man in front of her noticed the difference, too, and began to move more guardedly. But between the power of Eitan's song and the strength that bubbled up from inside Ilahna's soul, the invader had little chance. Ilahna drove him backward, again and again, drawing thin lines of blood with each flurry of her blade. The warrior parried most of her strikes, but there was panic there. Uncertainty. And, finally, almost before it actually happened, Ilahna saw him make a mistake. A swing too wide. An unbalanced gait.

Ilahna took the opportunity and ducked under the wide swing, sinking her blade into the other warrior's stomach. Her opponent gasped softly as the light faded from his eyes. Ilahna let him fall and pressed forward again, towards Kaiya.

Eitan's song was evidently inspiring the other revolutionaries too, and their steady lines of advance pushed back the invaders with sure, deliberate steps. Ilahna joined the advancing line, raising her sword to match those beside her, feeling the power that came from being part of something bigger than herself. There was a certain magic of its own in being part of a solid line of steel and determination. Something powerful in the way that every soldier stepped in unison.

Ilahna reveled in it, and the people they marched against apparently felt the strength and fury there, as many broke from their stances and tried to retreat into the trees. But they were too late, and with a ferocious, unified yell the revolutionists were on them, cutting the invaders down as they fled, or facing them with grim determination in their final moments of desperate fighting.

Kaiya had cut down most of her own opponents, her long braid swinging as she spun and ducked beneath their blows. But the Faoii was tiring, and Ilahna could see blood seeping across her leather breastplate and through her cloak. Ilahna forced herself to break away from the line and darted to Kai, ducking beneath an attacking woman's swing and lifting her fantoii to catch her in the soft tissue between the hip and ribcage. She forced it higher, underneath the ribs, and the woman toppled.

On instinct, Ilahna took up a stance she had never actually learned, but it felt so natural that she did not question it. She crouched, back to back with Kai, her feet mirroring the taller Faoii's with an instinctual grace.

Something in Kaiya's stance changed, too, as she stiffened in surprise. But if she had been a fluid shadow of grace and danger before, she was on the level of the Gods now. And, as Ilahna mirrored her movements, hardly in control of her own body, she could hardly believe her own dexterity and poise as their surrounding attackers fell beneath their twirling blades.

Soon, no invaders were left standing, and Ilahna turned towards Kaiya again. There was the faintest hint of a smile on the Faoii's lips. "I have not had a shieldsister for a long time. I had forgotten what it was like. You did well, girl." Ilahna was taken aback by the unexpected compliment and was trying to decide how to respond when Kaiya suddenly released a deep groan and staggered, hitting one knee as she pressed a hand into her side. Blood seeped between her fingers.

"Healer! We need a healer!" Ilahna screamed as she tore off her cloak and pressed it into the wound. Kaiya hissed, her dark skin turning grey. “Hold on, Faoii,” Ilahna pleaded. “I didn’t save you just to watch you die.” The Faoii chuckled a bit.

“My, how the tides change,” she gasped out before listing bonelessly into Ilahna’s arms.

41

There were several people in the camp gifted with healing magics, and a handful more who had learned their craft through more mundane schooling. Together, they were able to save most of the resistance fighters.

Most, but not all.

Heartbroken wails perforated the air that evening as Ilahna sat outside the tent where a healer was attending to Kaiya. On the other side of the clearing, Ilahna could see Risala standing over a young man's body, solemnly relaying his story to a small group that had gathered. With a heavy heart Ilahna recognized the body as that of Arati, the brother who could sense the rain. His sibling was not at the small ceremony, evidently trying to heal others in the camp. Ilahna hugged her legs to her chest and tried not to think about how many other funerals were being held by family and loved ones throughout the forest.

Tanner and a medic stepped out of the tent behind her, and Aurelius approached with long, sure steps. "What's her status?" he rumbled.

"She'll live, Your Majesty. Most of the injured will. Though we lost eleven warriors to the fray."

"We shouldn't have lost any!" one of Aurelius' guards roared. "You heard the old woman. They weren't here for us. They weren't a danger to anyone until that witch provoked them!"

"Quiet, Tiviren," Aurelius said, almost kindly. "Anyone that is able to get that close to us without anyone knowing is a danger. We will have better fortifications going forward. Tanner, go find any information you can on the first witch." Tiviren pressed his lips together and nodded. Tanner offered his bright smile.

"There is some good to this, Tivi. The soldiers know they can fight now. And our units worked well in cohesion. Better than I think we even expected."

Tiviren didn't say anything as Tanner walked away, and Aurelius ordered two guards to stand in front of the tent Kaiya had been deposited into. Tiviren looked less than happy about the order, but did as he was told, taking his position at the front of the tent.

"I don't think that's necessary." Jacir said softly as the guards took their post where he and Ilahna had been sitting. Aurelius sat and ran a weary hand over his face.

"Maybe not. But a lot of the soldiers and I will feel more comfortable with them there." He rested his arms on his knees and looked at Jacir. "You say we need her, and I won't question what you see in the Weave. But we do not know her. She brought a lot of pain here, to the one place we thought we were safe. So, we cannot trust her until we hear what she has to say. Until then, the guards stay." Jacir frowned but nodded.

"I don't think a hundred guards could hold her. Chains probably couldn't do it, either," Ilahna declared. Aurelius looked towards her, and she lowered her tone. "I don't think that treating her like a prisoner will make her want to talk to us, Your Majesty. But if you approve, I can sit with her until she wakes up. I think she hates me less than she used to."

Aurelius raised an eyebrow at Ilahna but didn't question her. "I saw the way you two fought together. I have seen veterans who don't move with their shieldmate that seamlessly. You may sit with her. But inform me the minute she wakes. There are questions we need answered."

Ilahna nodded and rose, but she stopped when she saw Tanner running across the camp. "Your Majesty!" he called, bowing as he approached. "I've spoken to the soldiers, sir. The old woman. The first one to enter the camp. We cannot find her among the dead. Several people remember seeing her wounded, but no one saw her leave."

Aurelius' shoulders stiffened, and his lips pulled into a thin line. "What of the plant she brought?"

"It is still there on the table."

"No one touch it. We'll wait until this Faoii wakes and question her about all of it." Tanner nodded and retreated again.

"You'd better hope your friend there has some answers, Miss Harkins" Aurelius said coldly. "If that woman escaped and knows our location then we're undone. The Betrayer might have ended our revolution before it could begin." Before Ilahna could reply, he stood and stormed off towards the other side of camp.

Ilahna chewed her lip. "Jacir," she asked, "can you find the woman that came to camp with the plant? Faoii-Calari?"

Jacir closed his eyes for a long moment, frowning in concentration. "I… I don't see her. And I can't find her in any of the threads out of the forest."

"How is that possible?"

"I don't know. But… I don't see Kai coming here on the threads, either. I see the other people that attacked us, now that I look. They walked here through the woods like normal soldiers. But Calari and Kaiya. They're just… there." He shook his head, frowning, then opened his eyes. "I don't know what that means. Maybe there's something wrong with me. Should I ask the other seers?" Ilahna shook her head.

"I don't think there's anything in the world they can see that you can't. Something is different about this. We'll have to wait until Kaiya wakes up to find out what."

Jacir thought for a moment. "You're the only person in existence who still calls her Kaiya instead of the Betrayer. I haven't looked across her entire story, but I know it's dark. She's done some truly terrible things. But… I still trust her. I can't explain why, but I do. And I don't think I trust that plant the other Faoii brought."

"The…tonicloran, right? You and Kaiya talked about that once before. On the rooftops when we went to save Eitan."

Jacir scrunched his eyes shut, concentrating. "Did we?"

"She didn't name it. Only said that there was once a plant that helped Weavers. You knew what it was." She put a hand on his shoulder. "Jacir, I know it might be tempting, depending on what comes next. But… I don't trust that plant, either. There must have been a reason Kai tried to destroy it, and maybe it should be left destroyed. Whatever comes, promise me you'll remember that."

Jacir's shoulder trembled under her hand. "I know, Lana. I… I can feel it from here." Some of the light faded from his eyes, and his voice became a little more distant. "The entire Weave and every world attached to it is wrapped up in those broad leaves. The Old Gods would kill for the power it promises. We mere mortals would do far worse. It offers many gifts… and many curses." Ilahna thought about the Faoii's extended lifespan and wondered which description Kaiya would use. She shuddered.

"Jacir. Promise me. Promise me you won't use the tonicloran no matter what it seems to offer."

"I promise. I… I don't want to know what's in that vine. I can hear dark voices beneath the tendrils." He trembled a bit more, and Ilahna drew her brother into a tight hug. Until now, she had been afraid to peer at a door that he had passed through without hesitation. She could not imagine what lurked beyond a door her brother would not even approach.

42

Kaiya dreamt.

No. Not dreamt.

Kaiya *remembered.*

She stood, watching the Great Tapestry, wringing a braid in her hands. She and Lyn had both cut their braids when they'd married, though both had grown long again over the years. But it was still a symbol. A physical sign that they would protect each other from here on, rather than dedicating themselves to the Faoii Order.

Or, that was what the exchange of braids was supposed to symbolize. The ending she thought they'd earned.

I promised her.

But the Tapestry had other ideas. And no matter where Kaiya looked, the lump was always there. It grew, beneath Lyn's scalp. Beneath the skull. No one saw it. No one knew. Lyn suspected. She knew something was wrong. But she never spoke.

It couldn't be. After everything they had done. All they had fought for. All they'd protected. They'd earned more than this. They were supposed to have more than this!

It wasn't fair!

There had to be something she could do.

Again and again Kaiya searched. Every route. Every outcome. For months she followed the threads in every direction. But there was no salvation. No easy end. A life of war and strength—a world that could not stop Lyn even with its strongest warriors—and the silky-haired Faoii would be brought low by something none of them could see. There would be no last battlecry. No real chance of fighting against this enemy. The fantoii above the fireplace was useless here.

It wasn't fair.

Lyn would fight. Even without looking at the Tapestry, Kaiya knew Lyn would fight. But she looked to the Weave, regardless, seeking a victory. Any hope at all.

In all the routes wherein she knew the stakes, Lyn fought back. Sometimes she left to save Kaiya from the pain, dying a slow and agonizing death far from the warmth of their hearth. In the few futures where Kaiya could convince her to stay, she died in their bed after months of agony, even though she tried to keep a strong smile until the last. There was no ending that did not end in death, and Kaiya broke again and again each time she watched her love face that oblivion.

Eventually Kaiya could not see through the tears or feel anything beyond the utter crushing of her heart, and she collapsed, weeping, before the Tapestry's eternal threads.

Who could tell how much time had passed before she stood again? Minutes? Days? But, at last, Kaiya rose and dried her eyes. There was one ending that offered Lyn a painless death. One ending where she could experience her last moments in the arms of someone who loved her. Where she could always remember that her last fight had been with a fantoii in hand and a battlecry on her lips.

"Tendaji. Asanali. Eili. If you wait somewhere beyond, hug her for me. Tell her that I love her. And, if she'll forgive me for what I am about to do… if she'll forgive me… tell her I will see her at the end."

Kaiya drew in one last shuddering breath, then steeled herself. The Tapestry swirled with a nonexistent breeze in her sudden absence.

43

Ilahna sat near Kaiya's cot. Behind her, the two guards whispered in low tones, glancing backwards at the unconscious woman and her long, white braid. While those gathered here in the forest were more accepting of people with gifts or talents… the words of the Proclaimers still ran deep. The stories and legends of the Faoii had spread much further than Clearwall. And it did seem that the old woman had come under the guise of offering assistance before Kaiya had interfered.

Things didn't look good for Kaiya, and Ilahna was worried.

Hopefully Aurelius would help to smooth things over. He seemed to listen to Jacir, and Jacir had said they needed Kai. The would-be king might not trust Kaiya, exactly, but Ilahna felt relatively sure he would at least spare her, despite everything.

Kaiya stirred on her cot. Ilahna swallowed hard.

She hoped so, anyway.

"She's waking up," Ilahna said to the guards as she lifted a waterskin to Kaiya's lips. The Faoii drank greedily as one of the men went to find Aurelius.

"Faoii—" Ilahna started, but Tiviren poked her hard in the back with the butt of his spear.

"Don't say anything until King Aurelius arrives. To do otherwise will be seen as conspiring." He gave Ilahna a look as pointed as the spear. She nodded, sitting back again.

Ilahna waited silently, and Jacir knelt next to her, his fingers fidgeting in his lap. But she saw him watch the Faoii out of the corner of his eye, and for a moment, she thought that, if she desired to, she could pull at the edge of that door and listen at the keyhole to hear what they were saying to each other across the Weave.

She shuddered and shook the thought away. If Jacir wanted to tell her about this conversation later, she would listen. But it was still not somewhere she wanted to venture. Now or ever.

Kaiya and Jacir both stiffened at the same time. A moment later, the posted guards opened the tent flap to reveal Aurelius marching towards them with a powerful gait. Behind him, Lucinda's footfalls were lighter and quieter, but no less sure. In her pale hands, she carried a simple wooden bowl, though she held it away from her body and with slightly trembling hands. Ilahna could see broad, flat leaves rising slightly above the rim.

"I expect she is well enough to speak?" Aurelius directed the question at Tiviren, but Ilahna bristled at the hostility there.

"Hey! Kaiya helped us! She's on our side!"

Aurelius and Kaiya turned to her in unison, and Ilahna wilted underneath their combined gazes.

"So far, I have only seen evidence that she is on her own side," Aurelius said as he ducked into the tent. Lucinda followed, and Ilahna and Jacir pressed themselves towards the canvas on either side of them as the little space became more crowded.

"You. Faoii. I do not truly care who you are or what you want. We have bigger plans than you. But you've come here and given away our position. And you have knowledge that may lead to even worse outcomes. I cannot allow my people to walk blindly into dangers that you bring or see." Kaiya rose slightly from her bedroll, her shoulders tense.

"'Your' people will walk blindly no matter what I tell you. Even with your fledging of Weavers watching the Tapestry. Even with all the powers you think your forces have combined. They are still but blind children." Ilahna sighed inwardly. It was too much to hope that Kaiya would be anything other than abrasive.

Aurelius stiffened, and the tension between the two of them grew.

"You think so, do you?" Aurelius ground out. "You think that you are so much more powerful than hundreds of men and women that have grown up with magic in their very veins?"

Kaiya shrugged. "It doesn't matter what I think. All that matters is that you think you are clever enough and knowledgeable enough to lead them on the right path. But you are not. And if you use that plant to the effects you're considering, you will doom them all."

She rose enough to point one dark finger at Aurelius' chest. "You think I toppled your petty revolution simply by following an insane witch into the woods? Imagine how it will feel to know that you not only offered *but encouraged* those that follow you to pick up the blade that will slay them all."

Lucinda's hands shook again and she watched the tonicloran like it was a snake posed to strike. Aurelius caught her eye before turning back to Kaiya. He seemed to make a conscious effort to soften his voice.

"Okay, Faoii. I am willing to listen. Tell me of the tonicloran."

Kaiya glared and forced herself to her feet. Ilahna thought she saw a tremble in the Faoii's legs as she stood, but if she did, the older woman hid it quickly.

It only took two steps for Kaiya to cross the small space that separated her from Aurelius and Lucinda. Without breaking eye contact, she reached with one hand and took the stalk from Lucinda's bowl. Aurelius almost made a move to stop her, but a strong, warning glance backed by the full power of the Faoii made him pause.

Ilahna studied Kaiya's face as the Faoii drew the broad-leafed plant from the bowl and looked it over. There were many emotions there. A deep, strong love for the thing, but also a stark and bitter hatred. For a moment, she thought that Kaiya was going to crush the plant in her hand, but Jacir, of all people, stopped her with a gentle touch.

"I will follow whatever you decide, Faoii-Kaiya. But if you do destroy the tonicloran, will you at least tell us why?" he whispered.

Kaiya turned to Jacir slowly, the ghosts of her eyes nearly glowing in the darkened tent.

"What did you just say?"

"Tell us why." Jacir's voice was a little stronger than the timid cadence he had always had before joining the resistance, but there was something new there, too. The tiniest hint of the power that colored Kaiya's words so often.

"No. Before that. You would follow me?"

Jacir shrugged. "Of course."

A thin, dark laugh slipped from between Kaiya's lips. "No. Never again. I am not one to be followed. That is your role, now, young Faoli. And you will do it with the gifts you have already been granted. You are more than strong enough without this poison that will destroy your mind and heart over centuries." With the hand that did not hold the tonicloran she lifted Jacir's chin and peered into his eyes. "You will find any of a thousand destinies, Faoli-Jacir. Some good, some great, some very dark. All worthy. But you will never reach them by following me. Or this."

Kaiya slipped the tonicloran into her belt pouch as though it were a mint leaf. Lucinda let out a small sound of shock, and Kaiya laughed her mirthless laugh again. "What? There is nothing more the tonicloran can offer me. Not even death. That is why it's safest with me."

Aurelius set a hand on his hilt and tried to rise to his full height, though he was hampered by the tent. But the glare in his eyes was unmistakable. "It is not your place to take that with you, Faoii. No matter your own experiences or lies, it is painfully obvious that the plant has great power. Our own seers will decide if it is too dangerous to keep. And, if so, we will be the ones to destroy it. But not you."

Kaiya squared her shoulders as well, and she was nearly as tall as Aurelius. "You don't know what you're getting into, Bastard of Clearwall. And I do not answer to you."

Aurelius' eyes darkened and his stance changed. Kaiya didn't drop her gaze, even as he drew his blade from its sheath a few inches. "You can be my ally or my captive. The choice is yours, Witch."

Ilahna stepped forward to protest, but he stopped her with a menacing glare. Kaiya's grey eyes darkened several shades as she eyed the partially drawn blade, and her entire body tensed like a caged panther. The air around the little group bristled with electricity and Ilahna held her breath, afraid of what was coming.

Then, suddenly, Kaiya was simply *gone*. Ilahna blinked once, and there was a series of gasps and shouts from the campsite outside. Aurelius nearly tore off the tent flap as he charged through.

"You do not get to tell me what choices I have," Kaiya said from across the campfire, her voice biting and filled with power. "I am here because *I* choose to be." She spread her arms, and power gathered around the Faoii as she narrowed pale green eyes. In the center of the growing circle, the fire leapt and danced. "I am known as the Betrayer. I have been known as the harbinger and as the destroyer of hope. I have served and toppled Gods. I can be your greatest ally or your greatest bane. And thus, you should know better than to cross me, *Your Majesty*."

All around them, people were picking up bows and swords, inching towards the witch with uncertain steps. Ilahna felt the prickling of electricity that comes just before a fight, felt her heartbeat in her ears. But then Jacir stepped from the tent with a quiet acceptance, and the tension softened a little.

"Your Majesty," he said, his voice gentle. "We need to let her go." Tiviren let out a sound of protest, but Jacir raised his hand for silence. He turned his attention to Kaiya. "Faoii, I want you to remember how many times you've told me and Ilahna that you don't want to lead. You don't want to make the decisions that shape entire worlds, anymore. And that's okay. But if you take the tonicloran with you, that means you're taking all of its responsibility off my shoulders and putting it on your own again. Are you sure that's the thread you want to follow?"

"It's better this way, young Faoli. Do not doubt me."

"I believe you. I will follow your decision if that is what you choose."

"Stop saying that!" Kaiya's eyes flashed, and an unnatural breeze pulled at her long braid as she stared at nothing, her eyes darting back and forth as she watched something no one else could see. It continued for seconds. Then minutes. The silence stretched out for what felt like an eternity.

"What is she doing?" Ilahna whispered to Jacir. His eyes never left Kaiya, but he gave a knowing smile.

"Watching the Tapestry. Trying to see if this really is the best way forward."

"Do you think it is?"

"I think she thinks it is. But I think that she is basing that on her own experiences and not on anything she's actually seen in the Tapestry. Nothing's set in stone, Lana. And nothing is inherently evil or good. Not even the tonicloran."

Suddenly, Kaiya came back to herself and stumbled backwards a step.

"Even after all this time, it is too big. There is too much. Every step, every decision. It can all lead to a million different paths. I will not be the cause of such waves again. Never again." She threw the piece of tonicloran to the ground, her hand shaking.

"Do what you want with it, young Faoli. You may start the ripples that cause monsoons or stop the tides altogether. But never think that I did not try to help you when you were still yourself."

With one last hateful look at the broad, flat leaves, Kaiya turned away and was gone.

Jacir carefully walked up to the little plant and bent to pick it up.

"Don't!" Ilahna cried, grabbing his arm. Jacir smiled at her and patted her hand, much like she had done for him a million times before, then bent over and picked up the stalk by the stem, careful of the broad, flat leaves and their tiny, razor-like edges. He turned it over carefully, holding it up to the light.

Lucinda approached him cautiously, standing next to Ilahna.

"I can still feel the power in it." Jacir whispered. "There is so much in it. I… I don't want it. But I don't want to destroy it, either. I don't want to destroy something so amazing. So… pure. All the things that make people and soil and planets and galaxies is hidden away in these tiny leaves. The whole Tapestry runs through its veins. I don't want to destroy it. But we cannot keep it here."

"Is there a vision to back up your claims?" Aurelius demanded as he stalked towards them, still angry at the disappearance of the Faoii.

"Both. There are a million possibilities tied to this plant. I couldn't describe them all even if we had years to discuss it. Most people cast a tiny ripple in the life pools, even with their strongest swings. This causes entire waves."

"Can it be used to bring Aurelius to the throne?" Lucinda asked quietly.

Jacir's eyes faded a little as he stared into the distance. "Of course. It can create him an entirely new kingdom if you knew which strands to pull. He could pull every remaining nation under his rule. Or spread them all to the winds. It's more powerful now than it was even in the Betrayer's time. Because the magic is already here. It can enhance it all."

When Jacir's eyes didn't refocus and he began rubbing his fingers along the stem with loving strokes, Ilahna grew worried. "Jacir." She shook his arm. "Jacir! Remember. You don't want to keep it!"

Jacir shook his head and appeared to come out of his stupor. He jerked away from Ilahna and the plant fell from his hand. He blinked several times before nodding.

"Ilahna?" Tears crept into the corners of his eyes, and he hugged her tightly. "You're right. It's too strong. It sucks you in too deep too fast. We can't use it. Even if it doesn't kill the person that tries—and the chances of that are very high—it *will* destroy them eventually. Or worse. Kaiya was right. It is more of a curse than a blessing."

Ilahna pet his hair and whispered soothing sounds to him, but as she thought of Kaiya's eyes that switched between crazed and empty, she knew that he was right.

Aurelius paced angrily, looking down at the little vine near his feet. "No! We can't just destroy it. It has too much potential. And, even for all our seers, we don't know what is still to come." Ilahna tried to protest, but he cut her off, his voice filled with power and finality. "For now, we return to our previous plans. We must retake Clearwall. But those Faoii witches have made this location unsafe. We need to find a new place to camp. Regroup. Train. And then we may finally bring the battle to Clearwall herself."

Aurelius stopped pacing, evidently making up his mind.

"We will bring the plant with us. If we are lucky, everything will go according to plan and we will not need it. But I will not destroy a potential weapon when we have so few to begin with."

Lucinda nodded silently and knelt down. She carefully placed the tonicloran back in the bowl and followed Aurelius to his tent on the other side of camp.

Ilahna watched them go and, as she continued stroking her brother's hair, wondered if maybe he'd been wrong this one time and that they should have let Kaiya take the tonicloran with her when they had the chance.

44

Ali and her mother both jumped when the front door suddenly crashed open, ushering in an icy wind. Her father slammed it shut behind him, leaning heavily against the wood. "Hide the trinkets! Quickly!"

"Danther, what is happening?" Ali's mother asked, gathering the Fallen Goddess symbols they'd been weaving and shoving them into a basket.

"The Monastery has been attacked! They're coming this way!" Danther shakily grabbed the basket clutched in his wife's hands and hurled it into the fire.

"Father! What are you doing?"

"You don't understand, Ali! The invaders are wearing that symbol!" He pointed at the fire with a shaking finger. Ali's mother paled and sank unsteadily into a chair.

"The symbol… Oh! What have we done?"

"We haven't done anything, mother! We made the trinkets of our forebearers. There's nothing wrong with that!" But Ali didn't even believe her own words as the sounds of fighting rang over the distant hills.

The trinkets were still visible in the blaze when there was a sudden shout and pounding on their door. Ali's mother timidly moved towards it, but Danther stopped her, shaking his head. But the pounding didn't stop, and the shouting increased.

"Traitors to the Faoii-Croeli Order! We see your trinket! We know you are in there! By the Monastery of the Horned Helm, you are called to answer for your crimes."

All three of them glanced, terrified, towards the window. They had forgotten to remove the symbol there. The original one that their ancestors had so lovingly crafted. The door banged louder.

"Ali! We know you're in there! Open the door or we *will* break it down!" The sound of Calari's demanding voice, backed by an audacity borne of power, turned Ali's heart to stone. As afraid as she was, she never thought she could turn against a friend. She never thought her hate and fear could be that strong.

She was wrong.

As the pounding increased and more armored warriors beat against the door, Danther gathered his courage and moved to barricade it. Just as he moved in front of the bulging wood, however, a sword finally bit through, cleaving into the top of his balding head.

Ali's mother screamed and fell to her knees as blood pooled around Danther's limp body. From the hewn door, Ali could see Calari's enraged face lit by the firelight.

"Mother! Run!" Ali forcefully pulled her mother to her feet, shoving her towards the bedrooms and the door at the back of the house. Her mother responded woodenly, and Ali tried to guide her as best she could.

Someone was already breaking down the back door, too, and Ali forced her mother through the hallway and into the nearest bedroom. It was hers, and Ali grabbed her dagger from the dresser as a Croeli finally broke through and charged around the corner, his sword drawn. Ali stepped in front of her mother and squared her shoulders, widening her feet into a stance she had long since drilled into her very being. If it was to end here, she would die protecting all that she loved from all that she hated.

The man before her was young, and he seemed less sure than she did in his posture. But he swung at her, and Ali ducked under his arm, spinning towards him in a maneuver she'd practiced a thousand times. At the apex of his too-wide swing, she was able to thrust her short dagger into his armpit. It slid in more easily than she'd imagined it would.

The Croeli screamed and dropped his blade, stumbling backwards. Ali stooped to pick the sword up, knowing already that his scream had drawn the others. She would not be able to face all of them, no matter how untrained some of them might be.

But as she lifted the fallen blade in her hands, something thrummed inside of her. The sword was larger than anything she had ever wielded before, but it did not seem any heavier than her own wooden practice sword had been. Instead, she only felt the steel of it spread through her limbs, grounding into the heels of her feet as the others drew into the doorway, their bronze breastplates forming a wall of anger and bloodlust. Calari stood at the forefront.

Ali could not win, but she would not go down without trying. "Drop your swords," she hissed, her voice shaking. "We haven't done anything to you! Leave us alone!" She planted her feet and raised the sword a little higher, forcing steel into her voice. "Leave us alone!"

Ali waited for the Faoii squadron to surge forward. To cut her and her mother down just as they had her father. She waited for the pain in her heart at Calari's stance to become a physical sensation as her old friend's blade bit into her flesh. But it never came. Instead, everything in the house went deathly silent. Then, there was the clatter of a dropped blade from somewhere in the back of the mob.

This stunned everyone, and the group of warriors turned to look at the Faoii that stood, staring in stark terror at Ali's raised blade, slowly backing away towards the door. Ali felt something strengthen in her and pressed harder, raising the sword higher.

"I said *leave!*"

She pumped all the anger and fear and hatred and thoughts of her father's pooling blood and sound of her mother's sobs into the command, and it flowed through her icy chest and stolen blade and out into those that had gathered around her. The air vibrated for a moment as the Faoii in the doorway fought her command. "*Get out!*" With a shrill scream Ali took her sword in both hands and pointed it directly at Calari's face.

Slowly, like puppets under the control of an inexperienced child, the other Faoii and Croeli turned and left, until Ali could only hear her mother's quiet sobs behind her. Calari was the only Faoii that remained, her sword still raised. She shook beneath her bronze breastplate, struggling to resist Ali's command, sweat beading on her forehead.

"Ali," Calari finally ground out, her voice trembling with strain. "How are you doing this?" Her eyes were piercing and filled with hatred, and Ali knew that if she relieved any of the pressure at all, her former friend would kill her in an instant. She forced more power through the sword, and knew in that instant that the power was not coming from it, but from *her.*

She had magic. And if the Faoii had only granted her a sword when she'd asked, they would have had it work for them and not against. They had dug this grave long before. She would lay them in it.

And they would know it before she came.

"Calari. Leave this room. Leave this house. And tell every Faoii or Croeli you ever come across that I will burn down their Order and return the Old Gods to Their thrones. The Faoii reign has ended." Calari held her ground, but her sword dipped further. Ali pushed harder. "*Tell them!*" she screamed.

Calari at last dropped her sword and turned woodenly towards the door. "You will regret this, Ali," she hissed through locked teeth.

"No." Ali declared, her voice drifting across the floor like smoke. "No, Calari. Ali is a child's name. From now on, you will call me Elise."

45

A ripple of fear spread across the camp during the next few days. Most of the seers were frightened, and they whispered about the witches who had found their way into the camp without being seen before disappearing just as mysteriously. The shadowy soldiers that had followed Calari could be seen in the Weave now that their presence and death were woven into the Great Tapestry, but it frightened the seers that the other two remained invisible to those who searched for them, Jacir included.

There were many theories amongst the seers, but nothing definite. They only knew that those who traveled through space and time without footfalls—as Kaiya had demonstrated when she'd teleported outside the tent—were an unknown in the Weave. And unknowns were rarely comforting. Unknowns could cut across the Tapestry's strands without warning, not needing to follow dedicated paths across time. They could not be watched or followed. And that made them dangerous.

"It has to be because of the tonicloran," Aurelius said to Lucinda one day, slamming his fist on the table. Ilahna nearly fell from her perch in a nearby tree at the power in his strike. But she repositioned, swinging her legs idly, pretending to focus on the bracer she was stitching.

Aurelius continued. "This is the power the witches were speaking of! They can do more and control more than those that wield only their natural abilities. We should use the tonicloran to enhance our own forces."

"There is not enough, Your Majesty," Lucinda replied with a soft murmur. "I can plant it, if you'd like. Nurture it until there is enough to start experimenting with its properties. But the few things I can find in the ancient texts say that it must be made into a tincture. And not every person who imbibed it survived."

Ilahna perked up her ears. She had not realized that Lucinda knew how to read.

Clearly, Aurelius knew of Lucinda's hidden talent. He was more distressed about the content of her message. "What do you mean?"

"Evidently, it is very dangerous. Only the most powerful of Faoii were able to survive the tonicloran poison even in the time of the Old Gods. Now that all magic has shifted since the Godfell War… I do not know what is required to do so."

Aurelius paced next to the table. "We do not have enough time to cultivate crops. But we need the same abilities that the intruder and the so-called Betrayer possess if we want to protect ourselves against them. And the Proclaimers."

"You think the Proclaimers can see the Weave, Your Majesty?"

Aurelius rubbed at his chin. "There have been too many coincidences for me to assume they are completely without powers of their own. But they seem suppressed. Either the Proclaimers are seeing hints of what the Weave holds and simply writing it off as intuition and gut feelings, or they're knowing hypocrites. Even if they don't actually have abilities and have burnt out all of the witches of their own order, we cannot deny that they have resources and decades of preparation on their side. At the very best, our acceptance of our people's gifts has allowed us to match them move-for-move, but we'll never be able to pull ahead as it is. We need an advantage. Something attainable in days to match what they have gathered over years."

Lucinda thought it over for a moment. "The tonicloran does seem to offer that advantage," she said thoughtfully. "Though, I do not know that we have anyone strong enough to survive the initiation, even if we do learn how to make the necessary tincture."

Aurelius softened for a moment, and he gave her a warm smile. "You know the people's gifts better than any of us, Lucy. See what you can find. We need someone strong enough to survive what the witches have."

"The presence of the intruder and the Betrayer does at least prove it is survivable. I will research what I can and see if we have anyone that might make it through the initiation. There is only one stalk left. We have only one chance. And if we're wrong, it will mean a truly terrible death for the poor soul that we condemn."

"I know it. And I don't like sending anyone to face something I would not. But we both know I'm not as gifted as you or any of the others."

Lucinda almost laughed. "You could command nearly anyone here to eat the tonicloran with a fork and they would obey you. Town criers will call you Aurelius of the Steel Cords one day."

"Please tell me you haven't actually seen that in the Weave." Lucinda only smiled and Aurelius shook his head. "I am glad I've been offered something with which to lead my people. Our people. But you and I both know that a voice is not the same as what the witches in the days of old commanded before they could become Weavers. I am not the one to risk that poison for the betterment of all. Find out who is. We need someone that can lead us past this darkness and into a light not made of pyres."

Lucinda cast a quick glance at Ilahna's perch, and Ilahna almost toppled from the branch again when she realized she'd been caught. Lucinda made no acknowledgement of her, however, as she lowered her eyes and nodded.

"Of course, Your Majesty. I'll see what I can do."

When Lucinda left Aurelius' table and took her small, gentle steps towards the far edges of the camp, Ilahna swung from her bough and moved to match her pace, though her footfalls were much harsher against the fallen pine needles.

"I heard what you and Aurelius were talking about."

"I am aware." Lucinda barely smiled, and Ilahna almost missed a step.

"You knew?"

"Of course. Even if I couldn't see your path on the Weave, you're not exactly subtle when you swing your legs and shower pine needles everywhere." Ilahna's cheeks reddened.

"Why didn't you tell Aurelius I was there? Or talk quieter?"

That sweet smile again. "I will not pretend that Aurelius and I do not discuss the young Jacir often. His guidance has been unmatched in the months since he's been accepted into the fold. He does not have the fear in his heart to worry about the things we say, but you are cautious and want to hear our plans for him before they are made. I cannot begrudge you that. I know what it is like to worry about a brother."

Something *clicked* in Ilahna's mind, and she stopped walking, pulling on Lucinda's willowy arm until the pale girl turned to face her. Ilahna narrowed her eyes at the frail young woman with her wispy, silver hair and moonlike face. Lucinda, in turn, met her eyes, and Ilahna saw that her gaze was filled with wisdom, pride, and a strength that seemed too great to fit within such a small frame. But the thing Ilahna was looking for was there, and she *knew*.

"You and Aurelius. You're siblings."

Lucinda nodded. "You are not a seer, but if you could follow the Weave, I think you would be surprised at how often the banner of change comes on four shoulders. So many siblings in the threads. You and Jacir. Aurelius and me. Even the Betrayer was known to have a brother. The old texts so often talk about duality. I wonder how many other siblings have walked the world, completely unaware that they are blessed by the Gods?" She set a soft hand on Ilahna's arm. "I should not be surprised that you, of all people, were able to discern Aurelius' and my relationship, but I am impressed. Very few people are able to put that together; my brother and I are so different." Ilahna shook her head, red curls bobbing.

"No. No, I think it's great. Jacir and I look so much alike you can tell from across the square. Not a lot of redheads in Clearwall, you know? It made it impossible to play any sort of ruse on merchants or traders. They knew we were together. And watching two of a pair split up is always suspicious. So, we could never use one as a face while the other got things done."

"Yes. Which is why you must not tell anyone what you know."

Ilahna frowned. "What? Why not?"

"Because if Clearwall is to survive, we need someone upon the Starlit Throne again. While illegitimate, my brother and I are heirs, and Aurelius' stature and features make that obvious. He could reclaim Clearwall easily, and with the support of the people. His ascension would set things right, and with the least amount of upset. The Proclaimers must fall, and that war will cause enough irreparable harm to Clearwall than even they have already caused. We do not want to create any more rifts beyond that."

"So? We can do that with people still knowing that the king has a sister. Lots of kings have sisters." Lucinda shook her head quietly.

"Do you not see? My brother is strong. And brave. And even intelligent. But he does not see the Weave like I do. He knows strategy better than almost any warrior alive, and even he is unable to best me at chess. If Clearwall is to endure, my brother must become her King. And I must be his advisor. But the people of Clearwall have already been taught that women with gifts such as ours are to be feared at best and, in many more cases, burnt quickly. Our group has learned to see beyond such things. We know that most people have some sort of gift. But old bigotries die hard. Tying him to me would only cause more duress after a battle we can already ill-afford. People will say he is fighting for witches first and the citizens second. So I cannot be his witch. Or his official advisor. Or his sister. But his servant? Or even his perceived concubine? There are many things a woman may be if not Faoii. And I will take that fall if it is for the betterment of Clearwall."

Ilahna was surprised. She had never heard anyone other than Kaiya refer to "Faoii" as anything other than evil. Lucinda must have read her face, because she smiled.

"I have read the old texts. 'Faoii' is not a good or bad word. Like any warrior, the perception of 'good' or 'bad' is attached to which side of the war you are on."

Ilahna pondered that for a moment, kicking pine needles with her feet as they continued walking. After a few minutes, she finally spoke again. "I know you can read. Will you help me with something?"

"What is it?"

Ilahna searched around for a fallen stick, then scraped pine needles away from the forest floor with her boot. Lucinda stood by silently and watched as she used the stick to draw irregular patters into the soft earth. She tried to remember back to Eitan's smithy as she gouged several harsh lines into the mud. Finally, she felt like she'd gotten the symbols right, and she stepped away, giving Lucinda room to see.

"What does it say?"

Lucinda pondered for a moment. "I don't think it says anything. It looks like gibberish to me."

Ilahna's face fell, but she huffed and reached back into her memory again. She made a few adjustments to the lines she'd already created. "Now?"

"It is very close to the word for Illindria. The main Faoii Goddess before the Godfell War." Lucinda beckoned for the stick, and Ilahna handed it to her. Lucinda frowned thoughtfully and began elongating some of the shorter lines and smoothing out some of the dips Ilahna had incorrectly placed. But she paused partway through one of the movements. She glanced over at Ilahna before continuing.

"Why do you want to know this? You are more warrior than scribe." Ilahna shifted uneasily.

"I want to reteach Clearwall how to read. Well, maybe not me, personally. But us. The resistance. We knew how to once. We can learn again. I think… I think that once, a long time ago, reading and writing tied us all together. I think it taught us more than we knew and brought people to a single cause from leagues away. But… maybe, more importantly, if we learn to read, then so much of what we've lost might be returned to us."

Suddenly, self-conscious, Ilahna spoke more quickly. "It'll take time. I know it will. But maybe if we can start here, with one word, it can become a symbol. Something to rekindle the flame that the Proclaimers keep putting out." She paused, thinking hard. Jacir would know how to say what she was trying to articulate. "Mostly… I don't know. I think we need knowledge and communication and hope more than we need anything else right now. I think we need that even more than the tonicloran." She gave Lucinda a pointed look, and the fair woman nodded.

"I understand. And I agree. We need a symbol. More than the symbol of the Clearwall Crest or any of the other things that the Proclaimers have tarnished. But I think, perhaps, that the name of a long-dead deity is not where we want to start. We want to move forward rather than back, do we not?" Ilahna nodded, and Lucinda used the toe of her slipper to wipe the mud smooth again. "Illindria wouldn't have worked for what you want, anyway. Too many of the letters look the same." She smiled as she used the stick to draw two clumps of symbols in the mud. A moment later, she leaned back, admiring her work.

"What do they say?" There was no reason to whisper, but Ilahna felt awed by the two little clusters of drawings peering at her from the earth.

Lucinda used the stick to point at both of the groups. "This one is HOPE. And this one is RISE."

Ilahna smiled. That was exactly what she wanted to hear.

46

Kaiya tried to outpace the fear and uncertainty that had nearly overwhelmed her in the camp. But, more than that, she tried to outrun the thrill of hope that the revolutionaries had felt at the pull of the tonicloran. It had rolled off them in waves. And part of her could not blame them. They'd all known the odds before the witch Calari had arrived. When put up against the Proclaimers, there was every chance that many or even all of them would fall beneath their blades, magic or no magic. So of course they would grasp at anything they could on what seemed like a quickly sinking ship. And the tonicloran did seem to offer an edge even the Proclaimers could not counter.

Kaiya spit to one side. They were all young. Foolish. They did not know what that plant meant. She had tried to warn them, but she also knew that destroying it would cause equally large waves in the Tapestry. And she would not be the one to start those ripples. Never again.

Her heart was less certain, though. As Kaiya tried to focus on the creaking wheels of the caravan wagon that bore her away from Clearwall and its dark forest (she refused to reopen the door to the Tapestry again and blink across its threads to far-off lands) a part of her begged to go back the way she'd come. She could feel the silver cords in her mind pulling her towards the young urchins that held so much of the future on their shoulders.

Her heart said they still needed her, but she refused to turn back. She was free now. After having called forth Calari, even without meaning to, Kai knew Jacir would lock that part of his powers away in order to protect his people. He would not compel her again.

She was free. She intended to use that freedom.

The Bastard King and his followers in the forest could be the ones to lead those children into battles they couldn't possibly know the outcome of, so sure that their path was good and true and right. Kaiya was less certain, and she did not want to see whatever final pattern those two powerful children eventually wove into the Tapestry's everlasting threads. She did not have it in her to hope that their ending would be better than her own had been.

The silver cords vibrated more urgently, and the hair on the back of Kai's neck stood on end. The Tapestry was calling to her. It once did this often when there was danger in the threads, and in her younger days she had bounced back and forth to the Hall constantly, trying to stop whatever was coming. Trying to protect her people from danger. Eventually she'd learned that there was always danger. The Goddess Illindria had gone mad by trying to keep her people from experiencing it. And, as the Proclaimers took power and killed the Faoii one by one, Kaiya thought she had, too.

Kai tried to bury the feeling as she pulled her cowl around her face. She had learned to ignore the pull once. She could learn to do it again.

She was done.

47

In the next several days, the camp was a flurry of motion and desperation. The seers searched for safety away from the prying eyes of the now-absent witches that had found them and then disappeared from the Tapestry's threads. They could be anywhere now; could reappear anywhere in the future. The camp was not safe, and tensions were high. But there were few places where they could find the protection they had here while still being near enough to Clearwall to plan their assault.

Ilahna had roamed more of the canopy than anyone else, and she showed Aurelius and the Weavers her careful maps of the forest. One location seemed adequate, and the growing army prepared to move. The revolutionaries gathered their belongings and trekked through the forest to a new camp with rocky outcroppings and dense foliage, and everyone seemed more comfortable once they'd settled.

They'd been at the new camp for several weeks when Aurelius looked around the new location approvingly for the hundredth time. "This is a good location, Miss Harkins," he said again. "The outcroppings force attackers to maneuver in ways we can predict." Ilahna tried not to smile too broadly at his praise.

"Thank you, Your Highness."

"Truly, Ilahna. You've done well. But now I have another task for you." Ilahna frowned. She had not finished mapping the forest, yet. What could Aurelius want from her that would be more important than that?

"What's that, Your Highness?"

Aurelius opened his mouth to respond, but Lucinda placed a gentle hand on his arm.

"Come now, Aurelius. At least wait until she has seen her surprise, first."

"What surprise?" Jacir asked from the branch he was perched on. Lucinda smiled up at him.

"There's a new group of recruits coming today. Maybe you should go meet them." She gave Ilahna a wink as Jacir fidgeted excitedly in the tree. Ilahna raised an eyebrow at Lucinda, but the wispy girl only smiled. "Go on," she whispered. "We'll talk tomorrow." Ilahna glanced at Jacir and shrugged.

"Okay. Come on, Jace." Together, they took to the trees.

They hadn't gone far when they found the small group coming from the direction of Clearwall. Tanner led them, but Ilahna looked past the roguish scout to a familiar figure who followed, staring wide-eyed at the surrounding trees.

"Trisha!" Jacir whooped as he hopped down and ran to the catlike girl, nearly knocking her over with his hug. Trisha squealed with delight as she hugged him back.

"Jacir! Ilahna! I'm so glad to see you!" Trisha smiled at them both, but she was quickly enthralled by the trees again. "Did you ever believe somewhere like this could exist?"

"You want us to show it to you?" Jacir asked excitedly, pulling on her arm. "The forest is amazing! Come with us! It's just like running through the Maze, but better! You'll see!"

Ilahna smiled at Jacir's enthusiasm. He'd grown so much during their time in the forest, and he'd often been forced to carry the entire revolution on his shoulders, but in moments like this Ilahna could still see him for what he was. A boy that liked to run and explore. A child who'd just reconnected with one of his only friends.

Trisha looked to Ilahna quizzically, and Ilahna winked back. "Actually, that's a good idea. We need a new test to see who's the best mazer in Clearwall, don't we?"

Trisha looked uncertain, and Ilahna took her other hand. "It'll be okay. I promise. Let us show you." Trisha relaxed a little, excitement creeping into her features as she looked at the branches overhead.

"Okay. Let's do it."

Whooping in exhilaration, the three mazers took to the trees.

Hours later, Ilahna, Jacir, and Trisha sat together in the tallest tree they'd been able to find. "What's it like in Clearwall these days?" Ilahna asked, swinging her legs idly.

"On the surface, it seems nearly the same," Trisha replied, pulling a leaf from the tree and rubbing it between her fingers. "But there's something coursing beneath the Maze. The urchins are angrier. Bolder. They started attacking guards that got too close to the inner wall. Now Proclaimers patrol the streets. A lot of the adults have disappeared. But the urchins are still too fast. Too slippery. And that means they're taking more chances."

Ilahna let out a low whistle. "Mazers against Proclaimers, huh? That's going to lead to a lot of dead kids sooner or later."

"Yeah. That's why I agreed to come out here when someone left an egg message in one of my nests. There's something on the horizon. Like the cracks that form on an egg right before the chick breaks through. And if all of my friends are going to be part of it, I want to at least give them a chance." She paused, not looking up. "But, it's more than that… I don't know, Ilahna. I wish I was like you. You gave a lot of the mazers hope. Your disappearance was a big part of the rage, I think." She tore the leaf up, watching the pieces fall to the forest floor. "Imagine if they'd known you were out here. They probably would have all scaled the walls to follow you. I think they would have followed you anywhere."

Ilahna laughed uncomfortably. "All I ever did was guide kids away from pyres and show them how to collect moss or steal trinkets. And after enough kids knew how to survive, I didn't even do that anymore." Trisha shook her head.

"I don't think it's what you did. I think it's what you were. Mazers have been betrayed and forgotten by everyone that they ever knew. But… not by you. You lied to merchants and guards when you needed something, but you never lied to any of us. You never forgot any of us, and you always told us exactly how things were. We could all hear the truth in your words… louder sometimes than the temple bells.

"Mazers still asked about you, after you disappeared. We all forget the names of the dead in a few weeks, you know? But not yours."

Ilahna didn't know how to answer that, and they sat in silence, watching birds in the trees.

"That reminds me," Trisha finally ventured. "I want to show you something. Is there somewhere that's… not grass and wood? Somewhere stone?"

"Hmm," Ilahna pondered, grateful for the change in topics. "There's an old tower not far from here. Kind of. More like a circle of rock with part of a wall on one side, but it still has a stone floor."

"That sounds like it will work. Will you show me?"

The urchins led Trisha to the ancient ruin Ilahna had found a few months before. The catlike girl circled it twice before nodding, satisfied. "You remember Corey and Belinda?" she asked as she dug into her trinket belt. Ilahna thought back to the siblings they'd led away from the pyre a lifetime ago. She nodded. "You did well finding those two. They're really bright. Learned to make this."

Carefully, Trisha pulled a large egg from the fur-lined pouch. Ilahna wrinkled her nose.

"Has it gone bad? It smells terrible."

"That's the silk strand moss they put inside. Watch." Trisha pulled out her flint and tinder and sent a single spark down the hollowed-out hole at the top of the egg. Then she immediately flung the entire thing as hard as she could against the stone floor of the crumbling ruins.

The eggshell cracked on impact, and the flaming silk strand moss began to unravel in fiery tendrils, spreading across the stone floor of the fallen tower rapidly. Ilahna and Jacir watched in frightened awe.

"That's… terrifying." Ilahna finally whispered. Trisha nodded.

"I know. But the mazers are playing with them more often. They're going to use them on the Proclaimers sooner or later, and it's going to start a bloody war the mazers can't win." Trisha watched as the last tendril finally climbed the stone wall and extinguished. "If I'm gone, maybe they won't find as many eggs. But if this revolution is going to happen, I hope it's soon. Otherwise, the mazers are going to start it for us from inside the walls."

"The Proclaimers wouldn't wage a war on a bunch of kids, would they?" Jacir whispered. Ilahna wanted to reassure him, but she remembered Jorthee's story, and her mouth went dry.

"We should get back to camp," was all she could respond.

The three former mazers of Clearwall ran through the forest in silence, chased by the darkness of approaching night.

48

"We need to ensure that we are more defended than we have been," Aurelius said solemnly as Ilahna, Eitan, and Trisha sat at his makeshift war table the next morning. Nearby, Jacir sat on the ground, letting a small red bug run across his fingers. "This is a good place you've found, Miss Harkins. The Weavers say that fewer threads lead to death, here, though there are always dangers. We need Jacir in camp to direct their gazes, but I have a new assignment for you."

"What is it?" Ilahna leaned forward, squeezing Eitan's hand.

"We want both of you," he motioned to her and Trisha, "to prepare traps in the trees. Things that our enemies won't expect and that can ensnare them even if they move past our patrols. You two are quick and sure enough to get it done."

"We can do that," Ilahna said quickly. "We can absolutely do that, right?" She nudged Trisha who nodded enthusiastically.

"Good." Aurelius leaned back in his chair. "This is an important responsibility. You will be the last line of defense in camp—on par with our strongest soldiers. Heart and mettle are useful, but never underestimate the power of a well-laid surprise. You'll have to be ready at a moment's notice if our camp is breached again. And you must follow my orders exactly."

"We will," Ilahna promised, though she knew that very few people were able to resist Aurelius' orders, regardless. But this was an oath she felt sure she could keep. "We won't fail you or the resistance." Next to her, Trisha nodded fervently.

"You can depend on us, Your Majesty."

Over the next several days, Trisha and Ilahna worked on making nets, poring over Ilahna's maps, and plotting the most strategic places to hang the traps Aurelius demanded. Meanwhile, Lucinda still ghosted through the camp, carrying her small bowl with its tonicloran stalk. She spoke to nearly everyone, learning about their abilities and nodding as they told her of their past experiences. Ilahna watched her, more out of curiosity than anything, but her heart grew a little cold when she saw the spark in Lucinda's eyes each time she spoke to Jacir.

If Jacir saw it, he never said anything. But Ilahna remembered the discussion about tonicloran, the way Jacir had been pulled towards it on the night the cursed plant had come to them. She shuddered. No matter what Aurelius wanted, Jacir would not be his poison-tipped spear in this war. She'd make sure of it.

Instead, Ilahna tried to make her own contributions to the movement, hoping they could find strength in something that was not the broad-leafed plant. In her spare time, she practiced the words Lucinda had taught her, carving them into trees where the nets would hang, into mud, into the leather of her halter. The oldest members of the alliance would sometimes come to see her carved scribbles, and their eyes would fill with tears at nearly-forgotten memories from long ago. Sometimes, they would help her to make the symbols stronger or straighter. Sometimes, they would show her how to embellish the lines and make the words look like they were dancing. And always, they left with their backs a little straighter, their steps a little lighter.

HOPE and RISE spread across the camp. It was not long before nearly every soldier in the resistance had either an H or R emblazoned on their leather breastplate. Like so many things before, that which had been taken by oppressors became a symbol of something even greater once it was taken back.

One evening, Ilahna was leaning against Eitan, carefully emblazoning the last symbol of HOPE on a set of bracers when Lucinda approached them. Ilahna tensed when she met her turquoise eyes. Next to her, Eitan set a steadying hand on her waist.

"You think Jacir's the one." Ilahna did not form it as a question, but her heart still hammered in her chest as she hoped with everything she had that Lucinda would deny her accusation. Instead, the wispy seer only nodded, turning a small vial over in her hands.

"He is, Miss Harkins. There is no one else that is half as powerful as Jacir, no matter how it seems. Even now he can already pull and change the Weave in ways the rest of us did not think possible. If he could be truly trained, then maybe this would not be necessary. But there is no one to train him, and we have no other options. If we are to succeed against the Proclaimers and the others that will come against us while we are still rebuilding Clearwall, we will need someone with true power to help lead us. Only the tonicloran can offer that."

"Kaiya could teach him."

Lucinda frowned thoughtfully. "I do not doubt that she could, Miss Harkins. But even you don't truly believe she will." Ilahna could not disagree, but she clenched a fist anyway.

"I won't let you poison my brother." Next to her, Eitan straightened, nodding. Ilahna's heart filled with steel at his silent support. Lucinda acknowledged the change in the air, but did not withdraw.

"I know," she said, still turning over the small vial. "But that is precisely why I am here. Our future king wants Jacir to take the rite. He and I both know that Jacir would be a powerful ally. But we also know that you would make an even more powerful enemy. All of the seers have agreed that giving Jacir the tonicloran without your blessing will lead to destruction. And we will listen." Lucinda smiled slightly, and Ilahna raised an eyebrow. She had never been told that the seers in camp talked about her, as well. And it certainly had never occurred to her that the seers saw her as someone formidable. No wonder she had never been forced to leave the camp to scout or train, as the others had, unless her brother could accompany her. She had always been allowed to remain near Jacir. His ever-present bodyguard.

And why not? She would have fought anyone who tried to keep her from that position, anyway. It seemed that everyone else in the camp already knew it.

Ilahna would have chuckled, but the serious look in Lucinda's eye sobered her. She eyed the vial in Lucinda's hand. "So where does that bring us?"

Lucinda bowed her head. "I give you the power of the tonicloran, Ilahna Harkins. There was only enough for this small vial, but it is more than enough to kill any man—or raise a Weaver wrapped within the safety of the Tapestry to a greater power. A Weaver like your brother." She took a deep, trembling breath. "There are no other stalks in the world that we know about, so the last of the Faoii's strongest magic is yours to command."

Ilahna started to reach for the vial, but withdrew her hand at the last moment. "Why trust me with this?" she asked.

That understated smile again. A twinkle in Lucinda's turquoise eye. "Because, Ilahna. You are the Keeper of Truth. We have all seen it, even if you have tried to bury it. And that has to be enough."

"The what?"

"Do not worry about it now. Knowing things too early changes the Weave. That's why your Faoii friend stopped watching the future. Just know that I trust you with this when I cannot trust anyone else in existence. We all depend on your brother. And your brother depends on you."

Softly, Lucinda pressed the vial into Ilahna's hand. It felt icy to the touch as Ilahna wrapped her fingers around it. She considered for a moment, then secured the small container between her leather harness and the soft fabric of her tunic.

After she finished, Ilahna looked up to speak to Lucinda again, but the pale girl had already walked back into the trees. Next to her, Eitan brushed a finger across her cheek.

"Are you okay, Ilahna?"

She didn't know how to respond.

49

Kaiya had forgotten that, once opened, the doors to the Tapestry's Hall could not be easily closed again. It had taken her decades to untangle herself from those ghostly threads when last she's stepped away from them. A lifetime to free her mind from the everlasting Weave. In the end, she had succeeded, plunging into a life of near-oblivion as her dreams finally quieted and she forgot how to access the Tapestry. After years of trying to bury it, she had finally been freed of her curses and promises.

But now the door was open again, and Kaiya's mortal body tossed fitfully on her bedroll. Her mind was already racing back through the twisted streets of Clearwall. She zoomed past the broken, forgotten homes filled with broken, forgotten people. Up through the dusty, abandoned corridors of Clearwall Keep. Down the twisting, blood-stained passageways beneath the floor. Through the torture chambers and back into the wide corridors of the old library.

No. It wasn't a library anymore. The temple. A place filled with smoke and secrets, its knowledge long-since burned to ash. Candles flickered in a darkness that wasn't borne of the shadows of her mind. There was something foreboding here. A presence she thought she had felt before. A deep, untouchable fear that lurked in the hearts of those who did not know what the future held—and in those who absolutely did.

An iron-willed and stalwart Proclaimer stood rigidly on the dais that had been installed sometime since Kaiya's last visit to this ancient haven of knowledge and curiosity. Now, its walls were composed of dutiful songs and fear-mongering sermons. And this—a tall, unbowed woman who could have so easily been a Faoii in a different life.

The First Proclaimer. Madame Elise.

In front of Madame Elise was the witch from the woods. Faoii-Calari. The woman who had somehow learned all of the secrets that Kaiya had tried to bury, who had escaped her notice for an untold number of years. Kaiya still cursed the threads that had first allowed her to miss such a pivotal point in a war she'd wanted nothing to do with, only to later force her to so easily find the same Gods-hated witch now that the damage was already done. Again she tried to pry her mind away from the Weave, determined to claim her independence from its unfaltering pull, refusing to watch whatever the damned Tapestry was now trying to thrust into her mind. But there was no escaping, and Kaiya found herself trapped—chained by invisible shackles to watch the scene unfolding before her.

"You can't deny me, Calari. Tell me what I want to know." Madame Elise hissed from her raised platform, resting one gauntleted fist on her sword hilt. Calari fought the command, but finally succumbed, her entire body shaking.

"The rebels are in the forest. They have many powerful seers and healers."

"What else?"

Calari fought against the question, clenching her teeth together so hard that Kaiya could smell blood."

"What else?" Elise bellowed, her voice reverberating around the room.

"And now they have a plant that can change the tides of history." Tears leaked from Calari's eyes as she spoke, dropping onto the marble floor.

"Tell me of this plant." Madame Elise's eyes sharpened in the candlelight, the steel-grey irises glinting like one of the fantoii of old.

"Ali, I—"

"You will call me Elise!" the Proclaimer screamed. Faoii-Calari bowed her head, compelled by Elise's power. "Tell me of the plant."

"It opens the doors between our world and that of the Old Gods. Very few can use it, and even those of us who have the gift can rarely use it to its full potential. But I saw the Weave. There is someone in that camp who could survive its use and do more than any of us could ever imagine. He could physically move between the worlds if he desired. He could bring others to that side, or pull something from there to here. He could move between the ages with his physical body, rather than just watch the passage of time as it spirals across the Tapestry. He could change anything. And once he tastes that power, he would not be able to relinquish it again. You could bend him to do anything."

Something sparked in Madame Elise's eyes. Hope? Something darker?

"You've done well, my old friend. When you stumbled to the gates of Clearwall, I could hardly believe my eyes. I could have let you bleed to death. But the Old Gods are merciful to those who ask for forgiveness."

Faoii-Calari barked out a mirthless, sobbing laugh. "They might have been, once. But you aren't, Ali. I never would have come here if I'd known what I was doing. You should have let me die."

"Perhaps. But I suppose there might still be time for that. Tell me of the other one. The one you were babbling about in your fever when we found you."

"She is the Betrayer."

Elise smiled wickedly. "Now, that is interesting. Your disgraced Order sought for the Betrayer for centuries… and failed. One more reason that I am everything your monasteries were not. Surely, she will be a fitting sacrifice to appease the Old Gods upon Their return. How lovely." Proclaimer Elise descended the steps of her pulpit, motioning for Calari to stand. The Faoii did, her eyes dark with distrust.

"Tell me something honestly, Calari. Without me forcing it from your lips. Do you still hate the Betrayer as much as you did when we were young?"

Calari narrowed her eyes and looked down at the chains that held her wrists. Finally, she nodded.

"I want the Betrayer to watch the dark Tapestry she's created unravel and burn. I want her to regret the day she condemned all of us to a life without Gods. She left us with magic but no guidance. We became rivers without currents. Now that I know that she yet lives, I want her to feel the weight of all she's done to us."

Kaiya could almost laugh in her ethereal form. Oh, how she regretted everything that had happened since the Faoii-Croeli war. Everything she had done, even then. The way her hopes and dreams for Clearwall and all of Imeriel had been twisted and tarnished. This woman wanted her to pay, completely unaware of what she had already given.

Madame Elise's voice took on a soft tone, but the unsettling glint did not leave her eyes. "To think that our goals would align after all this time," she whispered, pushing up Calari's chin until their eyes met. Calari spit at her cheek.

"We are nothing alike, Ali."

Elise wiped the spittle from her face and laughed. "Of course not. I am everything you could never be." With a flourish of her cloak, the First Proclaimer walked away from the pulpit and her chained prisoner, her sabatons ringing in the hall. "Return her to the dungeon," she ordered the Proclaimers stationed against the walls. "Everything depends on the plant and the boy, now. And we know where they are. The Old Gods will return before the seasons change. Prepare yourselves."

Kaiya bolted upright from her bedroll, her braid disheveled and damp with sweat. It had been a long time since she had seen through the veil, and even then, her visions had seldom been so clear. From across the expanse, the silver thread that was wrapped around her heart pulled her towards the forest.

No! I won't go back! I'm free! Just let me be free!

In the darkness, Kaiya cursed Jacir. How dare a child—*a child!*—twist her mind back into the Tapestry she had long abandoned? What gave him the right?

Kaiya rolled back into her bedroll. This wasn't her fight. She'd warned them. That was enough. *Why couldn't it just be enough?*

But then, for a moment, Kaiya saw a face she thought she had forgotten. He looked so like Jacir in many ways—kind, earnest, and thin lips that seemed thinner when he smiled. From across time and space some frenzied part of her mind suddenly wondered if Jacir would click his heels together if he ever had cause to salute.

Kaiya sat up again, slowly. She brought one hand to her head, and felt it tremble there. In all of that war, in all the people that were fighting for political gain or for sovereigns both mortal and not—one man had picked up his bow because something told him it was the right thing to do. At the time, Kaiya thought Illindria had been influencing him, but she'd realized later that she was mistaken. In all their time together, he'd never said an Oath, never heard a blade sing, never worshipped any of the Gods that would have laid claim to him. Instead, he'd always fought and lived and loved because it was the right thing to do. He was there because he cared about people more than the king he swore fealty to and the Gods that later usurped his throne. He followed orders and helped where he could, because that's who he was. And even though he'd become one of her closest friends, he always called her ma'am.

Oh, Emery.

Maybe the war didn't matter. Maybe the Proclaimers would win or the revolutionists would. But none of that what was important. What mattered was that the descendant of one of her closest friends was in danger. The Proclaimers knew of the woods, and those that hid there. Even if the children had been smart enough to convince the Bastard King to move their camp, there was no way they could have gotten far enough away by now to be safe from the Proclaimers, who would be right behind.

There were no reinforcements close enough to help the urchins. No one except for Kaiya.

She should have known she couldn't outrun this. That all her careful planning could fall apart as easily as a woven tapestry against a pair of shears. But it did not surprise her, anymore.

Kaiya vaguely wondered what the caravan leader would think when he found her empty bedroll in the morning, but the thought was quickly forgotten as she *blinked.*

50

Screaming.

Ilahna bolted upright from her bedroll, already reaching for her fantoii as Eitan grabbed his hammer. There was screaming in the trees.

The somewhat less jarring sound of steel against steel came more slowly, but Ilahna recognized it as she dashed into the night, one hand brandishing her sword and the other grasping Eitan's.

Outside, the camp was in chaos. Invaders were kicking over tents and waving torches in the darkness, lighting canvas with people still trapped inside. *This isn't right*, Ilahna thought frantically. *Why didn't we know this was coming? All the people in this camp who can see the Weave, and none of them could see it? How is that fair? Isn't magic supposed to be a gift?*

All of the old hatred against magic and Faoii rose against Ilahna's breast as she screamed, sweeping her blade up and deep into the back of an unfamiliar breastplate.

The Proclaimers. They've found us.

Next to her, Eitan was driving off another warrior. A sudden, barbaric yell tore Ilahna from her thoughts as another Proclaimer charged them. Ilahna just barely raised her blade in time to block, releasing Eitan's hand as she focused on each blow. He attacked again, and she twisted around his extended sword, kicking him in the knee before piercing his side with her fantoii. He made a sort of gurgling sound as he fell, but his death cry wasn't even noticed by the others who were attacking the resistance members scattered about the camp.

Aurelius bellowed from somewhere nearby, trying to rouse the scattered warriors into action. "Form ranks!" his gong-like voice boomed. "Use the trees to your advantage! And if you hear a seer, do what they say. Immediately!" Aurelius' hulking arms cut down the figures that came against him, and his piercing eyes took in everything with a quick and pragmatic certainty. "Third squadron, circle to points six and seven. Second Squadron. Take one and four. Their flanks are exposed! Herd them towards the sleeve."

Ilahna didn't know most of the terms, but she knew what the sleeve was. A series of traps she and Trisha had set amidst the rocky outcroppings to the south. She knew the plan: the resistance would herd the invaders, and she would drop one side as Trisha dropped the other Their timing would have to be perfect or the plan would fail. But if they did it right, if she and Trisha could work in perfect unison like they'd practiced, the sleeve could easily turn the entire battle in their favor.

"Come on!" Trisha yelled to her, already taking to the trees. "They'll need us soon!"

Ilahna moved to follow, her fantoii humming in response. She was needed there. She had her place and her orders. She had to go.

Jacir. Where was Jacir?

"Eitan!" she screamed. "Where's Jacir?" Eitan tried to respond, but he was fighting his own battle, locked in combat with two other Children of Truth.

It didn't matter. She already knew. *The stream.* She was sure of it even before she'd completely remembered the offshoot from the Starlit River that ran north of here. Jacir often sat next to the stream now that there was no clearing to meditate in. He would have to be there if he had not already found her in camp. And, if he heard the sound of fighting, he would be coming back. Alone. Unprotected.

Ilahna drove off another Proclaimer's blade and carved her fantoii deep into his stomach. She heard Trisha yell for her again, but another Proclaimer was in front of her, wielding a sword that was longer than Eitan was broad.

Ilahna tried to parry, but her thin fantoii could not compare to the Proclaimer's ferocious blows. Twice Ilahna was able to get her arm up in time to block an overhead swing, and both times her arm went numb with the force of the hit. She'd barely brought her arm up for the third assault, already aware that her numb fingers would not be able to hold the fantoii's hilt should it be struck again. She tried to move away, but it was too fast. There was no time.

Ilahna didn't realize she'd closed her eyes against her own coming death until she finally recognized that there was no new pain and that the yell she heard was not her own. Incredulous, she opened one eye.

A giant, tattooed warrior with a braided beard and piercing eyes stood over the Proclaimer, hacking at her with a curved, bloody axe. One of the tribesmen that Jacir had convinced them to seek out. She rose and tried to shout a word of thanks, but the tribesman was already turning to cleave at another Proclaimer.

"Ilahna! Are you okay?" Eitan gasped, running up to her. Blood seeped into his left eye.

"I'm fine. I have to find Jacir!"

Trisha's cries forgotten, Ilahna cut through the camp in the direction of the stream. Eitan followed, and they were nearly free of the main battle when two Proclaimers leapt from the bushes on either side of them, screaming for the glory of the Old Gods.

Ilahna had been born a mazer, and she somersaulted away from the Proclaimers on instinct, coming up behind one of them with her fantoii already poised to strike. But Eitan had never lived in the Maze, and he was caught by surprise, barely able to ward off the two assailants as they pressed their advantage.

Unleashing her battlecry, Ilahna shifted her grip and darted forward, bringing her fantoii down and around in a sweeping arc, cutting into the soft skin below one of the Proclaimer's breastplates. With a short scream, the Proclaimer dropped his blade and Ilahna drove her sword into his throat. The scream was enough to startle the other Proclaimer for a moment, and Eitan used the hesitation to slam his hammer downward, caving in the other man's skull.

They started to run deeper into the forest, but a sudden, booming command cut through the trees. "Stop! Eitan! Your song is needed. Find Tanner and lend your hammer and your voice to his men. Go!" Aurelius' order erupted from the sounds of battle, shaking the trees. Ilahna's heart sank a tiny bit. Eitan had always been good at taking orders. Following his father's commands as a child had taught him the craft more quickly than anything Ilahna had learned on her own. And she knew from experience that very few people could disobey Aurelius.

Eitan froze, looking torn. Ilahna placed a gentle kiss on his cheek. "Go, Eitan. The resistance needs you. I'll find Jacir. It'll be okay." Eitan wrapped his arms around her for a long moment.

"Be safe." Then he was dashing off to do as instructed.

Ilahna felt the pull of service. The deep desire to be part of something bigger than herself. The hum of her fantoii that directed her to the sleeve. But she shook it off, tearing herself away from the call of purpose. She had to find Jacir.

"Ilahna!" Aurelius' voice sounded like fire and crashing waves, forcing her to turn towards him even as she tried to push her legs to move towards her brother's favorite spot. "You're supposed to be in the sleeve! We need you! Go!"

Ilahna's body stiffened, Aurelius' piercing gaze from above his own battles catching her off guard. When she heard Aurelius' command, a deep part of Ilahna *wanted* to do as he said. She trusted his strategies and his orders. She trusted *him* in a way she never could have trusted the Proclaimers. She knew, deep in her being, that if she followed Aurelius then things would be okay.

Lucinda was right. He is meant to be our king.

But the sleeve wasn't in Jacir's direction.

With a heart-wrenching shake of her head, Ilahna broke eye contact with Aurelius and charged in the opposite direction, aiming for the stream. She wasn't sure if the cry that rose behind her was that of Aurelius or of her own sense of honor and purpose wailing against her betrayal. But some part of her felt the resistance fall in the darkness as she left it behind.

There were so many Proclaimers in the forest. Ilahna ducked underneath the swing of another man, barely putting a tree between them. She didn't have enough time to fight every person in her way. She had to find her brother.

Please be okay. Please be okay. You have to be okay.

Ilahna took to the trees. It was like being a mazer again, and the safety of the branches carried her across the battle like the crows that were already circling overhead, waiting for the feast that was sure to come. Ilahna tried not to think about the people the crows would feast on because of her. Shaking her head, she darted forward, leaving the sounds of battle behind.

There was no one next to the stream. A small fire was still lit in Jacir's favorite place, but her brother was clearly absent.

Her heart hammering in her ears, Ilahna leapt from tree to tree, searching for any sign of Jacir and praying to anyone who might or might not listen to her cries.

When she finally saw him, Ilahna's heart clenched in anger and sympathy. Jacir was bound and kneeling on the ground, a woman holding a knife to the back of his neck. He looked so small and frail, his shoulders shaking in the predawn air. Ilahna recognized the woman as the witch that had brought the tonicloran to camp, and her heart hardened at the sight of the Faoii that had brought them so much trouble. But nothing compared to the rage she felt when she saw who else was there.

The witch seemed to have no sympathy for Jacir, but even she seemed kind compared to the stalwart mound of iron and dignified anger that stood with her arms crossed at the head of the huddled group. Ilahna tensed and gripped her blade. Madame Elise.

"I've done as you commanded, First Proclaimer," the Faoii hissed without moving her weapon. "You have your prize. But, please. Ali. If you ever loved me as a child, I beseech you: release or kill me now. I will not be your slave any longer."

Madame Elise didn't even look at Calari, instead turning to survey the trees around them, snapping sharply as she did so. Several more warriors broke from the tree line to surround Jacir, and Ilahna's heart fell. There were too many for her to fight alone.

Calari tried again. "Ali. Please."

Madame Elise's lips curved upward in the faintest hint of a smile. "Fine."

With a single, fluid motion, Madame Elise drew her blade and swung it towards Calari. She missed Jacir's head by inches, and a spray of blood matted his hair as the decapitated Faoii slumped sideways behind him. Elise flicked the blood off her sword.

"Good. Now that that's finished, stand him up." Two of the Proclaimers kicked the twitching body away and pulled Jacir up by his arms.

Ilahna clenched her teeth but felt a flush of pride when her brother didn't even flinch as he was dragged to his feet. Madame

Elise turned to him slowly, using one long, thin finger to raise his chin until they were looking into each other's eyes.

"Be grateful, little one," she said, her voice like steel shards. "The Gods have need of you. You will meet fate today."

Madame Elise's cloak rustled as she spun on her heel. "Bring him. And find the sister. She is too troublesome to leave unbridled."

Ilahna bristled and tensed her muscles to spring, numbers be damned. She was not going to let them take her brother.

But a voice behind her made her freeze.

"I already have, Madame."

Everything was dark before Ilahna could respond.

51

Kaiya could hear the clash of swords and the cries of the dying before she could see the fray. She drew her fantoii with grim determination and charged forward, what little sense of optimism she still possessed whispering quietly that maybe she wasn't too late. Maybe she hadn't doomed the urchins and the world they'd tried to build with her inaction and uncertainty.

Kaiya's fantoii released a bone-chilling howl as she swung at the back of the first armored man she reached. He could not even turn away from the revolutionist in front of him before she had lobbed his head from his shoulders. The defending fighter paled and backed away from her and her screaming blade, dropping her short sword. Kaiya glared. It seemed this revolution was doomed to fail, anyway.

"Pick that up. Now is not the time to be useless."

The woman stuttered a reply and stooped to retrieve her sword, but Kaiya was already moving through the battle, hacking at Proclaimers as she passed. The combatants in the forest parted at her howling weapon, trembling at the sound. It was Aurelius' voice that seemed to break through their stupor, though it was thready and weak. A far cry from the commander the troops had been following until now.

"Do not give up! Bring these usurpers to their knees! We will restore Clearwall to glory!"

Something in Aurelius' voice stirred Kaiya to focus on the warriors around her, and she cut down two more before she could completely tear her mind free of his persuasion and remember her true purpose. Aurelius' followers were fighting on their own now, however, and she was easily able to disengage and make her way to the Bastard King's position. He was lying on the ground, his face ashen and his right arm completely severed. Several healers were working to stem the blood flow.

Kaiya didn't care. He was not why she was here. "You!" she barked at the dying man. "Where are the children? Ilahna and Jacir?"

Something darkened in Aurelius' eyes. "The girl is a defector. She abandoned her duties and escaped into the forest. I have not seen the boy."

"You fool! He is the strongest of you, and she is his guardian. She went to him!"

Aurelius' face paled another shade, and for a moment Kaiya was sure he would faint, but he opened his eyes again, and glared at her through the pain. "I know that, witch. I do. And it pains me to have lost them, but I cannot spare the men or time to search. Find them if you want to. In fact, I wish you whatever blessings the Gods might still bestow. But if we lose here, we lose everything. And I will not let that happen."

Kaiya looked at his severed arm and the blood that covered the ground. She knew they'd already lost, and something in Aurelius' eyes told her that he knew it, too. But he looked away from her and barked another order to his men. Kaiya left him there with his tendrils of hope and dashed deeper into the forest. She needed it to be quiet. She needed to focus. Distantly she realized that the boy who had accompanied them in the sewers—*Eitan. That was his name*—had broken from his own squadron and was following her. She ignored him, too. It made sense that he would care about what had happened to the siblings, but he was not her problem, either.

Find the boy.

Kaiya groaned in frustration. The tendrils of silver threads that she'd once been able to trace through the Tapestry to a million different Faoii and their connection to the Weave were harder to grasp than they once had been. They slipped through her fists like sand. With increasing desperation, she tried again.

Find him.

"Where are you, Faoli?" she nearly screamed into the trees.

But the threads woven around Jacir eluded her.

52

Ilahna came to herself slowly. The back of her head ached, and her stomach lurched as she tried to rise onto one elbow. But her body didn't want to work right, and she only flopped on the cold floor instead.

Oh. My arms are bound.

Things were becoming a little clearer now. She was able to figure out that the rough floor beneath her cheek was made of damp cobblestones. She could smell old torch smoke and stale air. *I'm inside. Or underground.* And, most importantly, she could hear the deep, demanding voice of Madame Elise somewhere nearby.

The Proclaimers. They found us.

Us.

"Jacir?" Ilahna's voice was hoarse, and bile rose in her throat as she tried to raise her head. She tried again. "Jacir?"

Nearby, someone groaned. Ilahna nearly collapsed with relief. "It's okay, Jacir. We're going to be okay." She didn't know what they were going to do, but at least they were going to do it together.

Ilahna squirmed her body and her bound limbs in the direction of the moan. It was hard without the use of her arms and legs, but finally her numb fingers brushed against something warm behind her. Almost reflexively, Jacir's fingers wrapped around hers.

"Ah. You are both awake. Wonderful." There was no joy in Madame Elise's steely voice. "Stand the boy up and put the girl in her place. There is much to do."

Someone yanked Ilahna up by her arms, and she was dragged backwards, her head spinning painfully as she tried to get her bearings. She heard Jacir yelp somewhere in front of her and she tried to pull free at his cry, but was quickly overpowered.

"Get *off of me!*" She screamed, struggling as the Proclaimers shoved her harshly onto a plain wooden stool, their bodies pressing against her on all sides. Ilahna clenched her jaw and wrung her hands behind her, but the ropes held. "*Let me go!*"

Ilahna struggled for what felt like ages, to no avail. When her blindfold was finally removed an indeterminable time later, she had to blink several times despite the darkness of the room she found herself in. She'd been right that they were underground, seemingly deep beneath the temple. A handful of Proclaimers, hoods drawn, stood in a circle around Jacir. Ilahna struggled harder, trying to see if he was alright. He seemed unharmed, but his shoulders were clutched in the clawed hands of Madame Elise.

The First Proclaimer stared at Jacir with a madness that could only come from true belief.

"Get your hands off of him!" Ilahna hissed through clenched teeth.

Madame Elise clicked her tongue at Ilahna. "Come now, child. You know that this tale doesn't end that way. Your brother is necessary."

Ilahna narrowed her eyes, her skin crawling at the madness in Elise's voice. "Jacir, are you hurt?" she finally asked.

Jacir shook his head, but Madame Elise answered, regardless. "Use your head, child. We would not harm our savior." The mad glint in her eye got stronger, and Madame Elise gesticulated wildly with one hand as she grasped Jacir with the other. "Do you not see? This perfect child will bring back the Gods. He can fix what the Faoii ruined. With the tonicloran, he will fix everything!"

Ilahna instinctually tried to clutch the hidden vial at her breast, but her bound hands stopped her.

"The Betrayer destroyed the tonicloran. She saw what you were planning and thwarted you again." Ilahna carefully arranged her features to hide her fib, but Madame Elise barely looked to her as she disregarded the comment.

"Your lies mean nothing to me, child. The Old Gods have whispered Their return to me for decades, and They have gotten louder." She ran a long nail along Jacir's cheekbone. "The traitorous witch, Calari, confirmed what I'd already known. If only she had brought the blessed plant to me rather than to your ragtag band of wretches. All of this could have been concluded without any further harm. But here we are. Pity." She finally looked up from Jacir's face and focused on Ilahna completely. "The Old

Gods whisper of Their return. And you know the secret of their release. You should be grateful to be part of such grand machinations." Madame Elise smiled almost kindly at Ilahna as she stroked Jacir's hair. Ilahna spit in her direction, and the smile faded.

"Come now, child. Why do you fight me so? Give me the tonicloran, and all of this will be over in an instant. This is not the end of worlds that your traitorous Faoii friends have convinced you of. It is merely a righting of the Betrayer's wrongs. And you can be the harbinger of that justice! You and your brother can live in elevated ease as the heralds of the most powerful beings in existence. Honored servants of the Gods! Is that not what you've always wanted? A life of ease?"

Madame Elise's words were like honey, and her free hand stroked the hilt of her blade. Ilahna's body froze, and for a moment she believed everything the First Proclaimer was saying. Just as she had when she'd held the effigy by the pyre. Just as the people of Clearwall had believed it all her life. It was so obvious. Why were they fighting against a current that would bring them to paradise?

Jacir struggled in Madame Elise's grasp. "No! Lana! Don't listen! We saw what lurks beneath those threads, remember? You made me promise!"

Something changed in Madame Elise's eyes, and the look of unfaltering faith flashed through her gaze with a dark intensity. Then, with a movement faster than Ilahna could follow, she lashed out for Jacir's bound hands. Even from across the room, Ilahna could hear the sickening *crack* of one of his fingers as the Proclaimer snapped it backwards against his wrist. Then there was only the sound of Jacir's pained scream and blood rushing in her ears as she tried to stand. But the surrounding Proclaimers shoved her back onto the stool.

"Jacir! *Jacir!*" Ilahna struggled under the Proclaimers' grasp, watching her crying brother with strained features, her heart tearing at his pain. "Jacir, look at me! *Look at me!*" Jacir sniffled and brought his head back up, breathing heavily. He still shook a little, but he was able to stop his tears as he grounded himself again, watching Ilahna's eyes.

"I'm okay," he whispered. "I'm okay."

"Aw. Such a strong, sweet child." Madame Elise's voice was filled with a false generosity. "I can see why the Gods would choose you as Their harbinger." She looked to Ilahna as she stroked Jacir's hair again. "Are you ready to do what is necessary, girl? Or do I need to break another finger?"

For a moment Ilahna felt like she could break the bonds at her wrists with just the strength of her hatred, but still the ropes held. She met Elise's eyes, her chin up and her gaze steely.

"Pyres take you."

Madame Elise studied Ilahna's face for a long moment, her gaze filled with fire and the unspoken desire to break the child that dare challenge her. But then, something in that hate-filled gaze shifted, and what was left chilled Ilahna to her very core.

"Very well," the Proclaimer said, almost casually. "I see I cannot reason with you. The boy is useless to me, then."

Before Ilahna could even comprehend what the Proclaimer meant, Madame Elise drew a dagger from her belt. With a flick of her wrist that was as fast as the finger break had been, the First Proclaimer jammed the twisted blade into Jacir's back.

"*NO!*" Ilahna's scream shook the walls and cracked the floor. The flames around them flickered violently, and she felt the ropes at her arms loosen a tiny bit. But still they held, and she could do nothing as Jacir took an unsteady step towards her, mouth agape and eyes wide...before stumbling forward onto the cold floor.

Madame Elise let him fall, and Ilahna watched Jacir's twitching limbs as he tried to crawl towards her stool. The bloody pool around him reflected the firelight, and she heard him try to call her name.

"No! Jacir! NO!" Ilahna shook on her stool, shouting incoherently as she watched her brother's twitching fingers finally still. Her unearthly scream caused the men around Ilahna to totter back a step, but Madame Elise seemed unaffected as she spread her hands, taking a careful step backwards to avoid the growing pool of blood.

"The tonicloran has many properties, my child. It can save him. Now his life is in your hands."

Ilahna wanted to strike the First Proclaimer. Wanted to tear the eyes out of her face. The rage built up in her chest until she couldn't contain it anymore, and finally exploded as she released a bubbling shriek directed at the Proclaimers, Madame Elise, the Betrayer, the Old Gods, and every part of every thread of whatever Tapestry had led to her watching her sweet, wonderful brother bleed out on the floor. The men behind her grasped their heads, and the bonds that tied her wrists finally unraveled into long strings that drifted to the ground behind her back.

Ilahna didn't even notice. She was already next to Jacir, cradling his head, whispering all the things that had comforted him as a child. His mouth moved slightly as he stared up to her, but even

Ilahna couldn't tell if he was looking at her or through her. Watching the door that had always been everywhere and nowhere for him. Then, his eyes unfocused completely, and something in Ilahna's heart broke into a million shattered shards made of moonlight and curses.

"No," she whispered, shaking him through her tears. "No. Jacir. Not like this. I won't let it happen. It can't. I'm sorry. I'm so sorry."

Even as she spoke, Ilahna dug beneath her armor and pulled out the chilled vial she'd held against her breast. It fogged immediately beneath the warmth of her touch. "I'm sorry. I'm so sorry," she repeated into the darkness.

Ilahna barely had time to process a piercing scream of protest from an unknown throat behind her before she popped the cork out of the vial and poured the contents down Jacir's throat.

The silence of the catacombs was replaced by screams.

53

Kaiya felt the threads shift and shimmer across the distance that separated her from the young Faoli. But the thing that tied her to the young boy was not physical, and the ripples that tore through the Tapestry shook the foundations of her understanding of existence nearly to the core. Kaiya staggered as the enormity of the sudden change hit her, as the ever-present tie to the Tapestry was suddenly severed and reforged, over and over again. Kaiya fell to her knees, clutching at the ground, at her head, at anything she could. Distantly, she heard the boy behind her say something, but she could not answer.

Kaiya had lived a long time. She had seen much. Many had accessed the tonicloran since she had learned of it in her youth.

Many had peeked at the Tapestry and its many threads. Many had tried to change it, and a few had even succeeded. But nothing had ever begun to compare to this. Had anyone ever changed the course of time as quickly and easily just by existing? What sort of being was this?

Jacir. His name is Jacir. He is a human child. And you must help him.

There. The sudden understanding of his name, of his existence, grounded Kaiya, and she began to piece her mind back together.

He is young. He is afraid. And he has been thrown to the Tapestry and everything it holds. He will need guidance.

"I am not the one to give it to him," she ground out, the words mixed with bile.

You have to be.

Finally, Kaiya was able to pull the scattered pieces of her mind together enough to shakily reach her feet. Behind her, Eitan was trying to help her up, but she shook him off.

"Faoii! What is going on?" Eitan was yelling over the rushing wind and shrieks of pain and fear coming from the camp. One of the Weavers who had trained with Jacir stumbled towards them through the trees, shrieking as she pulled out her hair in bloody clumps.

"The Tapestry is being destroyed and reformed over and over again. And young Jacir is at the center of it." Kaiya ground out the words, taking another unsteady step.

Eitan looked between Kaiya and the shrieking woman as she stumbled back in the other direction. "Is what was happening to you and… her… happening to him?"

"Worse. Be silent so I may find him."

Kaiya stopped searching for the faint glimmer of silver cords and instead followed the metaphorical volcanoes and earthquakes that shattered the Weave and restitched it in strange, blocky patterns. She shuddered. She had seen something like this once, long ago, when she had killed the Goddess Illindria. She had been shackled beneath the name "Betrayer" from that day forward, and her impact had been much smaller than this.

What was this child?

She supposed that the name people assigned to the little boy's legacy would have to be answer enough. Whether he survived to see it or not.

He must survive. Make sure of it.

There. Kaiya saw the center of the chaos. A maelstrom of tattered threads and a swirling, screaming void. Her head spun just to gaze upon it, and she stumbled to one knee. Somewhere far away, she heard Eitan trying to talk to her again, and she distantly rolled her eyes. He was safe on the physical plane. What did he have to worry about when this terrible existence was beyond his reach? The world he knew would change in its aftershocks, but he would never know the difference. And yet he had the audacity to seem afraid.

Kaiya tried to reach for the young mind at the center of the vortex, but it slipped through her consciousness like water through a sieve. She tried again, and again, but to no avail. She slammed her physical fist against a physical ground she could not see. She would have to build that bridge in a different way. And that meant crossing gaps she'd sworn she'd never bridge again.

But as the Tapestry and all of its thousands of strands surrounding the world restitched itself yet again, she realized she did not have a choice. More and more mages from across the world were falling beneath the strain of the noose the Weave had become. And everyone had some semblance of power now. Soon, there would be no one left, and if Kaiya could not forgive herself for being the death of one being, she would not let Jacir be the death of all of them.

"Grab on to me," she ground out with her mortal mouth even as she used her mind to search for the path she'd take through the ever-shifting Weave. "You're coming with me." She didn't know if Eitan heeded her instructions or not, but she didn't care. With a deep breath, she blinked to the center of the chaos that was already spreading across the empire like wildfire.

Hold on, Faoli. I am coming.

54

Ilahna tried to cradle Jack to her as his shrill shrieks of pain and fear pierced the tunnels. Around her, the Proclaimers had started their approach immediately, eyes hungry to behold the boy who would bring them all that they desired. But now the cloaked figures lay in a semicircle around her, writhing on the ground as they dug at their ears and eyes. Even Madame Elise had fallen to her knees, clawing at the cobblestones with nails that split, leaving behind bloody strands of flesh and muscle.

Ilahna felt something terrible and incomprehensible surge against the stone door at the back of her mind, the one she had so stubbornly refused to open. It surged again, and she focused all of her might on to the barricades she had created and reinforced over a lifetime. The pressure on her mind eased slowly.

"Oh, Jacir. I'm so sorry. What have I done?" With their captors incapacitated, Ilahna scooped her brother into her arms. He writhed and screamed in her grasp, nearly unbalancing her, but she straightened her legs and cradled him to her, staggering towards the corridors that would lead to freedom.

"I'll take you back to the sewers," she whispered to him in the dark. "Or to the Maze. I'll take you somewhere safe. I promise. Just hold on, Jacir. Hold on."

Ilahna didn't want to think about what she would do when she got to the ladder and the trapdoor. What she would do when Jacir's screams filled the streets of Clearwall. How she would escape the Proclaimers that had followed invisible trails through time and space to find them in the forest and return them here. But she didn't question it now. All she could focus on was the brother in her arms who screamed in agony and fear because of her.

She dragged her feet forward, nearly crippled as another surge of power beat against the barricaded doors in the back of her mind. Her focus slipped away. She wasn't even sure which way she was facing. She tried to take another step, and the door bulged again. Again Ilahna reinforced the barricade, piling every bit of stubborn refusal she still had against it. Blood leaked from her nose. What could she do? How was she going to get them out of here? How--? She spun in circles, trying to get her bearings, sobbing when she couldn't find a path.

Suddenly, Eitan was there. Ilahna's legs almost gave out in relief when he appeared beside her, hugging her close and pressing the edge of his sleeve against her bleeding nose, whispering to her in the darkness. Someone else took the screaming burden from her arms, and Ilahna shrieked in protest. She scrabbled for Jacir again.

"Give him back! *Give him back!*"

"Eternal Blade, girl. How are you still so annoying? Calm down." Ilahna was taken aback, and she sagged in Eitan's arms as she finally figured out how to open her eyes.

"Faoii? You're here?" It didn't seem real. Was she crazy? How'd she get here? How did any of them get here?

"Quiet, girl. You've done enough for now. Let me work." The Faoii's face tightened in a grimace, and she got a faraway look in her eyes. Ilahna wanted to demand what was happening, but she bit her tongue when Jacir quieted. Kaiya released a shaky breath. "Grab on to me. I don't even know if I can bring us out of this. I will leave you if I have to."

Ilahna clutched at Kaiya's arm and she suddenly had the feeling she was falling. The air was sucked out of her lungs as everything rushed away from her at a blurring speed that made her head spin sickeningly. She hadn't even realized that she'd closed her eyes, but when she opened them again, there was only blackness and the sound of Jacir's soft whimpers.

Ilahna breathed deeply, trying to calm the quaking in her head and stomach as she heard Eitan dry-heaving somewhere nearby. She recognized the dampness and dank odor of the long-forgotten sewers. The coolness of the air and the familiarity of the haven soothed her, as she tried to get her bearings. Her groping hands found Kaiya's shaking form.

"Faoii?" she asked uncertainly. "Are you all right?" As her eyes adjusted, she saw Kaiya on hands and knees, quaking viciously.

"*Blinking* has never been my strongest suit. Even in my prime, I never brought more than two others through the Weave. And that was when the threads were straight and smooth." The Faoii looked like she would stand, but she suddenly turned away from Ilahna, retching violently onto the worn stones. "See to your brother," she gasped out. "He needs comfort now, though there is little you can do. I need only a minute."

Ilahna's eyes could nearly make out Kaiya's dark skin now, and she was nervous at the greyish pallor the Faoii had taken on. But Kaiya was nothing compared to Jacir, who writhed in a sweaty heap on the slimy floor.

Ilahna crawled towards her brother, pulling him to her and shaking him gently. "Jacir. Jacir! Wake up." In response, Jacir only curled into his sister, his trembling hands grasping at her with weak fingers. Ilahna tried again, to no avail. Finally, desperately, she began to hum a song he'd enjoyed as a baby, and Jacir slowly stilled. Imploringly, Ilahna turned to Kai.

"What's wrong with him? Why won't he wake up?" Ilahna begged, hugging Jacir to her. Kaiya shook her head, looking up at Ilahna through her disheveled white hair.

"Many people have glimpsed the Tapestry before. But it is like seeing it through a reflection. Through a pane of glass. The tonicloran has forced your brother to see it in all its terrible glory. It has thrust the threads into his hands. It is a terrible experience even with proper training. His mind has likely been entangled in the strands of the Weave."

A cold anger filled Ilahna as something clicked into place, and she dug her fingernails into Jacir's limp arms without noticing as she rose to tower over the Faoii. "You saw this coming, didn't you?"

Kaiya nodded once and forced herself to stand. The height difference was nearly staggering, but Ilahna did not change her stance as she raised her chin to meet the Faoii's eyes.

"I do not look upon the Tapestry anymore," Kaiya said. "But even without seeing the threads I knew this was one possible fate for your brother—the strongest Faoli I've ever seen. I had hoped we could avoid this end."

Ilahna opened her mouth to speak, but Kaiya cut her off with a piercing stare. "Do not chide me, girl. You did not even have the strength to peek behind the door. As little as you think I've done, you did far less. I tried to take the tonicloran far from him. I tried to save you all from this fate." The Faoii's eyes flashed green in anger. "Had you even tried, you would have realized that the Tapestry is very real, and very large, and that old deities lurk beneath it. They pull at it, twist it, trying once again to control this world as They once did. They always reach for those few who could survive the tonicloran and set Them free. Now your young Faoli has seen it, and Them, and if he so chooses, he may draw Them forth. Just as the Proclaimers want. They may be misguided, but they are not wrong."

"You could have done it! You could have brought the Old Gods back! Then Jacir wouldn't have to be this way!"

The Betrayer's eyes swirled with a coldness that Ilahna had never seen before, and suddenly she was very afraid. She expected the woman to yell in response, but instead her silvery voice was very quiet, laced with ice and power.

"Listen very carefully, Ilahna Harkins of the Maze. I did not sacrifice everything to free our people just so I could enslave them again. I realized long ago that the loss of one will always be worth the salvation of a thousand."

Eitan, who had been silent until now, suddenly spoke. "If the swirling sound in my head has anything to do with Jacir, then I think there's more than one life at stake here." As he spoke, the buzzing, spinning sensation that had been trapped behind the doors at the back of Ilahna's mind grew in strength. With effort, she shoved it back again. She did not doubt that those in the world who had opened those doors, however slightly, were suffering greatly now.

Kaiya closed her eyes for a moment, the pallor in her face more prominent.

"The Tapestry is in disarray. The young Faoli has more power than anyone I've ever met. He can re-weave the Tapestry in any pattern he chooses. But no one has taught him to use the loom, and there are no Weavers or Gods left to show him how." She paused sadly. "It is not something you can learn without training. Even I had an insane woman in a pit."

Something in the words stirred Ilahna, and she pressed Jacir to her chest as she took another step towards Kaiya. Slowly, fearfully, she offered her little brother up with tears in her eyes.

"Please, Faoii… Jacir has an insane woman, too." Ilahna said quietly, imploringly.

Kaiya stared at the girl for a long moment before doing something Ilahna never would have expected.

The Faoii threw back her head and laughed.

"Yes, I suppose he does."

55

Faoii-Kaiya, the Betrayer and last of the Monastery of the Eternal Blade, swallowed back bile as she knelt next to the still form of Jacir.

No. Faoli-Jacir, now. He has earned his title.

It had been a long time since she had looked directly upon the Tapestry's threads. Decades since she had decided to pluck at some of the strings and try to shape the world in a kinder image than the one she had been born into. It had not worked then. She did not know if it would work now. But the little Faoli before her had a strength that even she had not had when she'd slain a goddess. Perhaps he was strong enough.

"How long has it been since you've done this?" the girl, Ilahna, asked beside her. Kaiya furrowed her brow, trying to remember, even though she had no plans to respond out loud. From the girl's standpoint, it would have been a long time. But she did not see the world as Kaiya did. As Jacir would now. A millennium had passed since she'd last walked the Tapestry's halls. Perhaps more. To Kaiya, it still was not long enough.

She tried to remember the roads that would connect her back to the Weave. Unbidden, her mind flashed back to the first time she had seen the Tapestry. She had been so young. It was too many lifetimes ago. But she remembered it. Every story. Every strand.

If he steals a loaf of bread here, it will force that woman there to go to another store tomorrow. A button on her dress will snag on the counter. The seamstress that sells her a needle and thread will be able to buy food for another day. She will share a bit of wisdom with a pair of twins . . . But the already disheartened baker will begin to hold resentment for other people in his heart. He will pass it on to his son over the next decade . . .

Their reactions shaded other stories, leading to a million other choices. A million other outcomes. She watched as uncountable versions of the unnamed boy's life passed before her. Death at a hundred different hands. Laughter at a million jokes. Love in the arms of a dozen different women. And each choice led somewhere else. A dozen different families. A million different lives. The choices colored generations, all created or destroyed by a single man who remained completely unaware of his impact.

If he meets the tailor's daughter, she will bear him two strong sons. They will become politicians and help shape their countries. But if he goes to the smithy first that day, she will be gone before he meets her, away to deliver her father's wares. Then he will marry one of the women in the next town over, and the tailor's daughter will marry a traveling salesman from . . .

"I'm still not sure I understand," the older boy, Eitan, said from somewhere behind Kaiya, yanking her back from the Weave even from across the centuries. "If he's there, how is he here?" Kaiya wasn't sure how Ilahna would respond, but she almost smiled at Preoii-Vonda's voice across the void:

"No, no! You're using your innate abilities. You have to use me.*"*

"I . . . I can't," Kaiya gasped out, her arms shaking.

"No? And why not? Come on, Faoii! You've already accomplished the impossible just by seeing those fading images! Your mind is there. The next part is easy. Even the brain-dead Croeli can do it."

Even the brain-dead Croeli could do it.

"Whatever happens, do not try to wake us. And if we vanish, do not be frightened." Kaiya's mortal voice echoed through the cavernous sewers where once she and Eili had trained an army. She didn't even feel her body list to the side as she sent her mind across the Weave, following the far-off whimpers of a frightened Faoli who should never have been forced into this position.

She found him, curled on his side next to a deep pool that had not been here when she had last entered this place. The hall had looked like a Faoii Monastery to her. Jacir had constructed the vast expanse with tall stone walls and no ceiling. It looked like the Maze of Clearwall.

Gingerly, Kaiya stepped around the pool and knelt next to the whimpering boy. She saw the edges of a frayed Tapestry clutched in his small fists, the ragged threads writhing like snakes in his palms.

"Faoli. Can you hear me?" The child hiccupped in response and nodded. "Talk to me, Faoli. Let me help you."

"I saw the Weave. I could touch and change every strand. I could go anywhere in it, physically or mentally. Past. Present. Future. It was open to me. And it… moved towards me. Begging to be changed. Begging to be controlled. I tried to keep it as it was. But it's so easy to change too much. If even one thread is different…"

"I know, Faoli. I know." Kaiya tried to be comforting, though that had never been something she was good at. But she remembered how terrible grasping that power had been in the beginning, even though she had only held a fraction of the power this poor child clutched now. Jacir whimpered again.

"I will help you, Faoli. As much as I can. Let me help you hold the threads." The boy shook his head.

"I looked across the entire Weave when I grasped them. There was no one else who could hold them. One a century ago, perhaps. Burnt by scared peasants. One in another decade, on the other side of Imeriel. I don't even know if she'll ever make it to Clearwall. There were a thousand different possible deaths. I watched them all." He shuddered, then whispered, "I don't think you can take them from me, Faoii-Kaiya."

"Then hold them with me. Relinquish some of the burden. You cannot lie here like this forever."

Slowly, Jacir rolled towards Kaiya, and he reached his little hands towards her. She took them in her own, the threads between them.

The power within those strands was staggering. It coursed through her, a million years and lives worth of thoughts, feelings, and memories blasting through her body. She hit one knee, hard, and focused on remaining conscious. As with seeing the Weave, the key was not to watch anything in particular, to just ride the river's course. Eventually, while it did not lessen, the sensation became easier to bear as she shared the burden with Jacir. He sagged in relief and finally struggled to his feet without releasing her.

"Now we're both trapped, though." His voice was thin.

Kaiya tried to smile for him. "In a manner of speaking, yes. But the Tapestry is acting this way because we are at a crossroads, young Weaver. If you make the decision to direct the Tapestry, the Weave will settle."

Jacir shuddered. "I don't want that power. I never wanted that power."

"No. None of us ever do. But, for whatever reason, you are the one who has received it, Faoli. You must decide what you want to do with it, or stand here in indecision for all eternity, while the world struggles on in the vortex of the chaos."

Jacir let out a heart-wrenching sob, large tears welling from his eyes. Kaiya let him grieve the death of whatever it was he felt he was losing and still didn't feel like he was grieving hard enough. He could not possibly know what sadness his future held now.

Eventually the boy blinked away his tears and peered at nothing.

"What is it?" Kaiya asked as kindly as she could.

"I… could cut them all off from the Weave," Jacir replied, watching the strands. "Then it could not control them anymore. They would be free. We would all be free." As he spoke, however, a new river coursed through them, slamming against their skulls as the possibility of change manifested itself. Kaiya saw a world where magic and intuition did not exist. Where people lived their lives like ghosts, drifting through a world without purpose. They made their own ambitions, and they thought they were happy, but always there was the sense of loss and nostalgia for a place none of them had seen. She shuddered. It was like the Clearwall she had seen when only the Faoii had magic. She had slain a Goddess to save them from that.

"You could do that, if you wish," she said, trying to ignore the Tapestry that was trying to stitch itself around them, but Jacir was already shaking his head violently.

"It's terrible! How could they live like that? How could they be happy?" He was shuddering again, and Kaiya squeezed his hands.

"Close your eyes, Faoli," she whispered. Jacir did, and Kaiya hummed a short tune she remembered from long ago, in a life she thought she had forgotten. It was something the Cleroii used to sing when their shieldmates were overwhelmed. Mollie had sung it for her before her first ranked swordfight as a girl. Cleroii-Belle had sung it to help young Faoii fall asleep. She'd hummed it to Lyn in those last moments…

I had forgotten.

As she finished the tune, the Weave quieted, and Jacir's face softened a little.

"It may not last long. See if you can answer my questions without imagining the Weave changing. I know it sounds impossible, but try. What do you want, Faoli?"

"I…" The threads began to writhe again, but with some concentration, he quieted them. "I do not want to have to decide anything at all."

Kaiya smiled, though he did not see. "That is an option, Little Faoli. You can give the decisions to those that crave them."

Without opening his eyes, Jacir turned his face towards the pool, paling at the beasts that writhed before the surface.

"What are they?"

"I think they are Gods. Or beings older than we are, anyway. Perhaps They were the first to make the Weave, or the first to be entwined in it. They were not here when Illindria was, but she spoke of Them. And They have grown more powerful as the Proclaimers have colored the great Tapestry with more and more strands painted in Their image." She paused, considering. "I do not think They are evil, necessarily. And They will become more and more like us over time, should we let Them walk amongst us. By the end, Illindria was nearly human." She did not mention that Illindria had been twisted until Her ambitions had narrowed simply to control. But that had always felt like the most human aspect of Illindria. The mindset that you are the only creature capable of doing things correctly.

Kaiya eyed the things within the pool. "You can give Them everything They want, Faoli. Those things you feel just beneath the Weave are hungry for that power. And They would not be as cruel as even the Proclaimers have been. They would provide for all your friends, all those attached to the Weave. Everyone. And the people of Imeriel would be happy, their smiles attached to upturned strings they have no control over."

"But it… it wouldn't be real."

"It would be real to them. Is that not enough?" Kaiya watched the young boy tremble at the enormity of what she was asking. The dark shapes beneath the pool drew closer to the surface.

"No." he finally mustered. "I… I think it's better to be sad at your own life than happy because of something you had nothing to do with. And… I know it's harder, but there's still a chance for happiness even if we do it ourselves, right?" Kaiya smiled sadly.

"I do not know anymore, Faoli. I believed so, once. But you have seen what became of that optimism." She squeezed his hands, forcing him to look at her again. "If you follow this path, Faoli, the people you are trying to help *will* hate you for it. The people of this world want to be handed an easy life. They will want what you are not giving them."

Jacir shook his head. "It's not the same, though. I have something you didn't have when you made this choice two hundred years ago."

"Oh? And what is that?"

"Ilahna."

Kaiya threw back her head and laughed. "Oh, foolish child. I had a sibling, too. So many people who have changed the threads of the Tapestry have done it with someone at their side. And nearly every sibling in history was far less insolent than yours is."

A ghost of a smile lightened Jacir's face for a moment, and he shook his head. "No. You're not listening, Faoii. You've seen Ilahna speak. The Weave pours through her mouth like a river even though she's dammed it up. She pulls truth from the threads and shakes the ground when someone tries to bury it. And people can *tell.* The urchins trust her, and they don't trust anybody. The rest of Imeriel will, too."

"Your sister won't even crack open the door to see what's she's capable of," Kaiya responded.

"But that's just the thing! She's been able to do all of that with only the faintest wisps of power that have seeped through the door." Jacir looked down. "I know you don't like Ilahna. But I promise, Faoii. She's a good person. The best. We…I can do this with her help."

Kaiya frowned for a moment, then sighed. She could not deny that the girl had stirred the hearts of many people they'd come across. Even hers. Her voice did not offer the commanding presence of Aurelius. It did not make you want to follow her. But it stirred something inside of you. The truth that was buried deep down. It made you want to follow *yourself* by waking up the parts that had lain dormant.

If Kaiya had had Ilahna Harkins' help in the days after the fall of Illindria, it was very possible that things could have turned out differently.

"Kaiya." Jacir said, pulling her attention back to him. "If we are going to break the cycle of what you've already seen, I need Ilahna here. I need to let her hold the threads in her hand like you are now. Can you bring her?"

Kaiya's tight smile was bitter on her lips. "You know she'll never come here, Faoli. Your sister is stubborn and afraid. And she'll never admit either."

"Please. We have to try."

Kaiya looked at the little child holding the unraveled strands of the Great Tapestry in his small, white-knuckled fists. He seemed more exhausted than he'd been when they'd started talking. Finally, she nodded.

"Hold on if you can. Hopefully, I will be back with your brat sister soon."

56

Ilahna crouched in front of Kaiya and Jacir, her gaze crossing between them time and again as she desperately prayed to the Gods she didn't even think existed that one of them would open their eyes. Eitan paced behind her, his footsteps the only sound in the otherwise silent catacombs that made up the twisted sewer. Every now and again he'd put a comforting hand on her shoulder or hum a bit of song, but she didn't move.

Open your eyes. Please open your eyes.

Despite her intense concentration, however, Ilahna wasn't prepared when Kaiya's eyes actually did pop open and the Faoii's long, dark fingers shot forward to grasp Ilahna's wrist. Ilahna stumbled backwards from her crouch, surprised by the intensity in Kaiya's now-green stare. It was piercing and—more surprisingly—desperate.

"Girl. You need to come with me."

Ilahna gathered herself and sat back up, pulling her arm away. "What do you mean 'come?' We can't just leave Jacir here! You said you were going to save him!" Kaiya rolled her eyes and hissed something under her breath as she forced herself to her feet.

"Daft girl. That's why I'm telling you to come with me. For once in your life don't question those wiser than you and just do as you're told." Ilahna raised her chin and narrowed her eyes.

"Where?"

"You wouldn't understand even if I explained it to you. But if you want to help your brother, then you need to go to him. He says he needs you. And I do not have the strength or the heart to dissuade him. Eternal Blade knows why he thinks someone like you could be of any use." The Faoii stumbled for a moment, and on instinct Ilahna reached for her arm to steady her.

"Are you all right?"

"Better than your brother is. And he is only suffering more for every second you choose not to help him."

Help Jacir. That's all Ilahna had ever wanted to do.

She knelt next to her brother's still form. His face was twisted in concentration or pain, and his forehead was beaded with sweat. Gently, she brushed a strand of matted hair out of his face. "I'm here, Jacir. I'm right here."

Kaiya stomped her foot. "Come on, girl! You aren't listening. He needs you. All of you. Not just this physical form you refuse to give up. You are so much more than you've allowed yourself to be. And your stupidity is costing him greatly."

Ilahna stood again, and suddenly she understood. Goosebumps prickled her skin and she felt the door at the back of her mind calling to her, albeit more quietly than it had a minute before. The forces that had surged against the barricade had lessened, and she knew that it was Jacir who was holding them back. For once, it was Jacir who was protecting *her*.

"Ilahna," Eitan approached her slowly, wrapping his arms around her. "Ilahna, you don't have to. I felt the dark things behind the wall. You don't have to face them."

"You do if you want to help your brother. Or have you given up on that already?" Kaiya planted her weight on one foot and put a hand on one hip. Ilahna pulled away from Eitan urgently.

"No! Never!"

"Really? You could have fooled me." Kaiya's voice was filled with scorn. "Come on, girl! Your brother is facing everything you will not even look at! What are you still afraid of? Open the door!" Ilahna closed her eyes, trembling. But the thought of Jacir suffering pushed past everything else.

"Okay," she finally whispered. "Okay. I'll do it."

"Ilahna…" Eitan whispered, putting a hand on her shoulder. Ilahna brought it up to her cheek, then kissed it softly.

"I have to, Eitan. I have to."

"Be careful."

Ilahna focused on the dark door at the back of her mind again. It stood there, towering above her consciousness, unyielding. She tried to picture it opening, tried to pry at the edge. Tried to chisel away its rough surface.

Nothing happened. The door would not budge.

No. No. Had she spent so much time trying to bar the door that now it was unreachable?

She tried again.

Nothing.

"It won't open! I can't do it!" she cried, her hearth thrumming at her ears. She scrambled at the stone, but still it remained closed. "I'm trying! But I can't do it!" Tears streamed down her face and she clutched at Eitan's chest for support. "What do I do? What do I do?" Eitan wrapped his arms around her and hummed into her hair. The Faoii nearly growled.

"Your brother has been opening that door since he was able to walk, and you have been closing it for nearly as long. Think. What made you barricade it so completely?" Kaiya narrowed her eyes at Ilahna when she opened her mouth to respond. "And do not lie to me. There is no time to unravel whatever words come from between your untrustworthy lips."

Ilahna swallowed down the lie she had been about to voice. It wasn't even really a lie, exactly. But it wasn't the full truth. Because she knew the truth was something she would never admit were the stakes not so high.

"I… I was afraid."

"Of course you were. And now that fear is going to drive your brother to death or madness. Are you not glad that you protected your own mind at the cost of his?"

"No! I mean, I didn't!"

"*Then why are you still here?*" Ilahna wasn't prepared for the thundering demand of Kaiya's question, though her voice hadn't risen more than a whisper's worth. She was about to respond with an equally biting retort, but she stopped herself.

Because the Faoii was right.

Jacir needed her, and she was still hiding behind her fear. A fear that, as Jacir had tried to explain to her a thousand times, was unwarranted. A fear that had been fed to her by Proclaimers since her birth. She was still clutching to things that had been ingrained in her over years of tangled schemes, propaganda, and lies. And, while she knew she might never be able to rid herself of them completely, she could at least try. For Jacir, she had to try.

With one more sour glare at the old Faoii, Ilahna reached deep inside herself and relinquished all the fears and hatred that had held her back before. Mentally, she scratched at the door that stood so foreboding in her mind, clawing at it with bloodied and bedraggled fingers, nails peeling away even as her physical body stood straight and still in Eitan's embrace. Part of her screamed that this way lay madness. This would lead to the pyre and all the evil the Proclaimers had warned her about. But It didn't matter. None of it mattered. Not if she could help Jacir.

With another terrified, defiant scream, Ilahna forced the door to yield to her, and it groaned open with a wail of wind and icy rain. Ilahna plunged forward through its gaping maw.

And she *saw.*

The door did not show her the same secrets and visions that had graced her brother. It did not offer her the songs that rose from Eitan's throat or the calming power of clarity Lucinda had. Instead, Ilahna faced all of the truths that she had suspected but refused to voice: that once, the powers behind this door had been siphoned and poured into a singular being, the overrun focused into monasteries that dotted the lands. With the death of Illindria, it had spread across the world, touching each person as a paintbrush touches a canvas. Some beings, like Jacir, received a heavier touch than those like Eitan, but magic had been allowed to gift the world again with one final, terrifying blow.

That was why it was so easy for the Proclaimers to find witches. Why everyone was so afraid. Magic was in everyone, and no one was willing to speak up about it, lest their own secrets come to light. And the Proclaimers thrived on fear. Found those whose magics could twist it. Command it.

All the times she'd tried to draw forth a truth buried under lies and laws. Every time she'd offered comfort and reality to those who had wandered a world woven out of falsehoods. The thousands of epiphanies that Ilahna had experienced in her lifetime, convincing herself it was only luck that her mind worked like it did. The little parts of grand puzzles that had been shifted into place by her mind's eye—these were only small examples of a larger power within her, the one she had always tried to barricade behind the door. But she had seen truth when no one else could, and she had used those little star drops of light to illuminate other people's paths.

Imagine what I could have done if I'd let more than a ray of this in at once? I could have convinced the people to question the Proclaimers so long ago. I could have found ways to help Jacir hone his gifts. I could have helped him find friends that knew his secret. I could have talked openly with Jorthee. Learned all his stories. I could have protected him from the Proclaimers by asking less and knowing more. So much of what has happened is because I tried to scrape the truth out of others' bowls. But I could have known it all. I could have shared it all. We could have lived with more than just snippets passed on through time. I had the power to tie all of Clearwall together with everything we've forgotten if I hadn't been afraid of what questions to ask. I could have changed everything.

Ilahna clenched her fists. There wasn't enough time to focus on everything she had done wrong up until this point. This was the path she had chosen to take, and it had finally brought her to the sense of belonging she had been searching for. The stories and truths of a thousand generations danced around her in a chorus that was both haunting and beautiful. Ilahna was finally who she had always wished she could be. Who she thought she should be. She was something bigger than herself.

"I am Ilahna Harkins, Keeper of Truth."

And the door was open to her.

Ilahna did not walk through that door so much as feel herself first shoved by Kaiya's demanding presence, then pulled by something softer, the direction of her acceleration beyond her control. She thought she should scream or cry or faint with how quickly the world and all within it passed away from her, but before she could completely formulate the thoughts, the journey was over. Ilahna found herself in a room filled with walls open to a blank sky.

Jacir stood in the center of their little tannery, a deep pool at his feet. His face was drawn into a tight grimace, and he had both hands clenched out in front of him. Long strands of silky fibers spilled from between his fingers.

"Jacir?" Ilahna took a tenuous step forward, wary of the Maze that was not the Maze. But when her brother did not answer she shrugged off the uncertainty like a too-large cloak and rushed to him, skirting the dark pool at his feet. "Jacir. I'm here. You asked me to come, so I did." Again, Jacir did not move except for a slight tightening of his hands, and Ilahna became more frantic.

"Please, Jacir. What can I do? What do you need? Talk to me." On instinct, she wrapped her arms around his shoulders, trying to comfort him as she always had in the past. Jacir did not move, and his still upright fists dug into her stomach. Eyes filling, Ilahna pulled away.

"Please. Tell me what you need. I came, Jacir. I'll always be there when you need me."

Imploringly, Ilahna grasped his hands, and the sudden weight of an entire universe slammed into her, ripping her fingers away with cries of fury on a howling wind. She fell backwards, screaming and shaking, her mind shredding into a thousand pieces of things she could not understand.

And still Jacir stood, his eyes scrunched tight, alone in a world devoid of anything except for the strength to keep standing.

With a shaky breath, Ilahna stood again. If Jacir could do this, she would help him. She had to. Because surely no one could bear all of that alone.

With a resolute heart, Ilahna gripped Jacir's hands again.

The torrent of memories and dreams and possible futures crashed into her again, but Ilahna forced steel into her legs and planted her feet. An ocean's worth of things she didn't want to know or see washed against her in wave after bludgeoning wave, each one enough to break bones and minds with ease. But Ilahna felt Jacir's hand underneath hers and held on.

Ilahna did not know how long they stood there as howling gales of future possibilities shredded the edges of her mind. She felt like she was drowning, being pulled apart, and flying all at once. She thought her mind and body would be torn to shreds with all the fear, hope, and strength that the people within the Tapestry held up to her. She didn't think that anyone could face that storm and survive.

The only thing that kept her from utter annihilation, of having her soul destroyed and her mind wiped clean, was the feeling of Jacir's tiny, frail hands holding her own. Those digits became her beacon. The familiar calluses became the rock on which she tried to build and rebuild her reality. Through the chaos, her senses still felt the familiar contours: The scar he had gotten on his finger when the swipe of an angry merchant's knife had lashed out at his escaping wares. The indent from when he broke his hand in an unlucky fall four summers before. She even noticed the new, slightly askew tilt of the finger that Elise had broken, as though months of healing had already taken place within the few hours of the tonicloran's effects.

At last the torrent fell into the background. A raging tempest, still, but now they stood in the calm eye of the storm. Ilahna opened her eyes to look at her little brother. His face was slightly less troubled than before.

"Jacir? Can you hear me?" Finally, he nodded. Then slowly, so slowly, he opened one eye.

"Lana! You came. I can't believe you came!" He opened his eyes completely and the relief in his voice filled Ilahna with shame. Had she ever known that this is what he needed more than protection and talk of hiding, she wanted to believe that she would have flung open those doors long ago. But she remembered the fear that had held her back only a few minutes before and the truth in her soul reminded her that she had not been ready then.

But she was now. "I'm here," she whispered to Jacir. "I'm here. What do you need? What can I do?"

Jacir stood in trembling silence for a long moment. "There are more paths we can take from here than there are bricks in the

Maze's walls, Ilahna. We can take any of them. We can do anything." He squeezed her hands, the threads still between them. "We can bring back the Gods or give humans more power than they would know what to do with. We can shift everything in a thousand different ways."

"Is that what you want?"

Jacir shook his head. "I just want to fix what's broken. And let people know that they can keep fixing broken things without other people telling them how."

Ilahna smiled, despite herself. "That sounds exactly like what the world needs."

"That's what Kaiya tried to do. But she couldn't do it alone. I…I need your help. If I open up a current to all the people connected to the Weave—connected to us—will you talk to them? Will you help me convince them that we need to fix this? By ourselves. That we need to stop waiting for Gods and miracles?"

"Why me, Jacir? You're the one who sees everything so clearly. You could do this."

Jacir tried to smile. "Come on, Ilahna. We've known my entire life that no one knows what I'm talking about until you translate."

Ilahna smiled too, and the Tapestry around them fluttered in a nonexistent and pleasant breeze, its colors shining and vibrant. Her heart lighter, she nodded.

"Okay, Jacir. Let's show Imeriel the truth."

57

It took several tries before Jacir could help to coax Ilahna across the web without her pulling out of the trance in fear or surprise. Her self-preservation kicked in automatically when her mind was pulled apart in a trillion directions, despite his gentle coaxing.

Ilahna stood, panting, and gripped his hands again.

"I'm sorry, Jacir. I'm trying."

Jacir was pale and weak looking, but he smiled. "I know. Let's try again."

Finally, slowly, Ilahna was able to swallow her fear and bile and, with Jacir's guidance, crept across the Weave, spreading herself across the infinite threads still gripped between their hands.

With each new mind she reached, Ilahna felt a shade of the emotions that made up Imeriel. There was so much anger and distrust. So much disgust at both outside forces and at oneself. But mostly there was an… emptiness. A sense of foreboding that sucked everything else out of people's minds except for the gaping chasm that all the people felt at their feet, but no one saw. Everyone knew an unstoppable change was coming, and the fear and dread was nearly palpable. But there were also the tiniest pinpricks of hope in the darkness.

Ilahna whispered into the pinpricks of hope, encouraging them to swell. She had been waiting for this spark her entire life. She knew there could be better futures on the horizon. But she had never guessed that her words would start it all.

Jorthee's words reached her from far away. *The Proclaimers always say that your tongue is the first step towards the flames. And that's true. But I want you to be very aware that the fires lit by words are stronger and brighter than anything the Proclaimers have ever built.*

Ilahna hoped that Jorthee would be proud of her if he could hear her now.

"People of Clearwall and all of Imeriel. I know you can hear me. All I ask is that you listen. The Proclaimers will tell you that this magic you are experiencing is evil. That you can hear me now because I am a witch. They will tell you to hide from those pieces of yourself you've kept secret for years and decades. They will make you fear and hate and bend to their control. But the truth is, Imeriel, if you can hear me, then you have magic within you. And that is wonderful. It's beautiful. And you should have never been told to be ashamed of it.

"I know it's hard. I know you're scared. But even as you cower at this knowledge, you've known it to be true your entire lives. You need to understand that we don't have to be afraid of symbols or magic or Old Gods or witches. And I don't care about what the Proclaimers will call me or what they'll say.

"Because here's what I care about: I care that every single one of us has watched someone we love die on the pyre. I care that children in the Maze have always had effigies to burn instead of real dolls. I care that I don't know how to read, that every opportunity to learn about the past has been stolen from me, and that I learned the word for hate before I learned the word for love. I care that the temples used to be libraries and that I don't know where we even come from because every record of those days has been destroyed. I care that I am so afraid right now, and all I'm doing is saying that we have a right to know about our history. Our heritage. Our homes. Each other. I care because I realize now that I was never allowed to care about anything before—just trained to hate and fear and cower. And I am *done*."

Ilahna took a breath, trying to stop the shaking in her voice. Jacir squeezed her hands and the crystal of power formed in her gut. From somewhere across the Weave she could hear Eitan singing, encouraging her, his love and pride evident. She pushed on, stronger than before. "We have to take back all the things we have a right to. The things that have been stolen from us. And we need to do it now, before it's too late. I know that there are people out there who once learned to read. Who learned of the past through word of mouth from their parents and elders. Storytellers and ancients who haven't had the truth burned out of them yet. I had someone who could have taught me. I should have asked him more. I should have cared when I had a chance. We cannot lose those who are left. They need to be allowed to teach, and the rest of us need to be allowed to learn."

She took a deep breath. "I know you are afraid. I know you think that just knowing or thinking these things will get you killed. But if we continue to do nothing, then we will have no future except for an ending on the pyre. We'll rot here in obscurity until the Proclaimers have enough call to burn us as witches. Our past will be gone forever, lost for future generations that only have ashes in the air to remember. Stolen by those who pretended they were doing what was right."

Her words were coming out in a flurry now, and the crystal built up, pouring from her lips as she spoke. "We can't even see what we've lost, anymore. But I know you all feel it, deep in your hearts. I know that fear and hatred and lies cover it, but we have more than this life we've been forced to live. We deserve more than this. Our ancestors and descendants deserve more than this. You know it. Have always known it. It is time to prove it."

Ilahna felt her message spread over the Weave like a wave as Jacir directed it forward, and at first she was dismayed as people drew back or even bristled at her words. Dread filled her as she realized that they were too late. The Proclaimers had dug in too deep. Had convinced people too thoroughly. Even though she had always known that the people of Clearwall were afraid, she had assumed it was because they thought they were outnumbered. Because they thought that they would be cut down if they tried to rise. But here they were all attached by the Weave. Everyone was caught in the same delicate tangles. They had to know that they were no longer alone. Surely there was strength in numbers?

But that wasn't the problem. Maybe it had been once, but the winds had long since shifted. Whether they had just said the same thing to themselves over and over enough times that they truly believed it or too many dissenters had been lashed to the pyres to tip the balance, the people of Imeriel no longer wanted to stand up and retake what they had lost. They no longer wanted to fight back. They were ready to die beneath this shadow they had convinced themselves resembled the sun.

Ilahna's heart dropped, and her eyes filled with tears. She clenched her fists so tightly around the strands that she could feel blood beneath her nails. They were too late. There was nothing left of Clearwall to save.

Then, softly, a faint cry of protest rang out across the strands. At first it was barely loud enough to be heard, but it gathered strength as more people joined in the rising tumult. Ilahna strained to hear, and Jacir pulled at the threads that held the discordant notes. The voices were filled, not with hope as Ilahna thought would be elicited from her battlecry—but rage. A scream of gut-wrenching fury.

It is not fair!

The cry rose into a shriek as more voices joined the chant, and Ilahna felt their screams of protest in her veins. A cacophony of pent up demands and cries of disgust.

We did not ask for this!

You expect us to fix your mess?

We did not start this!

We deserve more than this!

You brought us to this!

How dare you give up?

Do you not care?

The voices rose across the Weave, filled with anger and hatred and a desire for change so strong that Ilahna could imagine the people behind the voices tearing down entire cities brick by crumbling brick. They screamed their rage and disappointment. Their sense of abandonment. Under all of it was a cry of despair as the voices stepped into a fight they should not have been ready to face and take actions they should never have been forced into. Ilahna's heart tore for them as her soul matched their cries. Because she knew their hurt. She, too, had lived it.

From across the Weave, it was the children of Imeriel who rose to Ilahna's call. The urchins and orphans who had grown up with magic inside them and a society that had done everything it could to keep them from rising to the potential within that power. The children who had grown up in fear of what they were, and without a place to speak about what made them who they were and what they were worthy of. Who were taught to hate themselves and all people like them, because no one had ever bothered to ask the new generation what they thought, and killed those who showed their true selves without first asking for permission.

Ilahna could not blame the urchins as they gathered in strength, screaming across the Weave. Those who had discovered the power inside them drew upon those innate abilities, prepared to fight a war their parents had thrust upon them and then forfeit. Parents that no longer cared what would happen to the world they'd carved out of fires and fear.

Ilahna was bolstered by the strength of the voices that were not yet tainted by the sewage-laced propaganda of the Proclaimers and Madame Elise. They had not been dampened by the fear that the others still wrapped around themselves like a cloak. Maybe the children still had a chance, and she cursed the world that had forced them into a situation where they had to find out. She hated that it was necessary as she whispered across the Weave, letting Jacir direct her words only to the voices that cried out in protest and dismay.

"I hear you. And you are right. This isn't fair. It's not right. We should never have been forced to face this. But we have. For those in Clearwall, meet us in the temple courtyard. For those outside the walls, prepare for the waves that will follow. It's time we reclaim our future."

With the path of the Tapestry set, Jacir finally released the strands, and it spun forward into oblivion, weaving itself into something infinite and beautiful.

Neither urchin tried to look at what was coming, content in knowing that they would meet it head-on.

58

Ilahna, Jacir, Eitan, and Kaiya must have looked small and alone as they walked into the empty courtyard that surrounded the great temple at the center of Clearwall. Once, this had been a place of learning and thought, but it had been desecrated and twisted into a place of blind obedience and fear. Ilahna thought it was fitting that everything should end here.

The Proclaimers waited at the top of the stairs leading to the library. Madame Elise stood rigid in the center, staring down at the approaching group with cold eyes, her armor glinting in the moonlight.

"Children. You return." Madame Elise's voice billowed from her mouth like the smoke from her pyres, and it made Ilahna's skin crawl. "You have tried to change the course of the Gods' plans for far too long. All of that, and this tiny group is what you have to show for your trouble? You should have known that no one would back your evil callings. Even after all of your desperate actions, you are still alone."

Ilahna heard other Proclaimers marching through the streets of Clearwall, calling for the citizens to come to the courtyard. Ilahna realized for the first time that this tradition was not only used as a show to drive fear into the people, but to alienate those being sentenced. On the other side of the courtyard, she saw other Proclaimers erect the pyre and its four stakes. She took a deep breath and clenched her fists.

"What you have done is wrong, Madame Elise. The gifts of the world are not evil. And we will not let you kill us and shame us for who we are."

"Oh? And what are you if not just impetuous children?"

A quiet whisper called to Ilahna from across time. The voices from beyond the door whispered a phrase that had once meant something more than witches or magic or soldiers. A phrase that evoked the strength of unity. The call to be something greater than what you were when you stood alone.

Ilahna took a deep breath and looked Madame Elise in the eye as she reclaimed something that had been corrupted by an untold number of generations.

"We are Faoii."

Madame Elise threw back her head and laughed. "Little girl, look around you. The people of Clearwall do not want the change you are trying to bring. They know the danger in your words, the evil in your thoughts. We are stronger when the sickness is purged. They know this."

People were beginning to gather in the square, now. Ilahna watched the men and women she had known her entire life step forward with their torches and their apathy. But she also saw more than that. Tanner. Lucinda. The surviving members of the resistance appeared in the crowd, dispersed but ready. Even the man who'd attacked her in the Maze, whose jaw she'd broken months before stood with a glimmer of hope in his eyes. She squared her shoulders as smaller figures appeared on the roofs and in the alleyways that had been their playgrounds all their lives. Many of them dropped from their perches to fan out behind Ilahna, small fists gripping sticks and rocks. Many carried eggs.

Madame Elise's eyes were calculating as they passed over the groups of small bodies. She clicked her tongue.

"This is what you bring against the servants of Gods? Untrained whelps raised only on the lies of Faoii witchcraft? Oh, child. You tried to help these poor urchins with your sickening words, but you have only turned them against what is right. You've twisted them away from their own people. You have created monsters."

Something snapped inside Ilahna, and a wind picked up around her as she clenched her fists. "Us? You dare to call us monsters?" Ilahna's green eyes sparked with a deep-set fury she could barely contain. "We are *children*. And you have brought us to this war." The urchins behind her braced themselves, squaring their ragged shoulders. Ilahna's heart lurched at their determination, and she spit the next word at the Proclaimers in the square. "You're right. No one should lead children into war. No one should make them meet this kind of fate head-on. But I wasn't the one who did that." Ilahna drew her fantoii and swept it in a wide arc, gesturing to the town and its high, foreboding walls trapping its shrunken, hollow people.

"We are children. We should never have had to clean up the mess your generation created. We should never have had to lose our adolescence in a desperate attempt to collect the broken pieces of our lost future. The future that you carelessly flung against the cracked cobblestones we've used as beds. We should never have had to join this war. But we did. Because you were the ones that decided to leave us a world where death and sorrow and fear was the only outcome. And we had to decide that, if you were planning to let our hearts and minds and souls die regardless, then at least the sword is a more merciful end." The swarm of dirty, unfed bodies bristled behind her. "Clearwall will be ours sooner rather than later, Proclaimer. We will fight for it."

Madame Elise shrugged. "Then you will all burn together." She raised her hands above her head as she stepped onto her dais at the top of the stairs. "People of Clearwall! This sickness must be cleansed with fire! Bind the Faoii to their stakes. For the safety of all we are! For the Old Gods! For the greatness of Clearwall!"

"No! For the chance of what Clearwall will be!" Ilahna cried, raising her fantoii into the air.

And for the first time, it *screamed.*

Ilahna's blade sounded like a choir of angels. Like demons howling in the night. It was the strength of every truth and battlecry that had ever passed her lips. It was made of the fear and the despair she'd felt every time she'd heard Jacir's far-away voice talk about things he shouldn't know. It was a beacon for everything that could yet be and a spotlight on every injustice that had occurred under this tyranny.

For a moment Faoii-Kaiya, standing next to Ilahna, only stared in shocked silence at the blade's response. But then, with a smile and piercing gaze of her own, she drew her own fantoii. The blade did not scream in fury and loss as it had when Ilahna had heard its song before. Instead, it harmonized with a song of renewal and rebirth. Of flowers returning after a long winter. Or tyrants falling after too long a reign.

As one, Ilahna and Kaiya surged forward, and the surrounding mob of people rushed after them as the dissidents released their own haunted battle cries. The mazers of Clearwall leapt from their perches with little more than sticks and rocks. Eggs flew from rooftops, and fires spread across the cobblestones as the silk strand moss inside unfurled.

The people of Clearwall flocked to do Madame Elise's bidding, but there was hesitation. They'd been told their entire lives that eventually this battle would come, but instead of facing the witches with long braids and sharp swords, the enemy they had expected, their opponents were only children. A part of Ilahna held hope. Maybe these people who had once lived on something other than hate and fear would stand down in a war where children had been asked to raise arms in defense of their own futures.

"I don't know what I expected to come from a brainwashed and terrified city, but I knew, even then, that if Clearwall was going to change there had to be a turning point. And if it wasn't the pale faces of our own dead children, I don't know what else it could be."

Jorthee's forlorn words trickled across her mind as she clashed against one of the Proclaimers that separated her from Madame Elise. She was about to press her advantage, but Jacir's scream stopped her.

"Trisha! Watch out!"

Ilahna spun, time standing still. She saw the tiny, catlike girl in the crowd. Watched her hurl an egg in Madame Elise's direction with all her strength. Watched her fall limply onto the cobblestones when someone bashed her small head in with a frying pan. Not even a real weapon. The improvised arsenal of farmers and housewives who, Ilahna finally realized, also should have never been forced into this war. But they had arrived here by their inaction. They would have to live with the consequences of all they had and hadn't done.

And that included the lifeless body of the child now sprawled in the center of the square. Her blood dripping from a skillet that would be used to cook eggs for someone else's child the next morning. Unquenchable fires from the silk strand moss slithered towards her, sizzling the blood that pooled around her disheveled curls.

The battlefield seemed to freeze for a moment, an unseen impact radiating outward from a little dead girl with tangled hair and unblinking eyes. Then, there was a wail from the man who had felled her, and things resumed more quickly than before.

Some of the people in the square fought harder, determined to bring back the life they'd had the day before when death was not so prevalent. Others dropped their tools and makeshift weapons, broken by the sight of what their lives and world had become. But the urchins—those who had not lived with the privilege of a home and who'd faced the constant fear of persecution every day of their waking lives—refused to draw back now. Refused to let things return to what they had been. "Normal" wasn't good enough.

Over the lifeless body of Trisha, Belinda and Corey screamed their fury and threw more eggs. The battle raged on.

"Girl. Stay with me." Kaiya's voice cut through the din, and Ilahna straightened her shoulders and spun around the Proclaimer in front of her, sliding her fantoii across the back of his knee. He toppled with a scream, and she shifted her weight until she was back-to-back with Kaiya, their swords still screaming in the darkness.

"Eitan! Whatever happens, protect Jacir!" she shouted into the night. Eitan nodded, twirling his hammer in his right fist before swinging it overhead at a man wielding a pair of shears. Jacir stared straight through the man as he fell, his face serene. Ilahna briefly wondered what he was seeing through on the Weave.

As Ilahna and Kaiya circled slowly, back-to-back, they fought their way to the temple steps where Madame Elise watched the battle with steely eyes and a stern grimace. But still she did not draw her blade.

Here, next to the temple, most of their foes were Proclaimers, defending Madame Elise and the seat of all their power. Part of Ilahna was grateful as more of the resistance fighters she had met in the forest forced their way to this clump of armored bodies and clanging steel. They faced the Proclaimers, leaving the children to fight against the untrained and terrified masses—many of whom were already beginning to drop their makeshift weapons or turning to flee into the crumbling streets of Clearwall. But the backup still wasn't enough, and the terrified, pained screams of both children and adults drowned out the sound of Ilahna and Kaiya's swords.

But another sound rose from the din. Eitan's singing. Battle songs of healing and strength. And there, from deep in the crowd but getting closer—Aurelius' gong-like voice shouting encouragement.

The other side had their own mages, it seemed, and nothing about the Proclaimers hiding their own magic as they cut down "witches" surprised Ilahna. But her people had something that the Proclaimers didn't. Through it all, Jacir's and Lucinda's gentle fingers quietly stroked the strands of the Eternal Tapestry, sending quiet messages across the Weave, helping their warriors to form ranks and strategize even in the darkness of the temple square. Even the children were more unified under their administrations. Slowly, the tide of battle began to turn.

The Proclaimer at the bottom of the steps screamed her fury as Ilahna and Kaiya approached, and Ilahna ducked beneath her swing, raising her blade to parry the blow. Behind her, Kaiya slid her fantoii out from between another man's ribs and spun around Ilahna's left side to cleave off the Proclaimer's outstretched arm. She fell, screaming, to the cobblestones that were already slick with blood.

Three other Proclaimers, the last vanguards protecting the steps to the great temple, rushed at Ilahna and Kaiya, their swords raised. Both women dropped into readiness, but their foes were met instead by a group of revolutionists that swarmed in from the sides, screaming for freedom from tyranny. Aurelius was with them, and he forcefully shoved aside one of the heavily-armored Proclaimers with his remaining arm, clearing a path to the temple steps.

"Go!" he yelled above the battle, forcing power into his words. But his encouragement was not necessary. Ilahna did not need to be persuaded.

Ilahna and Kaiya took the stairs two at a time, and the ever-stoic Madame Elise watched them from the top. They slowed as they neared the landing on which she stood, and she glared at them with cold, calculating eyes.

"Quite the show you've put on, Faoii brat," Elise said, iron in her voice. "It is all for naught, of course. You are too young to remember why I control this city."

With an elaborate flourish of her cloak, Elise brought her massive sword up and planted her feet in a powerful stance. And Ilahna *felt* it. The strength and power that coursed through Elise and her sword was so similar to the silver cords that bound her arm to her fantoii. But it was different. This was a cold, icy power built out of a determination and hatred that Ilahna couldn't even begin to comprehend. It chilled her soul, and Ilahna found herself unable to move against that unstoppable force that waited at the top of the stairs.

This is why the first riot quieted so quickly. Why they were afraid to try again.

Ilahna tried to break free of the terror that bound her. Tried to move her feet. Behind her, the sounds of fighting had silenced as everyone froze in the presence of Elise's dark gifts.

Ilahna fought the force with everything she had. *Move. You have to move!* But her body refused to respond.

Next to her, Faoii-Kaiya also struggled to regain control. The woman's entire body shook with exertion. As Ilahna watched from the corner of her eye, a bubble of truth rose from her soul. She stopped fighting her legs and instead focused on her lips. The truth rolled off her tongue more easily than she'd expected.

"Faoii. You've toppled Gods and changed worlds. You're not going to be undone by a single woman's sword, are you? You're the Betrayer."

Kaiya cast a dark look in Ilahna's direction, but the words were evidently the fuel she needed.

"Impudent girl," Kaiya snarled as she closed her eyes. A rush of power exploded from her, and the Faoii broke free from the icy prison that held her, falling forward onto the base of the steps. Madame Elise's eyes darkened.

"Of course it would be you to face me, Kaiya the Betrayer. None other could expect to face the might of the Gods' Herald."

Kaiya released a chilling battlecry as she bolted up the last few steps, sword at the ready. Her cry and her fantoii's scream twisted around each other in dark chilling notes of ancient pain. Madame Elise parried her blow with ease, and the two women clashed and spun at the top of the temple steps in a flurry of parries and blocks.

If she can do it, so can you. Move. You have to move.

Damn it, Ilahna! Move!

Ilahna screamed internally, trying to draw all the power inside of herself to burst through the frigid prison. But still the power of Elise's domain over war and death held Ilahna rooted, and she shook as she tried to step forward, inching her boot towards the steps. Behind her, the silence was absolute. Ilahna shuddered. Elise had never ruled. She had controlled.

The fight in front of the temple raged on, the two most powerful fighters in Clearwall clashing in the light of the pyre. But Kaiya seemed to be tiring. Her attacks were a fraction less fluid, her parries barely fast enough. Elise had the advantage, fueled by self-assurance and war magic, and she pressed against the Faoii's attacks, drawing thin streaks of blood as she forced her towards the steps again. Again, Ilahna tried to push herself forward. Again, she failed.

Then, a quiet note rose from behind her. She felt the support and pride in that single lonely tone, and felt it wrap around her like a warm hug. The song continued, and Ilahna recognized it as one Eitan had often led in the resistance camp. One of the many symbols of camaraderie they had all adopted around the fire night after night.

Yes. Eitan! Sing!

He did, and slowly… oh, so slowly… other members of the resistance began to add their voices to the chorus, barely capable of moving their lips around the oppression of the icy grip of Elise's war magic. But they tried, each giving what they could. Slowly, Madame Elise's hold began to weaken.

Ilahna had always known that the Proclaimer's strength came from isolating those who could stand against her. But none of them were isolated anymore.

A ghostly whisper snaked its way to Ilahna's ears. *You cannot stop the choir.* It surprised her that the whisper came in Kaiya's voice. A young Kaiya's voice from long ago.

Kaiya.

The Faoii was still moving, but her legs wobbled. She bled from a dozen superficial wounds. Ilahna's heart twisted at the sight of her shaking sword and face of grim determination. But they both knew that it was only a matter of time until she weakened. As Ilahna's heart filled with the need to help the Faoii, pushed by the song that she had sung around a dozen campfires, the invisible shards of ice around her legs began to crack.

Even Madame Elise's face paled when Ilahna shattered the spell holding her in place. She took a step up the stairs. It was enough for Kaiya to find firmer footing away from the steps, and Elise tried to find a stance where she could watch both of her adversaries at once.

Ilahna didn't let her. As Kaiya swung again, forcing Elise to parry, Ilahna darted up the last few strides that separated them. Elise spun, her breastplate scraping against the tip of Kaiya's sword as she rotated around the outstretched fantoii. As she reached the height of her spin, she snapped her long, heavy blade outward with an impossible swiftness. It swished towards Ilahna's head, and the urchin hit her knees, sliding beneath it, though only just.

A normal fighter would have wasted precious seconds scrambling back to their feet, but Ilahna had spent her entire life in alley fights and the tight quarters of the Maze. As she slid past Elise's knees, she extended her fantoii, clipping the First Proclaimer right above her polished greaves. Madame Elise snarled and spun towards Ilahna, but Kaiya pulled her attention back, and Ilahna flipped back onto her feet, circling behind Elise with careful steps.

They fought like this, turning warily and dividing Elise's efforts, with Kaiya using her mastery at swordplay to keep the Proclaimer's attention while Ilahna jumped sporadically across the marble steps and dais. Madame Elise growled as she parried another of Kaiya's blows, simultaneously raising her gauntleted fist to shove Ilahna backwards as the urchin brought her booted foot down against Elise's pauldron.

Elise had been so focused on Kaiya as the greater threat that she had, until now, given Ilahna little more than a passing glance during the fight. Ilahna had succeeded in drawing a series of superficial wounds over what exposed skin she could see across Elise's body. Now, however, as Ilahna prepared to somersault away from Elise again, the First Proclaimer suddenly shifted her focus, yanking Ilahna downwards by the ankle before slamming her bodily onto the marble steps.

"Stay down, wretched girl."

Stunned, Ilahna tried to suck air into her lungs as the First Proclaimer stepped around her crumpled body like water sliding around a rock. Blood from an untold number of wounds dripped from Elise's breastplate and stained her white cloak as she turned her full attention to Faoii-Kaiya.

Kaiya did her best as Ilahna finally remembered how to move her legs and scrambled back onto her feet, pushing past the pain and dizziness. But the older Faoii was already tiring. Her movements were just a hair too slow. Ilahna tried to pick up her sword again and rejoin the fray in time, but already knew that it was too late. They both saw what was coming just before Elise sidestepped deftly and sunk her giant blade deep into the Faoii's shoulder.

The song of Kaiya's blade fell silent in the wake of the Faoii's piercing scream.

Ilahna's blood ran cold, and she met Elise's eyes as the Proclaimer turned to face her, the gruesome, blood-soaked sword flashing menacingly in the moonlight. Ilahna understood the glint in her eye. Even a trained Faoii could not beat the Proclaimer. There was no warrior that could match her.

But Ilahna wasn't a warrior. She was a mazer.

How many times had she plotted how she would surmount this temple and its jagged, broken face? A smile shone across her face as she squared with Madame Elise, planting her feet determinedly… before she spun on her heel to sprint in the opposite direction.

More out of instinct than conscious decision, Elise pursued her prey, driven by the need to end the girl that had cut down so much of her authority in front of so many. Ilahna picked up her pace, her trained eyes already seeing the faintest footholds in the column nearest her. Two steps up, and she spun and leapt to the next column that towered over Madame Elise.

For a normal person, even an urchin of Clearwall, it would have been too far. But Ilahna had grown up in the Maze. She had practiced in armor on roofs and trees. She was so much more than a soldier. And Madame Elise never should have forgotten that.

Ilahna's foot struck the opposite pillar, and below her, Madame Elise had to slow in order to spin towards her new location. It was enough. Ilahna was already pushing off from the column with all of her might, aiming *down.*

Madame Elise released an unearthly howl when Ilahna landed on top of her, knocking her sprawling against the alabaster floor. The Proclaimer's sword clanged as it tumbled down the steps and into the silent square below.

Ilahna knew how to fall as well as she knew how to climb, and she rolled to her feet with ease, her sword pressed against the back of Elise's neck as the Proclaimer lay stunned, her face pressed into the blood at Ilahna's feet.

"I concede," the First Proclaimer finally whispered, but a smile crept into her voice. "Are you prepared to finish it, little girl? In front of everyone? In front of your brother?"

Ilahna pushed her blade a little further into Elise's neck, drawing a bead of blood. A pale and shaky Kaiya stepped up behind her, clutching one shoulder, her braid undone.

"End it, girl. Make all of this worth it. This is what you wanted, is it not?"

"I only wanted Clearwall to be led by someone who cared about the people," Ilahna growled to the Proclaimer. She remembered how callously Elise had driven the dagger into Jacir's back. The way she'd lashed people to the pyre over braided hair and worn paint without blinking. The fear she and all of Clearwall had felt every time those thin, claw-like fingers had moved towards the hilt of her sword. "And that wasn't you, Madame Elise. It should never have been you."

Ilahna's breath came out in ragged gasps, sweat seeping into her eyes. She pressed her blade deeper into the First Proclaimer's neck, and a thin line of fresh blood dripped onto the shining breastplate. Something about the crimson droplets stopped her, and she had to forcefully remove the memory of Jacir's blood from her mind. It was so… human. Ilahna's shoulders shook as she resisted the overwhelming urge to decapitate the First Proclaimer and set her head on a stake in front of the temple for all to see. It was what the Proclaimer would have done. She looked up into the crowd. It was what any of them would have done.

Even now the mob of Clearwall watched her eagerly, enthralled by this new drama in the temple square, their eyes still reflecting the excitement of the pyres. Ilahna shuddered. They had grown too used to death. They had all grown too used to death.

"This life is not mine to take," she finally yelled across the square. "That decision is for the true leader of Clearwall. I call upon Aurelius, heir to the Starlit Throne!"

She felt the power in her voice. The tendrils of silver and light that accompanied words that she knew in her heart were true. The people of Clearwall must have heard it, too, because no one protested as Aurelius walked up the temple steps with a stately grace. The revolutionists that had been following him for years knelt without hesitation, and after a moment, the other people of Clearwall followed suit.

The remaining Proclaimers stood amidst the sea of kneeling bodies, staring in shock at the still-prone body of Madame Elise. Then, slowly, they, too, staggered to their knees.

Ilahna removed her sword and hauled Elise up with all her strength. The Proclaimer did not resist, and from her knees she lifted her chin to watch Aurelius approach. "Well, Your Majesty," she sneered, "what will you do? Do you require even more blood to be spilled in order to quench your thirst?"

For a moment, Aurelius' face was purple with rage and he moved behind her and wrenched the Proclaimer's head up by the hair with his remaining hand. "Look at this, Proclaimer. Look at what you've created. What you've done." Madame Elise's eyes roamed over the broken, bloody bodies scattered before the temple. Proclaimers. Peasants. Children. Dozens of corpses lit by the still-burning pyre and tendrils of silk strand moss. All around them were the wailing cries of the injured and dying. The cries of children who had never had anyone to dry their tears was the most haunting, because you could tell in their sobs that they expected no comfort. Aurelius lifted her head another inch, shaking her entire head with his fury. "This is all on your hands, Proclaimer."

Madame Elise squared her shoulders even from her kneeling position. "Some sacrifices are necessary to cleanse the whole. We must face hard decisions in order to sanctify this place for the return of the Gods."

"You still want to bring the Old Gods back?" Ilahna cried, her fists shaking. Madame Elise turned her eyes toward her.

"Of course. If not, then everything I have done—everything that we've accomplished and all of those precious lives that were lost—would have been in vain." She looked back over the crowd of bodies and the weeping people huddled in the shadowy edges of the square. "How do you not see that this is the result of a Godless existence?"

"I can show you." For the first time, Jacir rose from his kneeling position at the edge of the forum. His voice was quiet, but his back was straight and his footsteps sure. "This place you want to return to. I can show you what it was like before the Betrayer killed Illindria. And, if you decide that that is where you want to return to, I will help you make it happen."

Ilahna, Aurelius, and Kaiya simultaneously let out cries of protest, but Jacir only held up one hand. "Without Madame Elise, I wouldn't be able to manipulate the Weave at all. She deserves to see how her actions have colored the strands." He stepped up the stairs and reached his hand out to the First Proclaimer. "Come with me. Let me show you."

Aurelius frowned and looked between Jacir and Ilahna. But Ilahna had learned to trust her brother even more than she trusted herself. She nodded. Reluctantly, Aurelius released Madame Elise's hair and took a step back.

Madame Elise glared at Jacir's hand expectantly, as though she could read the description of a trap in his palm. Then she turned her eyes upward to match his gaze and, without breaking eye contact, placed her hand in his.

The two of them vanished from the temple steps.

59

Ali stared at the desolate city, where its citizens scurried through the streets without looking up. The sun was high in the sky, and she could tell that it was summer, but the surrounding air was… cold. Chilled in a way that had nothing to do with temperature.

"What is this place? Why does it feel so hollow?"

"This is Clearwall. In the days of Illindria. One of your Old Gods." Next to her, the witchy child Jacir knelt in the garden they stood in, and he pressed his palm against the earth. "Do you feel the difference?"

Ali pressed her palm down, too, but felt nothing of the life that had reverberated beneath her father's fields. The emptiness pricked at her fingers.

"It feels so dead. How does anything grow here?"

"Because it's not life and death you've felt all around you all this time," Jacir said softly, taking her hand. "It is the magic that seeped into the world when Illindria fell." He squeezed her hand as a tall woman on a dark horse passed them in the Maze. Ali recognized the long, black braid and pale green eyes.

"The Betrayer!" she hissed, reaching for a sword that wasn't there. She frowned.

"You know, you actually could kill her here, if you wanted to. Create all the timelines that you tried to forge. In a few minutes she will be chained by King Lucius IV and, tomorrow, she will be hunted by Croeli-Thinir. You could kill her now and create a Tapestry that aligns with all your goals. It would not be difficult. But who knows who will rise in her place?"

"Why are you telling me this, boy?"

"I'm trying to show you that you're not the first person to wipe the Faoii from Imeriel. Thinir tried. You tried. Someone else will probably try again. But the thing about Faoii is, they can't really be destroyed. They're not people. They're… more like an idea." He brushed the dirt from his hands and stood next to her. "Sometimes the words and temples change. Sometimes things get muddled and buried. Sometimes the idea gets covered by ceremony and stupid rules. But there's always someone that remembers the core tenets, even if they were never taught."

The Oath she'd practiced and sworn a thousand times as a child flashed across Ali's mind. "I am the harbinger of justice and truth. I am the strength of the weak and the voice of the silent," she whispered as she watched Kaiya the Betrayer guide her horse around a corner and out of sight.

"Right. Those were the things you believed in once, weren't they? And when the monasteries stopped living by those promises, you rose up to stand for all those who could not stand for themselves." He placed a hand on her arm. "You were Faoii then, no matter what the monasteries told you. You tried to burn out all the false Faoii, but you went too far. You see that, right?"

Ali tried to reply, but anger bubbled up from her throat. "No! The world was better when the Old Gods were there to watch us! To protect us!"

"Take my hand again."

Ali did, and suddenly they were in a cold room with crumbling walls, hidden in deep shadows. Jacir pulled aside a billowing curtain and Ali peered into the next chamber.

The Betrayer was there, and in front of her was a starkly beautiful woman with strawberry blonde hair and a sword that screamed like demons in a maelstrom. In front of her, the Betrayer lifted her blade higher.

"No! My Goddess! I don't want to see this!" Ali shrieked, though the scream did not seem to reach the others.

Jacir frowned. "Don't you?"

And Ali knew that a part of her did. She wanted to see the moment that had destroyed all of their lives. This was the moment that justified everything she'd done.

"You ungrateful *worm!*" the Fallen Goddess screamed. "I have given you everything! I have stayed in this form all this time for *you*—for all of you!"

"Look around you! You have provided only death and suffering!"

"Without my influence, you—all of you—would have known nothing but war and pain!"

"That's all we've known anyway!"

The battle raged on, but Ali couldn't hear anything else over the ringing of her ears. This beautiful, glorified past she'd slaved for. This wonderful ancient being she'd prepared to sacrifice everything in the name of—was just as flawed as she was. As any of them had ever been.

Suddenly, Ali and Jacir were in an impossibly large maze with an infinitely long tapestry weaving around them on all sides. Ali had not realized that she was crying on the ground, her head held in her hands.

"It's okay, Madame Elise. It's going to be okay." The urchin boy was standing next to her, patting her shoulder comfortingly. "Let's go back to the others. We can guide the path to a better place now. All of us together."

"No!" Ali screamed, surging to her feet and shoving the child out of the way. "There has to be more than this! The Old Gods have called to me! They've shown me the path! Illindria was flawed, but She was just one of many! The Old Gods are perfect! And I will heed Their words!"

Frantically, she clawed at the Infinite Tapestry—the beautiful Weave that the Old Gods had told her about but that she'd never been able to reach before. The secret to Their release was in the strands. She knew it.

Ali heard Jacir's frantic cries behind her to stop, but did not heed them as she gripped the Tapestry with clawed fingers. She would release Them. She'd show everyone that the Old Gods were better than Illindria had been. That the Faoii had been wrong to try and keep Them buried.

"All hail the Old Gods!" she screamed.

The writhing shapes beneath the pool surged and erupted in frantic waves, Their ancient, colossal minds pulling towards Ali as she connected with the threads. She felt Them trying to direct her. Trying to show her how to release Them.

But Ali couldn't hear or see anything other than what the strands in her hands displayed. Old Gods and oaths forgotten, her concepts of reality and time disintegrated as she spun ceaselessly through a thousand lives she did not recognize, past a million choices she'd never wanted to see. The Tapestry unfurled in all directions, and she lived and died innumerable lives in moments, unable to free herself from the tangled strands that were suddenly wrapped around her. Trapping her. Strangling her.

Ali screamed, trying to wrench away from the Tapestry, but it enveloped her, climbing into her eyes and ears and mouth. She thought she would go mad. That she would drown beneath the ceaseless waves. But then Ali began to recognize the threads that twisted in her fingers. In her mind. Hundreds of souls that had seen their ends on her pyres. A thousand beautifully colored threads that had been cut short by her hands. Ali screamed as she watched the million possible lives each one might have lived had she not sent them to the flames. And now… Now they were all just ghosts made of ash and sermons from her own cursed tongue.

Ali had never realized how much of an impact every person could make. How every creature could color the strands. And then there was the impact of their children. Their grandchildren. All their descendants down the line… it was unfathomable. Awesome in its scale and complexity. Beautiful in the ripples that flowed outward from a single action. The waves created by a single existence.

And she'd cut so many of them short, afraid that the waves would become bigger than her own.

What have I done? What have I done?

It seemed to Ali that she spent years tangled in the Threads, watching lives that she'd stamped out dance over a Tapestry that she'd shorn in the name of gods that suddenly seemed so small.

Surely even gods could not have changed the world in all the ways those people might have done. They are nothing compared to what we might be.

Suddenly, violently, Ali was thrown from the Weave, her fingers clawed like talons and her eyes streaming. She choked on her own sobs as the images faded by degrees, but she could not remove them from the back of her eyelids. She let out a trembling wail as she tried to roll over. Tried to stand. In front of her, Jacir carefully unwound the last of the threads of her fingers, then whispered something she could not hear. The Infinite Tapestry disappeared.

"Madame Elise?"

"What have I done? What have I done?" Ali wailed, the ghosts of threads still tracing across her eyelids, nearly strangling her as they crept between her ears and down her throat. She tried to dispel them, but they'd stretched too deeply into her mind. Into her soul.

"Everyone's life has an impact, Proclaimer. Did the Tapestry show you yours?"

Ali nodded, still crying. "And theirs! All of theirs! What have I done?" She scrambled upwards, grasping at the boy's hands. "Can we fix it? Can we go back? Remove all the death I've wrought? Repair the strands I cut?" The shorn strands slithered behind her eyelids. Jacir slowly shook his head.

"That would change the Weave even more. Cut jagged strips into it in ways we can't see. It would be so much worse than even this is. I'm sorry, Proclaimer."

Elise hung her head. "But… but if we can't go back, then… then what do we do?"

Jacir knelt in front of her, grasping her hand in both of his.

"Isn't it obvious, Madame Elise? We go forward."

60

Kaiya watched grimly from the back of the newly restored throne room at Aurelius' official coronation. The air felt lighter now. There was a buzzing excitement about the changes everyone expected to come. People seemed ready to move forward as a group. And, possibly more important, they seemed ready to *listen.*

She idly listened to Ilahna and Eitan argue in hushed whispers at the end of the row.

"I'm glad Jacir got Elise to understand," Eitan growled, "but her followers will still want what she wanted. No one's safe yet."

"Hush, Eitan. This is a good first step. You saw what she looks like now. How mad she's gone. No one wants to follow her into *that.* We'll erase some of the lines she drew. They're going to reopen the schools. We can teach them to read. We can uncover the old histories and let people learn from those who came before. Build upwards instead of razing everything and starting from inside Elise's sinkhole." Ilahna used a dagger to carve something into the freshly polished bench in front of her, and Eitan slapped her hand away. Kaiya looked over out of curiosity and smiled at the two words there. HOPE. RISE. Ilahna rolled her eyes and stuck the dagger back into her trinket belt. It looked ridiculous next to the fine dress Lucinda had picked out for the urchin, but a part of Kaiya liked it better this way. "It will take time," Ilahna whispered. "But we can start moving forward again now that people have stopped trying to go back."

"You're helping a lot, you know," Eitan replied, slinging an arm around her shoulders. "When you tell people how things should be. What it's like when the truth isn't buried. They hear you. They believe you."

Kaiya secretly agreed with the blacksmith. Ilahna's gifts were some of the most important in Clearwall right now, as she learned everything she could and then helped to spread it forward throughout Imeriel. When she spoke, the people found the parts of themselves that wanted to change and align with the universe—and they pulled at those strands from deep inside. It almost felt like things might turn out better this time.

Almost. Kaiya had lived long enough to know it wouldn't last. And that she did not want to be around when the winds shifted again.

She had no reason to stay. She knew with certainty that Ilahna and Jacir would be safe in her absence. Jacir would never compel her again. And she had doubtlessly fulfilled any unspoken promise to Emery.

She had been there to help the Harkins children reach the height of their existence. She would not be around to watch them fall again, as everything eventually did.

As the coronation finished, Kaiya quietly drifted out to one of the balconies of Clearwall Keep, inhaling the crisp air in a deep sigh. She shrugged uncomfortably at the sling that immobilized her wounded shoulder. It would take time for it to heal completely and would be an inconvenience wherever she chose to go next. But time was the one thing she had too much of and had become the biggest inconvenience of her existence. Once again, the world was open to her, and there was nowhere in it to which she wanted to disappear.

The light step through the doorway behind her was barely a brush of boot against stone, but Kaiya spun around to face the person that dared intrude upon her solitude. She was getting tired of such things. It would be good to disappear again, no matter where she went.

Jacir stood there, looking older and uncomfortable in the fine clothes he now wore as one of Aurelius' advisors. Kaiya had smiled when she'd seen him that morning and had nearly laughed out loud when Ilahna had called her floor-length gown a "torture device." Kaiya had said the same thing once, long ago.

"Greetings, Faoli," Kaiya said at Jacir's approach. "I am told that a bow is supposed to accompany your new title. Royal Arcanist, I believe?"

"Faoii bow to no one." Jacir replied, fisting his hands, one on top of the other, before her. "I have learned the old rules. I let people in the past teach me of my abilities. Of my duties."

"Oh? And what exactly have you learned?"

"That I don't want to use any of it."

Kaiya chuckled darkly. "Then maybe this age has a chance, after all."

Jacir took another step forward, his face thoughtful. "You do not want to stay and see for sure." It was not a question.

Kaiya shook her head. "No. I do not. This is your time. I do not want to see if the cycle restarts or if it is broken. I just want rest."

Jacir nodded, tilting his head to one side as he thought. After a long moment, he outstretched his hand. "Will you come with me, Faoii-Kaiya? One more time? Please?"

His question was so earnest that Kaiya could not bring herself to question why. Instead, she only put her dark hand in his small palm and nodded.

They appeared in the Tapestry Hall that now looked like the Maze. The pond that Jacir had conjured in the center of the room was still and calm, a serene reflecting pool that cast back images of the infinite walls all around them. Jacir stepped up to it, studying his finely-dressed image. Kaiya stood behind him, seeing the deep lines set under her eyes, the stark whiteness of her braid. She had finally grown as old as she had felt for nearly 200 years.

"I can do things with the Tapestry that none before me could do. There are others in the future who can learn. I will teach them before I go, but that is a long time from now. Even by your standards." He cocked a half smile, and Kaiya tried to match it, albeit halfheartedly.

Jacir let the smile drop and conjured the Infinite Tapestry. Its fine, beautiful, intricate Weave twisted through the infinite Maze, swirling around them like parchment in a soft wind. Jacir laid his finger on a particularly vibrant thread, and it radiated across a thousand events, solid and unbending. Kaiya looked more closely and gasped as she made out the images that the thread had been woven into.

The thread was hers.

"You know what's interesting?" Jacir asked, almost to himself. "This isn't the only Tapestry. This is just *our* Tapestry. But you've seen how many threads can come from a single choice. How many events can build from one moment in time. We see all the possibilities, and it's overwhelming. But that's because we're seeing all of the different Tapestries that exist throughout all the versions of the world."

Kaiya frowned and opened her mouth to speak, but Jacir shook his head. "No. I know it sounds crazy. I thought the same thing when I first realized it. But I have spent more time amid the threads in all versions of the Tapestry than I think you realize. I need you to trust me."

Kaiya frowned again. "What does this have to do with me, Faoli? I will not watch the Weave again. I am no Weaver."

"No. That's not what I want. I want to offer you a gift." He plucked at her thread once, and Kaiya watched it vibrate, shimmering against the Tapestry. "If you want… I can remove your thread from this Weave. I can tie it to one of your threads in another Tapestry. One where Lyn lives a long, full life. It would be…uncomfortable, I think. Your mind will fight as it tries to reconcile which memories it should consider real. You will have an ancient mind in a young body. The transition will be hard. But your mind has already survived more than most. I think you could adapt. Perhaps you could even be happy." He paused, offering her a sad smile. "And, if you would like, I can cut your thread when Lyn reaches the natural end of her life. You could be free of this immortality. Truly free. If that's what you want."

"Yes." Kaiya's response was immediate, the words escaping from her lips before she could even truly understand the full implications of what he was offering her. But if anyone in the Weave could release her, it was Jacir. "Yes to all of it." She grasped the young Faoli's hand with both of hers, the enormity of what he was saying causing her entire body to tremble and her eyes to flood with tears she no longer even realized she had left. "Please, Faoli. Please. Let me rest."

Jacir smiled and squeezed her hand gently. "I thought so. Safe journeys, Faoii-Kaiya. May you have no more battles needing guidance." Kaiya smiled slightly at the bastardization of a long-forgotten salutation, but Jacir was already carefully extracting her Thread from the Weave. With teary eyes and a soft whisper of gratitude, Kaiya the Betrayer, the final Faoii of Illindria...was gone.

61

Ilahna pulled uncomfortably at the neckline of her dress, her grimy trinket belt jangling obnoxiously against the silk. Next to her, Lucinda was much more graceful as they walked away from the throne room, leaving Aurelius behind to discuss banquet plans with Tanner. Ilahna knew she was expected to stay in her regalia for the feast, but she'd begged Lucinda to help her unlace the ridiculous gown that she'd already had to suffer in for long enough, and the wispy girl had finally relented. Now they spoke quietly as they walked to one of the few rooms that had been restored within the Keep.

"So," Ilahna said as she tried to walk. "I have to ask. Now that you've seen more of the people connected to the Weave—people all across Imeriel—do you know if there was someone else who could have done all of this? Someone beside Jacir?" Even after all this time, some part of Ilahna still wanted to know if they had been tied to this entire mess by fate or birthrights or just coincidence. She didn't say any of this to Lucinda, however, as the other woman considered the question thoughtfully.

"I..." Lucinda finally ventured quietly. "I don't know if it mattered, Miss Harkins. There are so many people in the world who can at least glimpse the Weave now. We weren't aware, before, but now that they are not afraid, they are starting to come forward. And I don't think the Faoii of old ever considered that possibility. They were all so afraid of taking the tonicloran. Of spreading something that was so famously evil. Hurtful. Poisonous. Everything in the ancient texts describes it causing people's flesh to peel off in ribbons. That it was a painful, slow, agonizing death. The Faoii of old said only a handful of people could survive it—those that had seen the Weave without training or help. Who had an innate ability." She paused, pulling one of the heavy gems from her hair. "It used to be so rare. But you've seen how things are now. Magic has spread through the world more than it ever did when the ancient texts were written. Our minds and bodies and souls have changed. It's possible that anyone could have taken it and survived. Maybe anyone could have helped to guide the Weave as he did. Or maybe it was only ever Jacir."

"Aren't you curious, though?"

Lucinda shook her head. "I do not think so. I think it's good that the last of the tonicloran is gone. Maybe we never actually needed it. Maybe the Faoii of old did. Maybe the Goddess that Kaiya destroyed demanded its use. Maybe things were different. But... I do not know. It seems like just one more way to get caught in the Weave. One more way to fall into a well that so few are able to get out of again. The Betrayer was right. If you spend your life watching what might happen, nothing ever does. You miss out on your entire life."

Ilahna looked past the wispy girl to focus on Eitan, who was laughing with another revolutionist. Now that she knew Jacir was going to be okay, she thought she might have a chance to focus on a life she'd never really believed she'd be allowed to live. She hoped so.

"Perhaps young Jacir has the power to go back and try again," Lucinda continued. "Make better choices. Improve upon the world we see around us. But he also seems like the only one out of all of us who would never choose to do that. Who would rather move forward and watch life unravel in all of its beauty and terror without him pulling the strings. And maybe that's why it had to be him, all along."

Ilahna rubbed her forehead. "Wait. So do you believe in destiny or our control over… everything?"

"Can't the answer be both?" Lucinda's turquoise eyes sparkled in the moonlight. "I've seen a million threads all leading to one place. And I've seen your brother do things that none of the threads even hinted at. Maybe some of us are tied to certain threads. Maybe none of us are and the Tapestry is just a map guided by likelihoods. Or maybe thinking about it too much tangles the strings."

Ilahna shook her head and caught a glimpse of something out of the corner of her eye. Jacir was standing on one of the balconies, staring out over Clearwall.

"Jacir!" she called. "I thought you were with Kaiya. Where'd she go?"

Jacir turned to Ilahna with a soft smile.

"Home."

Epilogue

Teilithia took careful steps through Her forest. Glowing tendrils that reflected moonlight grew beneath Her unshod feet. They fell away from Her as She took another step, wilting in the darkness and disintegrating into starry ash. Next to Her, one of Her companions nuzzled Her hand, and She pet him fondly. It was not much further, now.

The tendrils fell away as She stepped out of the trees, and Her companions shook their antlers and stomped their hooves as they watched Her walk across a sandy beach onto which they dared not tread. She smiled patiently back at them, promising Her return.

She walked across the beach of white sand, watching the waves in the moonlight roll forward toward Her pale toes. As She stepped, the tides changed their pattern, no longer shackled to the moon as they had been before Her arrival. Riding upon a wave that even a mortal could not see as natural, another Goddess glided from the sea.

"Hail, Sister," Teilithia whispered in the moonlight. Both Goddesses clasped Their hands in front of Them, though neither lowered Their eyes. She waited a moment before dropping Her hands. "It has been a long time."

"Why have you called me here?" There was no hatred or love in Her sister's flowing voice, which sounded like the color of shells.

For a moment Teilithia looked up to the moon that She and all of Her sisters shared.

Had shared. There was one less, now.

"Illindria is dead."

Her sister showed no outward emotion, but the waves behind Her surged a little more forcefully than before.

"How long ago?"

"Not long. Her slayer has also fallen."

Her sister tilted Her head in thought. "And the others?"

"Nearly released, though locked below the Weave for now."

Her sister considered, the liquid of Her eyes scanning the horizon beyond Her waves. "The mortals of Imeriel are very resourceful," She finally relented.

"It was Our youngest sister that propelled them forward in Her impatience. In Her naivety."

"What will We do?"

Teilithia refocused Her gaze on the moon for a moment more.

"Prepare for what comes. The winds and tides are changing, Sister. The Weave will follow in kind."

Acknowledgements

I'd like to thank everyone that helped me to make this book a reality. I will not pretend that my initial road to publication was easy, and there were many times when I wanted to give up. But so many of you convinced me to keep going. I have the deepest gratitude and respect for each and every one of you for picking up a sword when I could not. Thank you, my warriors.

There are several people in particular I'd like to thank. My husband for being the person that listened to every errant thought, whisper of self-doubt, and curse word I had throughout the entire process of creating this novel. It didn't matter what I was saying, he was willing to listen and then edit whatever I finally put to paper. My father, for being my biggest supporter and promptest editor since I was old enough to hold a pen. Evan Graham for creating the amazing covers for these books and for yelling at me every time I tried to make my own using PowerPoint. The incredibly talented Becca Dobias for wading through every twisted sentence and story arc so we could corral them into something comprehensible. And Carolyn Dubiel for teaching me that I don't know the difference between "that" and "who," among other things. Without them, this book would still be a jumble of words and sketches of swords. Thank you.

For More Information

about Tahani Nelson and the Faoii

Please Visit

TahaniNelson.com

Made in the USA
Coppell, TX
24 November 2020

42009984R00267